James H. Graff, William Harrison Ainsworth

Saint James's

The Court of Queen Anne

James H. Graff, William Harrison Ainsworth

Saint James's
The Court of Queen Anne

ISBN/EAN: 9783337348762

Printed in Europe, USA, Canada, Australia, Japan

Cover: Foto ©Andreas Hilbeck / pixelio.de

More available books at **www.hansebooks.com**

SAINT JAMES'S:

OR,

THE COURT OF QUEEN ANNE.

An Historical Romance.

BY

WILLIAM HARRISON AINSWORTH, Esq.

AUTHOR OF "THE TOWER OF LONDON,"
"WINDSOR CASTLE," ETC.

NEW EDITION.

LONDON:

GEORGE ROUTLEDGE AND SONS,

THE BROADWAY, LUDGATE.

NEW YORK: 416, BROOME STREET.

BY W. HARRISON AINSWORTH.

SAINT JAMES'S:

OR,

THE COURT OF QUEEN ANNE.

Book the First.

THE DUCHESS OF MARLBOROUGH.

CHAPTER I.

A GLANCE AT THE COURT AND CABINET OF QUEEN ANNE IN 1707.

THE commencement of the year Seventeen Hundred and Seven saw Queen Anne, to all outward appearance, in the most enviable position of any sovereign in Europe. Secure of the affections of her subjects, to whom the wisdom and beneficence of her five years' sway had endeared her, and who had begun to bestow upon her the affectionate appellation of the "good Queen;" dreaded by her enemies, and who had everywhere felt and acknowledged the prowess of her arms; cheered by the constant cry of victory; surrounded by able and devoted counsellors; served by one of the greatest commanders that England had then ever known; encircled by a brilliant court, distinguished alike for its grace, its polish, and its wit; fortunate in flourishing at an age when every branch of literature and science was cultivated with the most eminent success; thus fortunately circumstanced, with all around prosperous and promising, the Union with Scotland recently effected, the pride of France humbled, the balance of power in Europe established, and the Protestant succession firmly secured, nothing appeared wanting to Anne's grandeur and happiness.

And yet under this mask of glory she concealed an anxious heart. The power seemed valueless, which rarely, if ever, availed to carry into effect a favourite measure. The constitutional indolence of her royal consort, Prince George of Denmark, to whom she was tenderly attached, and his incompetency to the due fulfilment of the high offices he had been appointed to, and which not unfrequently drew upon him the sarcastic censure of the party in opposition, were sources of grievance. The loss of all her family, and especially of the Duke of Gloucester, at the age of eleven, preyed upon her spirits, and in seasons of depression, to which she was subject, made her regard the bereavement as a judgment for her desertion of her father, the deposed and exiled James the Second. The situation of her brother, the Chevalier de Saint George, as he styled himself, also troubled her, and sometimes awakened scruples within her breast, as to whether she was not usurping a throne which, of right, belonged to him. Added to this, her cabinet was secretly disunited, while party warfare raged with so much violence, that she herself was but little respected in its attacks and reprisals.

Not the least of her annoyances was the state of thraldom in which she was kept by the Duchess of Marlborough. Her friendship for this illustrious lady was of early date, and had been confirmed by the zeal and warmth displayed by the latter during the differences between Anne, while Princess of Denmark, and her sister, Queen Mary. So strong did the princess's attachment to her favourite become, and so anxious was she to lay aside form and ceremony with her, and put her on an equality with herself, that in her correspondence and private intercourse, she chose to assume the name of Mrs. Morley, while Lady Marlborough was permitted to adopt that of Mrs. Freeman.

Of an imperious and ambitious nature, endowed with high mental qualifications, and a sound and clear judgment, when not distorted or obscured by passion, the Duchess of Marlborough, as she became immediately after Anne's elevation to the throne on the 8th March, 1702, determined to leave no means untried to aggrandize and enrich her husband and her family. Her views were seconded by her royal mistress, from whom she obtained, besides large pensions, the places of groom of the stole, mistress of the robes, and keeper of the great and home parks, and of the privy purse, while she extended her family influence by uniting her eldest daughter, the Lady Henrietta Churchill, to Lord Ryalton, eldest son of the Earl of Godolphin, lord high treasurer; her second daughter, Lady Anne, to the Earl of Sunderland; her third, Lady Elizabeth, to the Earl of Bridgewater; and her fourth and youngest, Lady Mary, to the Marquis of Monthermer, afterwards, by her interest, created Duke of Montague. Hence the Marlborough and Godolphin party were called, by their opponents, "THE FAMILY."

Anne's great bounty to the duchess and constant concession to her opinions, made the latter suppose she had only to ask and have; only to bear down in argument to convince, or, at least, gain her point. And for awhile she was successful. The queen's good-nature yielded to her demands, while her timidity shrank before her threats. But these submissions were purchased by the duchess at the price of her royal mistress's regard; and more than one quarrel having occurred between them, it became evident to all, except the favourite herself, that her sway was on the decline. Blinded, however, by confidence in the mastery she had obtained over the queen, she conceived her position to be as firm as that of the sovereign herself, and defied her enemies to displace her.

A coalition having occurred two years before between Marlborough and Godolphin, and the Whigs, the ministry was now almost wholly supported by that party, into whose confidence, notwithstanding her former disagreement with them, the queen had surrendered herself on the meeting of the second parliament, in 1705, in consequence of the affront she had received from the Tories, when the motion whether the Princess Sophia should be invited to England, was made; upon which occasion she wrote to the Duchess of Marlborough—"I believe we shall not disagree, as we have formerly done; for I am sensible of the services those people (the Whigs) have done me that you have a good opinion of, and will countenance them, and am thoroughly convinced of the malice and insolence of them (the Tories) that you have always been speaking against."

The leaders of the Whig cabinet, distinguished by the title of "The Junta," were the Lords Somers, Halifax, Wharton, Orford, and Sunderland,—all five statesmen of great and varied abilities and approved zeal in behalf of the Protestant succession, while Halifax's zealous patronage and promotion of men of letters and science, as exhibited towards Addison, Prior, Locke, Steele, Congreve, and Newton, is too well known to need recapitulation here.

To most of the Junta, however, the queen entertained a strong dislike, and notwithstanding the repeated requests of the Duchess of Marlborough for the appointment of her son-in-law, the Earl of Sunderland, to the office of secretary of state, it was only on the personal solicitation of the duke himself, on his return from his last glorious campaign, that the earl received the place on the dismissal of Sir Charles Hedges. The Tory opposition was headed by the Lords Rochester, Jersey, Nottingham, Haversham, Sir Edward Seymour, Sir Nathan Wright, and the above-mentioned Sir Charles Hedges.

The Earl of Godolphin, whose interests, as well from family connexion as from community of sentiment, were co-existent with those of the Duke of Marlborough, was a person, if not of dazzling talent, of such industry and capacity for business as more than compensated for any want of brilliancy, and admirably adapted him to his office of high-treasurer. Methodical in management, and exact in payment, he raised the credit of the country to a higher point than it had ever before attained, and was consequently enabled to procure supplies whenever they were required. A man of the strictest honour, he never failed in his engagements; and though forbidding in manner and difficult of access, was generally esteemed.

There were two other members of the cabinet who were closely united in friendship, and of whom the highest expectations were formed. These were Mr. Saint-John and Mr. Harley. Both were Tories, and belonged to the high church party, having taken office in 1704, when Harley consented to succeed the Earl of Nottingham as secretary of state, on condition that his friend Saint-John should be made secretary at war. This was readily acceded to; for Saint-John's wit and eloquence, combined with his brilliant abilitie-

and graceful manners, had long recommended him to notice, and must have ensured him promotion earlier if his unbridled profligacy had not stood in his way. Since his appointment, however, he had applied to business with as much ardour as he had heretofore devoted himself to pleasure, and so wonderful were the powers he displayed, so clear and comprehensive was his judgment, so inexhaustible were his resources, that the highest post in the administration seemed within his reach. Among wits and men of letters, he ruled supreme, and was an arbiter of taste and fashion, as well as a political leader.

A very different man was Robert Harley. Without the meteoric splendour, the fervid eloquence, the classical learning, the searching philosophy of Saint-John; but he had, nevertheless, a quick and keen understanding, great subtlety, and ever-stirring, though deep-seated ambition. Though enjoying a high reputation with all parties for skill in financial matters, for lucid, if not profound judgment, and for excellent habits of business, he was held to be somewhat uncertain. and was in reality a trimmer. To his indefatigable exertions was mainly owing the accomplishment of the Union with Scotland, the advantages of which measure have been subsequently felt to be so important.

Harley affected great moderation in his views, by which means he succeeded in veiling his fickleness; and it was a favourite maxim with him, that "the name of party ought to be abolished." Professing great independency and liberality, however, he merely held himself aloof with the view of securing a certain influence with both parties. His agreeable and polished manners, tried abilities, and experience, had caused him to be chosen Speaker of the House of Commons during the two last parliaments of William the Third, and he was continued in the office on the accession of Anne, until his appointment as secretary of state, in 1704.

From many causes, Harley had rendered himself obnoxious to Godolphin; amongst others, it was supposed that he had supplanted the lord treasurer in the favour of a certain Mrs. Oglethorpe, through whom important secrets, relative to the clandestine intrigues of the court of Saint-Germains, had been obtained. By the Duchess of Marlborough he was always treated with contempt, and such was the haughtiness and distance with which she comported herself towards him, that it was surmised he must have dared to breathe dishonourable proposals to her; and as it was known that he would allow few scruples to stand in the way of his advancement, the path of which would have been cleared, if he could have obtained the favour of the omnipotent duchess, the story obtained some credit. From whatever cause, however, whether from baffled hopes or wounded vanity, he conceived a strong antipathy to the duchess, and determined to destroy her influence with the queen, and, at the same time, overthrow her husband and Godolphin, and replace the Whig cabinet with a Tory ministry, of which he himself should be the head.

With these bold resolutions, and while revolving the means of secretly reaching the ears of royalty, which was essential to the accomplishment of his project, but which appeared almost impossible, owing to the vigilance and caution of the duchess, an instrument was unexpectedly offered him.

One day, while waiting upon the queen at St. James's, in his official capacity, he perceived among her attendants his cousin, Abigail Hill, the eldest daughter of a bankrupt Turkey merchant, who stood related to the Duchess of Marlborough in the same degree as to himself, and had very recently been preferred to her present situation by her grace's interest. Though Harley had hitherto, in consequence of the misfortunes of her family, wholly neglected her, he now instantly saw the use she might be to him; and congratulating her upon her appointment, professed the utmost desire to serve her.

New to a court, and unsuspicious of his designs, Abigail believed him, and forgave his previous coolness. The artful secretary took every means of ingratiating himself with her, and contrived to sow the seeds of enmity between her and the duchess. At the same time, he pointed out the course she ought to pursue to win the queen's favour; and his advice, which was most judiciously given, and with a full knowledge of Anne's foibles, being carefully followed, the anticipated consequences occurred. Abigail Hill speedily became her royal mistress's favourite and confidante.

Many accidental circumstances contributed to assist Abigail's progress in favour. Exasperated against the duchess, who had left her, upon some trifling misunderstanding between them, with bitter reproaches, the queen burst into tears before her new attendant, who exerted herself so assiduously and so successfully to soothe her, that from that moment her subsequent hold upon the royal regard may be dated.

Apprehensive of the jealousy and anger of her old favourite, Anne was careful to conceal her growing partiality for the new one, and thus the duchess was kept in ignorance of the mischief that had occurred until too late to remedy it; while Abigail, on her part, though she had already become the receptacle of the queen's innermost thoughts, and thoroughly understood the importance of the position she had acquired, had the good sense to restrain any outward exhibition of her influence, knowing that the slightest indiscretion might be prejudicial to her rising fortunes.

Through the channel he had thus opened, Harley now ventured to propose to the queen his willingness to liberate her from the bondage of the duchess, if she was willing to commit the task to him; but Anne hesitated. She dreaded the shock which the separation would necessarily occasion; and about this time, the glorious battle of Ramilies being won, an important change was wrought by it in the duchess's favour.

Incomparably the most distinguished ornament of Anne's court, or of any court in Europe, whether as a commander or a statesman, though chiefly, of course, in the former capacity, was the Duke of Marlborough. His great military genius, approved in four glorious campaigns, and signalized by the victories of Schellenberg, Blenheim, and Ramilies, had raised him to a pinnacle of fame unattained by any living commander, and had won for him, in addition to more substantial honours at home, the congratulations of most of the potentates of Europe. The dignity of prince had been conferred upon him by the Emperor Joseph, and he had been repeatedly thanked for his services by both houses of parliament.

No general had ever advanced the military glory of England to such an extent as Marlborough, and his popularity was unbounded. His achievements were the theme of every tongue, his praises were upon every lip; and however he might be secretly opposed, in public he was universally applauded. And well did he merit the highest praise bestowed upon him; well did he merit the highest reward he obtained. His were all the noblest qualities of a general; and his courage and skill were not greater than his magnanimity and lenity. Perfect master of strategics, in enterprise and action he was alike unequalled. In the heat of battle he was calm and composed as in the tent; and a slight advantage gained was by him rapidly improved into a victory, while the victory itself was carried out to its full extent, not in needless slaughter, for no man showed greater consideration and mercy than he did, but in preventing the enemy from rallying. England might well be proud of Marlborough, for he was among the greatest of her sons.

Nor were his abilities confined merely to the camp. He shone with almost equal splendour as a diplomatist, and his acute perception of character, his sagacity and extensive political knowledge, combined with his fascination of address and manner, admirably qualified him for negotiation with foreign courts. Marlborough's absence with the army in Flanders prevented him from taking an active part, except by correspondence, in affairs at home, but he was ably represented by his wife and Godolphin.

The Duke returned to London towards the end of November, 1706, after completing his fourth campaign in the Low Countries, distinguished, among other important achievements, by the victory of Ramilies, above mentioned, which was followed by the submission of the chief cities of Flanders and Brabant, and the acknowledgment of Charles the Third as king.

Immediately on his arrival, Marlborough proceeded in a chair to St. James's, but in spite of his attempt at privacy he was discovered, and in an incredibly short space of time surrounded by eager thousands, who rent the air with their acclamations. Nor was his reception by the sovereign and her illustrious consort less flattering. Prince George embraced him; and the queen, after thanking him, with much emotion, said, she should never feel easy till she had proved her gratitude for his unparalleled services.

Magnificent entertainments were subsequently given him by the lord mayor and the heads of the city, and as the colours and standards won at Blenheim were placed within Westminster Hall, so the trophies obtained at Ramilies were now borne by a large cavalcade of horse and foot, amid the roar of artillery and the shouts of myriads of spectators, to Guildhall, and there deposited. The duke's popularity was at its zenith. To oppose him would have been as dangerous as to attempt the dethronement of the queen herself. The voice of faction was drowned amid the thunder of general applause; and for the moment, the efforts of his enemies were paralyzed.

Such was the state of affairs at the beginning of the year 1707;—such Anne's position. Externally, all seemed smiling and prosperous, and the queen the happiest, as she was the best, if not the greatest sovereign in Europe. That she suffered from private grief has been shown, as well as that she felt annoyance at the state of bondage in which she was kept; and it has also been shown, that she was no stranger to the cabals and dissensions in her cabinet. To one bosom alone did she confide her secret sorrows,—to one ear alone breathe her wishes or designs. And the person so favoured, it is almost needless to repeat, was Abigail Hill.

———

CHAPTER II.

THE FRENCH ADVENTURER, AND THE QUEEN'S FAVOURITE.

THE royal birthday was usually kept with extraordinary splendour during the reign of Anne, but on no previous occasion was it accompanied with so much magnificence and rejoicing as on the 6th of February, 1707. Preparations were made for a general illumination, and the bent of popular feeling was proved by the fact, that wherever the queen's name appeared, it was sure to be followed by that of the hero of Blenheim and Ramilies, while transparencies were placed in the most conspicuous situations, representing the chief events of the recent campaign. Bonfires were lighted at an early hour, and the French king, the pope, the pretender, and the devil, were paraded in effigy through the streets, and subsequently burnt.

The weather was in unison with the general festivity, being unusually fine for the season. The sky was bright and sunny, and the air had all the delicious balminess and freshness of spring. Martial music resounded within the courts of the palace, and the trampling of the guard was heard, accompanied by the clank of their accoutrements as they took their station in Saint James's-street, where a vast crowd was already collected.

About an hour before noon, the patience of those who had taken up their positions betimes promised to be rewarded, and the company began to appear, at first somewhat scantily, but speedily in great numbers. The science of the whip was not so well understood in those days as in our own times, or perhaps the gorgeous and convenient, though somewhat cumbersome vehicles then in vogue were not so manageable: but, from whatever cause, it is certain that many quarrels took place among the drivers, and frequent and loud oaths and ejaculations were poured forth.

The footpath was invaded by the chairmen, who forcibly pushed the crowd aside, and seemed utterly regardless of the ribs or toes of those who did not instantly make way for them. Some confusion necessarily ensued; but though the crowd were put to considerable inconvenience, jostled here, and squeezed there, the utmost mirth and good humour prevailed.

Before long, the tide of visitors had greatly increased, and coaches, chariots, and sedans, were descending in four unbroken lines towards the palace. The curtains of the chairs being for the most part drawn down, the attention of the spectators was chiefly directed to the coaches, in which sat resplendent beauties, bedecked with jewels and lace, beaux in their costliest and most splendid attire, grave judges and reverend divines in their respective habiliments, military and naval commanders in their full accoutrements, foreign ambassadors, and every variety of character that a court can exhibit. The equipages were most of them new, and exceedingly sumptuous, as were the liveries of the servants clustering behind them.

The dresses of the occupants of the coaches were varied in colour, as well as rich in material, and added to the gaiety and glitter of the scene. Silks and velvets of as many hues as the rainbow might be discovered, while there was every kind of peruke, from the courtly and modish Ramilies just introduced, to the somewhat antiquated but graceful and flowing French campaign. Neither was there any lack of feathered hats, point-lace cravats and ruffles, diamond snuff-boxes and buckles, clouded canes, and all the et cetera of beauish decoration.

Hard by the corner of Pall Mall, stood a little group, consisting of a tall, thin, plainly-dressed man, apparently belonging to the middle class of society, and a rosy-faced, short-necked individual, whose cassock and band proclaimed his reverend calling, and who had a comely woman of some forty years old under one arm, and a pretty, shy-looking damsel of less than half that age under the other.

"Here comes Sir Nathan Wright, late lord keeper of the great seal," said the tall, thin man, addressing his reverend companion, to whom he appeared to act as cicerone.

"Is that Sir Nathan, Mr. Greg?" asked the divine, gazing at a sharp-featured, well-wigged person in the coach.

"The same, Mr. Hyde," replied the other; "and as I live, he is followed by his successor, Lord Cowper, whom I needn't tell you is one of the ablest lawyers that ever wore a gown. His lordship is pretty certain, ere long, to take his seat upon the woolsack."

"Save us! who's he in the gilt charrot?" cried the young damsel just mentioned. "What a curious fine gentleman he is, and what pure fine clothes he wears!"

"That's the Earl of Sunderland, Miss Angelica," replied Greg; "secretary of state, and son-in-law to his grace of Marlborough. The countess is by his side. That angry-looking nobleman, who is thrusting his head out of the window and rating his coachman for driving so slowly, is Lord Orford, another of the ministers, and one of the ablest of them, but no great favourite with her majesty, for the reproof he administered the Prince of Denmark, on the score of his highness's mismanagement of the navy. Behind him comes the Duke of Devonshire, and after the duke, his grace of Newcastle. Next follows my master, Mr. Harley, who, if he doesn't become lord treasurer one day, wont meet with his desert. Take note of him, I pray you, Miss Angelica, for he's worth looking at."

"Oh, yes! I see him," replied Angelica; "but I can't see much to admire about him."

"Many of your sex have entertained a different opinion," replied Greg, with a smile. "But how do you like the young gentleman with him?"

"Purely," replied Angelica; "purely. He's another guess sort of body."

"Who may the young man be, friend Greg?" inquired Parson Hyde.

"His name is Masham," replied Greg; "he is one of the Prince of Denmark's equerries, and considered the handsomest man at court."

"I'm sure he's the purest-handsome man I've seen," cried Angelica, her eyes sparkling as she spoke. "O lud! if he isn't getting out of the coach. I hope he isn't coming to speak to me. Mother, lend me your fan to hide my face."

"Peace, you silly thing!" cried Mrs. Hyde, with a reproving look.

As she spoke, the carriage stopped, and Masham, stepping forth, closed the door after him. Greg's eulogium was not unmerited. The young equerry possessed a figure of perfect symmetry, and a countenance remarkable for delicacy and beauty. His eyes were of liquid blue, and it would seem of great power over the female heart; for as he fixed them upon Angelica, as he was detained beside her for a moment by the press, she felt hers flutter within her bosom.

His attire was not remarkable for richness, but it was tasteful, consisting of a green velvet coat, laced with gold, and a white satin waistcoat, made so low as to descend half way down the thigh, as was the mode. In lieu of a peruke, he wore his own dark-brown hair gathered from the forehead, and tied with a riband behind.

Samuel Masham was of a good Essex family, his father being Sir Francis Masham, of High-Laver, Bart., and his mother a daughter of Sir William Scott, of Rouen, in Normandy, who enjoyed the title of Marquis de la Mezansene in France; but as he was an eighth son, he had little expectation either of title or property. He was not more than twenty-three, or four at most, but had been for some time about court, having been page to the queen while Princess of Denmark, and was now equerry and gentleman of the bed-chamber to Prince George.

"By your leave, my pretty lass," said he, addressing Angelica in tones which thrilled her with delight, "I would pass."

"This way, Mr. Masham, this way," said Greg, retiring, and endeavouring to clear a passage.

"Ah! Mr. Greg," cried Masham, "what are you doing here?"

"Merely come with some country cousins to see the quality go to court, sir," replied Greg.

"Faith, you'll find no brighter eyes, nor cheeks more blooming, than those you've with you," said Masham, chucking Angelica under the chin. "Those lips are cherries indeed, but I must not be seduced by them to linger here. I've a word to say to the Comte de Briançon before I enter the palace."

So saying, and with a laughing glance at Angelica, he pushed through the crowd, and entered the house at the corner of Pall Mall.

"The Comte de Briançon, whose hotel he has just entered, is the envoy-extraordinary from the Duke of Savoy," observed Greg, not a little elated at the notice taken of him and his pretty country cousin by the handsome equerry. "I am well acquainted with his confidential secretary, Monsieur Claude Baude, who is to his master what I am to Mr. Harley. He's a charming man, Mr. Masham—eh, Miss Angelica?"

"Curiously charming," simpered the damsel.

"All the ladies think so," pursued Greg; "they're all in love with him."

"I should be surprised if they weren't," said Angelica.

"But see!" pursued Greg, "here comes another handsome man, Mr. Saint-John, secretary at war. He's a terrible rake."

"A rake, is he!" cried Angelica. "Oh! gemini! then I wont look at him, for mother says a rake is worse than a roaring lion, and sure to eat one up. Tell me when he's gone, Mr. Greg, for I don't desire to lose any more of the sight than I can help."

"The roaring lion has departed," replied Greg, laughing; "and here you have the Duke of Beaufort and his beautiful duchess. Has not her grace a noble presence? The bold, proud-looking dame who follows, is the Lady di Cecil. The three ladies laughing so loudly in yonder large coach are Lady Carlisle, Lady Effingham, and Mrs. Cross. Next comes my Lord Ross, to whom, they *do* say, Lady Sunderland is kinder than she should be; but that, I dare say, is mere scandal. Whom have we here? Faith, my Lady Fitzharding, at whose house more foolish spendthrifts are ruined at ombre and basset than at the groom-porter's."

"Oh, blind and perverse generation!" exclaimed Hyde, lifting up his eyes.

"Ah! you may well denounce them, reverend sir," replied Greg; "and here comes further food for a homily in the shape of his grace of Grafton. Look with what an air he lolls back in his coach. His good looks have made desperate havoc among the ladies, and no one but Mrs. Onslow has been found to resist him. Next comes fat Mrs. Knight, of whom I could, if I chose, tell you a diverting history. To her succeeds my Lord Nottingham, who appears as grave as if he had not recovered his dismissal from office, though he has tried to console himself with the Signora Margaretta. In the next coach sits the proudest dame at court—her grace of Marlborough, whose daughter she is, not excepted—it is the Duchess of Montague. Isn't she a magnificent creature? The lady who whisks past next, covered with diamonds, is Mrs. Long, Sir William Raby's sister. That handsome equipage belongs to Sir Richard Temple—you may see him, and a fine-looking man he is. People talk of him and Mrs. Centlivre—but I say nothing. Ah! here come a brace of wits. The one nearest this way is the famous Mr. Congreve, and the other the no less famous Captain Steele. I wonder which of the two owns the chariot—neither, most probably. The fine lady who succeeds them is Mrs. Hammond, whose husband is as much of a roaring lion as Mr. Saint-John, while she is said to console herself for his neglect by the attentions of my Lord Dursley, vice-admiral of the blue, and whom you may see leaning out of the next chariot window kissing his hand to her."

While he was thus running on, Greg felt his arm pulled by Angelica, who asked him in an under-tone if he knew the strange gentleman who had just taken up his station near them.

"To be sure I do," replied Greg, looking in the direction indicated, and raising his hat as he caught the eye of the individual alluded to; "it is the Marquis de Guiscard."

"Lawk, how he stares!" whispered Angelica. "I declare he quite puts a body out of countenance."

The marquis was tall and well-formed, though somewhat meagre, with dark, piercing eyes, black, bushy brows, and a pale, olive face, which looked perfectly blue where the beard had been shaven from it. His features were prominent, and would have been handsome but for a certain sinister expression, the disagreeable effect of which was heightened by an insolent and rakish air. His attire was the court-dress of an officer of high rank—namely, a scarlet coat, richly embroidered with gold, and having large cuffs; white satin waistcoat, likewise worked with gold; a point-lace cravat and ruffles, and a diamond-hilted sword. A full-flowing French peruke, a feathered hat, and a clouded cane, completed his costume.

Antoine de Guiscard, Abbé de la Bourlie, or, as he chose to style himself, Marquis de Guiscard, a scion of an ancient and noble French family, was born in the year 1658, and was consequently not far from fifty, at the period under consideration. Destined for the church, and possessed of considerable learning, he must, from his abilities and connexions, have obtained high preferment in it, if he could have placed due control on his passions. But amongst the depraved of a licentious court, he was the most depraved; and finding a priestly life too tame for him, he accompanied his brother, the Chevalier de Guiscard, to the scene of war in Flanders. On his return from this campaign, he resumed his wild courses, and assisted the chevalier to carry off a married woman, of whom the latter became enamoured. This affair was scarcely hushed up, when he got into fresh trouble, having wounded a gentleman, a near relation of Madame de Maintenon, and killed two of his servants, while shooting; and he put the climax to his folly and violence by subjecting a serjeant in his own regiment whom he had suspected of theft to the military rack—a species of torture administered by placing burning matches between the fingers of the accused. Orders being issued for his apprehension, he consulted his safety by flight, and escaped into Switzerland, where he conceived the notion of making himself the head of the malcontents in France, and with this view concerted measures with the leaders of the allies to produce a general insurrection, both of Protestants and Catholics, among the Camisars, who were then in a state of agitation. The plausible representations of the marquis procured him the commission of lieutenant-general from the emperor, and thus armed, he proceeded to Turin, where, with the assistance of the Duke of Savoy, he procured four small vessels of war, which were fitted up and manned at Nice, and with which he meditated a descent on the coast of Languedoc. But tempestuous weather, and, it may be, other causes, interfered with the expedition, and the marquis, after losing one of his ships and running great risks, returned to the court of Savoy. Here his underhand proceedings having excited the suspicion of the duke, he removed, towards the latter end of the year 1704, to the Hague, and had several conferences with the grand-pensionary, Heinsius, and the Duke of Marlborough, who were so well satisfied with his representations, that the States-General agreed to allow him the monthly pay of a hundred ducatoons. Intelligence being soon afterwards received of the Earl of Peterborough's expedition to Catalonia, the marquis hastened to join him at Barcelona, and meeting with the same success which had hitherto attended his projects, he contrived to obtain letters of recommendation from the King of Spain to the Queen of England, with which he embarked for that country. During the voyage, which was remarkably stormy, the vessel he sailed in engaged with a French privateer, and afforded the marquis a good opportunity of displaying his valour and skill, for it was mainly owing to his resolution capture was avoided. On reaching London he was graciously received by the queen, and the royal countenance procured him the entrée to the houses of the Dukes of Devonshire and Ormond. He also speedily managed to gain the good opinion of some of the ministers, particularly Mr. Saint-John. When, therefore, a descent upon France was proposed, and troops were raised for the purpose, to be commanded by the Earl of Rivers, Guiscard received the commission of lieutenant-colonel, and had a thousand pounds furnished him for his equipments. But fortune, which had hitherto smiled upon him, began now to waver. While the confederate fleet lay at Torbay, waiting for a favourable wind, disputes arose between him and the English generals, who refused to allow him the command which he claimed, and his ignorance of military affairs, as well as his imperfect acquaintance with the state of France, becoming apparent to Lord Rivers, he was recalled, and, returning to London, remained for some time in privacy. Though his pay as lieutenant-general was discontinued, he had still his regiment as well as his pension from the States; and taking a good house in Pall Mall, he set up a showy equipage, kept a host of servants, and commenced a career of extravagance and dissipation, which he contrived to support by play and other expedients, while he was constant in his attendance upon court, and at the levées of ministers, in search of employment and preferment.

Anxious, like most adventurers, to strengthen his precarious fortunes by an advantageous match, Guiscard had paid court to several heiresses and wealthy widows, but hitherto without success. It was also suspected that he had other and deeper schemes in hand; and that, having made his peace with France, he had contrived to open a clandestine correspondence with the court of Saint-Germains. Though a successful gamester, the marquis indulged in other profligate excesses, which ran away with all his gains at play. Audacious and insolent in general, he could yet be cringing and supple enough, if it suited his purpose. From some of his creatures employed about the palace, he had ascertained how well Abigail Hill stood with the queen, and at once discerning her future ascendancy, he turned all his attention to winning her regard. But his efforts were fruitless. Whether she divined his scheme, or had been warned against him by Harley, she repulsed his advances, and on the rare occasions of their meeting, scarcely treated him with civility. Guiscard, however, was not a man to be easily turned aside. Though his vanity was mortified by his rejection, he resolved to persevere, and to wait some favourable opportunity for the prosecution of his design.

Soon after the marquis had posted himself in the manner described, another slight disturbance occurred in the rear of Greg and his party. It was occasioned by the issuing forth of several lacqueys in gay liveries from the house at the corner of Pall Mall, before alluded to, who pushed aside the crowd with their gold-headeds, to make way for a superbly-gilt chair, emblazoned with the arms of Savoy. As this chair was borne past the Marquis de Guiscard, the window was let down, and, amidst an atmosphere of perfume, a handsome, but dissipated-looking man, wearing a magnificent French peruke, put out his head and addressed him.

"It is the Comte de Briançon himself," said Greg to his companions.

"How purely sweet he smells, to be sure," remarked Angelica. "I declare, he's just like a great scent-bottle!"

"Well, my dear Marquis! how speed you? Is the adventure over?" inquired the comte, laughing, and displaying a brilliant set of teeth.

"The lady has not yet passed," returned Guiscard. "What have you done with Masham? I thought he was in the chair with you."

"He has stayed behind to read a letter," said the comte. "You have secured the coachman, you say."

"Five guineas has done his business," answered Guiscard. "But, by Saint Michael! here she comes. Away, count!"

"Adieu, then, and success attend you," cried Briançon. And giving the signal to the chairmen, they moved on towards the palace.

The foregoing brief conversation, though conducted in French, was not lost upon Greg, who perfectly understood the language, and who being also well aware of the Marquis's character, at once comprehended the nature of the project on which he was engaged. He looked, therefore, with some curiosity towards the approaching coaches, to see which of them contained the heroine of the expected adventure, and he was not long in making the discovery. As he scanned the line, he observed a stout, rosy-faced fellow, in a full-bottomed, powdered wig, and sky-blue livery with yellow facings, who was seated on the hammer-cloth of a magnificent chariot, slightly raise his whip, and give a nod of intelligence to the marquis.

"There she is, I'll be sworn!" he exclaimed, stepping forward to get a better view of the equipage. "As I live! 'tis Lady Rivers. He cannot mean to give her a billet-doux in this public place. But who has she with her?—Miss Abigail Hill. Oh! I now see his mark. Egad! she looks uncommonly well."

Abigail Hill could not be called positively beautiful, and yet the expression of her countenance was so agreeable, that she deserved the epithet quite as much as many persons whose features were more classically moulded. Fine eyes of a clear blue, a radiantly white skin, auburn hair, round dimpling cheeks, and teeth as white as pearls, constituted her attractions. Looking at her narrowly, it was seen that there was a good deal of firmness about the brow and mouth, and a steady expression in the eye, that argued determination, the proper bent of which seemed guaranteed by the rest of her face. Her quickness of manner, and vivacity of look, proclaimed the possession of a ready wit; nor were these outward indications delusive. Her figure was extremely good, slight, tall, and graceful. It was displayed in court dress of white satin, trimmed with lace, and made low, with short loose sleeves. Her age might be about four-and-twenty.

By this time the chariot in which she rode approached within a short distance of the Marquis de Guiscard, when the coachman, who had watched his opportunity, contrived to run against the vehicle moving in a line with him. He was instantly assailed with the most vehement abuse for his carelessness by the neighbouring Jehu, to whom he responded in appropriate terms, charging him with being the cause of the collision. This, as he anticipated, roused the other's ire so much, that he threatened to knock him off the box. Whereupon the offender replied by an oath of defiance, accompanied by a cut with his whip. The aggrieved coachman instantly rose on his box and lashed furiously at his adversary, who, while defending himself, had much ado to restrain his horses, which began to plunge desperately.

Greatly amused by the conflict, the spectators cheered lustily, while the ladies within the carriage becoming alarmed by the noise, Abigail Hill put her head out of the window to see what was the cause of the stoppage. At this moment, the Marquis de Guiscard rushed forward, and opening the door offered to assist her out, but on seeing him, she instinctively drew back.

Guiscard then addressed himself to Lady Rivers, but with no better success.

"Obliged to you for your offer of assistance, marquis," replied her ladyship, "but we will stay where we are. Do tell the coachman to drive on, or I will discharge him."

"Pardon, miladi," cried Guiscard. "The fellow refuses to attend to me. His island blood is up. Come, Miss Hill, I must be peremptory, and insist on your getting out. I am fearful some accident may occur"

"You are very attentive, marquis," said Abigail; "but Lady Rivers's servants are at hand, and will take care of us. Ditchley," she added, to a footman, who had now approached the door—"your arm."

The man would have advanced, but the marquis motioned him angrily off. The fight, meanwhile, between the two coachmen, raged with increased fury.

"Ditchley!" screamed Lady Rivers, who now began to be seriously alarmed.

"Comin', your la'asip," replied the footman, trying to push past the marquis.

"Back, fellow!" cried Guiscard. "I warn you not to interfere."

But seeing the man resolute, and exasperated at the failure of his plan, he raised his cane, and with a well-dealt blow on the sconce, stretched the unlucky Ditchley on the ground.

Both ladies now screamed, not knowing how far the violence of the marquis might extend. At this, the three other footmen who were clinging behind the chariot, flew to their assistanse, but another protector anticipated them. Just as Ditchley fell, Masham, who, a few moments previously, had issued from the Comte de Briançon's hotel, seeing what was going forward, made his way through the crowd, and rushing up to the carriage, caught the marquis by the collar, and thrust him forcibly aside.

"Ha! what in the devil's name brings you here, sir!" cried Guiscard, in tones almost inarticulate with rage.

"I am come to protect these ladies from affront," replied Masham, sternly, and laying his hand upon his sword.

"'Sdeath, sir!—how do you know they have been affronted?— And who constituted you their defender?" demanded Guiscard, furiously.

"I will render you a full account for my interference hereafter, marquis," replied Masham; "but if you have any pretension to the character of a gentleman, you will not carry on this dispute further in the presence of ladies."

"Be it so!" replied Guiscard, between his teeth. "But be assured, you shall not escape chastisement."

"Do not involve yourself in a quarrel on my account, I pray, Mr. Masham," said Abigail, who, meanwhile, had descended from the coach, the door having been opened by one of the footmen.

"I am very happy to have been of the slightest use to you, Miss Hill," replied Masham, bowing; "and as to the quarrel, I beg you will give yourself no concern about it."

"I have seen all that passed," said a soldier, advancing, with his musket over his shoulder, "and if it is your pleasure, sir, or that of the ladies, I will take these two quarrelsome coachmen to the guard-house."

"That would scarcely mend the matter, my good fellow," replied Masham; "but the disturbance is at an end."

"Unquestionably, so far as I am concerned," said the marquis, seeing the disadvantage in which he had placed himself, and suddenly assuming an apologetic tone. "I have been altogether in

B

the wrong. I meant only to offer you assistance, Miss Hill, and have to implore your pardon for suffering my passion to carry me to such absurd lengths. It was yon fellow's rudeness that caused my anger. However, I am sorry for him, and hope a guinea will mend his broken pate. Mr. Masham, you have cause to thank me for the service I have rendered you—unintentionally, it is true—but a service not the less important on that account. Ladies, I salute you." And with a bow of supercilious politeness he marched off towards the palace, amid the murmurs of the bystanders.

Seeing the turn matters had taken, and the discomfiture of his employer, the coachman now thought proper to listen to reason, and to beg pardon for his share of the misadventure, while his adversary drove off. Thus reassured, Abigail resumed her seat in the coach, warmly thanking the young equerry, who assisted her into it, for his gallantry.

"Only promise me one thing, Mr. Masham," she said—"that you wont accept the marquis's challenge, if he sends one. If anything should happen to you, I shall never forgive myself."

"Have no fear," he replied, laughingly. "I shall run no risk."

"But promise me not to fight," cried Abigail. "Nay, if you hesitate, I must procure a mediator in the queen. You dare not disobey her."

"It is scarcely worth while to trouble her majesty on so unimportant a matter," returned Masham.

"The matter is not so unimportant to me," replied Abigail. And then checking herself, and blushing, she leaned back in the carriage, which rolled on towards the gateway of the palace.

"You expressed great concern for Mr. Masham, my dear," observed Lady Rivers. "If he has any vanity,—and what handsome young fellow has not?—he will fancy he has made a conquest."

"Nay, I only expressed a natural concern for him, I'm sure," replied Abigail. "I should be terribly distressed if he were to fight this odious Marquis de Guiscard."

"And still more terribly distressed, if he should chance to get run through the body by the odious marquis, who, they say, is the most expert swordsman about town," rejoined Lady Rivers.

"Don't suppose anything so dreadful," cried Abigail, turning pale. "I will certainly mention the matter to the queen; that will be the surest way to prevent mischief."

"But take care not to betray the state of your heart to her majesty at the same time, my dear," said Lady Rivers, somewhat maliciously.

Abigail blushed again, but attempted no reply; and at this juncture the carriage stopped, the door was opened, and they were ushered into the palace.

CHAPTER III.

A TÊTE-À-TÊTE AT MARLBOROUGH HOUSE.

NEVER had a drawing-room at Saint-James's been more numerously or brilliantly attended than on the present occasion. It was remarked, however, that the queen looked somewhat jaded and out of spirits, while a slight inflammation about the eyes increased her general appearance of indisposition. Noticing these symptoms with concern, the Duke of Marlborough alluded to them to the Prince of Denmark, who replied hastily and heedlessly, as was his wont, "The queen owes her illness to herself. If she did not sit up so late at night, her eyes would not be so red, nor her spirits so indifferent."

"Indeed!" exclaimed the duke; "I thought her majesty retired to rest early."

"So she does, generally," replied the prince, in some confusion at the indiscretion he now perceived he had committed; "but sometimes she will sit up talking for an hour or two—talking to me, your grace—merely to me—asking my opinion on matters before the cabinet—much better go to bed—late hours don't agree with either of us—ha! ha!" And he thrust his snuff-box into the duke's hand to put an end to the discourse.

Marlborough acknowledged the attention with a bow, but he muttered to himself—"She sits up o' nights, ha! Some one besides the duchess is in her confidence. This must be looked to."

Later on in the day, when the drawing-room was over, the duke was alone with his illustrious lady, at Marlborough house.

The duchess was radiant. Her fine eyes sparkled with pleasure, and her cheeks were flushed with triumph. Her step, as she crossed the chamber towards a sofa at the further end of it, was prouder than usual, and her mien statelier. A magnificent woman still was Sarah of Marlborough, and little of decay was visible about her. There was something queenly in her look and deportment. Her figure was tall and commanding, and her features cast in that superb mould which seems reserved only for the great. All emotions could those features well portray, but the expression which they habitually wore was that of pride. And yet they were soft and feminine, and not destitute of a certain character of voluptuousness, chiefly discernible in the rich fulness of the lips, and the melting languor of the eyes, which, when not lighted into fire, had inexpressible tenderness. Her forehead was exceedingly fine, and her dark hair, which was gathered like a tiara over her brow, descending in ringlets behind, retained all its original glossiness and profusion. Her proportions were full; the rounded neck, arm, and shoulder, being all of marble whiteness. Her attire corresponded in magnificence with her person, and blazed with diamonds and precious stones. Among other ornaments, she wore a ring of great value, which had been presented to her by Charles the Third of Spain, when he visited

England four years before. The Duchess of Marlborough was a woman to inspire a grand passion, and to maintain it. Neither absence nor irritation could shake the devoted attachment entertained for her by the duke, and now, after their long union, he was as much her lover as when he wooed her as Sarah Jennings.

And well was she matched by her noble lord. Not more distinguished for his mental qualifications than for his personal graces and accomplishments, was the Duke of Marlborough. A perfect courtier, in the best sense of the word, which means that he was a most refined gentleman, the duke superadded the soldier to the courtier, making a matchless combination. Nothing more polished, more graceful, more easy, or which set others more at ease, can be imagined than Marlborough's manner, while at the same time it was dignified and imposing. His figure was lofty, and nobly proportioned; and what with his renown, his stateliness of presence, and his handsome form and features, it was impossible to look at him without admiration. True, the duke was no longer young— true, he had undergone excessive fatigue of all kinds, had been harassed in every way, and for years had known but few and brief intervals of repose; despite all this, however, he preserved his good looks in a most astonishing manner, and though no longer the fair youth who had captivated the Duchess of Cleveland in Charles the Second's day, he was still a model of manly beauty. He was habited in his general's uniform, and was richly decorated with orders, amongst which was the George, in a sardonyx set with diamonds of immense value. His spirits were by no means so high as those of the duchess. On the contrary, he looked thoughtful, and followed her slowly and musingly to the sofa.

"What ails your grace?" cried the duchess, seating herself. "Methinks if anything could make you cheerful, it should be the acclamations with which you were greeted by the crowd as you left the palace. Their deafening cries of, 'God save the queen and the Duke of Marlborough!' can almost be heard here, and I fancy must have reached even the ears of Anne herself. The sweetest music to me, is the applausive shouting of the people, and the most gladsome and stirring sight, their beaming faces and waving hats. But both seem to have lost their charm for you to-day. Custom has staled them, as it has staled me."

"Popular applause may indeed fail to move me," replied the duke, affectionately—"perhaps does so; but the day is far distant, sweetheart, when I shall be insensible to your love. I am somewhat overcome by the tumult, and wish I had returned from the palace privately."

"Better as it is," said the duchess; "you cannot show yourself too much. Has anything happened at the drawing-room to annoy you? I thought you looked somewhat grave there."

"Well, then, I must own I have been disturbed by a few words let fall by the prince, respecting the queen. I told him I was sorry to see her look ill, and he said it was her own fault, for she would sit up late at night."

"Did he tell you with whom?" demanded the duchess.

"No," answered the duke. "Like a poor chess-player, he tried to repair his inadvertence, and therefore exposed himself further. But I could not learn who was the queen's companion, beside himself."

"Then I will tell you," replied the duchess; "it is our cousin, Abigail Hill."

"What, the dresser and bed-chamber woman?" cried the duke; "if that be all, it is of little moment,"

"It is not of such little moment as your grace imagines," replied the duchess; "and if I had known what I now know of Abigail, when I placed her near the queen, I would never have put it in her power to do me an injury. Who would have thought so artless a creature, to all appearance, could play her cards so cunningly! But the jade has discerned the queen's weak points, and seeing how much she is the slave of those who feign to love her, and will condescend to fawn upon her and flatter her for her wit and understanding—*her* wit and understanding, forsooth!—she has resorted to all these mean arts to win her confidence."

"If she *has* won it, you cannot blame her," replied the duke; "and I cannot help saying, if you yourself, madam, were to study the queen's temper and peculiarities more, it would be better."

"I am surprised to hear your grace talk thus," replied the duchess, bridling up. "Would you have me sacrifice my opinions to one to whom I have been accustomed to dictate? Would you have me approve measures when I disapprove them! Would you have me cringe, protest, and lie, or copy the manners of this servile creature? Would you have me listen to every childish complaint, every whim, every caprice,—or affect sympathy when I feel none? Would you have me solicit when I can command,—kneel, when I can sit,— obey, when I can exact obedience?"

"Nay—but, madam," said the duke, "the duties to your queen make what might appear servility and flattery to another, rightful homage and respect to her."

"I shall never be wanting in loyalty and devotion to the queen," replied the duchess; "and whatever opinions I offer, shall be consistent with her honour. I can never reproach myself with advising aught derogatory to her station or to the welfare of the country, and with that conviction I shall continue to act as I have begun. I may lose her regard, but I will never lose my own respect."

"I know you to be a high-minded woman, madam," replied the duke, "and that all your actions are directed by the best and noblest principles; but I still conceive that, without any sacrifice of moral dignity or self-respect, you might more effectually retain her majesty's regard."

"Your grace mistakes the queen altogether," replied the duchess, impatiently: "and were I to yield to her humour, or subscribe to her opinion, things would be in a far worse position than they are now. Anne is one of those persons who, if allowed to have her own way, or act upon her own impulses, would be sure to go wrong. Without energy or decision, she is so short-sighted that she can only discern what is immediately before her, and even then is pretty sure to err in judgment. To serve her well, she must be led—to make her reign prosperous and glorious, she must be ruled."

"My own experience leads me to the same conclusion as yourself, madam," said the duke; "but this principle must not be carried too far. Weak natures like that of Anne must not be pressed too hardly, or they will rebel against the hand that governs them. I have observed some indications of this sort of late about the queen. She seems displeased with you."

"And what matter if she be displeased with me?" replied the duchess, somewhat contemptuously; "she may be piqued for the moment, but I am too necessary to her, and, indeed, too much her mistress, for any lasting breach to occur between us."

"Be not over-confident, madam," returned the duke. "Security is often fatal. Security lost the battle of Blenheim to Tallard; and to Villeroy's security I owe the victory of Ramilies. To trust too much is to give your enemy an advantage, and defeat may occur when there is least appearance of danger. It is true that the queen has hitherto submitted to your governance in all things, but her advisers may turn your very power against you. I am so much of a Jesuit, in one sense, that if the object I had in view were praiseworthy, and I was satisfied on that score, I should not look too scrupulously at the means by which the great end was to be accomplished. Some concessions must be made to the queen—some change in your deportment towards her, or I am apprehensive you will lose her favour."

"If I must lose it, I must," replied the duchess. "But I will never retain it by imitating these truckling slaves—these minions who would crouch to the earth for a smile. It shall never be said of Sarah of Marlborough, that she adopted the abject policy of Abigail Hill,—and she only feels surprised that her lord should give her such counsel."

"I recommend no abject policy," replied the duke, a little nettled by her tone. "But firmness is one thing, imperiousness another. It is not in human nature, still less in the nature of one of such exalted rank, to submit to the control you impose upon Anne."

"Be content to rule in the camp, my lord," said the duchess, "and leave the queen to me. I have hitherto proved successful."

"But you are on the eve of a defeat," cried the duke. "I warn you of that, madam."

"Your grace is as impatient as her majesty," said the duchess, tauntingly.

"And with as much reason," cried the duke, rising and pacing the apartment.

"I have been a faithful and loving wife to you, my lord, and a faithful and loving friend and servant to the queen," replied the duchess, "and I cannot alter my conduct to please either of you."

"You rule us both with an iron rod," cried Marlborough; "and my own feelings of irritation make me perfectly comprehend those of the queen."

"As I do not desire to quarrel with your grace, I will leave you till you are cooler," said the duchess, rising, and moving towards the door.

"Nay, you shall not go," cried the duke, catching her hand. "I have been hasty—wrong. By Heaven! I do not wonder you govern Anne so absolutely, for I have no will but yours."

"Nor I any law but yours, my lord," answered the duchess, smiling. "You know that, and therefore yield to me—*sometimes*. And so does her majesty."

"If she loves you as truly as I do, Sarah," returned Marlborough, tenderly, "you have nothing to fear. My passion borders on idolatry, and I could be anything in your hands, if the reward for it was to be your love. The letters I have sent you, written amid the hurry and exhaustion of rapid marches—amid the vexations of opposing interests—on the agitating eve of battle, or in the intoxication of victory, would prove to you that you were ever foremost in my thoughts, but they could not speak the full extent of my feelings. Oh, Sarah! fortunate as my career has been, and much as I ought yet to do to serve my queen and country, I would far rather retire with you to some quiet retreat, where we might pass the remainder of our life undisturbed by faction, or the cares of public life."

"Your grace would not be happy in such an existence,—nor should I," replied the duchess. "We were made for greatness. The quiet retreat you propose would become a prison, where you would be tormented by a thousand stirring thoughts of conquests yet unachieved, and laurels yet unwon; while I should lament the ascendancy I had lost, and the power I had thrown aside. No, no, my lord—much is to be done—much to be won before we retire. It will be time to quit our posts when our acquisitions can no longer be increased. When I have made you the wealthiest noble, as you are the first in Europe, I shall be satisfied; but not till then."

"You are a woman in a thousand," cried the duke, in admiration.

"I am worthy to be the wife of the Duke of Marlborough," she answered, proudly; "and my lord may safely repose his honour and interests with me, I will watch well over both."

"I doubt it not, madam," cried the duke, in a voice of emotion, and pressing her hand to his lips—"I doubt it not. But I would you had never placed Abigail near the queen."

"My motive for doing so was this," replied the duchess. "I was fatigued to death with attendance upon her majesty; and to speak truth, after your grace's elevation to a principality of the empire, I thought the office derogatory. Abigail was therefore introduced as the fittest and safest person to fill my place. That I could not have made a worse selection I now find. The wench has begun to comport herself towards me with a degree of insolence that argues the reliance she places on the queen's protection. Add to which, I have discovered that an understanding subsists between her and her kinsman, Harley."

"Godolphin and I have for some time doubted Harley," returned the duke, "and have been anxious for his removal from the ministry. But the queen has clung to him with a tenacity till now unaccountable."

" Your grace had once a high opinion of this secretary," said the duchess, " but I always warned you against him as a smooth-tongued hypocrite, who had merely his own advancement in view. Now, I hope you are convinced?"

" Most unpleasantly so," rejoined the duke. " But how do you suppose Harley communicates with Abigail?"

" I intercepted a note from her to him this morning at the drawing-room," said the duchess.

" A love letter?" asked Marlborough.

" No; a few words hastily traced in pencil, desiring him to be at the garden gate of the palace at eleven to-morrow night," said the duchess.

" That sounds like an appointment!" cried the duke.

" Ay, but it is not with herself," said the duchess. " He is to come there to see the queen. Of that I am well assured. But I will surprise them. Having the key of the back staircase, I can easily be present at the conference."

" You had better think this over," said Marlborough. " The queen may resent the intrusion."

" I have already told your grace you know her not. She is far more in awe of me than I am of her, and with reason. If she were not ashamed of Harley, she would not receive him thus clandestinely. My discovery of the intercourse will be quite sufficient to put an end to it."

" I hope so," replied the duke. " But while Abigail enjoys her favour, there will always be danger. Can we not provide her a husband?"

" Hum!" exclaimed the duchess.

At this juncture, a servant entered and announced the Earl of Sunderland.

" Glad to see you, son-in-law," said the duke, extending his hand to him. " We were talking of marrying our cousin, Abigail Hill."

" What, to the Marquis de Guiscard! who attempted to carry her off in the face of all the world this morning," cried Sunderland, " and was only prevented by the interference of young Masham, the prince's equerry?"

" Ah! how was that?" inquired the duchess.

And the earl proceeded to detail the occurrence.

" Guiscard is a dangerous man," said the duke; " and if he cannot rid himself of a rival by fair means, will not hesitate to have recourse to foul. I heard a strange character of him at the Hague; but he is brave, and useful for certain purposes. I'll warrant me it is suspicion of Abigail's favour with the queen that makes him pay court to her. Otherwise, she could have no attraction to an adventurer like him."

" Lord Ross, who mentioned the circumstance to Lady Sunderland," said the earl, " and who had it from Lady Rivers, declared that Abigail was quite taken by Masham."

" Ah, indeed!" said the duchess. " Something may be made of this hint. Are you acquainted with Mr. Masham, my lord?"

"Quite sufficiently for any purpose your grace may require," replied Sunderland.

"Make it your business to find him out, then, and bring him here to dinner," rejoined the duchess.

"You forget the ball this evening at the palace?" interposed the duke.

"No I do not," replied the duchess; "and I will thank your grace to send a card of invitation, without delay, to the Marquis de Guiscard. I will explain my motives presently. I depend upon you, Sunderland."

"Your behests shall be obeyed, madam, if possible," replied the earl, who was accustomed, like all the duchess's family, to render blind obedience to her. "I think I heard Masham was gone with Harley and some others to the Cocoa Tree. I'll seek him there at once."

CHAPTER IV.

THE BALL AT THE PALACE, AND WHAT HAPPENED AT IT.

THE ball at the palace in the evening was as brilliantly attended as the drawing-room had been, though of course less numerously. Adjoining the grand saloon where dancing was going forward, was a small apartment hung with green silk, woven with gold, whence it obtained the name of the "green chamber," in which, by the subdued light of shaded candles, might be discovered, seated on a fauteuil, a finely-formed but somewhat full proportioned lady, attired in a robe of purple velvet, of the particular die devoted to royalty. Around her smooth throat, which lost little by the contrast, was twined a string of the largest and most beautiful pearls, while across her fair rounded shoulders glittered the collar of the George. Her dress was worn low in front, as was the mode—and the style perfectly suited the wearer, who was remarkable for the beauty of her bust. The upper part of the stomacher was edged with stiffened point lace, as were the short loose sleeves of the gown. Here again the mode was favourable to the wearer, whose arms were of Junonian roundness and whiteness. Her hair, dark brown in colour, and of a fine texture, was divided in the centre, but raised in high and ample curls above the head, and being looped behind by a string of pearls as magnificent as those encircling her throat, descended in thick waving ringlets down her back. Her complexion was fresh and rosy—its bloom derived from health and nature only—her features regular, with a small, delicate mouth, and agreeably-moulded chin. Her eyes were good, but disfigured by a slight contraction of the lids, while a heaviness about the brow gave a somewhat cloudy expression to her countenance. The Duchess of Marlborough says, in the character bequeathed by her of Anne—"There was something of majesty in her look, but mixed with a sullen and constant frown, that plainly betrayed a gloominess of soul, and a cloudiness of disposition within." But this was written after the painter of the portrait had, by her own imprudence, called a "constant frown" to the countenance.

Anne's manners were dignified, graceful, and easy, and her embonpoint rather added to the majesty of her deportment than detracted from it. In stature, she was of the middle size In a much less exalted sphere of life, Anne would have been admired for her accomplishments and personal attractions, which were by no means inconsiderable. In earlier days she had danced remarkably well, and accompanied herself in singing on the guitar—an instrument then much in vogue, which she played with consummate skill. The tones of her voice were singularly clear and harmonious, and, like her illustrious successor in modern times, she was distinguished by the admirable delivery of her speeches to parliament.

Anne's private virtues have already been dwelt upon. She was a model of conjugal affection, amiable, devout, charitable, and an excellent economist; insomuch that her treasury was always well provided. A lover of polite letters, and a true friend to the church, her bounty in surrendering the tithes and first-fruits in augmentation of poor vicarages, must ever cause her name to be held in grateful remembrance by the clergy. At the period in question she was in her forty-third year.

Not far from the queen, at a small card-table, sat her consort, Prince George of Denmark, playing at picquet with Mr. Harley. A slight description must suffice for the prince. Stout, with large, handsome, good-humoured features, he seemed to be fonder of play, and the pleasures of the table, than the cares and perplexities of sovereignty. Apart from his constitutional apathy and indolence the prince had many good qualities. He was humane, just, affable, and had the welfare of the country sincerely at heart. Rarely offering advice to the queen, or interfering between her and her ministers; when he did so, his opinion was well considered. His was a character rather to inspire esteem than respect, and Anne loved him more for the qualities of his heart than regarded him for those of his head. He was dressed in black velvet, with a star upon his breast, and wore the blue riband, and the garter.

The Duchess of Ormond, Lady Portmore, and Lady Rivers, were in attendance on the queen; and somewhat nearer to her than the rest, stood Abigail Hill, with whom she was conversing. A concert of singers from the Italian Opera, with which Anne had been much diverted, was just over, and she was still talking of the pleasure she had received from it when the Duchess of Marlborough entered.

"Ah! you are come at last," said Anne. "I feared I was not to see your grace to-night."

"Your majesty knows I have little taste for music," returned the duchess, "and I therefore postponed my arrival till after the concert, which I knew would take place at ten."

"Better late than not at all, certainly," rejoined Anne; "but I have missed you."

"Your majesty is infinitely obliging," said the duchess, sarcastically—"and I fear sacrifices your sincerity at the shrine of complaisance; for I can scarcely believe I can have been missed when I find you in company so much more congenial to your taste than mine has become."

"If you mean Abigail," replied the queen, slightly colouring, "she has indeed proved herself pleasant company, for she loves music as much as myself, and we have been talking over the charming songs we have just heard."

"You have heard of Abigail's adventure on her way to the drawing-room this morning, I presume, madam?" said the duchess.

"I have," replied the queen, "and have taken care that the quarrel between the Marquis de Guiscard and Mr. Masham shall proceed no further."

"Your majesty is very considerate," said the duchess; "but it would have been as well, methinks, if the young lady had made me, her kinswoman, acquainted with the occurrence."

"In imparting the matter to her majesty, I thought I had done all that was needful," rejoined Abigail; "and I should not have interfered in the matter if I had not feared that harm might befal——"

"Mr. Masham," supplied the duchess, maliciously. "But you need not have given yourself uneasiness. The Marquis de Guiscard has been with me to express his regret at what has occurred, and I must confess his explanation appears satisfactory. He says that some misapprehension of his intention, on your part, made you treat him in such manner as led to the violence which he regrets, and for which he is most anxious to apologize."

"I had no misapprehension of his intentions," said Abigail—"none whatever."

"If you mean to insinuate that he is in love with you," returned the duchess, "I must admit that you are in the right, for he owned as much to me, and entreated me to plead his cause with you. For my own part, I think the offer a good one, and, as your relation, should be pleased to see the union take place. If you yourself are willing, cousin, her majesty, I am persuaded, will not refuse her consent."

"I certainly should not refuse my consent if I thought Abigail's happiness at all concerned," replied the queen; "but in the present instance such does not appear to be the case. Nay, I almost fancy I should please her best by withholding it."

"Your majesty is in the right," replied Abigail; "and even if you were to lay your injunctions upon me to wed the Marquis de Guiscard, I do not think I could obey you."

"Your devotion shall not be so severely taxed," said the queen, smiling.

"Yet the Marquis should not be rejected too hastily," said the duchess. "You behaved somewhat rudely to him this morning, Abigail—his gallantry deserved a better return."

"It is easy for the contriver of a scheme to play it out,' said

Abigail. "What if I tell your grace that Lady Rivers's coachman has since confessed to being bribed by the marquis to act as he did?"

"The fellow must lie!" cried the duchess, angrily. "But the truth shall be instantly ascertained, for the marquis is without. May he be permitted to enter the presence?"

"Why—yes," replied the queen, reluctantly, "if your grace desires it."

"I *do* desire it," returned the duchess. And stepping into the ball-room, she returned the next moment with Guiscard.

Notwithstanding his effrontery, the marquis looked abashed at the presence in which he stood; he glanced uneasily towards the queen, and from her to Abigail, beneath whose steadfast contemptuous look, he quailed.

"My cousin Abigail declares you bribed Lady Rivers's coachman to occasion this disturbance, marquis," said the duchess. "Is it so?"

"I will frankly confess it is," replied Guiscard, with an air of candour; "and the impulse that prompted me to the act, I will with equal frankness admit, was my passion for the lovely Abigail. I hoped by this means to make a favourable impression upon her. But I have been sufficiently punished for my temerity by failure."

There was a moment's pause, during which a glance passed between the queen and the Duchess of Marlborough.

"You did wrong, marquis," said the former, at length; "but the admission of the motive is something."

"I have nothing to plead in extenuation of my conduct, but the excess of my passion, madam," rejoined the marquis, penitently. "I entreat Miss Hill's forgiveness."

"I would willingly accord it," she answered, "if I felt assured there would be no repetition of the annoyance."

"Let me play the mediator, Abigail," interposed the duchess.

"Your grace will waste time," rejoined Abigail. "I am surprised that a person of the marquis's spirit should persevere, where he sees there is no chance of success. A well-executed retreat, as the Duke of Marlborough would tell him, is equal to a victory. Let him retire while he can do so with a good grace."

"You have had your answer, marquis," said the queen, smiling.

"I have, madam," replied Guiscard, bowing to hide his mortification; "but a monarch of my own country, and one who had the reputation of understanding your sex thoroughly, having left it on record that woman is changeable, and that he is a fool who takes her at her word, and my own experience serving to prove the truth of the assertion, I shall not be discouraged, though at present rebuffed."

"I must at least interdict you from pressing your suit further," said the queen.

"Agreed, madam," returned Guiscard; "but what if I have the fair Abigail's consent?"

"In that case, of course, the interdiction is withdrawn;" replied the queen.

"She shall yet be yours," said the duchess, in a whisper to Guiscard.

"I know on whom I rely," returned the marquis, in the same tone. "I would rather have your grace's word than the lady's own promise."

"And you would choose rightly," said the duchess, smiling

As the words were uttered, the party was increased by the entrance of the Earl of Sunderland and Masham. The latter looked somewhat flushed and excited.

"Ah, Mr. Masham!" cried the queen, "you are come most opportunely. I wish to make you friends with the Marquis de Guiscard."

"Your majesty is very kind and condescending," replied Masham, "but I am already reconciled to him."

"I am happy to hear it," rejoined Anne; "but I was not aware you had met."

"Oh dear, yes, madam!" returned Masham; "we both dined at Marlborough House, and are the best friends imaginable. Instead of quarrelling, we have laughed heartily at the adventure of the morning. If I had known the marquis's motive, I should not have interfered."

"Indeed!" exclaimed Abigail, with a look of ill-disguised vexation.

"You surely do not think he was justified in what he did, Mr. Masham?" said the queen.

"In love and war, I need not remind your majesty, all stratagems are fair," replied Masham, bowing.

"You are a very unaccountable person, Mr. Masham," said Abigail, in a tone of pique.

"I am not the only unaccountable person in the world, Miss Hill," he replied, significantly.

"There seems to be some misunderstanding here," interposed Harley, who had just finished his game, rising from the card-table; "can I set it right?"

"Where others fail, doubtless Mr. Harley can succeed," observed the duchess, sarcastically.

"I will try, madam, at all events," replied the secretary. "You appear put out of the way, my dear?" he added, to Abigail.

"Oh, not in the least, cousin," she replied, quickly.

"And you?" he continued, turning to Masham.

"Oh, not in the least," was the answer; "unless, indeed, he added, "for making a fool of myself, and spoiling sport."

"But you really appear to require some explanation," said Harley; "and I am sure Miss Hill will afford it."

"You are giving yourself very needless trouble, sir," said Masham, coolly; "I have had all the explanation I require."

"And I have given all I design to afford," said Abigail, with affected indifference.

"Very adroitly managed, indeed, Mr. Secretary," laughed the duchess. "You have set matters right very expeditiously, it must be owned."

"Perhaps I might be more successful," interposed Anne, good-naturedly.

"Oh, no, indeed, your majesty!" said Abigail. "I begin to think I was wrong, after all, about the Marquis de Guiscard."

"She relents!" whispered the duchess to the marquis.

"Not so," he replied, in the same tone; "that was merely said to pique Masham."

"Never mind why it was said, if it promotes your object," rejoined the duchess. "Go to her at once. If you succeed in irritating Masham past reconciliation, all will be well."

"There's my hand, marquis, in token of forgiveness," said Abigail to Guiscard.

"You are wrong, cousin," whispered Harley, "and will repent what you are doing."

"No, I sha'n't," she replied, in the same tone.

Further asides were interrupted by the advance of the marquis, who took Abigail's hand and pressed it respectfully to his lips.

"You were right; she is a mere coquette," said Masham to Sunderland, in a tone almost sufficiently loud to be audible to the others.

"Why—yes. I thought you could easily discover it," replied the earl.

"May I be permitted to claim your hand for the dance, Miss Hill, now that I have possession of it?" said the marquis.

"If her majesty will allow me, yes"—hesitated Abigail.

"You see I have the young lady's consent, madam," said Guiscard to the queen. "I trust, therefore, you will graciously withdraw your interdiction?"

"Abigail must use her own discretion," replied Anne. "I think you are wrong in dancing with him," she added, in an undertone to her.

"I have a motive for it, madam," replied Abigail, in the same voice. "I have succeeded in vexing him," she added, aside, to Harley, as she passed.

"You have lost him," he rejoined, angrily.

"Well, no matter, I shall not break my heart about him," she returned. And dropping a profound courtesy to the queen, she tripped into the ball-room with Guiscard.

"On my soul, I begin to think her a coquette myself," muttered Harley. "She will ruin all my plans, I must speak to Masham."

"I will myself proceed to the ball-room," said the queen, rising, and taking the arm of her royal consort. "Your grace will attend me?"

The duchess bowed, and extending her hand to Masham, said—"Come, sir, you must go with me."

And, with a glance of triumph at the discomfited secretary, she followed the queen into the ball-room.

Another attempt was made by Harley to bring about a reconciliation between Abigail and Masham, but it proved as unsuccessful as the first. The young equerry was so piqued that he devoted himself exclusively to the beautiful Countess of Sunderland, who, having received a hint to that effect from her mother, took care not to discourage his attentions, and finally carried him away in triumph with her and the earl to supper. Foiled in this quarter, Harley turned to Abigail; but she was equally engrossed by the marquis, laughed loudly at his remarks, and appeared so much amused and interested by him, that the secretary was completely puzzled, and began to consider what course he should adopt.

"If she really likes Guiscard," he thought, "I must make a friend of him betimes. But I cannot believe it. She admitted to me that she was pleased with Masham—and her looks said more than her words. And yet she acts in this unaccountable manner. But a woman never knows her own mind for an hour together, and why should I expect more from her than from the rest of her sex? I never knew a plot miscarry, but a woman had some share in it. I have no special regard for Masham, but he would be better than this intriguing Frenchman, who will speedily ruin Abigail and himself. And this the duchess well knows, and therefore she befriends him. I must put an end to the silly scene at once."

But he found it no such easy matter. Abigail would neither attend to his glances, nor listen to his whispered remonstrances, and he was forced to retire in some confusion, for he felt that the eyes of the duchess were upon him. Venting his anger in muttered maledictions against the sex, he returned to the green closet, which was now entirely deserted, and pondered over what had occurred, and upon the best means of retaliating upon his enemy.

While occupied with these reflections, he was surprised by the entrance of Guiscard and the Comte de Briançon. The latter threw himself into a chair near the picquet table, and taking up the cards, affected to examine them, while the marquis hastily advanced to Harley.

"What! quitted your fair partner already, marquis?" cried the secretary. "I thought it was an engagement for the evening."

"Miss Hill has rejoined the queen," answered Guiscard, "and, seeing you enter this room, I thought it a favourable opportunity to have a word with you, Mr. Harley."

The secretary bowed somewhat stiffly.

"I have reasons to think my attentions are not disagreeable to Miss Hill," pursued the marquis; "you are her cousin, Mr. Harley."

"Miss Hill will dispose of herself without consulting me, marquis," replied the secretary, drily; "but you had better address yourself to her other cousin, the Duchess of Marlborough."

"I am sure of the duchess' consent," rejoined Guiscard; "but as I have a particular regard for you, Mr. Harley, and would not do anything for the world disagreeable to you, I wish to ascertain your sentiments as to the connexion."

"The alliance is too advantageous, and too exalted, not to be gratifying to me, marquis," said Harley, sarcastically.

"Apart from my regard for Miss Hill," continued Guiscard "one of my chief pleasures in the union,—should I be so fortunate as to obtain her hand,—would be that it would enable me to serve you, Mr. Harley, as effectually as I desire to do."

"Really, marquis, I am more indebted to you than I can well express," rejoined Harley, in a tone of incredulous contempt; "but I apprehend that your understanding with a certain great lady, with whom I have the misfortune to differ on some points, will rather interfere with your obliging desire to serve me."

"There is no understanding between the duchess and me, I assure you, Mr. Harley," replied Guiscard, "or if there is," he added, lowering his tone, and assuming a confidential manner, "I do not consider myself bound by it. The duchess only uses me for her own purposes, and I am, therefore, under no obligation to her. But I *could* be grateful to one who would serve me from a better motive."

"You would need a clearer lantern than that of Diogenes to find out a disinterested friend at a court, marquis," replied Harley, with a sneer. "If I were to aid you, it would be upon the same terms as the duchess."

"Will you aid me upon her terms?" asked Guiscard, eagerly.

"Hum!" exclaimed Harley. "What faith have I in your professions?"

"This is no place for explanation, sir," replied Guiscard, hurriedly and earnestly, "but though my conduct may appear that of a double-dealer, I can easily prove my sincerity. Our sentiments on many points I know to be the same. We have each of us a secret regard for an exiled family——"

"Hush!" exclaimed Harley, raising his finger to his lips, and glancing uneasily at the Comte de Briançon, whose back was towards them, and who still appeared occupied with the cards.

"He hears us not," said Guiscard, "and if he does, nothing is to be feared from him. He is in my confidence. Whenever you please, you shall receive satisfactory assurances of my good faith, and, in the meantime, I entreat you to place reliance in me. Motives of policy, which must be obvious to you, have induced me to join, apparently, with the duchess. I now offer myself to you, being persuaded that without you I shall never obtain Miss Hill's hand."

"It would be unfair to contradict you, marquis," replied the secretary. "Without my aid, I do not think you will obtain it."

"Then hear me, Mr. Harley," said Guiscard; "if I am successful in gaining my object through you, I will devote myself wholly to your service. If you do not drive out Lord Godolphin, and occupy his post, it shall not be my fault."

"While you and Madame la Maréchale supplant the Duke and Duchess of Marlborough—eh, marquis! Egad, Saint James's will then really boast its Concini and Galigai, and our gracious sovereign shine forth a second Marie de Medicis."

"Sir!" exclaimed Guiscard, angrily.

"Nay, I am but jesting," replied Harley seriously. "I must have time to think the proposal over. You have taken me by surprise. Come to me to-morrow, and you shall have an answer."

" At what hour ?" asked the marquis.

"About noon," replied Harley.

" I will not fail," said Guiscard ; " and remember it rests with yourself to make me an assured friend or a determined enemy."

" I perfectly understand you, marquis," rejoined Harley ; " and now we will separate, or we may be observed. Ah ! the duchess."

" What ! in close conference with Mr. Harley, marquis?" cried the duchess, entering the closet. " You are talking treason, I am certain."

" Not of your grace, at all events," replied Guiscard, with perfect assurance ; " nor, indeed, of any one. Mr. Harley has been professing an obliging interest in my suit to Miss Hill."

"And you believe him ?" said the duchess. " If he speaks the truth, he must have suddenly changed his mind."

" Sudden changes of opinion *do* occur, your grace," rejoined the secretary.

" You are right," replied the duchess, significantly. " And it is well when we know from the first whom we have to deal with," she added, glancing at Guiscard ; " one cannot then be deceived."

" True," replied the marquis. " She suspects me," he added to himself.

At this moment, the queen and her ladies, together with the prince and his attendants, entered the closet, and while Anne seated herself on the fauteuil, the duchess drew near the Earl of Sunderland, and said to him in an undertone—

" I have just overheard a perfidious proposal made by Guiscard to Harley. Whether it has been accepted or not I could not ascertain ; but it is clear the fellow is not to be trusted."

" I could have told your grace that before," replied the earl ; " but he will answer your present purpose as well as a better man, and will be more easily shaken off afterwards. It will enchant me if he persuades Harley to league with him. There can be little doubt, then, of the match taking place, and equal certainty of Abigail's immediate dismissal. To further this, let me entreat you not to let either Guiscard or Harley perceive that you suspect the existence of an understanding between them. Both are eyeing you narrowly."

The duchess nodded, and, quitting her son-in-law, beckoned the marquis to her, and by the carelessness of her manner, and the friendly remarks she made upon the prosperous progress of his suit with Abigail, speedily removed his misgivings. No so Harley. His constant practice of dissimulation rendered him distrustful of others, and he said to himself—

" I am not to be so easily duped. I saw by the duchess's looks when she came in, that she had overheard what passed between us, or suspected it, and set down Guiscard as a traitor. She has changed her plans since, probably owing to Sunderland's advice. But it wont do—at least with me. What if I mislead them, and seem to combine with this intriguing Frenchman ? It shall be so.

c

Where practicable, one should never fail to play off an adversary's card against himself."

Soon after this, the queen retired, the company dispersed, and the duchess returned to Marlborough House well satisfied with the result of her schemes.

CHAPTER V.

A PEEP BELOW STAIRS AT MARLBOROUGH HOUSE.

On the morning after the ball at the palace, and just as the clock of old St. Martin's Church (for the present structure was not then erected) was striking eight, Mr. Proddy, the queen's coachman, issued from the Royal Mews at Charing-cross, and bent his steps towards Marlborough House.

A little man was Mr. Proddy—a very little man—but great, exceedingly great, in his own estimation; indeed, it may be doubted whether the lord-treasurer entertained a higher opinion of his post or himself, than did Mr. Proddy. Nature had been singularly kind to him, and if she did not actually design him for his exalted situation, she formed him in such a manner as ensured his elevation to it. She coloured his gills with the blushing hues ordinarily bestowed on the turkey-cock; moulded him after the fashion of a Bacchus on a rum-puncheon; and kindly limited his growth to four feet nothing

Not insensible, it has been said, to these natural advantages, was Mr. Proddy. No man was prouder of his calves, or set greater value on his paunch, or took more pains to nourish the genial tinting of his cheek. He felt it incumbent upon him to strut in his gait, when called upon by necessity to walk; to nod slightly, very slightly, if he encountered a friend; to eye disdainfully all other persons who might cross his path; and to cock his nose, which being small and snubby, suited the action well, and thrust out his under lip and double-chin in a manner that should leave no one in doubt as to his self-importance.

Great was little Mr. Proddy on his feet, but he was greater far on the box. To see him seated on the hammer-cloth of the royal state-carriage, in all the glories of his rich livery, his laced three-cornered hat, his bouquet, and his flaxen wig, contrasting so happily with his rubicund face, with his little fat legs fixed upon the splashing-board, and his eight milk-white horses in hand,—this was a sight worth beholding. All the dignity of all the coachmen in the kingdom seemed then to be concentrated in Mr Proddy. He was deaf to the shouts of admiring crowds; but you saw a smile of ineffable consequence irradiate his cheek and chin, and twinkle in his round protruding eyes, while he now and then addressed a brief injunction to the grooms at the horses' heads in the tone of a general issuing orders to his aides-de-camp. Once, and once only, did he forget himself, and this was on the occasion of the queen's recent visit to Saint Paul's, to return thanks for the victory of Ramilies, when the name of Proddy being shouted forth iu feminine accents near Temple Bar, he looked up for a moment, and recognising some familiar face, winked in reply. But this discomposure was momentary, and is merely mentioned to show that the great are not entirely free from the infirmities that beset other less distinguished mortals.

We must now follow Mr. Proddy up Pall Mall, along which he was slowly marching, or to speak more correctly, waddling, with one hand thrust up to the thumb in his waistcoat-pocket, and the other sustaining the stem of a yard of clay, from which he was drawing huge whiffs, and expelling them at the noses of the casual passengers. The hour being early, he was somewhat in dishabille, and wore only a white calico jacket, crimson plush breeches, and stockings, drawn above the knee. His shirt was unbuttoned, and as his little white wig merely covered the top of his head, it gave to view the back of a neck, precisely resembling in colour and expanse the same region in a scalded pig. The wig was crowned by a velvet cap, bound with gold, and having an immense neb.

On arriving at the first street running into St. James's-square, Mr. Proddy halted, and dispatched a youthful shoeblack, who had posted himself there with his implements, for a mug of ale; armed with which he crossed over the way, and entered the gates of Marlborough House.

Descending the area, he paused for a moment at the open door of a room adjoining the kitchen, where a prodigious clatter of knives and forks arose from a side-table, at which a number of servants were seated, headed by a stout, red-faced personage, in a white night-cap, white jacket, and white apron, who was occupied, at the moment, in carving a magnificent sirloin of beef.

"What, hard at work, I perceive, Mr. Fishwick," said Proddy, nodding graciously at the cook; "beginning the day well."

"Tolerably, Mr. Proddy — tolerably," replied Fishwick, returning the other's salutation by taking off his nightcap, and replacing it on his bald pate. "Wont you sit down, sir, and eat a mouthful with us? This beef is delicious, and as fat and juicy as a haunch of ven'son."

"I've not much appetite, Mr. Fishwick," returned Proddy, despondingly;—"not much, sir."

"Sorry to hear it," said Fishwick, shaking his head. "Should be afraid I was in a bad way, if I made a poor breakfast. Sit down and try. Here's a cold pork-pie—or some fried sassages, or a slice of ham or tongue may tempt you."

"Take a cup o' chocolate with me, Mr. Proddy," said a buxom, middle-aged woman, who might possibly be the housekeeper, at the lower end of the table, "it'll fortify you."

"Better have a dish o' tea with me, Mr. Proddy," interposed a much younger person, with a good deal of the air of a lady's-maid in her dress and manner; "it's good for the narves, you know."

"Obleeged to you, Mrs. Tipping; and to you, too, Mrs. Plumpton," replied Proddy; "but I'm not troubled with narves, and I don't want fortifyin'. Thank'ee all the same as though I did. But I'll tell 'ee what I *will* take, Mr. Fishwick, if you'll allow me, and that's a toast with my ale."

"You shall have it in a trice," replied the cook, issuing the necessary orders to one of his subalterns. And having done this, he relinquished his knife and fork to a footman near him, and went up to Proddy.

"Truth is, I drank rather too much punch last night, Mr. Fishwick," said the latter, in a low tone, "in wishin' the queen— God bless her!—many happy returns of the day; and I feel rather queasy this mornin', in consequence. Serjeant Scales and I supped together, and right jolly we were, I can promise you. We became sworn brothers at last, and I'm come to talk matters over wi' him now. Adzookers, he's a man of information, the serjeant."

"By the mass, is he!" returned Fishwick—"a man of parts, as one may say. He loves his glass a little too well; but that's his only fault."

"I cannot account that a fault, Fishwick," rejoined Proddy. "Serjeant Scales seems of a cheerful and conwivial turn, like myself. But nothin' more,—nothin' more."

"Far be it from me to blame him for his conviviality," said the cook, laughing. "He's a pleasant man always; but never so pleasant as with a glass in his hand, for then he loves to fight his battles over again; and to hear him tell what he has seen and done is as good as reading a newspaper. Lord love you, he has been with the duke in all his campaigns in the Low Countries, and elsewhere, and has received as many as seventeen wounds in different parts of the body! I've seen 'em myself, so I can speak to it. He has a bullet in each of his legs, and another in his shoulder; and you yourself must have remarked the great cut across his nose. I believe his nose was sliced right off, and afterwards pieced to the face; but however that may be, he had the satisfaction of killing the Bavarian dragoon that wounded him. As to the Mounseers, he has sent a score of 'em, at least, to the devil. He hates a Frenchman as heartily as he loves brandy."

"I honour him for the feeling, Mr. Fishwick," said Proddy. "I ate them Mounseers myself, consumedly."

"The serjeant's a perfect gazette in himself," pursued Fishwick, "and can relate all the duke said at this place, and all he did at that; how he marched here, and encamped there; what force he had at all his engagements; how he planned his battles, and what skilful manœuvres he executed; how, if numbers could have gained the day, the French ought to have beaten *him*, but how, on the contrary, they always got beaten *themselves*. In short, he'll show you, as plain as a pikestaff, what it is that makes the Duke of Marlborough the great general he is."

"I can tell you that, Fishwick"—rejoined Proddy;—"it's SKILL. Just the same as makes me a better coachman than any other man. The duke is cut out for the head of an army, just as I'm cut out for the queen's coach-box."

"Exactly!" replied Fishwick, scarcely able to suppress a laugh.
"But I haven't quite done with the serjeant yet. His memory's
so good, that he can tell you how many of the enemy were killed in
each battle—how many standards were taken, how many cannon,
how many firelocks, how many swords, how many pikes, gorgets,
and bayonets—and I shouldn't wonder if he could give a shrewd
guess at the number of bullets fired."

"The serjeant's a wonderful man, Mr. Fishwick," observed
Proddy, in admiration.

"You may say that, Mr. Proddy," returned the cook—"he *is* a
wonderful man. I don't know such another. You'll see his room
presently, and you'll find it a perfect museum."

"He told me he had something to show me," said Proddy.

"And he told you the truth," rejoined Fishwick. "The duke is
uncommonly partial to the serjeant, and chooses to have him constantly near him; and having perfect confidence in him, employs
him on any business where secrecy is required. The serjeant, on
his part, shows his attachment to his noble master in a curious
way. He wont let any one clean his boots but himself."

"Just like me!" cried Proddy. "I wouldn't let any one clean
the queen's carriage but myself. The serjeant's a man after my
own heart."

"The serjeant is too fond of drumming to please me," remarked
Mrs. Tipping, who, being a lady's maid, was somewhat of a fine
lady herself. "Rat-a-tat-atat-atat,—rat-a-tat-atat-atat! he's at
it from mornin' to night, so that it's a mercy the drums of one's
ears aint split with the noise. I wonder my lady stands it. I'm
sure I wouldn't, if I were a duchess."

"The duchess is a soldier's wife, Mrs. Tipping," said the cook, in
a tone of slight rebuke; "and our noble master is indulgent to his
faithful follower, and humours his whims. The serjeant, you must
know, Mr. Proddy, first served as a drummer, and though he has
risen as you see, he still loves his old occupation."

"Quite nat'ral, Mr. Fishwick," replied Proddy; "an old coachman always likes the smack of the whip."

"Well, my dear, if you object to the serjeant's drumming,"
remarked Mrs. Plumpton to Mrs. Tipping, "I'm sure you can't find
fault with his singing. He's as melodious as a nightingale."

"He croaks like a raven, in my opinion," rejoined pretty Mrs.
Tipping; "but we can easily understand why *you* find his singing
so sweet, Mrs. Plumpton."

"And why, pray, I should like to know, Mrs. Saucebox?" cried
the housekeeper, angrily.

"Fie, ladies, fie!" interposed Fishwick—"quarrelling so early
in the day. Mr. Proddy will have a pretty idea of your tempers."

"I should be ashamed to quarrel with a creature like Tipping,"
cried Mrs. Plumpton; "but if it must be told, there was a time
when she liked both the serjeant's drumming and singing."

"I wont degrade myself by answering a spiteful old thing like
Plumpton," replied Mrs. Tipping, "but I cast her vile insinuations
'n her teeth. Like his drumming and singing, forsooth! Marry,

come up! she'll try to persuade you I like the serjeant himself next."

"So you do," retorted Mrs. Plumpton: "so you do! And you're jealous of his attentions to me, though I'm sure I give him no encouragement. And that's why you abuse him so."

"Ladies, ladies, I must again call you to order," cried Fishwick. "It's a pity that a question of harmony, like the present, should lead to discord—ha! ha! But here's the toast, Mr. Proddy. If you wish to see the serjeant, I'll show you the way to his room."

Plunging the toast into the ale, and swallowing a huge mouthful or two, Mr. Proddy left the rest to soak, and resuming his pipe, which he had replenished during the preceding discourse, followed his conductor down a passage, leading apparently to the other side of the house. They had not proceeded far, when their ears were saluted by the loud rattan of a drum.

"That's the serjeant," cried Fishwick, with a laugh; "you'll have no difficulty in finding him now."

Whereupon he retraced his steps, while the other proceeded in the direction of the sound, which grew louder and louder each moment, until, as he reached a small chamber whence it issued, he was well-nigh stunned.

Rat-a-tat-atat-a-r-r-r-a-r-a—Rat-a-tat-atat-a-r-r-r-a-r-a!

CHAPTER VI.

INTRODUCES SERJEANT SCALES, AND SHOWS HOW THE DUKE OF MARLBOROUGH'S BOOTS WERE CLEANED.

"WHAT a devil of a din," thought Proddy. "I begin to think Mrs. Tipping was right. The serjeant is *rayther* too fond of drumming. I've come at an unlucky moment. But it can't last for ever."

It lasted longer than he expected though, and became so intolerably loud towards the close, that he wondered whether he should ever hear distinctly afterwards. The door being partially open, gave to view a sparely-made but athletic-looking man, who must have been more than six feet high when he stood erect, seated on a joint stool, with a large drum between his legs, which he was beating in the furious manner above described. Little flesh, but a vast deal of muscle, had Serjeant Scales; his hands were large and bony, so were his feet, so was his face, and his whole frame seemed knotted and compact, and built for a stout resistance against attacks of all kinds, whether from without or within. That he must have undergone much wear and tear was evident; but the freshness of his complexion, which was streaked with red, like an apple, bore testimony that neither the fatigues of a soldier's life, nor the addiction to good liquor, which was laid to his charge, had impaired his constitution. His nose was of unusual magnitude, and it was probably owing to its prominence that he had received the severe cut across it, which had so nearly robbed him of this remarkable feature. Nothing, indeed, but the skill of the surgeon of the regiment saved him from complete disfigurement, for his nose had actually been sliced off, and was only found and re-applied to the face some little time after its excision.* The restoration, however, was perfect; and though the point of junction to the parent stock could certainly be discovered, the nose was as firmly fixed, as ornamental, and as useful, to all intents and purposes, as ever. The serjeant had a pair of kindly gray eyes, shaded by grizzled brows; his forehead was bald and scarred in several places, while a black patch just above the left temple showed where a recent wound had been received. There was an air of military cleanliness about him. His face was shaved with scrupulous nicety, the scanty locks that graced the sides of his head were carefully powdered, and a tolerably thick pig-tail hung down his shoulders. A regimental waistcoat of blue cloth, fitting tight to the shape, and braided with white at the pockets and button-holes; tight white gaiters, ascending above the knee, and fastened beneath it with a black strap; square-toed shoes; a leathern stock; and a little cap of the same material, constituted his attire.

At the further end of the room hung two prints, the one representing the victory of Ramilies, in which the prowess of the British troops was represented in a very lively manner, and the other being a plan of the battle of Blenheim. Underneath was a map of the Netherlands, and a plan of the camp and entrenchments on the Schellenberg. Between these plans, from a peg, hung the serjeant's regimental coat, carefully brushed, and with the buttons polished as bright as silver, together with his three-cornered hat. On the left stood a large black military chest, with the owner's name inscribed upon it. Above it was a print of the recent royal visit of thanksgiving to St. Paul's. Opposite was a portrait of the Duke of Marlborough on horseback, enveloped in clouds of smoke, and calling to his men to charge. Near the duke was a broken sword, to which, doubtless, some history was attached; and beneath the sword hung a pair of buff-coloured, and seemingly blood-stained gloves, and a meerschaum. There were also two other caricatures, purporting to be portraits of Marshals Villars and Tallard, placed, intentionally no doubt, immediately under the picture of their great conqueror. From the centre of the roof hung, suspended by a stout cord, a twenty-pound-weight piece of shot. On a small deal table, on the right, stood a pair of jack-boots (WHOSE, Mr. Proddy could easily divine), a pot of blacking, a box of brushes, a pair of spurs, a knife, and some other trifling matters. On the floor lay a piece of music recently composed, and entitled, "A new

---

* Some curious cases, in which severed noses have been successfully restored are mentioned in Mr. PETTIGREW'S recent very amusing treatise on "Medical Superstitions."

health to the Duke of Marlborough, in three glasses," a map of Flanders, and a roll of popular ballads.

Having finished his reveillée, very much, as it appeared, to his own satisfaction, the serjeant got up, and putting the drum aside, proceeded to tie an apron round his waist. After which he took up a boot and began to brush it, clearing up his pipes at the same time for the following stave :—

MARLBROOK TO THE WARS IS COMING.

MARLBROOK to the wars is coming!
I fancy I hear his drumming;
'Twill put an end to the mumming
   Of our priest-ridden Monarque!
For the moment he enters Flanders,
He'll scare all our brave commanders,
They'll fly like so many ganders,
   Disturb'd by a mastiff's bark.

He comes; and at SCHELLENBERG licks 'em,
At BLENHEIM next, how he kicks 'em,
And on RAMILIES' plain how he sticks 'em
   With bay'net to the ground!
For, says he, "Those saucy Mounseers,
I'll thoroughly—thoroughly trounce, sirs,
As long as there's an ounce, sirs,
   Of powder to be found.

Now he's gone home so jolly
And we're left melancholy,
Lamenting of our folly
   That such a part we took.
For bitterly has he drubb'd us,
And cruelly has he snubb'd us,
And against the grain has rubb'd us,
   This terrible Turk, MARLBROOK.

We hope he will never come back, sirs,
Our generals to attack, sirs,
And thrash them all in a crack, sirs,
   As he has done before.
But in case QUEEN ANNE should send him,
We trust she'll kindly lend him
Some Tories* to attend him,
   Then he'll return no more!

At the close of the ditty, Mr. Proddy walked into the room.

"Serjeant Scales, your most obedient," he said; "man of my word, you see."

"So I perceive," rejoined the serjeant; "glad to see you. How are you, comrade? Excuse me. Can't shake hands. Busy."

---

* It will be remembered that the Tories of those days were pretty nearly the Whigs of ours; and that they were violently opposed to Marlborough, and the war with France.

"Don't mind me," replied Proddy; "*I'm* never interrupted. Go on."

"I like the sentiment," rejoined the serjeant. "Take a seat. This stool."

"Thank'ee, no," replied Proddy; "I prefer sitting here." And setting the mug on the chest, he clambered up beside it with some difficulty. When he was comfortably settled, the serjeant remarked—

"You know what I hold in my hand, comrade?"

The coachman nodded significantly.

"Yes, it's HIS boot, comrade—HIS boot!" cried the serjeant, emphatically. "I should like to see any man clean this boot but me."

"So I always say, when I wash down the royal carriage," observed Mr. Proddy. "I should like to see any man clean this carriage but me. That's my observation."

"But the duke is the duke," cried the serjeant, not quite pleased with the remark.

"And the queen is the queen," retorted Proddy.

"But which is the greater?" demanded Scales, with some asperity. "Which is the greater, I ask?"

"Why, the queen, to be sure," replied Proddy.

"No such thing," rejoined the serjeant. "The duke is the greater. Where 'ud the queen be without him? Doesn't he win all her battles for her?—doesn't he keep her on her throne?—doesn't he direct everything? Zounds! comrade, doesn't he govern the kingdom?"

"Not that I'm aware of," replied Proddy, opening his round eyes to their widest extent; "but they say the duchess does."

"Proddy, you're a Tory," said the serjeant, disdainfully.

"Dash my wig, if I am," replied Proddy; "but though I like the duke, I must stick up for my royal missis."

"Well, you're right," returned the serjeant, after a pause; "and I like you the better for it. Give us your hand, my boy. And now, look at this boot, Proddy. Observe it well. Do you see anything extraordinary about it."

"About the heel, or the toe?" asked the coachman.

"You're devoid of soul to make such a reply, Proddy," said the serjeant. "This is a remarkable boot—a very remarkable boot—an historical boot, as I may say. It was worn by the Duke of Marlborough at the battle of Ramilies."

"Odsbodikins! you don't say so," exclaimed the coachman.

"Yes, I do," replied Scales; "and I could say a great deal more about it, if I chose. But that one fact's enough."

"I suppose he wore t'other boot at the battle o' Blenheim," remarked the coachman, innocently.

"Nonsense!" cried the serjeant, angrily. And brushing away at the boot with great vigour, to hide his vexation, he once more lifted up his voice in song :—

KING FROG AND QUEEN CRANE.

Old King Frog, he swore begar!
  Croakledom cree!—croakledom croo!
That he with Queen Crane would go to war,
  Blusterem hoo!—thrusterem through!
With that, he summon'd his fiercest Frogs,
With great cock'd hats, and with queues like logs,
And says he, "Thrash these Cranes, you ugly dogs!
  Sing, Ventre-saint-gris!—Parbleu!"

To fight they went; but alack! full soon,
  Croakledom cree!—croakledom croo!
Messieurs the Frogs then changed their tune,
  Of blusterem hoo!—thrusterem through!
For Queen Crane had a leader stout and strong,
With a bill like a fire-spit, six yards long,
And the Froggies he gobbled up all day long,
  With their "Ventre-saint-gris!—Parbleu!"

"Bravo! serjeant," exclaimed Proddy. "You sing as well as you drum. The drum's a warlike instrument, serjeant."

"I believe you," replied Scales, with sudden animation, "the most warlike instrument as is, except the fife. But I prefer the drum. You should hear me beat the different calls, comrade."

"How many calls may there be, serjeant?" asked Proddy.

"I never counted 'em," replied Scales; "but let me see—there's the morning call, or reveillée—one; the assembly call, for the troops to fall in—two; foot-march—three; and there used to be another beat, called the long-march, for the men to club their fire-locks—that may count as four; then there's the grenadier's march—five; the retreat——"

"You never beat that, I'm sure, serjeant," interposed Proddy.

"Often," replied Scales; "though not in the way you imagine. The retreat is beaten at sunset, or gun-fire, when the pickets are formed—that makes six; the tattoo—seven; the call to arms—the church call—the pioneer's call—the serjeant's call—the drummer's call—the preparative, which gives the signal to the men to get ready for firing—the chamade, which means that a parley is de-sired—and the rogue's march, which is beaten when a soldier is drummed out of the regiment. In all fifteen."

"You amaze me!" said Proddy. "I should as soon ha' thought o' there bein' fifteen different ways of cracking a whip."

"So there are, no doubt, to him who can find 'em out," observed Scales, somewhat contemptuously. And having polished the boot to his entire satisfaction, he put it carefully down on the floor, and took up the other.

"I say, serjeant," cried Proddy, "do you know what you're doin'? You'll spoil that map."

"Never mind if I do, comrade," replied Scales, smiling. "It's not by accident that map of Flanders lies there. And it's not by accident that the Duke of Marlborough's boot is set upon it."

"I take," cried Proddy. "You mean to show that the duke has planted his foot on Flanders, eh?"

"Exactly," replied the serjeant. "You've hit the mark as neatly as I did the Bavarian trooper, at the battle of Schellenberg, when he was in the act of levelling a pistol at the duke's head. That boot precisely covers Bruges, Ghent, Antwerp, Oudenarde, Mechlin, and Brussels; all which cities his grace has lately subjected. I never do anything without a meaning, comrade. Look at those spurs," he added, pausing in his work, and pointing to them with the brush. "You might think it accident that they're leaning against the picters of them two French generals. But it's not. Guess why I put 'em there."

"To show how woundily the duke goads 'em, I s'pose," replied Proddy.

"Right," rejoined the serjeant; "you take me exactly, comrade. "It's a pleasure to talk to a man of your discernment. Those two queer-looking chaps have given us a world o' trouble. Both are brave men,—for we mustn't disparage an enemy,—but the bravest of the two, as well as the best general, is old Tallard. A well-fought battle was that of Blenheim,—and well do I remember the day! I needn't tell you it was the glorious Thirteenth of August, 1704. Many and many a boon and brave companion did I leave on that bloody field. The duke himself had a narrow escape, as you shall hear. About two o'clock in the morning, our camp between Erlingshofen and Kessel-Ostheim was broken up, and the troops were put in motion; the right wing of the army being commanded by Prince Eugene, and the left by the Duke of Marlborough. We marched forward in silence, and the morning being hazy, the enemy did not suspect our approach. As we drew near, the two generals rode forward with a strong escort to reconnoitre; and from this rising ground,"—pointing to the plan,—"near Wolperstetten, they descried the whole of the hostile camp. The duke then, after some consideration, laid out his plan of battle. By this time, the mist having cleared off, our propinquity was discovered, and the alarm being instantly given, preparations were made by Tallard and the Elector of Bavaria for the approaching strife. I shan't go through all our preparations, or the dispositions of the enemy, because you mightn't care to hear about 'em, or wouldn't understand 'em if you did, but shall pass to the event in question. It having been agreed between the two generals that the battle should begin on both wings at the same moment, Prince Eugene rode off, and the duke, while awaiting his signal, ordered service to be performed at the head of each regiment. This done, he appointed posts for the wounded, and gave special instructions to the surgeons; after which, he mounted his horse, and riding along the lines, seemed well pleased to find us all in such good heart, and so eager to begin. "You shan't have to wait long, my lads," he said. Scarcely were the words uttered, when a ball from one of the batteries struck the ground close beside him, and covered him from head to foot with dust. We all thought he was hit, and a cry was raised, but he shook the dust from his shoulders, raised his hat, and rode on as if nothing had happened."

"Just what I should have done under similar circumstances," observed Proddy. "Pray, serjeant, whose sword may that have been?" he added, glancing at the broken weapon hanging against the wall.

"That sword belonged to a brave man, comrade—a very brave man," replied Scales; "no less a person than General Rowe, who was killed on the memorable day I've just mentioned. I was near him when he fell. The brigade under his command had to cross the Nebel, the little river you see here," again referring to the plan, "under so dreadful a discharge of grape, that the clear water was turned to blood. But not a shot was allowed to be fired in return. On gaining the opposite bank, General Rowe drew his sword, and, in the teeth of the enemy's guns, with the balls whistling about his ears like hail, advanced to the enclosures, and striking his blade against the pallisades, gave the word to fire. At the same moment, a bullet pierced his breast; but, though mortally wounded, he waved his broken blade above his head, for he had shivered it against the wood, and called to his men to advance. The sword that fell from his grasp I picked up and preserved. Poor fellow! if he had died later in the day I should have grieved for him less. As it was, his last moments were cheered by the certainty of victory."

"A great consolation," observed Proddy. "I should like to die in harness myself. But I observe a pair of gloves there. They've a history, I dare say!"

"They have," replied Scales. "The dark stains you see upon them are blood—*my* blood, comrade. Those gloves were once the property of a Bavarian officer, whom I captured at the battle of Schellenberg. He had fled towards the Danube, but I overtook him in a wood, captured him after a struggle, and was returning with my prisoner, when two of his own men came up. Scared as they were, they saw how matters stood, and halted. The officer instantly broke from me, though he had yielded—rescue or no rescue,—and all three prepared to attack me. Before they could touch me, however, I shot one of them, and having my bayonet fixed, contrived to keep off the other two; and not merely keep 'em off, but to give 'em some awkward pokes into the bargain. At last, the second man fell, and the officer alone was left. He was severely wounded, but making a desperate blow at me, he cut through my cap, and brought down the blood over my face like rain, and then closing with me, seized me by the throat with both hands. Millions of sparkles danced in my eyes, and I could feel my tongue coming out between my teeth. But just when I believed all was over, his grasp relaxed, I shook him off, and he fell to the ground—stark dead! I kept his gloves, stained as you see 'em, in memory of the event."

"You'd a narrow escape, serjeant," observed Proddy; "that's a death I don't desire. It seems too like hangin'"

"Perhaps you would prefer to die like poor Colonel Bingfield, whose head was carried off by that cannon-ball, at the battle of Ramilies?" rejoined Scales.

"No, I shouldn't," replied Proddy, looking up with astonishment, mixed with alarm, at the huge piece of shot hanging above his head. "Has that cannon-ball actually taken off a man's head?"

"As clean as an axe could do it," returned Scales.

"Lor!" exclaimed Proddy, involuntarily putting his hand to his neck, and wondering how he should feel without his head. "If it wouldn't be tirin' you, serjeant, I should like to hear about *that*."

"You must know, then," replied Scales, "that during the heat of the conflict, the Duke of Marlborough, seeing some of the cavalry in disorder, dashed amongst them, to encourage them by his presence; but, being recognised by the French dragoons, with whom they were engaged, he was surrounded, and exposed to the greatest danger. Providence, however, had decreed that he was not to be taken, and extricating himself from them, he leaped a wide ditch; but in doing so, his horse fell, and he was hurled to the ground. In an instant, another horse was offered him by his aide-de-camp, Captain Molesworth, while Colonel Bingfield, his equerry, held the stirrup. As the duke sprung to the saddle, he uttered a cry of horror. The colonel fell back, *headless!*—while he himself was bespattered with blood and brains. This cannon-ball, which I afterwards dug out of the bank, and brought away, had acted the part of the poor colonel's executioner."

"Did you find the poor colonel's head?" inquired Proddy, who had turned extremely pale during the latter relation.

"No," replied Scales, "it was blown, as we say, to smash."

"Lord bless us, how shockin'!" ejaculated Proddy, recruiting himself by a prolonged pull at the mug.

"By way of changing the subject, I'll sing you a song which I myself composed on these boots," said the serjeant. And he forthwith commenced the following ditty, accompanying the chorus with a quick and appropriate movement of the brush:

THE BOOTS OF MARLBROOK.

Four marshals of France vow'd their monarch to guard,
Bragging BOUFFLERS, vain VILLARS, VILLEROY, and TALLARD;
These four gasconaders in jest undertook
To pull off the boots of the mighty MARLBROOK.
      Brush—brush away!

The field was first taken by BOUFFLERS and VILLARS,
But though they were the chaffers, yet we were the millers;
BONN, LIMBURGH, and HUY, soon our general took,—
'Twas not easy to pull off the boots of MARLBROOK.
      Brush—brush away

TALLARD next essayed with BAVARIA'S Elector,
But the latter turn'd out an indifferent protector;
For he SCHELLENBERG lost, while at BLENHEIM both shook
In their shoes, at the sight of the boots of MARLBROOK,
                          Brush—brush away!

To RAMILIES next came the vaunting VILLEROY,
In his own esteem equal to Hector of Troy;
But he found, like the rest, that his man he mistook—
And fled at the sight of the boots of MARLBROOK.
                          Brush—brush away!

Then here's to the boots, made of stout English leather,
Well soled, and well heel'd, and right well put together!
He deserves not the name of a Briton, who'd brook
A word 'gainst the fame of the boots of MARLBROOK.
                          Brush—brush away!

Of Gallia the dread, and of Europe the wonder,
These boots, like their master, will never knock under;
We'll bequeath 'em our sons, and our sons' sons shall look
With pride and delight on the boots of MARLBROOK.
                          Brush—brush away!

"Brush—brush away!" chorused Proddy, breaking his pipe in his enthusiasm.

"Hang it!" cried the serjeant, "I don't know how it is, but the thought o' the duke's goodness always brings the water to my eyes. I wish you could see him visitin' the wounded, as I've so often seen him. He's just as considerate to the enemy as to his own men. Or, if you could meet him making the rounds of the camp at night. He's as free and easy, and as like——"

At this moment, a tall figure appeared at the door. Proddy looked round in dismay, and instantly slipped off the chest.

"It's the victor of Ramilies himself," whispered Scales. "Stand at ease, comrade."

"I *am* standin' as easy as I can," replied Proddy.

"Don't disturb yourself," said the duke, good-naturedly. "I've a little commission for you, serjeant."

"Always ready to obey orders, general," replied Scales, standing bolt upright, and saluting.

"Who is this person?" asked Marlborough, regarding Proddy, who was imitating the serjeant as well as he could. "I seem to know him."

"The queen's coachman, Mr. Proddy, your grace," replied Scales.

"I thought I recollected the face. Her majesty has a good servant in you, no doubt, Mr. Proddy?" observed the duke.

"None better, your grace, though I say it, who shouldn't," rejoined Proddy.

"You know the Marquis de Guiscard, serjeant!" said the duke, turning to him.

"Perfectly, general."

"And are acquainted with his residence?" pursued Marlborough.

"No. 29, Pall Mall."

"Good," returned the duke. "Watch him, and let me know where he goes to-day."

"Any more commands, general?"

The duke replied in the negative.

"Your grace is probably aware that the marquis attempted to carry off Miss Hill, in St. James's-street, yesterday?" observed Proddy.

"Some such report reached me, certainly," replied the duke, carelessly; "but I believe it to be a mistake."

"It was no mistake, beggin' your grace's pardon," replied Proddy. "I heard all partic'lars from parties who saw what happened. A country parson, Mr. Hyde, together with his wife and daughter, are lodgin' in the house of a gentleman of my acquaintaince, Mr. Greg, and they told me what occurred."

"That Greg is a clerk with Mr. Secretary Harley—ha?" cried the duke, quickly.

"He is, your grace," replied Proddy.

"Do you see much of him?" asked Marlborough.

"At times, your grace. He comes to question me as to what happens in the palace. And that's what has brought about our acquaintance. He's always very curious to know if her majesty speaks of the Pretender."

"Well, and what can you tell him?" asked the duke, with apparent indifference.

"Little or nothin', your grace," replied Proddy. "Now and then a word may reach me,—but that's all."

"You were saying last night, that you had promised to deliver a letter from Mr. Greg to her majesty," observed Scales.

"To her majesty!" exclaimed the duke, bending his brows. "Does he dare——"

"He has often entreated me to undertake the task for him," stammered Proddy; and "at last I consented."

"Have you got the letter?" asked the duke.

"Y—e—e—s," rejoined the coachman.

"Give it me," cried Marlborough.

"Shall I search him, general?" asked Scales.

"No, it aint necessary, serjeant," replied Proddy, producing a letter from the crown of his cap, and delivering it to the duke.

"You may not be aware of the risk you have run," observed the duke, sternly. "This Greg is suspected of being an agent of the Pretender's, and is believed to be in communication with M. Chamillard, the French secretary of state, for the purpose of revealing the secrets of our cabinet. If this letter had been delivered, you would probably have been hanged."

"Spare me, your grace, spare me!" cried Proddy, trembling from head to foot. "It was done in ignorance—in pure ignorance. The serjeant knows I hate the Pretender and popery as I abominate Satan, and all his works, and am ready to fight to the last gasp for the Protestant secession."

"Succession, you mean, Proddy," whispered Scales.

"No harm shall befal you if you are silent," said Marlborough.

"I'll be as silent as the grave," replied Proddy.

"Do nothing to alarm Greg," pursued the duke, "for I suspect he is not the only person engaged in this treasonable design, and it is necessary to secure all the guilty parties. You may tell him with a safe conscience, that his letter shall be delivered to the queen, for I myself will place it in her hands."

"I will do whatever your grace commands me," said the coachman, recovering a little from his terror.

"Enough," replied the duke. "I will not fail to take your devotion into account. But I must remind you, that the slightest indiscretion will be fatal. Keep strict guard over your tongue. You say Greg has friends staying with him—a country parson and his wife. They must be watched."

"Nay, your grace, I could take my Bible oath they're no traitors," replied Proddy.

"You are easily imposed upon, I fear, my good man," said the duke; "but we shall see. Serjeant, come to me at two, and report what you have seen of the marquis."

"Odsbobs! now I think of it, the marquis is known to Greg," cried Proddy. "I've seen 'em together, and one Monsieur Claude Baud, the Count de Briançon's secretary."

"Indeed!" exclaimed the duke, "the plot thickens! Serjeant, go with the coachman in the evening, and try what you can make of Greg. You understand what to do in the other matter. Mr. Proddy, I must again impress upon you the absolute necessity of caution."

So saying, he quitted the room.

"Gracious me!" exclaimed Proddy, sinking upon the stool. "What a fright I've been in, to be sure. A treasonable correspondence with the Pretender! A hangin' affair. And poor innocent I to be lugged into it without my knowledge. Oh lor! oh lor!"

"Hush!" exclaimed the serjeant. "Recollect his grace's caution. Not a word of what you've heard to a living soul. Don't breathe it even to yourself, for you're not to be trusted. But I must now call Mr. Timperley, his grace's valet, and send up his boots."

CHAPTER VII.

OF THE MORTAL DEFIANCE OFFERED TO SERJEANT SCALES BY MONSIEUR HIPPOLYTE BIMBELOT.

THE boots being delivered, the serjeant next put on his hat and coat, and, accompanied by Proddy, sallied forth to Pall Mall, where, after agreeing to meet in the evening to visit Greg, pursuant to the orders they had received, the companions separated—the one betaking himself to the palace, and the other directing his steps towards No. 29.

Scales was soon there, and by good luck, finding Monsieur Hippolyte Bimbelot, the marquis's valet, with whom he had some acquaintance, at the door, he entered into conversation with him, and made himself so amusing, that he was speedily invited into the house. Monsieur Bimbelot had not breakfasted; and though the serjeant had consumed a couple of pounds of rump-steaks some two hours before, he was easily prevailed upon to take his place at table, and in the exhibition of his masticatory powers far outdid his entertainer. The drumming, singing, and boot-cleaning had given him an appetite. As to Monsieur Bimbelot, he was far too fine a gentleman to eat much. The wing of a chicken, the crumby part of a French roll, and a pint of Bourdeaux, contented him, while the serjeant carved away at the ham, sliced the loaf, explored the unctuous recesses of a Strasbourg pie, cracked the domes of a couple of eggs à la coq,—but shook his head at the claret.

In vain Monsieur Bimbelot assured him that it was of an excellent vintage, and that his master had imported it himself;—the serjeant replied, somewhat gruffly, that he never drunk such sour French stuff, though he admitted that his anti-gallican prejudices did not extend to an equal dislike of the brandy of that country. At last, his views were completely met by a bottle of Canary, which he lauded to the skies as a fine corroborative and strengthener of the stomach.

Like most of the fashionable valets of the period, Monsieur Bimbelot modelled himself upon his master. Like his master, therefore, he was a rake, a gamester, a beau, and, in a small way, an intriguant in politics. He wrote love-verses, execrable enough, to be sure, halting in their feet, slightly erring in grammatical construction, and containing, like his discourse, a comical admixture of French and English; affected to be a wit; lampooned his companions; and retailed all the scandal of Saint James's. He dressed gaily, that is, he wore his master's cast-off clothes; was nice in his perfumes; took Spanish snuff; covered his face with patches; played ombre and picquet; and was great in the galleries of the theatres. Monsieur Bimbelot was a little man, but he possessed a tolerably good figure, of which he was inordinately vain; his features resembled those of a baboon, with an enormous mouth, frightful projecting teeth, a clubbed nose, and a complexion like brick-dust. He used, indeed, to observe of himself, when standing before the glass to adjust his cravat, to put on a patch, or merely to contemplate his figure, " Pas beau, mais diablement gentil!"

The serjeant was too much engrossed by the viands before him to talk, but he made an excellent listener, and Monsieur Bimbelot rattled away about the theatres, the coffee-houses, the taverns, and the gaming-tables, and spoke with the greatest familiarity as well of actresses and orange-women, as of ladies of the first rank and fashion. He was especially eloquent on the subject of the play-houses; and spoke critically of the merits of Mrs. Bracegirdle and Mrs. Oldfield—those rival queens—deciding in favour of the former, though he confessed she was a little on the decline—Mrs. Barry, Betterton,

D

Booth, Wilks, Cibber, Verbruggen, and other stars of the then theatrical hemisphere.

"You've seen Madame Bracegirdle at de Haymarket, sans doute, sergent?" he said. "You shake your head. Den let me recommend you to lose no time in doing so. Ma foi! qu'elle est charmante, delicieuse, ravissante. She play Stifania, in 'Rule a Wife and Have a Wife,' to-night, and Mrs. Barry, Margarita. Don't fail to go. Dere's Weeks, too, in de 'Copper Capitaine.' Je vous donne ma parole d'honneur que vous serez enchanté. Apropos, sergent, your duke should see dat comedy, for dey say it is all 'rule a wife' at Marlbrook House."

"No jesting about the duke, Bamby," said Scales, sternly; "I don't allow it."

"Pardon, mon cher sergent," cried Bimbelot. "I have de highest possible respect for Lady Marlbrook. C'est une dame magnifique, superbe comme une reine, et adorable comme une ange. If ever I commit de folly of marriage, I should wish to be govern by my wife, for I make de observation dat men are alvays happy under vat you call de petticoat government. Est ce que vous sçavez le raison de cela, mon brave? Ce n'est pas clair, mais c'est indubitable."

"If you wish me to digest my breakfast, you wont talk so much French to me, Bamby," said Scales. "You can speak English well enough, if you like."

"Ver good in you to say so, sergent," replied the valet; "but I talk so mush to my master, dat I quite lose my English."

"I say, Bamby, what sort of master do you find the marquis?" asked Scales.

"Oh, ver good!" replied the valet, "suit me exactly, or I'd dissharshe him. Sacrebleu! c'est un excellent maitre; pas trop riche; mais follement prodigue, et excessivement genereux quand il gagne, ce que fait la fortune d'un valet. Non, sergent, I have no reason to be dissatisfy wid de marquis. Shall I tell you a secret? Il va marier."

"Curse that lingo!" cried the serjeant. "Talk English, can't you! Who's he going to marry?"

"Jure moi que vous tiendrez le secret, sergent, si je vous le dis," said Bimbelot, mysteriously.

"Swords and bayonets! I shall lose all patience," cried Scales. "Is the lady rich?"

"Mais non," answered Bimbelot.

"Young?"

"Pas trop—une peu avancée."

"Handsome?"

"Mais non—selon mon gout."

"Neither young, rich, nor handsome," cried Scales. "Then what the devil does he marry her for?"

"Ay, dere it is, sergent," returned Bimbelot. "Il a un motif— un très bon motif. Je vous conjure d'être secret. C'est la favorite de la reine—la nouvelle favorite, sergent. Qu'en pensez vous de cela?"

"Think of it?" cried Scales—"I don't know what to think of it! What between your gibberish and the news, I'm fairly bewildered."

"You'll see some shanges, by by, dat vill stonish your veak nerves, sergent," rejoined Bimbelot. "On my master's return from de ball at de palace, last night, he tell me dat Mademoiselle Hill has accept him, and order me to call him at eleven—instead of twelve, his usual hour—dis morning, as he have to attend Mr. Harley, the lady's cousin, pour arranger les fiançailles."

"Arrange the devil!" cried the serjeant, angrily "I don't believe a word of it."

"Comment donc—est ce que vous me doutez, sergent?" cried the valet, angrily. "Am I to understand dat my veracity is question, sare?"

"I don't doubt you, Bamby," replied Scales, "but I do your master. Miss Hill will never marry a cursed Frenchman."

"Ah, sacré nom! c'est trop fort," cried the valet, starting up, and gesticulating with fury. "I am a Frenchman, sare, as vell as my master, and my master's honour is dear to me as my own. Il faut que le sang coule—you shall lend me satisfaction for dis insult, sergent."

"Whenever you please, Bamby," replied Scales, coolly.

"Pas Bamby—Bimbelot, sare—*Monsieur* Bimbelot!" rejoined the valet, slapping his breast with dignity. "Nous battrons donc demain matin au point du jour, dans Hyde Park, avec des epées?"

"Good, Bamby," replied the imperturbable serjeant.

"Nous aurons des temoins," pursued Bimbelot. "I sall bring a second wid me. You had better arrange your worldly fair, sergent, for I sall certainly cut your troat unless you shoose to apologize."

"I must take my chance of that, Bamby," rejoined Scales; "but I am not in the habit of eating my words, whatever your country-men may be. But with your permission, now that the meeting is arranged, I'll finish the bottle."

"Ah, oui, je vous prie," replied Bimbelot, instantly resuming his former politeness. "Vous trouvez ce vin bon, sergent?"

"Excellent!" replied Scales. "Your health, Bamby."

"Mille remercimens," cried the valet. "May you live a tousand year—dat is, if I don't keel you to-morrow."

The serjeant acknowledged the compliment, and emptying the bottle into a tumbler, drained it at a draught. He then rose to depart.

"Je vous prierais de rester, et de prendre une autre bouteille," said Bimbelot, "mais j'ai entendu la sonnette de mon maitre. Laissez moi vous conduire à la porte. Adieu, mon sergent. A demain."

"Count on me, Bamby," replied Scales. And with ceremonious bows on either side, the serjeant took his departure.

Before going home, however, he wished to satisfy himself that the intelligence he had picked up was correct, and accordingly, he loitered about Pall Mall for nearly an hour, with his eye on the door of No. 29, until, at a little before twelve, the marquis came forth, and proceeded towards Saint James's-square.

Scales followed him at a cautious distance, saw him enter a house on the north side of the square, which he knew to be Harley's residence, and, convinced from this that he had not been deceived, he returned to Marlborough House.

CHAPTER VIII.

THE SECRETARY'S LEVEE.

THE Marquis de Guiscard, though he expected to be instantly admitted, was ushered into an ante-room, where several persons were seated, awaiting, like himself, an audience of the secretary.

Among them were three individuals, with whose faces he was familiar, having noticed them among the crowd of spectators in Saint James's-street, on the morning of the drawing-room, just before his own unsuccessful attempt to obtain an interview with Abigail Hill. These were Parson Hyde, his wife and daughter. Angelica's freshness and beauty had attracted Guiscard's attention when he first beheld her, but he was too much occupied by his project then to bestow more than a thought upon her; but now that he beheld her under different circumstances, he wondered he had not been more struck by her.

Angelica was plainly and modestly, yet not unbecomingly attired in a flat, low-crowned bonnet, with large brims, which sat on the top of her head, and which, while it shaded her face, displayed very charmingly her luxuriant auburn hair, gathered in a cluster of ringlets behind. A scarlet silk petticoat, seen through a white calico dress, which was tucked up at the side; bodice of the same colour as the petticoat; a white muslin apron; long white silk mittens, that came up nearly to the elbow, and high-heeled shoes, which suited her little feet to perfection, formed the sum of her dress. Her mother, who, it has before been mentioned, had not lost her comeliness, wore a black silk gown, a little faded, a furbelowed scarf, and ruffles, a spotted hood, and laced clogs.

Parson Hyde was conversing with a brother divine, whose rank in the church was higher than his own, as was evident from his attire, as well as from the doctor's hat which he held upon his knee. The features of the latter were handsome and prepossessing, his complexion sanguine, and his figure portly and commanding. He looked hard at Guiscard as he entered, returned the marquis's supercilious glance with a frown, and then continued his conversation with Hyde, by whom he was addressed as Doctor Sacheverell.

Soon after this, and while the marquis was ogling the pretty Angelica, who flustered and blushed beneath his regards, looked this way and that, giggled to her mother, and crumpled up her apron between her fingers, in her agitation, the inner door was opened, and amid loud peals of laughter two persons came forth from it. An usher at the same time stepped up to Guiscard, and told him that Mr. Harley was disengaged ; upon which the marquis kissing his hand to Angelica, and courteously saluting the new-comers, passed into the inner chamber.

The foremost of the persons who had just quitted the secretary, and considerably the younger of the two, was a very distinguished-looking man indeed. In stature, he was above the middle height, and his figure, though slight almost to effeminacy, was admirably proportioned. His features corresponded with his form, and were singularly beautiful and delicate, with a brow smooth and white as Parian marble, a slightly-rising but finely-chiselled nose, a curled and quivering lip, and a classically moulded chin. His eyes were large and dark, and as full of fire and softness as a woman's. An indescribable grace pervaded his slightest actions; his deportment was noble, though somewhat reckless; and but for a slight sneering air, and a certain libertine expression, his countenance would have been eminently pleasing. Indeed, it is but fair to say, that this expression was not habitual to it, and that there were occasions, and not unfrequent occasions either, when the sneer and the licentious glance were exchanged for quick and earnest sensibility, and for the loftiest and most impassioned look and demeanour. His age was under thirty, but such was the youthfulness of his aspect and figure, that it might have been guessed at three or four and twenty. He was dressed in the extremity of the fashion, and wore a light blue velvet coat with immense cuffs, richly embroidered with silver, amber-coloured stockings, crimson leather shoes, fastened with diamond buckles, and a diamond-hilted sword, with a long silken tassel dangling from the handle. His cravat was of point lace, and his hands were almost hidden by exaggerated ruffles of the same material. His hat was laced with silver, and feathered at the edges, and he wore his own brown hair in ringlets of some eighteen or twenty inches in length, tied behind with a long streaming red ribbon—a mode which he himself had introduced. His handkerchief, which he carried in his hand, and occasionally applied to his lips as he spoke, was strongly perfumed, and he diffused an odour around him as he walked, as if he had just risen from a bath of flowers. Such was the statesman, the orator, the poet, the philosopher, the wit, the beau, the sybarite, the all-accomplished Henry Saint-John, her majesty's secretary-at-war.

His companion, whom he familiarly called Mat, and who was no other than the eminent poet, Matthew Prior, was a thin, rather hollow-cheeked, dark-complexioned man, the natural swarthiness of whose skin was deepened by the extreme blackness of his beard. His features were sharp and somewhat prominent, and his eyes dark and yellowed in the ball by an attack of jaundice, but very brilliant and intelligent, and glistening with fun and good-humour. His mouth had rather a caustic expression; but there was great jocularity and freedom in his manner, and the tones of his ringing and laughing voice fell pleasantly on the ear. His age was forty-two, but he looked fifty. He had lost his situation of under-secretary of state, but was one of the commissioners of trade, and sat in parliament as member for East Grinstead. He was plainly attired in a black riding-suit, with boots, wig, and hat to match, and carried a whip in his hand.

After chattering together for a few minutes, the pair were about to quit the room, when Saint-John chanced to notice Sacheverell, and instantly stopped.

"Ah, doctor," he cried, "I am delighted to see you. I have to congratulate you, and the church at the same time, on your recent nomination to the rectorship of Saint Saviour's. To my shame be it spoken, I have not yet been to hear you. What are you laughing at, Mat, you rogue? But I am told that the sermons you have recently delivered there have been uncommonly powerful."

"Poppy-juice not more so,—they are undoubted soporifics," whispered Prior.

"Ah, Mr. Saint-John, you do me too much honour," said Sacheverell, bowing; "this praise from you is as gratifying as unexpected."

"It is richly merited, at all events, my dear doctor," replied Saint-John. "The effect of your sermons has already been felt in quarters where you would most desire it."

"Yes, because he has seasoned them strongly with politics," whispered Prior. "Personality is their chief merit."

Saint-John nudged his friend to be quiet, while Sacheverell bowed to the ground.

"The high church party owes you much, doctor," pursued Saint-John, "and I will venture to say it will not prove ungrateful."

"Let the Whigs bribe him with a bishopric, and he will preach up non-conformity or any other formity," whispered Prior.

"You attach more importance to my humble services than they merit, Mr. Saint-John," said Sacheverell; "but believing that I may do good, I shall persevere in the course I have begun. What I want in ability I shall make up in zeal, and I shall shrink from no menaces, as I would stoop to no corrupt rewards, though both, I do not hesitate to say, have been held out to me."

"What! can't you take a hint, Harry?" whispered Prior. "Offer him Lincoln or Chester at once."

"I shall go on, I say, sir, undeterred," pursued Sacheverell; "and I make no doubt I shall in time rouse the lukewarm among the labourers at the vineyard to greater exertion. It is needed: for now, if it has ever been, the Church of England is in danger. You smile, Mr. Prior, but the subject is not one to be treated with levity. I repeat, the church is in danger. And it is a cry I will raise till it is echoed from every part of the country—till it shakes the present ministry from their places."

"'Sdeath! if he can do that he will richly deserve a mitre," whispered Prior. "I begin to think the fellow may prove useful. He is not deficient in energy."

"Excellent, doctor—excellent!" cried Saint-John, trying to drown his friend's remarks by the loudness of his applause. "The church has a stanch champion in you."

"Too much toleration has been shown its enemies, and its friends have too feebly supported it," cried Sacheverell, warming as he spoke. "I will wage war against the nonconformists—war to extermination, Mr. Saint-John."

"Rekindle the fires at Smithfield," whispered Prior.

"Any support we can render you, doctor, shall not be wanting, I assure you," said Saint-John, with affected ardour. "You had better explain your views fully to Mr. Harley."

"I have come with that intention, sir," replied Sacheverell, "and from the message I have received from the secretary, I have no doubt he will co-operate with me. Mr. Harley is a true friend of the church."

"He is a true friend to himself," said Prior, half aside; "and his religion is self-advancement; but if he belongs to any sect, it is to that of the dissenters. However, to uphold the high church suits his present game, and he could not be addressed at a more favourable moment."

"What is that you are saying, Mr. Prior?" asked Sacheverell.

"I was merely observing, doctor, that Mr. Harley will be glad of an ally like yourself, and will support you through thick and thin," replied Prior.

"I am in right earnest in the cause, Mr. Prior," said Sacheverell, "and am prepared to undergo martyrdom for my opinions, if need be."

"We will hope you will only undergo translation—to a better see, doctor," replied Prior, in a slightly sarcastic tone.

Saint-John hastened to interpose; but at this moment the inner door again opened, and Guiscard, with a radiant countenance, emerged from it. At the same time, the usher informed Sacheverell that he could have an audience of the secretary. The doctor took a ceremonious leave of Saint-John and Prior, and as soon as the door had closed upon him, the pair, wholly regardless of those around them, burst into a loud fit of laughter.

"Capital!" exclaimed Saint-John. "If the church is saved by Sacheverell, he will deserve canonizing, at the least."

"If the Whig ministry are expelled by him, he shall be made Archbishop of Canterbury, if I have any voice in the matter," rejoined Prior.

"You are laughing at Doctor Sacheverell, gentlemen," said Guiscard, approaching them; "but let me tell you he does not deserve your ridicule. He is not to be despised, as you will see. The fire is low, but he will blow it into flame."

"Like a pair of bellows," said Prior; "the implements are homely, but indispensable."

"Guiscard is right, I believe," said Saint-John, seriously. "By the by, marquis, I ought to congratulate you. You are likely, it seems, to marry the queen's new favourite. We shall have to solicit places from you next, eh?"

"And not in vain, Mr. Saint-John, if I have any to bestow," replied Guiscard, condescendingly. "There is no one who would lead an administration more brilliantly than yourself."

"Oh, marquis!"

"True, 'pon my honour."

"If I might venture to prefer a claim," said Prior, "that of a humble poet—"

"The only claim Mr. Prior need make," replied the marquis, "and in itself sufficient to ensure my best exertions in his behalf. But he has other, though not better claims, to which he may not attach sufficient importance, but which, nevertheless, must be taken into consideration; I mean, his talents as a statesman. For a man of Mr. Prior's ability, an *under*-secretaryship would be inadequate."

"Oh! marquis!" exclaimed the poet. But he added to himself, "'Pon my soul, he is a man of discernment, and deserves to succeed."

Remarking the mock attention paid to the marquis, Parson Hyde thought it incumbent upon him to get up and make him a low bow.

"I had the honour of seeing you yesterday, when you stopped Miss Hill in Saint James's-street, marquis," he said. "I little imagined it would lead to this result. In fact, I thought the lady very much averse to your attentions."

"A little more experience of the world, reverend sir, would have taught you that a lady's opinion is as changeable as her dress," replied Guiscard.

"I am fully aware of that, marquis," replied Hyde, with a glance at his wife, "and I am glad the wind has shifted in your favour. Since you are likely to have so much to bestow, let me solicit some slight preferment for myself. I have a living in Essex, but it only brings me in forty pounds a-year."

"You may be sure of my interest, if only for the sake of your pretty daughter, my reverend friend," replied Guiscard, darting a tender look at Angelica.

"'Fore gad, a remarkably pretty girl," said Prior, whose attention was thus called to the parson's daughter. "Look at her, Harry. She's almost as beautiful as my Chloe."

"Troth is she," replied Saint-John. "You are come to ask preferment from Mr. Harley, eh, parson?"

"I am, sir," replied Hyde. "Understanding from my friend, Mr. Greg, that his chaplain has just left him, I have come to beg the place."

"Mr. Harley has a chaplain for every day in the week," said Prior, "and confers with each in turn. Thus, on Sunday he takes the established church; on Monday, the presbyterian; on Tuesday, the Roman; on Wednesday, the quaker; and so throughout the week."

"You amaze me, sir," cried Hyde.

"It's true, I assure you," replied Prior.

"If you fail with Harley, come to me," said Saint-John. "I have no chaplain at present."

"Allow me to present to you the Right Honourable Henry Saint-John, secretary-at-war," said Prior to the parson.

"You lay me under everlasting obligation, sir," rejoined Hyde, with a respectful bow to Saint-John.

"No such thing, my good sir," replied the latter, "the obligation will be on my side. These are your two daughters, I presume," he added, advancing towards them.

"Lord bless you, no, sir!" cried the elderly lady. "I'm Mrs. Hyde, and this is my daughter, Angelica."

"I certainly took you for her sister, madam," replied Saint-John. "Why, you're not afraid of me, surely, that you turn away your head, my pretty Angelica?" he added to her. "I wont eat you.

"I'm not so sure of that, sir," she replied. "Mr. Greg said you were a terrible rake, and mother says that rakes are as bad as roaring lions."

"Oh, Mr. Greg called me a rake, did he?" cried Saint-John, forcing a laugh—"ha! ha! Mr. Greg is a facetious fellow, and was amusing himself at my expense—ha! ha! Here's my friend Mr. Prior, the first poet of the age, as well as the greatest moralist, will tell you a very different tale. How say you, Mat, do I deserve to be called a rake, eh?"

"Certainly not, Harry, any more than the great Alcibiades deserves to be so characterized," replied Prior. "Whoever said so, calumniated you shamefully."

"I begin to think so too," said Angelica, in an under-tone, to her mother. "He's a pure handsome gentleman, and doesn't look a bit as if he could do one a mischief."

"That he doesn't," replied her mother. "Mr. Greg must be quite out in his reckoning. It's quite clear the gentleman's no rake, for he doesn't know an old woman from a young one."

"That decides it," said Angelica.

"I see you have altered your opinion of me, Angelica," observed Saint-John. "You'll find, when you know me better, that I'm the modestest man breathing. If I have a fault, it is on that side."

"I would trust myself with him, though he does think me so young, without hesitation," said Mrs. Hyde.

"So you might, and without the slightest apprehension," remarked Prior, aside.

"Well, my pretty Angelica, I must now wish you good day," said Saint-John, "for I have business that calls me hence. But be assured," he added, lowering his tone, "that I shall not lose sight of you. Your charms have produced a deep effect upon me."

Angelica coloured to the temples, and cast down her eyes.

"Good morning to you, madam," pursued Saint-John, turning to Mrs. Hyde. "Even after the assurance I have received, I can scarcely believe you to be Angelica's mother. You must have married preposterously early. Mr. Hyde, your humble servant. You wont forget my promise, in case you fail with Mr. Harley?"

"I shall not neglect to remind you of it, sir," replied the parson, bowing.

And kissing his hand to Angelica, Saint-John quitted the room with Prior and the marquis.

"What did he say to you at parting, my dear?" inquired Mrs. Hyde of her daughter.

"Only how much he was struck by your extreme youthfulness, mother," replied Angelica.

"Well, it's very curious," simpered Mrs. Hyde. "I never heard anybody say I looked so young before—not even your father. But here comes Doctor Sacheverell. Now we shall have an audience of Mr. Harley. I almost hope the chaplaincy may be given away, for then we shall go to Mr. Saint-John."

Angelica looked as if she quite concurred with her in opinion, and the usher advanced to conduct them to his master.

CHAPTER IX.

IN WHICH IT IS SHOWN THAT THE DUCHESS OF MARLBOROUGH HAD NOT ENTIRELY LOST HER INFLUENCE OVER THE QUEEN.

No communication had passed between Harley and Abigail since the ball; but, at eleven o'clock, wrapped in a roquelaure, the secretary tracked the garden wall of the palace fronting Saint James's Park, until he came to a door. Scarcely had he reached it, when it was opened, by Abigail herself, it seemed—but the night was too dark to allow him to distinguish clearly—and he was admitted into the garden. Not a word was said, but his conductress hurried along a walk in the direction of the palace, and he followed her at the same quick pace. She presently entered a door, and after he had passed through it, closed and fastened it noiselessly, and traversing a passage, ascended a staircase, which brought them to a room, where there was a light.

"I am almost frightened at what I have done," said Abigail, sinking into a chair; "for though I know I am only serving the queen, yet a clandestine interview, and especially at such an hour as this, is not at all to my taste."

"There is nothing to be alarmed at," replied Harley, divesting himself of his roquelaure, and showing that he was in a full-dress suit of rich brown velvet. "If anybody need be alarmed," he added, adjusting his point-lace cravat before a glass, and arranging his peruke, which had got a little disordered in the walk, "it is myself."

"You don't exhibit much uneasiness,' observed Abigail, laughing.

"Truth is, I feel none," replied Harley, "and my only sentiment is that of gratitude to you."

"A minister never remembers a favour, they say," rejoined Abigail.

"That may hold good with others, but not with me—at least, in your instance," returned Harley. "But may I ask, sweet coz, if you are still in the same mind with respect to young Masham?"

"I don't know," replied Abigail, carelessly. "Have you seen him to-day?"

"I have not," returned Harley; "but I have seen the Marquis de Guiscard."

"The odious wretch!" cried Abigail.

"Then you don't love him!" said Harley, in affected amazement.

"I can't abide him," cried Abigail.

"You have persuaded him to the contrary," said Harley.

"You know my motive," replied Abigail. "I was vexed with Masham, and resolved to pique him."

"And you have succeeded so well, that I fear you have got rid of him altogether," said Harley.

"Not so, cousin," rejoined Abigail. "I shall have him at my feet to-morrow."

"You are very confident," said Harley; "so confident, that I presume you have heard from him?"

"Not a word—not a line," she replied. "Harkee, cousin, we must understand each other. As yet I have made no compact with you. It is through me you are about to see the queen; but if you hope to repeat the visit, you must aid me in my plans respecting Masham. I have said I expect to have him at my feet to-morrow. It must be your business to place him there."

"But, cousin——"

"No buts," interrupted Abigail, peremptorily. "My will must be obeyed, or there are no more private interviews for you. I don't say I will forgive Mr. Masham. I don't say I mean ultimately to accept him—but I long to humble him—to torment him—to—in short, here he must be, at these feet to-morrow, full of penitence and affection."

"I will do my best, cousin, but——"

"Your best will not do," cried Abigail. "It *must be*, I tell you, or you don't see the queen now. I'm resolute, as you will find."

"Well, then, I give you my word it *shall be*," replied Harley. "Will that content you?"

"Perfectly," replied Abigail; "and now follow me. The queen awaits us."

So saying, she led the way along a narrow corridor, and entering an ante-chamber, proceeded to a door at the further end of it, against which she tapped gently, and was bidden by a sweet voice to come in. The next moment, she and her companion found themselves in the presence of the queen.

Anne was seated in an armed-chair, with a velvet footstool before her, and was attired in a white satin dress trimmed with the richest lace. She wore the blue riband across her shoulder, and a star upon her breast. The room in which she sat was a small closet, well adapted for an interview like the present, and was somewhat scantily furnished, containing no other chair except that occupied by her majesty. A few pictures were hung against the walls, amongst the most conspicuous of which was a portrait of Prince George of Denmark.

"I have most ardently desired this interview, madam," said

Harley, advancing towards the queen, and making a profound obeisance to her, "because, though my feelings of loyalty and devotion have for some time prompted me to address your majesty on a subject nearest my heart, yet the occasion for a full explanation has hitherto been wanting. I can now speak out, if I have your majesty's gracious permission to do so."

"I am well satisfied of your loyalty and devotion, Mr. Harley, and would gladly hear what you have to say," replied Anne.

"In a word, then, madam," said Harley, "it is with inexpressible concern that I regard your present situation. Forgive me if I speak boldly, but it will little avail if I do not utter the truth; and at every hazard I will do so. The kindness of your nature has been abused by a violent and ambitious lady on whom you have bestowed your regard, to such an extent, that you are no longer sole mistress of your kingdom."

"This is indeed bold language, sir," said Anne, tapping her fan —a gesture habitual to her when displeased.

"I see I give offence, madam," pursued Harley; "but I entreat you to bear with me. My language can scarcely be too strong, when the Duchess of Marlborough proclaims everywhere that you can do nothing without her."

"Ah! does she so?" cried Anne, tapping her fan more impatiently than before. "It is time she were silenced."

"In good truth it is, madam," said Harley, "both for your own sake, and for the welfare of your country, so grievously oppressed by this rapacious dame, who, notwithstanding the numberless favours you have heaped upon her, complains of being inadequately rewarded."

"I knew she was ungrateful, but I did not believe to such an extent as this," cried the queen, angrily.

"But what I and all your majesty's loyal subjects chiefly complain of," pursued Harley, "is, that the imperious duchess, by her menaces, forces you into actions which you yourself disapprove, and which are eminently prejudicial to the interests of the country. On this ground, if on no other, I would urge her dismissal."

"I will think about it, sir," replied Anne, irresolutely. "At all events, it cannot be now."

"If not now, madam, it will never be," said Harley, earnestly. "I pray you, pardon me, and attribute my importunity to my zeal. If you would indeed be a queen, the duchess must go. She stands between you and your nobles—between you and your parliaments— between you and your people. Far be it from me to adopt a course of conduct which I so strongly deprecate in this violent lady. Far be it from me to hold out threats. But my duty to your majesty requires that I should tell you plainly that if you do not rid yourself of the duchess you will rue it. You feel the annoyance occasioned by her imperious temper, but you cannot understand the mischief she does you."

"You are mistaken, sir. I *can* comprehend it, and I deplore it," replied Anne. "Oh, if I could remove her easily! But the scene will be terrible."

"Not if you will deign to follow my councils, madam," said Harley. "I have already expressed, through Abigail, my willingness to undertake the task of your liberation, and I have drawn up a plan which I will now submit to you. If this is exactly followed," he added, unfolding a piece of paper, "the duchess will save your majesty the trouble of dismissal, for she herself must retire."

"Let me hear it," cried the queen. "Ah!" she added, in alarm, as the noise of a key turning in a lock was heard, "the secret door! 'tis she!"

"Confusion!" exclaimed Harley, crushing the paper in his hand.

And as the exclamation was uttered, a small side-door was thrown open, and the duchess burst into the room.

"So," she exclaimed, "you *are* here, Mr. Harley. I could not believe it, but I find it true. Knaves will dare anything. Your majesty does well to give secret audience to this double-dealing trickster."

After enjoying for a few seconds the confusion into which the party was thrown by her sudden and unexpected appearance, and darting a scornful and indignant glance at Harley, the Duchess of Marlborough advanced towards the queen, and said, in a tone of deep reproach, "Is it come to this, madam? Are my long and faithful services to be thus rewarded?"

"What mean you, duchess?" demanded Anne, vainly endeavouring to hide her embarrassment.

"Do not affect ignorance, madam," replied the duchess, contemptuously. "It will not avail you. I know how, and by whom, Mr. Harley was brought here, and why. The scheme was worthy of him—worthy of his hypocritical ally; but unworthy, most unworthy of you. What must be the object of an interview that requires to be clandestinely conducted? What must it be when the Queen of England blushes—ay, blushes—to be detected in it!"

"No more of this, duchess!" exclaimed Anne, angrily.

"Nay, I *will* speak out, madam," returned the other; "if they are the last words I shall ever utter to you. I will show you how much you have been deceived by this double-dealing, insidious fellow, who stands abashed in my presence, though he dared just now to lift up his head loftily enough in yours. This miserable turncoat, I say, who now comes to you, would have been glad to make any terms with me. But I rejected his proffer with disdain. I would not use him even as a tool. In revenge, he has recourse to the vilest stratagems, and having reached your majesty by means which only *he*, or some one equally base, would resort to, pours his poison in your ear, which luckily proves as innocuous as it was malignantly and murtherously intended. Let him deny this if he can."

"I *do* deny it," replied Harley, who by this time had fully recovered his composure; "most unequivocally deny it. Your majesty has now heard the duchess out, and I could not desire a better advocate for my cause than she has proved. Setting aside her false and frivolous charges against myself, which I utterly repudiate and contemn, I would ask your majesty whether my complaint is not fully borne out by her present behaviour? Is her language towards you that of a subject? Is her tone that of a subject? Is her deportment that of a subject? What warrant has she for this intrusion? It is not for the Duchess of Marlborough to dictate to your majesty whom you shall receive, and at what hour you shall receive them. Neither is it for the duchess to thrust herself unasked into your secret conferences. If she knew I was here, and with your gracious permission, she should have carefully kept away. But I rejoice that she has come. I rejoice to be enabled to meet her face to face before your majesty, to tell her that she is wanting in gratitude and respect towards you, and to repeat my flat contradiction to her assertion, which I defy her to prove."

"You lie," cried the duchess, transported beyond all bounds, and striking him in the face with her fan.

"Duchess, you forget yourself," interposed the queen, quickly, but with dignity.

"I must crave your majesty's permission to retire," said Harley, almost white with constrained passion. "The duchess's tongue is sharp enough, as you have heard; but when she employs weapons which I cannot use, the contest is too unequal to be carried on further."

"I pray you remain, sir," said Anne, beseechingly; "and if the duchess has any desire to please me, she will ask your pardon for her violence."

"I am sorry to disobey you, madam," replied the duchess; "but till Mr. Harley retracts the falsehood he has uttered, I shall do no such thing. Ask his pardon, forsooth! Not I. Let him bear the blow as well as he can. He has borne as much ere now, I'll warrant, and in silence. But I have yet a word more for him. His presence at this clandestine interview, and the arts he has used towards your majesty, constitute a direct breach of faith towards the cabinet to which he belongs; and no honourable alternative remains to him, but retirement."

"I shall take leave to hold my post in defiance of your grace, as long as I can be serviceable to her majesty," replied Harley.

"Precisely what might be expected from you, sir," said the duchess; "but your dismissal *will* follow, nevertheless."

"Your grace's may possibly precede it," retorted Harley.

"An end must be put to this altercation," interposed Anne, peremptorily.

"I crave your majesty's pardon for the share I have been compelled to take in it," rejoined Harley; "and if I venture to prolong it for a few moments, it is because I think some explanation absolutely necessary after the scandalous remarks of the duchess. Whether I adopted unfair means to reach your majesty, you best know; but if I have not proceeded more directly, it has been because you are so surrounded by the duchess's creatures, that such a course must have been unsuccessful. Of the manner in which this system of espionage is carried on by the duchess, your majesty can form an idea from the fact that the private interview you condescended to grant me to-night, has been disclosed to her. And now, madam, with your gracious permission, I will proceed with what I was saying when this interruption occurred. You yourself have admitted an anxiety to shake off the yoke which your too confiding nature has imposed upon you."

"This cannot be true, madam?" cried the duchess. "Give him the lie—give him the lie."

"Her majesty's silence is sufficient answer," replied Harley. "Does not your grace perceive that by your overweening pride—by your violence, and by your rapacity, you have alienated the affections of a too-indulgent mistress? Nothing but the good-nature you have presumed upon, has enabled you to retain your place. But I tell you, in the queen's presence, and in her voice, that it is her wish, her command, that you should retire from it."

"Ha!" exclaimed the duchess, with a roar like that of a lioness.

"Mr. Harley, you go too far," said the queen, much alarmed.

"No, your majesty," replied Harley, "I will take all upon my head. I will tell this imperious woman that her reign is over—that you are determined to emancipate yourself from her thraldom—and be the great queen you ought to be, and are. A moment's resolution will do it. The step is taken. The scene you dreaded *has* occurred. Bid her leave the room, and surrender her places, and you are indeed mistress of your kingdom. Bid her go."

"That word will never be pronounced by the queen, sir," said the duchess, undauntedly.

"Your majesty's freedom hangs on a breath," whispered Abigail. "Recollect how much you have suffered."

"Duchess," said the queen, in a voice of emotion, "I must——"

"Before you proceed, madam," interrupted the duchess, "let me have a word. I will not wrong myself by any comparison with the persons I have found in your presence. I hold them as nothing, except so far as your majesty deigns to make them of importance. I will not remind you how unceasingly my energies have been devoted to your service—how, ever since you mounted the throne, I have had but one thought—the advancement of your glory——"

"With an occasional bye-reflection as to your own aggrandizement," remarked Harley, sarcastically.

"I will not remind you of my great husband's services in the field and in the state," pursued the duchess, disregarding the remark; "but I will confine myself to the friendship with which I have been honoured for many—many years, and which refers, not to public, but to domestic affairs. Our secret feelings have been interchanged—our joys, our afflictions, have been shared. We have each mourned—mourned in concert—a son lost. Love made us equals. Mrs. Freeman and Mrs. Morley were once dear to each other—very—very dear."

"They were—they were," said Anne, much moved.

"And shall it all be forgotten?" asked the duchess.

"It is Mrs. Freeman's own fault," replied the queen. "She has driven her friend to it."

"She will make any atonement her friend pleases," said the duchess, penitentially; "nay, more, she will promise not to offend again."

"Is it possible!" cried Anne; "if such were really the case——"

"Doubt it not," replied the duchess, throwing herself at the queen's feet, who instantly raised her, and embraced her affectionately.

"Dear Mrs. Freeman," exclaimed Anne.

"Dearest Mrs. Morley," cried the duchess.

"This coup de théâtre has ruined all," muttered Harley, with a significant glance at Abigail. "Madam," he added to the queen, "I presume I may now retire. My further presence can neither be necessary nor desirable."

"Before you go, sir, I must insist upon a reconciliation between you and the duchess," said the queen. "Nay, duchess, you were wrong, and it is for you to make the advance. What! you hesitate? Will Mrs. Freeman refuse Mrs. Morley's request?"

"That appeal is irresistible," replied the duchess. "Mr. Harley, I was too hasty." And she extended her hand to him.

"I take your grace's hand as it is given," replied Harley, advancing towards her. "This is a harder blow than the other," he added, in a low tone.

The duchess smiled triumphantly.

"Henceforth, all hostilities must cease between you," said the queen.

"Willingly, on condition that this is the last private interview between your majesty and Mr. Harley," rejoined the duchess.

"Willingly, on condition that her grace always maintains her present amiable deportment," subjoined Harley. "Mrs. Freeman is infinitely to be preferred to the Duchess of Marlborough."

"Peace being restored, I shall retire," said the queen, smiling.

"What, without a word in private with your poor faithful Freeman," whispered the duchess, coaxingly.

"To-morrow," replied the queen. "I am too much fatigued now. This interview has quite exhausted me. Good night, Mr. Harley. Abigail will see you forth."

So saying, and returning the secretary's profound bow, she withdrew with her attendant.

The duchess and Harley regarded each other for some moments fixedly in silence.

"Either you or I must retire from this contest, Mr. Harley," said the former, at length.

"It is not for me to tell your grace which of the two it shall be," he replied. "But I have no intention of withdrawing."

"Then I know how to act," said the duchess.

"There is no chance of a coalition, I suppose?" he insinuated, in his smoothest tones.

"With you—never!" replied the duchess, contemptuously.

At this moment, Abigail returned.

"I wish your grace good night," said the secretary, bowing ceremoniously.

" Good night, sir," replied the duchess. " I will take care this is the last time you are seen here."

" Heed her not," said Abigail, as they quitted the room ; " the queen is as much your friend as ever. Fulfil my injunctions respecting Mr. Masham implicitly, and you shall have another interview as soon as you please."

CHAPTER X.

OF THE PROVOCATION OFFERED BY MASHAM TO THE MARQUIS DE GUISCARD AT THE SAINT JAMES'S COFFEE-HOUSE ; AND OF THE CHALLENGE THAT ENSUED.

A DEEPER impression had been made by Abigail upon Masham than he cared to acknowledge. He could not render himself indifferent to her, and her very capriciousness seemed to make her more attractive. A ride in the park failing to distract his thoughts, he repaired to the Saint James's Coffee-house, where he found the Earl of Sunderland conversing very eagerly with a gentleman of good figure, and remarkably intelligent countenance, who was well known to him as Mr. Arthur Maynwaring.

Descended from a branch of a very old Cheshire family, which had settled at Ightfield, in Shropshire, and connected on the maternal side with the ancient and important families of the Egertons and Cholmondeleys, Mr. Maynwaring was as much distinguished for his high breeding and polished exterior, as for his wit, scholarship, and general ability. An admirable political writer ; a keen satirist and critic ; and an authority on all matters of taste and learning,—Maynwaring had recently received a lucrative appointment as auditor of the imprests from Lord Godolphin. He sat in parliament as member for Preston in Lancashire, and being completely in the confidence of the Duchess of Marlborough, frequently acted as her private secretary. In age, Maynwaring was nearly forty. He was a member of the Kit-Cat-Club, and accounted one of its chief ornaments.

The earl and his companion looked up on Masham's entrance, and their manner made him fancy that he himself formed the subject of their discourse. Nor was he mistaken ; for as he was passing on to another part of the coffee-room, Sunderland called to him, and said, " We were speaking of you, Masham, and I have been diverting Maynwaring with an account of what occurred at the palace last night."

" Just the way Abigail serves every one," laughed Maynwaring. " And I have no doubt, in spite of the encouragement she gave Guiscard, who has a right now to fancy himself the suitor elect, she will scarcely deign to notice him to-day. Who would be a slave to such a capricious creature ?"

" Ay, who indeed ?" echoed Sunderland, laughing.

Masham could not repress a sigh.

"For the credit of our sex, I hope you wont let her perceive the power she has over you," said Maynwaring, noticing the other's emotion.

"If Masham feels himself in danger, let him absent himself from court for a few days," observed Sunderland.

"That would never do," rejoined Maynwaring. "A thousand jests would be in circulation at his expense, and he would never survive the ridicule. No, he must stay and boldly face the enemy. The true way to mortify her will be to affect perfect indifference, and whatever lures she may throw out, whatever wiles practise, appear utterly insensible to them."

"I should be better pleased to pique her as she piqued me," returned Masham.

"You are not master enough of yourself for that," said Maynwaring. "Indifference, real or affected, must be your game. He is in love with her," he observed in a low voice to Sunderland, as Masham stepped aside for a moment.

"Evidently so," replied the other in the same tone. "If they meet, a reconciliation will infallibly take place. It must be our business to prevent it till she is fully compromised with Guiscard. If we could but get him away for a week."

"Ah! but he wont go," returned Maynwaring, laughing.

"Again amusing yourselves at my expense, gentlemen," observed Masham, returning.

"I was merely observing to Sunderland," replied Maynwaring, "that I think Abigail's influence with the queen vastly over-rated."

"I'm sure of it," replied the earl; "Guiscard will find out his error if he thinks to secure his own advancement by marrying her. When she weds, she will of course lose her place."

"Not of course, I believe," observed Masham.

"Oh, yes," rejoined Maynwaring. "But what matters it? The French adventurer will be rightly served."

"I should not mind the loss of place, if she had a heart," sighed Masham; "but she evidently has none."

"Not a bit more than Guiscard himself," replied Maynwaring, "so they will be nicely matched. Adsdeath! here comes the marquis."

As the exclamation was uttered, Guiscard, accompanied by Saint-John and Prior, entered the coffee-room. As the new comers drew near, Saint-John said, laughingly, "Good day, gentlemen. I've a piece of news which will delight you all, especially Masham. We are to have a marriage at court."

"A marriage!" exclaimed Maynwaring. "Between whom?"

"Between Monsieur le Marquis de Guiscard and the fair Abigail Hill," replied Saint-John. "Here is the marquis to receive your congratulations."

"Is it settled, then?" asked Masham, hastily.

"Mr. Saint-John is, perhaps, going a little too far in saying that it is actually arranged," replied Guiscard; "but I hope the marriage will not be long delayed."

" Accept our best wishes for the speedy completion of your happiness, marquis," said Sunderland and Maynwaring together.

" 'Sdeath, Masham," cried Prior, " why don't you offer your congratulations likewise? The marquis will be a great man presently, and it is prudent and proper to worship the rising sun."

" Let those worship it who like. I want nothing from him," replied the young equerry, walking moodily away.

" A disappointed rival!" said Sunderland to Guiscard. " Ah, marquis, you are a lucky fellow!"

" Deuced lucky!" cried Maynwaring. " You haven't decided yet for Whig or Tory, I presume?"

" Pardon me," replied Prior. " Guiscard is with us. And if Sunderland finds some one in his post within a month, he will know who placed him there."

A loud laugh followed this sally.

" Gentlemen," said Masham, returning quickly, and looking angrily round, " I should be glad to know the cause of your merriment."

A general burst of merriment was the response.

" This young Masham thinks everybody is laughing at him to-day," said Sunderland. " On the contrary, my good fellow, we sincerely condole with you—Ha! ha!"

" Your mirth has but slight grounds for it, my lord," replied Masham, sternly. " You are willing to take Guiscard's word for his acceptance by Miss Hill. For my own part, I doubt it."

" How, sir?" cried the marquis.

" I more than doubt it," pursued Masham, loudly and emphatically,—" I believe it to be wholly false!"

The laughter was instantly hushed, and some other persons, who chanced to be in the coffee-room at the time, gathered round th group.

" Pshaw, my dear Masham," said Maynwaring, " you let your vexation at our friend's success carry you too far. Marquis, you will make due allowance for his disappointed feelings."

" Most assuredly," replied Guiscard ; " I am willing to take no notice of the affront. Masham knows not what he says."

" You shall not get off thus, marquis," rejoined Masham, with increasing anger. " I repeat—deliberately repeat—that you have imposed upon this company."

" Mr. Masham hopes to cut my throat, in order to remove an obstacle between him and Miss Hill," observed Guiscard, with suppressed anger, " but I will disappoint him."

" You are quite in the wrong, Masham," said Sunderland, taking the young equerry aside,—" on my honour, you are. Granting this vain-glorious Frenchman has advanced more than he has warrant for, you will only give Abigail new cause for triumph by thus playing the Quixote for her. Allow me to reconcile matters. I can do so at once, without compromising you in the slightest degree."

" I can only retract what I have said on receiving from Miss

E 2

Hill's own lips a confirmation of the marquis's statement," replied Masham, sullenly.

"Pshaw, you know that to be impossible," said the earl. "Be reasonable."

The young equerry shook his head.

"Since there is no help for it, gentlemen, I suppose you must meet," said Sunderland, turning round.

"Most certainly, my lord," replied the marquis,—"most certainly we *must* meet. And I trust no one here will attempt to interfere. We are all men of honour."

There was a slight responsive murmur among the company, and those who were strangers immediately withdrew.

"Mr. Maynwaring, may I count upon you as my friend?" said Masham.

"Unquestionably," was the reply, "though I confess I would rather assist to settle the matter in any other way. But since that may not be, I shall be happy to attend you."

"And I conclude I may calculate on you, Mr. Saint-John?" said the marquis.

Saint-John bowed.

"Where, and at what hour, shall the meeting take place, gentlemen?" he inquired.

"As early as agreeable to the marquis," replied Masham, "and in Hyde Park, if he has no objection."

"Hyde Park will suit me as well as any other place," replied Guiscard, "and the earlier the better; because, as I shall sit up till the hour of meeting, I shall get to bed the sooner."

"These preliminaries arranged, gentlemen," said Saint-John, "I presume you can meet without annoyance to each other; and I therefore beg the favour of your company at supper to-night, as well as that of all our friends here. A few choice spirits have promised to come to me; and when I tell you I expect Mrs. Bracegirdle and Mrs. Oldfield, I am sure I need offer you no further inducement."

The invitation was eagerly accepted by all except Masham, who would willingly have declined it, but Maynwaring whispering him that his refusal might be misconstrued, he reluctantly assented; and, after a little further conversation, the party separated.

CHAPTER XI.

OF THE ASSEMBLAGE OF WITS MET BY MASHAM AT SUPPER AT MR.
SAINT-JOHN'S, AND OF THE MEANS PROPOSED BY HIM OF ADJUST-
ING A QUARREL BETWEEN MRS. BRACEGIRDLE AND MRS. OLDFIELD.

HAVING dined alone, and made such preparations as he thought
necessary for the meeting of the morrow, Masham betook himself,
about ten o'clock, to Saint-John's residence in Saint-James's-place.
The party, which was more numerous than he expected, had
already sat down to table, but a place was reserved for him between
Maynwaring and Prior, into which he slipped as quietly as he
could. Most of the guests were known to Masham personally, and
all by reputation ; and as he surveyed the assemblage, which com-
prised many of the most eminent wits of the day, he could not but
feel that he had little title to the place among them.

At the head of the table, as a matter of course, sat Saint-John,
who appeared in most buoyant spirits, and on his right was a lady
with a most fascinating expression of countenance, fine dark eyes
of extraordinary brilliancy, and hair and eyebrows of the same
shade. Though a brunette, her complexion had a rich bloom in it,
and though in the maturity of life, her charms had lost none of
their attraction. Her smile was witchery itself, as thousands who
had felt it make its way at once to the heart could testify. This
was the admirable actress, Mrs. Anne Bracegirdle, than whom a
lovelier or more accomplished woman never trod the boards.

On her right sat a gentleman of very courtly appearance, possess-
ing smooth, handsome features, who paid her the most devoted
attention, and who was addressed by her as Mr. Congreve. Next
to Congreve sat another wit, but scarcely so polished in manner, or
so regularly handsome, though his features were fine and interesting notwithstanding, and he was quite equal to the other in comic
genius.

Sir John Vanbrugh—for he it was—was conversing with an
elderly man, who, notwithstanding a stoop in the shoulders, the
total absence of teeth, and deep wrinkles in the cheeks, which
defied the power of rouge and paint to efface, affected the air of a
youthful beau, and wore a dress made in the extravagance of the
fashion, with a point-lace cravat, point-lace ruffles, and a flowing
peruke, while costly rings bedecked his fingers. In this antiquated
figure, whose shaking limbs and blear eyes seemed ill fitted for the
revel, could scarcely be recognised the once handsome, and still
witty friend of Sedley, Rochester, Etheridge, and Buckingham,
the boon companion of the Merry Monarch himself, whose good
looks and brilliant reputation had won him the hand of the young,
wealthy, and beautiful Countess of Drogheda, and whose comedies
are scarcely, if at all, inferior to those of Congreve and Vanbrugh
—namely, William Wycherley.

On Wycherley's other hand was a young man of rather prim air, and plain attire, but whose looks bespoke shrewdness and good sense, and whose name was Tickell. He was paying profound attention to the discourse of his neighbour, a handsome man, with a florid complexion, and a somewhat stout person, displayed to advantage in a suit of peach-coloured velvet, and who was no less distinguished an individual than Joseph Addison.

The great essayist, who had not, however, at that time, given to the world the full assurance of his unequalled powers, but was chiefly known by his travels, his poem entitled the "Campaign," and a trifling opera called "Rosamond," filled the post of under-secretary to the Earl of Sunderland, who had continued him in the office on his succession to Sir Charles Hedges, from whom Addison originally received the appointment.

Addison's neighbour, on the right, was the gay, the social, the kindly, the thoughtless Richard Steele, upon whose excitable temperament the pleasures of the table, and the deep libations that succeeded (for those were hard drinking days,) had already produced a far more pernicious effect than upon his phlegmatic friend, the under-secretary. Captain Steele, for he had recently procured a commission in Lord Lucas's regiment, through the interest of his friend, the brave Lord Cutts, was chiefly occupied at that time in conducting the *Gazette*, in which his chief aim, according to his own account, was to be "as innocent and insipid as possible;" and it must be owned his success was fully equal to his intentions. Steele had been for some time a widower, but was, at this particular period of his life, paying court to Miss Scurlock, to whom he was subsequently united. The dissolute courses he had indulged in had left their impression on his features, which, though puffy and cadaverous, were nevertheless expressive. Black overhanging brows, deep-set eyes, a broad and somewhat coarse visage, a figure thickset and square, and a military attire, may give some idea of his personal appearance.

Captain Steele's attentions were directed towards his neighbour, a young and singularly beautiful woman, with a slight and graceful figure, and an archness of look and manner perfectly irresistible. This was Mrs. Bracegirdle's rival, Mrs. Oldfield, who had lately risen into fame, and divided the town with her. All Steele's gallantries, however, were thrown away. Mrs. Oldfield had ears and eyes only for the soft speeches and tender glances of Mr. Maynwaring, who sat on her right, and with whom, it may be mentioned in passing, she afterwards formed a long and lasting attachment, only closed by his death.

Passing over Maynwaring, Masham, Prior, and Sunderland, we come to the tragic poet, Nicholas Rowe, the author of the "Fair Penitent," whose somewhat saturnine countenance was convulsed with laughter at the jests of his neighbour, the facetious Tom D'Urfey, who, like Wycherley, was one of the wits of the previous century, and, upon whose shoulders, Charles the Second himself had often leaned, to hum a snatch. No one, indeed, in former days could troll a ditty more merrily than old Tom; nor could any one write a choicer song of the amorous and convivial description in vogue when he was in his prime.

Like Wycherley, Tom D'Urfey was a good deal the worse for wear. The wonder would have been if he were not, considering the rollicking, reckless life he had led; but in spite of rheumatism, flying gout, and other aches and pains, it would be difficult to find a jollier old fellow than Tom, or one who enjoyed the good things of life more, or deserved them better. He was somewhat shabbily attired, it is true, for Tom was not one of your prosperous wits. But what of that? His coat might be threadbare, but his jests were fresh and glossy, and far more genial than those of the refined and freezing Congreve; and as to his laugh, it was joviality itself.

Tom D'Urfey had truly a lyrical genius, and was utterly free from the affectation which is the besetting sin of modern ballad-mongers; but he was besides an indefatigable labourer for the stage, and composed in his time above thirty comedies, all, or most of which, are forgotten. Alas! poor Tom! there is but a faint and far-off echo of thee and thy pleasantries in these degenerate days.

Guiscard was D'Urfey's neighbour, and next to the marquis sat Mrs. Centlivre, the witty authoress of several excellent but licentious comedies,—though no more licentious than the taste of the time required,—three of which, "The Busy-Body," "The Wonder: a Woman keeps a Secret," and "A Bold Stroke for a Wife," still keep their hold on the stage. Mrs. Centlivre had some little personal beauty, and had been thrice married, her last husband, Mr. Joseph Centlivre, being yeoman of the mouth, otherwise cook, to King William the Third. Her latest comedy, the "Platonic Lady," had just been produced with some success at the Haymarket.

Mrs. Centlivre's right-hand neighbour was Sir Samuel Garth, the celebrated poet and physician, a man as much esteemed for his amiable and social qualities as for his professional talent and poetical ability. Garth was a stout, handsome-looking man, with large features, of the mould which seems so peculiar to the period in which he flourished, and was attired in black velvet. On his further side sat another lady, the fourth and last that the party comprehended, and who was likewise a writer of dramatic works, which had procured her some reputation, though she subsequently became far more notorious by the production of the "New Atalantis."

Though in the hey-day of her life, Mrs. Manley had little more than her wit to recommend her; but she had great conversational powers, and a turn for satire which, combined with an intimate acquaintance (how derived is not worth inquiring) with what was going on in the political world, and the world generally, gave great piquancy to her discourse. In our own days, she would unquestionably have made a first-rate fashionable novelist.

Next to Mrs. Centlivre, sat Mr. Godfrey Kneller, the great painter, (Kneller, it may incidentally be mentioned, received his baronetage from George the First,)—a man of courtly appearance, handsome person and features, though a little on the decline, and most refined manners; and next to Kneller was Mr. Hughes, a scholar and a poet, then chiefly known by his elegant translations of Horace and Lucan, but subsequently distinguished by his tragedy, called the "Siege of Damascus," and the papers he contributed to the Tatler, the Spectator, and the Guardian. With him the circuit of the table is completed.

The repast was magnificently served, as well as admirable and abundant. A crowd of lacqueys in Saint-John's sumptuous livery were in attendance. The table groaned with the finest chased silver dishes, and sparkled with crystal glass; and as dish after dish of exquisite flavour disappeared, delicacies still more tempting succeeded. The wines were poured forth in equal profusion, and the produce of the choicest vintages of France, Spain, Germany, and even Hungary, was quaffed in bumpers. The glasses were not allowed to stand empty a moment, and there was a constant discharge of champagne corks.

An incomparable host was Saint-John. He had none of the airs of a petit-maitre, leaving his guests to shift for themselves, but did the honours of his table hospitably and well. By his sprightly sallies he kept up an incessant roar of laughter, and the only person upon whose brow a slight cloud could be discerned, and who appeared to have no zest for the rich viands or the delicious wines, was Masham.

"Mr. Masham looks like the rejected lover in a comedy," observed Mrs. Bracegirdle, in her exquisite voice, which gave to words of little import significance the most extraordinary.

"Nay, by my faith," cried Saint-John, "it is not acting with him. Masham is foolish enough to love a woman after she has agreed to give her hand to another; and, what is more, nothing will content him but the life of his fortunate rival."

"You are too hard upon the young gentleman, Mr. Saint-John," said Mrs. Oldfield, whose accents were quite as musical and delicious as those of Mrs. Bracegirdle; "if he is really in love, he is much to be pitied. I vow he is the only person here who knows anything of the passion, unless it be Mr. Tickell. If your lady-love has jilted you, sir," she added to Masham, "forget her, or supply her place with another."

"I could easily do that, Mrs. Oldfield," replied the young equerry, gallantly.

"I hope you don't mean to be so silly as to risk your life for her?" pursued the lady.

"Permit me the honour of wine with you," rejoined Masham, evasively.

"With great pleasure," she replied; "but I must have an answer to my question. Some women like to be the cause of a duel; but I should hate the man who fought for me; or rather I should hate myself, which would come to the same thing. Ladies, let us take Mr. Masham under our special protection. It would be a thousand pities if so pretty a fellow were cut off in the flower of his youth, and all for a senseless jilt. Your voices, I'm sure, will be with me. Fight he must not."

"Certainly not," cried the three other ladies, in a breath.

"You hear, sir," said Mrs. Oldfield. "We are four to one. You cannot disoblige so many fair supplicants. And now, let us know who is your rival?"

"You will make me his rival, if you go on thus," remarked Maynwaring, somewhat petulantly.

"Mrs. Oldfield is bent upon a conquest, it seems," observed Mrs. Bracegirdle, in a low tone to Saint-John.

"A glance from you will win him from her," replied the other: "you have often carried off a whole house in the same way."

"I'll try," said Mrs. Bracegirdle, "if only to mortify the vain thing.—Mr. Masham," she continued, aloud, and throwing one of her irresistible glances at him, "I am curious to know what sort of person it is that has inspired you with so deep a passion."

"Ay, do tell us, Mr. Masham?" said Mrs. Centlivre.

"She is young and beautiful, of course?" cried Mrs. Manley.

"And wealthy, also, it is to be hoped?" added Mrs. Centlivre.

"Do—do describe her?" cried Mrs. Oldfield. "Does she resemble any of us—Mrs. Bracegirdle, for instance?"

"Or Mrs. Oldfield?" rejoined the other actress.

Here was a general laugh.

"Masham will have a second duel on his hands ere long, I begin to think," said Congreve, glancing at Mrs. Bracegirdle.

"He will have a third," rejoined Maynwaring, "and will have to provide himself with another second, for I shall be obliged to take part as a principal."

"Really, gentlemen, I am unconscious of giving you offence," said Masham.

"I'll take Mr. Congreve's quarrel off your hands," said Mrs. Bracegirdle. "If he fights any one it shall be me."

"And since Mr. Maynwaring has thrown up his office, I shall be happy to attend you as second," said Mrs. Oldfield. "I can manage an affair of the kind quite as well as him. As for swords, I've plenty at your service, and pistols too, if needed. You shan't blush for your second, for I'll come in my town gallant's apparel. You remember *Betty Goodfield*, in the 'Woman turned Bully?' 'Udsbud, sir,' she added, assuming the look and tone of the character, "'do you come here only to ask questions? This is not to be endured. You have wasted my whole stock of patience, and now you shall find me an errant lion. Come, sir, draw!'"

This speech, delivered in the liveliest manner imaginable, elicited thunders of applause from the assemblage.

"Mr. Masham will prove irresistible, if so attended," said Wycherly. "'Gad! I thought the modern stage degenerate, but I find the old spirit of Nell Gwyn and Mrs. Kneppe revived in Mrs. Oldfield."

"With a little more discretion, I hope, Mr. Wycherley," replied the pretty actress.

"Ah! Mr. Wycherley," cried Tom D'Urfey, "things are greatly changed since those inimitable plays, the 'Country Wife' and the 'Plain Dealer' were given to the world. It's full thirty years since the last made its appearance; and if you had had any industry, or any necessity, you would have given us a comedy every successive year, and then how rich our drama would have been! Talking of the 'Plain Dealer,' how well I recollect Hart as *Manly*, Kynaston as *Freeman*, Mrs. Cory as *Widow Blackacre*—wondrous *Widow Blackacre!*—and Kneppe, pretty Mrs. Kneppe, as *Eliza!* You should give us another comedy before you quit the stage altogether, sir."

"I shall marry, and give you a farce, Tom," replied Wycherley, with some acerbity. "But why don't you appeal to Mr. Congreve? No man has written such comedies, and yet he has forsworn the stage."

"Don't remind me of the indiscretions of my youth, Wycherley," replied Congreve. "I've seen the error of my ways, and mean to avoid it in future."

"Congreve has been converted by Collier, though he answered him so sharply at the time of the attack," said Vanbrugh, laughing, "and thinks the theatres licentious and profane."

"Their morals will certainly remain questionable as long as you continue to write for them, Van," rejoined Congreve.

"'Sdeath!" cried Vanbrugh, "am I to paint men and manners as they *are*, or as they *are not?*"

"You paint them in colours so true, that your portraits will endure for ever, Sir John," observed Kneller. "When people become over-fastidious, it is a bad sign of the morality of the times."

"One thing is quite certain," remarked Addison, "that the English stage owes its revival to the genius of the two great comic writers here present, and if they had not exerted their matchless powers for its support, it is doubtful whether we should not have altogether been deprived of a most delightful and intellectual amusement. No, Mr. Congreve, the stage owes you too much to allow you to disown your connexion with it."

"I am sorry to say it in the presence of so many distinguished dramatists," cried Congreve, "but on my soul I cannot think writing for the stage the employment of a gentleman."

"Oh, fie, Mr. Congreve!" rejoined Rowe; "this is rank heresy in you, and worse than abusing a woman who has bestowed her favours upon you. A fine play is the noblest achievement of the human mind."

"The author of the 'Fair Penitent' and 'Tamerlane' has a right to say so," remarked Garth. "I can well understand that Mr. Congreve, having obtained so high a reputation, should not care to shake it; but that he should underrate the drama, for which he has done so much, passes my comprehension."

"I do not underrate the drama, Sir Samuel," replied Congreve, 'nor do I shrink from the stage from fear of failure, but from distaste. I dislike notoriety, and if I could do twenty times better than I have done, I would not write again; nay, I am sorry I ever wrote a line."

"Is he sincere, think you?" asked Guiscard of Prior.

"As sincere as you would be," replied the poet, "if, after winning ten thousand pounds at hazard, you were to say you would never play again, and protest you wished you never *had* played. He is prudent, and does not wish to lose what he has gained. Besides, with a strange kind of vanity, he values himself more upon being thought a fine gentleman than an author."

"Fortunately for us, my dear Congreve, your wish not to have written comes too late for fulfilment," said Saint-John. "It would be well, perhaps, if some of us could recal our early effusions, but you are not of the number. Meantime we are neglecting the wine. Captain Steele, I pledge you."

"My service to you," replied Steele, taking off a brimmer. "Congreve is right on one point," he continued. "The great secret is to know when to leave off. An entrance is more easily made than an exit. But though I hold this to be a sound rule, I don't mean to act up to it myself, but shall go on as long as I can find an audience to listen to me, or a bookseller to purchase my wares. Both will soon let me know when they have had enough."

"Ay, it was ever your rule, Dick, to declaim like a philosopher, and to act like a rake," rejoined Addison.

"There I only imitate you, Joe," replied Steele, "who write in praise of temperance in a style as pure and clear as water itself, with a bottle of old Oporto before you."

"That shan't prevent my taking a glass with you now, you scandalous dog," replied Addison; "what shall it be—burgundy?"

"Ay, burgundy," replied Steele; "'tis a generous wine, and floods one's veins like the hot blood of youth."

Soon after this, the cloth was removed, and bowls of punch, mulled burgundy, and claret were placed on the board. Tom D'Urfey volunteered a song, and although his voice was a little cracked, executed one of his old anacreontic melodies very creditably.

Mrs. Bracegirdle was next prevailed upon to sing, and roused her hearers to a state of rapture, which was by no means lessened when her fair rival, Mrs. Oldfield, followed her in a voice of surpassing richness and sweetness. Both ladies were most vociferously applauded in their turns, their mutual supporters trying to outvie each other in the expression of their admiration.

Saint-John, whose spirits appeared inexhaustible, and who was the soul of a revel, as of aught else he engaged in, took care that the exhilaration of the party should receive no check; and so well did he fan the flame of mirth, that it blazed up more joyously each moment, and spread so fast and freely, that even Masham caught the infection, forgot his anxieties, and laughed as loudly and heartily as the rest.

By this time, the various generous liquors had begun to produce an effect upon the company; the conversation became a little more noisy, and the laughter rather more uproarious. Perfect decorum, however, was observed; but there were more talkers than listeners, and Tom D'Urfey, in spite of the assistance of the host, could not obtain attention for another stave. To hide his disappointment, during a momentary lull of the clatter, he called upon Mrs. Oldfield, but an opposition was instantly made by the supporters of Mrs. Bracegirdle, who said she was under a promise to them, and their rights could not be deferred. In vain Saint-John interposed; the dispute instantly rose to a fiery heat, and many sharp speeches were interchanged, when a happy idea suggested itself to the host.

"A means of settling this matter occurs to me, ladies," he said. Will you leave it to Mr. Masham to decide who shall sing first?"

Both immediately expressed their assent, and turned to the young equerry, who looked as much puzzled as the shepherd Paris, when required to bestow the golden apple upon the fairest goddess. Without giving himself, however, more than a moment's consideration, he named Mrs. Bracegirdle, who, radiant with triumph, began to pour forth strains like those of a syren. But she was not allowed to proceed far, for Mrs. Oldfield, who was deeply mortified, began to talk and laugh aloud to Maynwaring, upon which the fair singer instantly stopped, and in spite of Saint-John's entreaties refused to proceed—her anger being increased by the insulting looks of her rival.

"We have been talking of duels just now," she cried; "I wish they were allowed amongst women. I should like to punish the insolence of that creature."

"Don't balk yourself, if you are so disposed, my dear," rejoined Mrs. Oldfield, with a sarcastic laugh. "I will meet you whenever and wherever you please; and as we are both accustomed to male attire, we can so array ourselves for the occasion."

"I wish you would dare to make good your word, madam," replied Mrs. Bracegirdle.

"If you doubt me, and are in a hurry, my dear," replied Mrs. Oldfield, "you have but to step into the next room, and we can settle the matter at once."

"Here will be a pretty piece of work," cried Prior; "a duel between our two fairest actresses. Whoever survives, we shall be losers."

"'Sdeath, this passes a jest," exclaimed Saint-John.

"We will fight with pistols," cried Mrs. Oldfield, heedless of Maynwaring's remonstrances. "I have practised at the mark, and am a dead shot."

"Agreed," replied Mrs. Bracegirdle; "I am as good a shot as yourself."

"What say you to arranging the affair in this way, ladies?" interposed Masham. "You both profess to be good shots. I will hold a candle, and you shall post yourselves at the extremity of the room, and she who snuffs it shall be adjudged the victor."

"I assent," said Mrs. Oldfield.

"But you will run a great risk, Mr. Masham," cried Mrs. Bracegirdle.

"Oh! I'll take my chance," he replied, laughingly. "Better I should receive a slight wound than the stage be deprived of one of its brightest ornaments."

The young equerry's gallantry was much applauded, and Mrs. Bracegirdle assenting with some reluctance to the arrangement, a brace of pistols were produced, and all impediments being quickly cleared away, Masham took up a candle, and marched to the further end of the room, where he took up a position, and stretched out his arm. All being now ready, Mrs. Bracegirdle begged her rival to shoot first. Mrs. Oldfield instantly raised her pistol, levelled, and fired.

The shot was so true that the flame wavered, and a burst of applause followed.

As soon as this had subsided, Mrs. Bracegirdle took her rival's place. But just as she had levelled her pistol, a trembling seized her, and she dropped her arm.

"I cannot do this," she cried. "I should never forgive myself if I hurt that young man, and would rather own myself vanquished than put him in danger."

On this, the applause was louder and more vehement than before, and at its close Mrs. Bracegirdle said, "To show that I am not without some skill, I will make an attempt, which can endanger no one. There is a small white spot on the upper panel of you door, not larger than a shilling. Be that my mark."

And as she spoke, she again raised the pistol quickly, and drew the trigger. The wood was perforated in the precise spot indicated by the fair shooter, but there was a general expression of consternation and surprise, as the door opened, and Harley walked into the room.

CHAPTER XII.

THE PARTY IS INCREASED BY THE UNEXPECTED ARRIVAL OF MRS. HYDE AND HER DAUGHTER—THE CAUSE OF THEIR VISIT EXPLAINED.

"An inch lower," cried the secretary, taking off his hat, which was pierced quite through with a small round hole, "and that bullet would have lodged in my brain. Another time, pretty Mrs. Bracegirdle must choose a safer place for pistol-practice, or she may chance to do a mischief."

The fair actress eagerly tendered her apologies to Harley, while the others congratulated him upon his narrow escape; and the cause of the shot having been explained, he laughed heartily.

"The victory must be adjudged to you, my dear Mrs. Bracegirdle," he said to her; "for though Mrs. Oldfield has displayed equal skill, you have shown the most feeling."

"It is very generous in you to say so, at all events, Mr. Harley," observed Mrs. Oldfield pettishly.

"Expert as you are, ladies," said Saint-John, "I hope that henceforth you will abandon pistols, and confine yourselves to those scarcely less dangerous weapons, your eyes."

"Glances may do very well for your sex, but for our own, powder and ball are required," rejoined Mrs. Bracegirdle.

"Well, the quarrel is honourably adjusted," said Saint-John. "So kiss and be friends."

Thus urged, the ladies complied. But it was easy to see from the toss of the head on one side, and the shrug of the shoulder on the other, that the truce was a hollow one.

The company then resumed their seats at table, and Harley placed himself by the host, who, while he circulated the glass as rapidly as before, and promoted the conversation as much as was requisite, contrived to hold a whispered discourse with him. Harley's brow became clouded at some information he received, and his glance taking the direction of Masham, showed that what he had heard related to him.

Soon after this, Sunderland and Kneller arose, declaring they had drunk enough; while Guiscard called for cards, upon which Saint-John rang for the attendants, and the folding-doors being thrown open, disclosed a magnificent saloon, blazing with lustres, and in which stood several card-tables.

Into this room most of the company adjourned, but Steele, Addison, D'Urfey, Prior, and Rowe, who professed to care little for play, remained behind to finish a large bowl of punch which had just made its appearance, and which they pronounced incomparably better than any that had preceded it. Coffee and liqueurs were next handed round, after which, the greater part of the guests sat down to ombre and basset, and Harley, supposing Guiscard engaged, drew Masham aside, and said to him, "I have just heard from Saint-John of the foolish meeting you intend to have with the marquis. It must not take place."

"Pardon me, Mr. Harley," replied Masham, "I see nothing to prevent it."

"*I* will prevent it," returned Harley, "and without the slightest discredit to yourself. On the contrary, you shall come off with flying colours. But you must submit yourself wholly to my guidance."

"I regret that I cannot comply with your request, Mr. Harley," replied Masham.

"Pshaw, sir, I say you must comply," cried the secretary, peremptorily, "unless you would for ever mar your fortunes. You must go with me to Abigail to-morrow."

"*Must* go, Mr. Harley!"

"Ay, *must*, sir, MUST," cried Harley; "you must not merely go, but throw yourself at her feet, and implore her pardon."

"And wherefore, in the name of wonder?" demanded Masham, in extremity of surprise.

"I will tell you," replied the other, smiling; "because— 'Sdeath!" he exclaimed, suddenly pausing, as Guiscard stood before them.

"Your pardon, Mr. Harley, if I interrupt you," said the marquis, who, guessing what was going forward, determined to thwart the secretary's plan; "but as Mr. Masham has doubted my word, for which he will have to render me an account to-morrow, I wish him to be made aware that you are favourable to my proposed union with your fair cousin, Miss Hill."

"Confound the fellow!" muttered Harley.

"You will not hesitate to give him an assurance that you are anxious to promote it," pursued Guiscard; "and that you have pledged yourself to use your best efforts with the queen for the speedy solemnization of the nuptials."

"Not exactly pledged myself, marquis," said Harley, looking at Masham.

"Surely I cannot have misunderstood you?" rejoined Guiscard, sternly.

"No, no; you have not misunderstood me, marquis," replied Harley; "but——"

"But what, sir?" interrupted Guiscard, impatiently. "If it has escaped your memory, fortunately I have a memorandum to remind you."

"Oh, no, I recollect it all perfectly," said the secretary. "It is just as you say—just as you say."

This he spoke with so significant a look at Masham, that he hoped the latter would comprehend him. The young equerry, however, paid no attention to his glances and gestures, but bowing stiffly, walked away; and Harley, annoyed at the marquis's ill-timed interference, abruptly left him, and proceeded to one of the card-tables.

At this moment, a servant entered the room, and approaching Saint-John, informed him in a low tone that two ladies desired to see him.

"Two ladies at this hour!" exclaimed Saint-John. "What the devil do they want?"

"I don't know, sir," replied the man; "but they appear in great distress, and one of them is young and very pretty."

"Ah!" exclaimed Saint-John, "that promises well. I will see them anon. Take them to the study, and send Mrs. Turnbull to them."

"I think, sir," said the man, "that the young lady's name is Angelica, and that her mother is a country parson's wife."

"What, my pretty Angelica!" cried Saint-John, transported with delight. "This is a rare piece of fortune! Show them up directly."

As the servant disappeared, Saint-John arose and communicated the intelligence he had just received to Harley and Guiscard, and all three were laughing and speculating upon the cause of the visit, when the door opened, and Mrs. Hyde and her daughter were ushered into the room. Both had handkerchiefs to their eyes, and Angelica looked as if she would sink with embarrassment at finding herself in so gay an assemblage.

"To what am I indebted for the honour of this unexpected visit, ladies?" asked Saint-John.

"Oh! dear sir!" replied Mrs. Hyde, "such a calamity as has happened! My poor dear husband!"

"What of him?" cried Saint-John, with affected concern.

"He has been—oh!—oh!" sobbed Mrs. Hyde. "Do tell, Angelica, for I cannot."

"I can scarcely bring it out, sir," said the younger lady. "He has been ar-ar-ar—ested."

"Arrested!" echoed Saint-John, in surprise—"for what?"

"For doing nothing—nothing at all," replied Mrs. Hyde. "That's his crime."

"And a very terrible crime it is," said Saint-John, smiling. "But surely something must be laid to his charge?"

"They say it's a plot," replied Angelica—"some treasonable correspondence with French ministers. Oh dear! oh dear!"

"Treasonable correspondence with French ministers!" echoed Saint-John. "Is he a Jacobite?"

"Lord love you, no, sir!—no more than yourself," replied Mrs. Hyde; "but it's all owing to Mr. Greg. Mr. Harley knows who I mean, for he's one of his clerks."

"Greg! what of him?" cried Harley, uneasily.

"Why, he has been arrested by a queen's messenger," replied Angelica, "and conveyed away to be kept in safe custody till he's examined by the privy-council to-morrow. All his papers have been seized."

Harley and Saint-John exchanged glances of ill-disguised anxiety; and Guiscard, stepping forward, said, with a look of consternation,

"What is this I hear?—Greg arrested?"

"Yes, sir," replied Angelica; "and I heard the messenger say, that the papers he seized would implicate some great persons. Your name was mentioned."

"Mine!" exclaimed the marquis; "mine! Impossible! I know nothing of the fellow,—that is, very little."

"This is an untoward occurrence, Harley," said Saint-John, in a low tone.

"Very untoward," replied the other; "for though I have nothing to fear, yet, as the villain was my clerk, it will give a handle to our enemies, which they will not fail to use."

"It is cursedly unlucky, indeed," cried Saint-John. "Well, my pretty Angelica," he added, "you may make yourself perfectly easy about your father—no harm shall befal him. I will answer for that. But how did all this happen?"

"Why you see, sir," she replied, "a serjeant, a great tall man, with a patch upon his nose, and as ugly as sin, came with Mr. Proddy, the queen's coachman, to see Mr. Greg this evening, and was invited by him to stay supper, to which he readily agreed. Well, in the course of the evening, Mr. Greg asked the serjeant a great many questions about the Duke of Marlborough, and Mr. Proddy a great many questions about the queen, and plied them both with brandy, which soon got into their heads, and made them talk nonsense about the Revolution, and so forth. My father paid no attention to what they said, but smoked his pipe quietly by the fire, and soon fell into a doze. By and by, they spoke in whispers, and I couldn't, of course, hear what passed, but I caught the words James the Third—court of Saint Germains—and Monsieur Chamillard—which made me suspect they were talking treason."

"And you were right in the suspicion," observed Saint-John.

"What a fool Greg must be to act so unguardedly!" muttered Guiscard.

"I rather think from what followed, that the serjeant and coachman were spies," pursued Angelica; "for after talking thus for some time, they got up, and staggered off; but though the serjeant pretended to be very tipsy, I saw him look round stealthily. About half-an-hour afterwards, and just as we were going to bed, a knock was heard at the door, and Mr. Greg, who turned very pale, hesitated to open it; but as the summons was repeated, he obeyed, and a queen's messenger, as he announced himself, together with a couple of officers, rushed in, seized him, and secured his papers, as I told you before."

"Did the messenger say who sent him?" asked Harley.

"Yes; the Duke of Marlborough," she replied; "and he declared that the duke possessed certain proofs of Mr. Greg's guilt."

Again Harley and Saint-John exchanged looks of intelligence, whilst Guiscard's countenance became darker and more troubled than ever.

"But on what plea was your father arrested?" asked Saint-John.

"Indeed, sir, I don't know," answered Angelica; "but as the officers took him, he bade us not be alarmed, for he had nothing to fear, as the queen hadn't a more loyal subject than he was, and his innocence would presently appear."

"And so it will," cried Mrs. Hyde. "He's as innocent as the babe unborn. I can answer for that."

"It seems a most unjustifiable proceeding," said Saint-John, "and shall be inquired into strictly. But what brought you here, child?"

"We've done very wrong, I fear," replied Angelica, blushing, and in great confusion, "but we were quite at our wits' ends, and having no friends in London, and thinking you a pure, good-natured gentleman, we came here in the hope that you would befriend us."

"Well, I wont disappoint you," rejoined Saint-John. "And now pray take some refreshment, while I order a room to be prepared for you. I'll undertake to procure your father's liberation in the morning."

With this, he conducted them to another room, where Mrs. Turn-bull soon appeared, to attend upon them, and on his return entered into a close and anxious conference with Harley. Guiscard sat down to basset, but played so distractedly that he lost a considerable sum, and at last rose and took his departure.

About the same time, the ladies' chairs arrived, and Mrs. Brace-girdle was escorted home by Congreve, and Mrs. Oldfield by Mayn-waring. Steele and Wycherley walked after Mrs. Manley's chair, and being rather excited by what they had taken, assaulted the watch, and got lodged in Saint James's round-house. Mrs. Centlivre was attended by Prior, who called her Chloe all the way, and vowed he would write a prologue to her next play.

Having finished his conference with Saint-John, Harley looked round for Masham, but could not see him, and on inquiry found he had been gone long since. Addison, Garth, and the rest, sat late, and drank another bowl of punch, and another after that, and it was nearly four o'clock when Saint-John found himself alone.

CHAPTER XIII.

TREATS OF THE SERJEANT'S EARLY BREAKFAST; AND OF THREE DUELS.

AN hour before daybreak, on the morning on which his duel with Monsieur Bimbelot was to come off, Serjeant Scales arose, and as he had drunk a good deal of brandy over night, as may have been gathered from the fair Angelica's relation, the first thing he did was to allay his thirst with a huge jug of water; after which, he proceeded to attire himself, singing and whistling the while, as was his wont, but in a somewhat lower key than usual, for fear of disturbing the house.

Accustomed to shave in the dark, he got through that necessary operation without accident; jumped into a pair of old jack-boots, which had been bestowed upon him by the Duke of Marlborough; threw a belt over his shoulders; experimented the temper of his sword against the floor; thrust it into the scabbard; and having put on his hat and regimental coat, marched with a tread, like that of the ghost of the commandant in Don Juan, to the kitchen, with the intention of preparing himself a cup of coffee before he sallied forth. The fire was blazing cheerily as he entered, and to his surprise, he perceived Mrs. Plumpton, the buxom under-house-keeper, standing beside it.

"My gracious, serjeant!" cried Mrs. Plumpton, in affected confusion, "who would ha' thought o' seein' you? Why, you're up betimes, indeed."

"You've got the start of me, any how, Mrs. Plumpton," replied Scales. "I'm obliged to go out on duty. But you're not generally up so soon."

"Not generally, serjeant," she replied; "but I felt a little qualmish, and thinking a dish of chocolate might do me good, I got up to make it, and was just beginnin', when you came in. But, good gracious! only think! why, if I haven't got my nightcap on!"

"Never mind the nightcap, Mrs. Plumpton," rejoined the serjeant; "I'm an old soldier, you know. If you hadn't mentioned

it, I shouldn't have found it out. But now I look at it, I declare
it's the most becoming eap I ever saw you wear."

"La, serjeant!—but you military men are *so* polite! Wont you
take a dish o' ehoeolate with me before you go out?"

"That I will, and thank you too, Mrs. Plumpton," replied Seales.
"I was going to take coffee, but I should prefer chocolate all to
nothing."

The chocolate was milled, and set upon the fire, and the buxom
housekeeper was about to give it a final frothing up, when, she
knew not how it was, but her waist was encircled by the gallant
serjeant's arm, and before she could utter even the slightest ery, he
had imprinted half a dozen hearty kisses upon her lips. A terrible
fellow was the serjeant, and as formidable in love as in war.

While this was going forward, the ehoeolate boiled over into the
fire, and a terrible hissing, sputtering, and smoking ensued, while
at the same moment a sharp, derisive laugh was heard near the
door, and looking up, the diseoncerted pair beheld Mrs. Tipping.

"So, this is what you get up for so early, Plumpton, eh?" eried
the lady's-maid. "Pretty doings, indeed! No wonder you like
the serjeant's drumming so mueh! But my lady shall know of it
—that she shall."

"Hadn't you better tell her at the same time how often the serjeant has kissed you, Tipping," replied Mrs. Plumpton, removing
the choeolate-pot from the fire. "Our meeting was quite accidental."

"Oh, quite aceidental, no doubt," retorted Mrs. Tipping. "As
if Mr. Timperley didn't tell you last night that the serjeant was
going out at daybreak, and would want some coffee. You got up
on purpose to meet him."

"Well, and pray what did *you* get up for?" asked Mrs. Plumpton,
sharply.

"To surprise you," replied Mrs. Tipping, "and I *have* surprised
you nieely. Oh! serjeant," she added, sinking into a ehair, "I
didn't expeet this of you. To make love to an old fright like
Plumpton!"

"Neither so old, nor so frightful, for that matter," rejoined the
under housekeeper, bridling up. "And the serjeant is too good a
judge to think mere youth, if it has nothing else to recommend it,
an attraetion."

"Ladies," said Seales, "having a great regard for you both, I
should like to see peaee restored; and having, also, a pressing
engagement on hand, you'll exeuse my sitting down to breakfast."

So saying, he took a seat, and Mrs. Plumpton poured out a large
cup of ehoeolate for him, while Mrs. Tipping, notwithstanding her
displeasure, proceeded to eut slices of bread and butter, whieh he
disposed of as fast as she eould prepare them. Three eups of ehoco-
late swallowed, and half a loaf eonsumed, the serjeant arose, and
wiping his lips, kissed first Mrs. Plumpton, and then Mrs. Tipping,
who submitted to the infliction with a better graee than might
have been expeeted, and quitting the house, passed through the
garden, into the Green Park.

It was just getting light, and he saw seated on a bench, in the avenue of trees immediately before him, a stout little personage, in a white coat, striped waistcoat, and velvet cap with a huge neb, whom he had no difficulty in recognising as Proddy.

The serjeant whistled a call, and the coachman instantly arose, and walked towards him. Proddy had a pipe in his mouth, and a sword under his arm, and strode with unusual dignity. After exchanging salutations, the pair shaped their course in the direction of Hyde Park. The morning was fine, but extremely cold, and the serjeant would have walked forward more briskly, but that he feared to outstrip his companion.

"I think I told you who was to be Bamby's second, didn't I, Proddy?" he observed, at length.

"One John Savage, a French corporal, who was brought over a prisoner with Marshal Tallard," replied the coachman.

"Sauvageon, not John Savage," rejoined Scales. "A brave fellow he is, too. I should esteem it a greater honour to cross swords with him than with poor little Bamby."

"I tell you what, serjeant," said Proddy, "I've been thinkin' the matter over. I shan't like to stand idle, and if he has no objection, I'll take a turn with Savagejohn myself."

"Why, zounds, Proddy," cried Scales, "he'll be through you in less than no time! He's perfect master of the sword, and earns his livelihood as a fencing-master."

"I don't mind that, serjeant," said Proddy. "An Englishman is always a match for a Frenchman."

"Why, yes," replied Scales, "provided—but I'd advise you to leave the honour of your country to me."

"No, I'm resolved to fight," said Proddy. "I've brought my sword for that purpose."

"Well, if that's your humour, I'm not the man to hinder you," said Scales; "but take care of yourself, that's all. I'll help you if I can."

Whereupon he began to hum "Lillebullero," caroling forth the following snatch, with lusty lungs:—

" Hero, hero, sing the brave hero,
    Victor of Blenheim and Ramilies' plains!
Marlbro' the glorious, ever victorious,
    Sing him, ye Britons, in rapturous strains!"

"We're both heroes ourselves, serjeant," said Proddy, proudly. "We're goin' to fight the mounseers, and I feel as you might have done before the battle of Blenheim."

"You're a brave little fellow, Proddy," replied Scales, clapping him on the shoulder, "and I honour you for your spirit; but you can't tell how a soldier feels before going to battle, especially when he has to fight the French. Why, on the morning of that battle, I felt like a war-horse reined in, champing and churning against the bit." And he again began to sing:—

" On the thirteenth day of August, seventeen hundred years and four,
   Was a famous battle fought on the Danube's rugged shore:
   Never since the Gallic legions to black Edward's might did yield,
   Has their pride so low been humbled as on Blenheim's well-fought field."

"If you go on in this way, serjeant, I shall long to engage both these mounseers," said Proddy. "I'm sure my real wocation is war. I should prefer the cartouche-box to the coach-box."

"Good!" exclaimed Scales, laughing. "Body-o-me! Proddy, how well we played our parts last night, and how completely we obfuscated that traitor, Greg! What a villain the fellow must be to betray his country to its enemies? He deserves to be rammed into one of the great guns at Dover Castle, and blown across the Channel to Calais. But, thank Heaven, he'll meet his desert! I hope they'll be able to touch his master, Mr. Harley."

"I never meddle with state matters when I can help it, serjeant," replied Proddy, whose terrors of the preceding day were somewhat revived by the remark. "I shall be glad when Greg's hanged out of the way."

The serjeant concurring in this wish, they once more marched forward in silence.

Soon afterwards they entered Hyde Park, the gates of which were just opened; and, striking off in the direction of Kensington Gardens, kept on the higher ground, till they reached the head of a long glade bordered by a natural avenue of fine trees, chiefly elms, and sweeping down to the edge of the broad and beautiful sheet of water, which has since received the appellation of the Serpentine,—for the very excellent reason that it is as straight as a canal. Broken into lovely little dells, and shaded by clumps of timber, the ground had a secluded appearance very fitting to their purpose. About half-way down the avenue were two springs, celebrated for their virtues, to which even in those days, when hydropathy had not commenced as a practice, numbers used to resort to drink and wash, and which were protected by wooden frames. At a later period, the waters of Saint Anne's Well—for such is the designation of the chief spring—used to be dispensed by an ancient dame, who sat beside it with a small table and glasses; while persons afflicted with ophthalmia found relief by bathing the eyes in the sister fountain. A pump now occupies the spot, but the waters are supposed to have lost none of their efficacy. Is it not strange that in these water-drinking times the wells of Hampstead, Kilburn, and Bagnigge, should not again come into vogue?

The sun had just risen, and his beams glanced through the branches of the tall and spreading trees, sparkled upon the surface of the distant water, which glistened like silver, and shone with diamond lustre on the dewy sod. Well may we be proud of Hyde Park, for no capital but our own can boast aught like it. The sylvan and sequestered character of the scene was wholly undisturbed, and but for the actual knowledge of the fact, no one would have dreamed that the metropolis was within a mile's distance. Screened by the trees, the mighty city was completely

hidden from view, while on the Kensington road, visible through
the glade which looked towards the south-west, not a house was to
be seen. To add to the secluded character of the place, a herd of
noble red-deer were couching beneath an oak, that crowned a gentle
acclivity on the right, and a flock of rooks were cawing loudly on
the summits of the high trees near Kensington Gardens.

"Well, we're first in the field at all events, Proddy," said Scales,
halting. "This is the place of rendezvous."

"I'm glad of it," replied the coachman, taking off his wig and
cap, and mopping up the moisture that was streaming down his
puffy cheeks; "you walked a little too fast for me."

"Why didn't you say so?" rejoined the serjeant. "But we're
not much too soon, for here they come."

Hastily replacing his wig and cap, Proddy turned to regard the
new comers. Little Monsieur Bimbelot appeared to be dressed with
extraordinary care, and wore a velvet coat, a brocade waistcoat, and
a full, flowing peruke. He was attended by a middle-aged man,
almost as tall as the serjeant himself, with a weasen, hatchet face,
a tremendously long, hooked nose, a sharp chin, and a beard as blue
as that of the great Wife-Killer of the fairy tale, which, together
with his nose, formed what is vulgarly termed a pair of nutcrackers. Then he had a long, scraggy neck, with the pomum
Adami largely developed, black, bristling brows, and great, staring
black eyes, that shot forth terrible glances. He was wrapped in a
loose white regimental coat, from beneath which the point of a
sword, and a pair of brown leathern gaiters appeared. His hat was
cocked very fiercely, and his wig was terminated by an immense
queue. Altogether, the appearance of the corporal seemed to justify
the opinion pronounced by Scales as to his prowess.

Drawing himself up to his full height, the serjeant awaited the
advance of his opponent, while Proddy emulated his example, and
by way of giving himself additional altitude, sprang upon an ant-
hillock, and stood on tiptoe as long as he could.

"Messieurs," said Bimbelot, tripping nimbly forward, and taking
off his hat, "j'ai l'honneur de vous presenter mon ami, Achille de
L'Epée Sauvageon, feu Caporal à sa majesté Louis-le-Grand, mais
à present prisonnier de la guerre en Angleterre."

"What does all that mean?" cried Proddy.

"Silence !" said Scales, sternly. "Corporal, your servant," he
added, taking off his hat to Sauvageon.

"Le votre monsieur le sergent," replied the other, returning the
salute.

"And now, gentlemen, to business," cried Scales. "I'll be ready
for you in a twinkling, Bamby," he added, taking off his coat.

"I sall not detain you long, sergent," replied Bimbelot, likewise
divesting himself of his upper garment.

The corporal then advanced to his principal, and delivered him
his sword, adding a few words in au under-tone, during which
Proddy addressed Scales.

"I say, serjeant, if you wont tell Savagejohn I want to fight him,
I'll do it myself." he said.

"You had better not," replied Scales. "At all events not till I've done."

"But I don't like to wait," rejoined the valorous coachman. "I say, Corporal Achilles Savagejohn," he added, in a loud voice, "since our friends are goin' to set to, we may as well have a bout together as stand idle."

"Avec beaucoup de plasir, mon gros tonneau," replied the corporal, grinning.

"What does he say?" asked Proddy.

"Mocks you, that's all," replied Scales.

"Does he!" cried Proddy, furiously. "Odsbodikins! I'll make him laugh on the wrong side of his ugly mouth. Mocks me—ha! Hark'ee, you spindle-shanked, black-muzzled Colossus—you half-starved may-pole, who look as if you had fed all your days upon nothing but frogs and cheese-parings—draw and defend yourself, I say, or I'll slit your scraggy weasand for you. Do you understand that?"

"Parfaitement, monsieur," replied the corporal, his teeth chattering with rage. "You are too full of good liquor, mon petit brave. If I don't spill some of your claret, may I never wield sword again."

"Since you needs must fight, Proddy," said the serjeant, in a low tone to him, "mind what I say. As your adversary is much taller than you, come to half sword as soon as you can."

"Half sword!" exclaimed Proddy. "What's that? I've got a whole sword, and a good long one, too. Look at it."

"Why, zounds and the devil!" exclaimed Scales. "Are you going to fight without any knowledge of the art of fence?"

"To be sure I am," replied Proddy.

"You'll be killed, as sure as a gun. However, since there's no help for it, get as near the corporal as you can, and when he thrusts at you, don't attempt to parry—you understand that—but thrust again, and ten to one but you may hit him. It will be *contre-tente*, as he would say, but no matter, if you succeed. It's your only chance."

"I'll do it," replied Proddy resolutely.

The serjeant then stepped aside a few paces, to select an open spot, and was followed by Bimbelot. They were about to take up a position, when the polite valet, remarking Scales' equipments, said, "Mais ces bottes, sergent? Wont you take dem off? You'll find dem ver inconvenient."

"Not in the least, Bamby, I'm obliged to you," replied Scales. "These boots once belonged to the Duke of Marlborough," he added, proudly; "I always wear them upon great occasions like the present."

"Ah—yes—I understand," replied Bimbelot, flattered by the implied compliment. "As you please, den. Commençons."

Swords were then drawn, appeals beaten, salutes made, and both stood upon guard; but before beginning the assault, the serjeant could not help glancing in the direction of Proddy, for whose safety he felt much uneasiness. He saw the poor coachman standing opposite his fierce antagonist, who now looked doubly formidable, and putting himself in guard in tierce, in imitation of the others whom he had watched, while with his left hand he was trying to take off his cap gracefully. All this Scales saw at a glance, and he then turned his attention to his own opponent, who made a thrust at him in carte, which he instantly parried, with a reposte in seconde. Though anxious on Proddy's account to terminate the fight as speedily as possible, Scales found it no such easy matter, for Bimbelot was a very skilful fencer, and pass after pass was exchanged without any decided advantage being obtained. At last, as the valet made a thrust in carte, Scales parried quickly in prime, and immediately passing his right arm swiftly over the forte of his adversary's blade, and presenting his own point at the same time, disarmed him.

Without bestowing further thought on his discomfited adversary, whom he left in an attitude of ludicrous despair, the serjeant dashed with a sword in either hand, to the assistance of Proddy. He was just in time. Vainly had the valiant coachman essayed to make a thrust at his skilful opponent, and he had only avoided the other's desperate lounges by springing back whenever a pass was made at him. Vainly, also, had the corporal, as he pushed him on, called upon him, with furious oaths, to confess himself vanquished. Proddy would not yield, and though much longer defence seemed hopeless, he still held out. Thrust after thrust did the corporal make at him, and leap after leap did he give, when just as his adversary's blade was within an inch of his breast, and he winced at the idea of feeling its horrid point in his flesh, he heard the cheering voice of the serjeant. Upon this, he gave a convulsive spring backwards, and in the effort fell, while the sword flew out of his hand to a couple of yards distance.

Seeing this, Scales hurried forward as quickly as his heavy jackboots would allow, and before the corporal could improve his advantage, dashed between him and his prostrate foe. Sauvageon, with a loud oath, made a thrust at him; but the serjeant parried in prime, and beating the feeble of his adversary's blade smartly and strongly with the forte of his own, sent the sword whizzing aloft.

"Ah! sacre bleu! dat I should be beat in dis way," cried Sauvageon, grinning with rage.

"Pick up your sword again, if you are dissatisfied, corporal," said Scales, magnanimously, "and we'll have another bout."

"Ah, non, vous êtes le diable, sergent," replied the corporal; "but you must admit dat I fairly conquer de little cosheman."

"It's false, Savagejohn!" cried Proddy, who by this time had got upon his feet, and regained possession of his sword. "I've never yielded, and never meant to yield. If you say that I did, I'll run you through the body."

As he spoke, he ran at the unarmed Frenchman, who seeing him advance in this truculent fashion, with slaughter painted in his countenance, was fain to take to his heels and fly. In vain Scales, who could scarcely speak for laughing, called him back. Heedless of his shouts, Proddy pursued the flying corporal with a velocity which the desire of vengeance alone could inspire, and which was wonderful in a person of his bulk, and contrived to prick him twice or thrice with the point of his sword behind, when his foot catching in the root of a tree, he was once more stretched upon the ground. Still, though he fell, the corporal continued his flight, and fancying his blood-thirsty foe at his heels, ran blindly and furiously on, till coming in contact with the wooden framework round Saint Anne's well, which he had not remarked in his haste, he was precipitated head foremost into the water.

Meanwhile, the victorious serjeant, having sheathed his sword, beckoned Bimbelot to him, and complimenting him upon his conduct in the affair, they shook hands very cordially. A few minutes afterwards, Proddy joined them, but was unable to speak for some time, the breath being completely knocked out of him by the last fall; and ere long, the corporal came up, with his wig plastered to his face, his clothes drenched, and presenting altogether a strong resemblance to a drowned rat. He was very angry with Proddy, whom he accused of taking a cowardly and dishonourable advantage of him, and expressed great anxiety to renew the fight. Nor was the coachman anything loth, so that it required all the efforts of the serjeant and Bimbelot to restore peace, which being at last effected, the disputants shook hands, and so warmed towards each other, that in less than five minutes they embraced, and swore an eternal friendship.

Bimbelot, who really was a very good-natured little fellow, asked the whole party to breakfast, and they were just walking off, when, as if struck by a sudden thought, he halted, and cried aloud, "Ah! I just recollect. Stupid dat I was to forget. My master has an affair of honour on his hands dis morning, and hereabouts. Let us go see for him. Our assistance may be needed."

"Who is your master going to fight, Bamby?" asked the serjeant.

"Monsieur Masham," replied Bimbelot; "de young equerry who pretend to de hand of Mademoiselle Hill."

Scales appeared to reflect upon the information, and the party commenced their search, shaping their course in a north-westerly direction. They had not proceeded far, when, guided by the clash of steel, they perceived, in a hollow among the trees, five persons, two of whom were stripped to the shirt, and engaged in conflict, while their companions stood at a little distance from them.

"Ah! voilà mon maître!" exclaimed Bimbelot, halting with the others under the shelter of a tree at the edge of the hollow, where they could see what was passing, without being noticed.

The two principals in the conflict, as had been rightly conjectured, were Guiscard and Masham, and the seconds Saint-John and Maynwaring. The fifth person was a surgeon, with a case of instruments under his arm. The combatants were extremely well matched, and the rapidity and skill with which the various thrusts were made and parried, elicited the applause of the serjeant.

"How beautifully that quinte-thrust was parried by Mr. Masham, Bamby," he cried. "Did you see how he held his wrist in high-carte, with a low point, and put by his adversary's point, by opposing the forte of his outside edge?"

"Vraiment, c'est bon," replied Bimbelot — "mais voyez avec quelle adresse mon maître forme la parade d'octave."

"But see," cried the serjeant, "Mr. Masham makes the cavé, and reversing his edge from the inside to the outside, throws off the thrust. And look—look! the marquis makes a pass in carte over the arm — Mr. Masham parries, and quickly returns in seconde, thrusting and opposing and outward edge. Ah, that pass has told—his point enters his adversary's breast."

As the last pass was delivered, the whole party ran down the side of the dell, but before they reached the bottom, the marquis had fallen. Bimbelot immediately went up to him, and the shirt being opened, the wound was examined by the surgeon, who pronounced that it was not dangerous, the sword having glanced across the ribs under the arm. The pain of the wound, and the effusion that ensued, had caused faintness, but restoratives being applied, by the aid of Bimbelot and the serjeant, he was conveyed to a chair, which was in waiting at a little distance among the trees.

"You have behaved like a man of honour, Masham," said Saint-John, at the close of the combat. "You and Maynwaring must come and breakfast with me, and afterwards I will go with you to Harley. You were perfectly right about Abigail, though I couldn't tell you so before. She detests Guiscard, and I think has a tenderness for you."

"In that case I have not fought in vain," replied Masham, sheathing his sword.

CHAPTER XIV

HARLEY DISCOVERS THAT CERTAIN IMPORTANT DOCUMENTS HAVE BEEN ABSTRACTED BY GREG — HIS UNEASINESS IS INCREASED BY A MESSAGE FROM THE MARQUIS DE GUISCARD.

ON their return from the duel, it being still very early, Saint-John proposed to the others that they should repose themselves for a short time before breakfast, to which both readily agreeing, Masham was shown to a chamber, where, being much fatigued—for he had not closed his eyes during the night—he threw himself upon a couch, and almost instantly fell asleep.

Aroused by the entrance of a servant, who told him breakfast was served, and assisted him to repair his toilette, he descended to the lower room, and was greeted as he approached it by the sound of merry voices and laughter. He found Mrs. Hyde and Angelica at table with the host and Maynwaring, and some progress seemed to have been already made in the meal.

A blooming countenance is always a pleasant object of contemplation in a morning; and notwithstanding her embarrassment. Angelica looked quite charming,—her complexion was so fresh, her eyes so liquid, and her teeth so white. She gazed with ill-concealed admiration at all around her—at the silver covers, shrouding the savoury omelette, the piquant cutlet, and the well-peppered grill; at the eggs reposing in the snowy napkin; at the exquisitely chased silver tea-kettle, with its spirit lamp, and still more exquisite chocolate-pot; at the delicious little blue tea-cups of the choicest porcelain; at the silver flagons for those who preferred claret to the simpler beverages; and having surveyed all this, her eyes wandered to the sideboard, with its well-ordered array of cold chicken, cold ham, tongue, raised pie, and potted meats; while, hard by, a portly butler met her gaze, ready to carve the viands, or to dispense the contents of certain long-necked flasks, with which an adjoining cooler was filled.

Like all country girls who enjoy good health, Angelica had a tolerable appetite; and she knew too little of modish manners to put any restraint upon it. She took, therefore, with gratitude all that was offered her; but her doings in the eating line were mere child's play compared with those of her mother, who was in ecstasies with the repast, and devoured everything before her.

"Dear me!" cried Mrs. Hyde, "why this is a much grander breakfast than we had at Squire Clavering's when his daughter Sukey was married. Do taste the ham, Jelly! I'm a good hand at curing a ham myself, but this beats me. The tongue, too, is boiled to a bubble—there's a great art in boiling a tongue, as I'm sure your cook knows, Mr. Saint-John—another slice, if you please, sir. Well, I don't mind a kidney, since you're so pressing. Jelly, my love, you don't eat! Bless the poor thing! she has fretted so much about her father, that she has quite lost her appetite. Try a little of this apricot marmalade, my dear. It'll do you good. Mr. Saint-John says he'll soon procure the dear man's liberation, so you may be perfectly easy. You see, I'm quite comfortable. Well, I've eaten a great deal, but I can't refuse a cutlet—it looks so nice. A few mushrooms with it, by all means. Another dish of tea, if you please, sir," to the footman. "You're very good. I shouldn't objet to a drop of brandy in it. But it must only be a drop—mind that! You've a design upon me, Mr. Saint-John, or you wouldn't offer me some of the omelette. The first and last omelette I tasted was at the squire's, and I thought it so good then, that I can't refuse now. Jelly, my dear, you're doing nothing. Do eat, child; and recollect you don't get such a breakfast as this every day. You're quite right, Mr. Saint-John, an egg can do nobody any harm. Ah! there we country folk have the advantage of you. You should taste *our* eggs, sir,—fresh laid, white as snow,—they *are* a treat. Jelly fetches them every morning from the nest. You've such a way with you, Mr. Saint-John, that I can't say no. I must taste the pigeon-pie, though positively I've eaten so much, that I begin to feel quite uncomfortable. Don't look at me, Jelly, but take care of yourself. A little gravy, sir," to the butler, "while you are about it."

It was at this juncture that Masham entered the room.

"I'm afraid Mr. Masham will find little to eat," cried Mrs. Hyde. "We've got half an hour's start of him."

"Don't distress yourself about me, madam," he replied. "Abundance is still left upon the table, and I'll soon make up for lost time."

"Angelica says she should have broken her heart if Guiscard had killed you, Masham," Saint-John observed.

"Nay, I said another lady would break her heart," she replied. "But I should have been purely sorry myself, I must own."

The young equerry bowed.

"You awaken a tender interest in all the ladies, Masham," remarked Maynwaring.

"It's not to be wondered at," said Angelica, "considering——"

And she blushed and hesitated.

"Pray finish your speech, my dear," cried Maynwaring. "Considering what?"

"I don't know what I was going to say," she rejoined, with increased confusion.

"Do let Mr. Masham eat his breakfast, Jelly," said Mrs. Hyde. "Try one of these cutlets, sir; you'll find 'em excellent — or these kidneys, they're broiled to perfection. And so you have killed the marquis? My worthy husband declares that a duellist is a murderer, and ought to be hanged. But then he's rather too severe; and, as I tell him, if that was to be the case, we should hang some of the first quality; and would you believe it, he answered, ' And a good thing, too.' Do take a little of this peach-preserve, sir; you'll find it delicious."

"How far Masham deserves hanging, I know not," said Saint-John, laughing; "but you are mistaken, madam, in supposing he has killed the marquis. He has only very slightly wounded him."

"More's the pity, I think," cried Mrs. Hyde. "But if the officer spoke the truth last night, he has only been saved from one death for another more ignominious."

"May be," observed Saint-John, somewhat gloomily.

But instantly resuming his former gaiety, he turned the conversation to the various amusements and attractions of town-life—expatiating upon the theatres, the opera, the concerts, the public gardens, the balls, the masquerades, the drives in the park, the promenades on the Mall, and drew such a captivating picture of fashionable existence, that it quite charmed Angelica's fancy.

"Dear me!" she sighed, "how purely happy those fine ladies must be, who can lie a-bed as late as they like; and have nothing to do but amuse themselves when they get up. How I wish I had been born to such a lot! I should like of all things to have a little black page with a white turban and feathers on his head—a nice room with great japan screens, and cabinets full of lovely chayney monsters—a French perruquier to dress my hair—the richest silks and satins for my gowns, and the finest lace for my caps and pinners; but most of all I should like to have a grand gilt charrot, with three footmen behind it, and a fat coachman on the box. Oh, it would be purely nice!"

" Save us! how sinfully the wench talks!" cried Mrs. Hyde.
" It's very well your father doesn't hear you, or he would reprove
you for your vanity."

" All this may be yours, Angelica," said Saint-John, in a low
tone to her. " You have only to say the word."

" I think I had better give up the gilt charrot, and the fat coachman," sighed Angelica, looking down.

" You'll be a great deal happier and healthier if you continue to
get up at five o'clock of a morning, to help Dolly to milk the
cows, Jelly," said Mrs Hyde, "than if you were to lie a-bed till
eleven or twelve, and then get up with the vapours and a head-
ache; and Tom the farming lad will wait upon you as well as the
little black boy; and as to the chayney gimcracks and monsters,
I'm sure my delf is prettier by half, and my pewter plates brighter
than any silver; and if you must ride, you know you can always
have the cart and the old mare; or if you want to go to Thaxted,
Phil Tredget will be too happy to give you a seat behind him on
the pillion. You seem to have forgotten poor Phil."

" No, I haven't," replied Angelica, with a look of mingled vexation and shame, and who had vainly endeavoured to check her
mother's volubility; "I think of him as much as he deserves.
But nobody knows him here."

" Phil's as honest a lad as any in Essex," said Mrs. Hyde; "and
as good-looking, too, though I say it to you, Mr. Masham, who're
an Essex gentleman yourself. He's about your height, sir; but a
good deal broader across the shoulders, and with fine curly auburn
hair, with a red tinge in it."

" His hair's as red as carrots," cried Angelica.

" Oh, I've no doubt he has the advantage of me immeasurably,"
replied Masham, laughing heartily.

" And so you've given your heart to Phil Tredget, eh—Angelica?'
inquired Saint-John.

" Not quite," she replied, blushing.

" Then Phil deceived himself strangely, Jelly," rejoined her
mother.

" I didn't know my own mind then," said Angelica, with a furtive glance at Saint-John.

" To be sure not," he replied, with a meaning look. " Well,
since you have finished breakfast, Masham, we'll proceed to business. Pray amuse yourselves here in the best way you can, ladies,
till I send Mr. Hyde to you." So saying he arose, and, accompanied
by his two friends, quitted the room.

" What do you mean to do with the girl?" asked Maynwaring,
as they issued into the street.

" Faith, I don't know," replied Saint-John; "but she's devilish
pretty."

Maynwaring acquiesced in the opinion, and quitted them at the
corner of King-street, while the two others proceeding to Mr.
Harley's residence in Saint James's-square, were without delay
ushered into his presence.

They found Harley alone, and engaged in writing. His looks
were troubled, and after congratulating Masham on the result of

the duel, he took Saint-John into an inner-room, and said to him,
—"This arrest of Greg gives me great uneasiness. I have been
revolving the matter all the morning, and am still full of per
plexity."

"Have you in any way trusted him?" asked Saint-John.

"No," replied Harley; "but it is impossible to say what the
villain has done. He may have opened my boxes—my letters;
and secrets of vital importance may have become known to him."

"Rest easy," replied Saint-John. "No credit will be attached
to any statements he may make, unless borne out by proof."

"But I fear he *has* proof," replied Harley. "I have examined
the escritoir in which I keep my secret papers, and there is one
packet missing, which if it should fall into the hands of Godolphin
and Marlborough, would ruin me."

"Cursed unlucky, indeed!" exclaimed Saint-John. "I would
almost recommend a flight to France."

"No, I will stay and confront the danger, whatever it may be,"
replied Harley. "Would I could know the worst! But I dare not
hold any communication with Greg."

The silence into which both fell was broken by the entrance of
the usher, who said that Parson Hyde was in the ante-room, and
begged an immediate interview with Mr. Harley, his business being
of the utmost importance.

"Show him in at once," cried the secretary. "As this man was
arrested with Greg, we shall now probably learn something," he
added to Saint-John, as the usher left the room.

The next moment Hyde was introduced.

"You have heard of my arrest, gentlemen, I presume?" he said,
bowing respectfully.

"We have, sir," answered Harley; "and are glad to see you at
liberty."

"My detention was the result of misrepresentation, as it turns
out," the divine replied; "but the consciousness of innocence supported me; and my confinement for the night in the Gate-house
has been the sole inconvenience I have endured."

"But what of your fellow-prisoner, Greg? Has he been released,
too?" asked Harley, hastily.

"No, sir," returned Hyde. "It is on his account I have come
to you."

"Well, sir, proceed. What have you to say concerning him?"
demanded Harley.

"I scarcely know how to justify what I have done," replied
Hyde; "but I could not refuse to aid a friend in misfortune. As
I have said, I was locked up in a chamber at the Gate-house
with my poor friend, and as soon as the door was closed upon
us, he extorted from me, by urgent solicitations, a promise to do
him a service, provided I was set at liberty, which he foresaw I
should be, the first thing in the morning. This was to go to the
Marquis de Guiscard, whose address in Pall Mall he gave me, and
tell him what had happened."

"Is that all?" cried Harley, impatiently.

" No, sir," replied Hyde. " He bade me tell the marquis to open a small box which he had entrusted to his care a few days ago, and with its contents purchase safety for him from you."

" That box contains the missing packet, I'll be sworn," whispered Harley to Saint-John. " Well, sir," he added, to the divine, " you went to the marquis, I suppose—but you did not see him? He has been wounded in a duel this morning."

" Pardon me, Mr. Harley," replied Hyde; " I *did* see him. On learning that I wished to speak with him, the marquis caused me to be introduced to his bedside, and dismissed his attendants. I then delivered poor Greg's message to him, upon which he instantly rang for his French valet, and bade him take a small box from a cabinet to which he pointed, and break it open. This was done, and a packet of letters was found within it. Having examined them, the marquis's countenance brightened up, and he cried, ' A thousand thanks, reverend sir! You have done me infinitely more good than the surgeon who has just quitted me. These letters will save our poor friend, and I am glad of it. But do me a further favour. Go to Mr. Harley, and tell him, as he values himself, to come to me instantly. I would go to him, but I cannot quit my chamber, and not a moment is to be lost. Observe the greatest caution.' And with a few words more, he dismissed me. This is all I have to relate."

" And enough, too," muttered Saint-John.

" The marquis is the dupe of some trickery on the part of Greg, I fear," said Harley, vainly trying to mask his uneasiness. " Nevertheless, I will comply with his request."

" You will do well," observed Saint-John: " for though I cannot conceive how these letters can serve Greg, yet it may be desirable to see them. You will find your wife and daughter at my house in Saint James's-place, hard by, Mr. Hyde; and as they have been much alarmed by your arrest, it will be well to set their minds at ease as soon as possible. Pray make my house your home for the present."

" I return you my humble thanks, sir," replied Hyde, bowing respectfully, and quitting the room.

" I will go to this rascal marquis at once," said Harley. " I shall have to buy these letters dearly,—but buy them I will. I have a plan which I think will succeed. Remain with Masham, my dear friend, till I return. I shall not be long."

CHAPTER XV.

THE PRICE PAID FOR THE LETTERS.

FOLLOWED by a queen's-messenger, whom he had hastily summoned, and to whom he gave certain instructions, Harley proceeded to Pall Mall. On arriving at the marquis's, he posted the messenger

near the door, and knocking, was admitted by the grinning and
obsequious Bimbelot, who, in reply to his inquiries, informed him
that his master was somewhat easier, but, expecting the honour of
a visit from Mr. Harley, hoped he would excuse being shown to his
bed-room, as he was unable to leave it.

With these, and many more apologies, the valet led the way, with
much ceremony, to a most luxurious chamber, in which stood a
large canopy-bed with brocade hangings, a superbly-appointed
toilette table, a cheval·glass, hung with muslin, two magnificent
wardrobes in one corner, and a range of peruke-stands. Over the
chimney-piece was a fine picture of the Judgment of Paris, and
there were other pieces of a similar nature hung about the room.

On a couch, and partly covered by a loose silk dressing-gown, lay
the marquis. The swarthy hue of his complexion had given place
to a deathly pallor, and, notwithstanding Bimbelot's assurance that
he was free from pain, he seemed to suffer acutely. He made an
effort, however, to raise himself on Harley's appearance, begged him
to be seated, and motioned the valet to retire.

" I am glad to see you, Mr. Harley," he said, with a smile, which
communicated a sinister effect to his ghastly features ; " I was sure
you would come. You have been told by the worthy clergyman I
dispatched to you what has happened?"

" I have been informed by him that certain letters, which I have
reason to believe have been purloined from my escritoir by the
villain Greg, have come into your possession," replied the secretary.

" You have been correctly informed, sir," rejoined Guiscard.
" Those letters, which are of the last importance, as proving that
a correspondence subsists between one of Queen Anne's ministers
and an exiled royal family, were entrusted to me by the poor devil
you mention, who now wishes me to make terms by means of them
for his safety; but I need scarcely say I require them for myself."

" You are sufficiently unscrupulous, I am aware, marquis," replied Harley, bitterly.

" Would you do otherwise if you were similarly circumstanced,
Mr. Secretary?" rejoined Guiscard, in a derisive tone. " But to
the point. No matter how obtained, these documents are in my
possession. With them I can purchase perfect security from
Godolphin and Marlborough, so that I have no further uneasiness.
Before doing so, however, I offer them to you, as they are of more
value to you than to any one else."

" Let me hear the price you put upon them?" said Harley, coldly.

" First, protection to myself," replied Guiscard, " in case Greg's
examination should at all implicate me."

" Accorded," rejoined the secretary. " What more ?"

" Secondly, the hand of Abigail Hill," said the marquis.

" Refused," replied Harley, in a determined tone.

" Then I shall be compelled to treat with your enemies," said
Guiscard.

" Now hear me, marquis," rejoined Harley—" those letters must
be mine, and upon my own terms. Knowing with whom I have to
deal, I have taken measures accordingly. A queen's messenger

awaits my orders at your door, and I have only to speak the word, and your instant arrest will follow. This will effectually prevent you from negotiating with Godolphin and Marlborough; and even if the letters should be laid before the council, I have little fear of the consequences, so well am I provided against every difficulty. Like a prudent man, therefore, after weighing the chances, and seeing on which side the advantage preponderates, you will incline that way. What I offer is this—freedom from your present jeopardy, and two thousand pounds."

And, as he spoke, he produced a pocket-book, and opening it, displayed a roll of bank-notes. Guiscard leaned back his head, and appeared to reflect.

" I would as lieve perish, as yield Abigail to that accursed Masham !" he cried, at length, with a frightful expression of hatred and bodily anguish.

" She will be his in any case," replied Harley; " and your wisest, and indeed only course, will be to abandon all idea of her, and instantly close with my proposition."

" Say three thousand," rejoined Guiscard; " your post is well worth that sum, and you are certain to lose it, if not your head, if these letters are given up. Say three thousand, and I consent."

" I have gone as far as I care to go, and further than I need have gone," replied Harley, closing the pocket-book. " Make up your mind at once. Mine is made up already."

And he arose from his seat, as if with the intention of leaving the room.

" I have your solemn pledge for my own safety ?" said Guiscard.

" So far as I can secure it—undoubtedly," replied the secretary.

" Then here are the letters," said the marquis, delivering the packet to him.

" And here are the notes," replied the other, handing him in exchange the pocket-book.

And while the one examined the letters to see that they were all right, the other told over the notes. Both were apparently satisfied with their scrutiny.

" You need fear no revelations from Greg, Mr. Harley," said Guiscard. " Your enemies, no doubt, will attempt to tamper with him ; but I will give him to understand, through Parson Hyde, whose simplicity will render him a serviceable agent, that his sole hope of escape depends upon his silence. The gallows will set all to rest. Leave him to me."

" Adieu, marquis," replied Harley. " You have seldom made a luckier hit—even at hazard—than this, and it may console you for your defeat by Masham, and for the loss of Abigail."

CHAPTER XVI.

HARLEY's triumphant looks on his return announced his success to
Saint-John; and after a word or two in private, they separated, relieved of much of the anxiety that had previously oppressed them,—
the one to return home, and the other to repair with Masham to
Saint James's Palace.

On arriving there, they were conducted to the ante-room of the
queen's private apartments, where they found Abigail and Lady
Rivers. The manner of the former was much more cold and constrained towards Masham than he expected, and somewhat disconcerted Harley.

"I have just left her majesty, Mr. Masham," she said. "She has
heard of your duel with the Marquis de Guiscard, and is much
offended at it. She expressed herself so strongly on the subject to
me, that I feel I am hazarding her favour in consenting to see you
now."

"If I had been aware of it, I would not have exposed you to any
such risk," replied Masham, much piqued. "And I will instantly
relieve you from further responsibility."

"That is not at all what Abigail intends, Mr. Masham," cried
Lady Rivers, bursting into a laugh; "and if you were not a very
young man, you would not require to be told so. She only wishes
you to understand that she would rather displease the queen than
not see you."

"I mean no such thing, Lady Rivers," said Abigail, pettishly.

"Then what *do* you mean, my dear?" rejoined Lady Rivers;
"for I'm sure you were dying for an interview with Mr. Masham
just now, and since you've got your wish, you almost tell him
to go."

"On my soul, you are enough to drive a man to distraction,
cousin," added Harley; "and I thank my stars I am not in love
with you. You seem to blame Masham for this duel, when you
know, or ought to know, that you were the cause of it."

"Exactly what her majesty says," replied Abigail. "She rates
me as if I could have helped it; while nobody knows better than
Mr. Masham, that he did not consult me when he went to fight."

"No; but he consulted your reputation, cousin," said Harley.

"I can take care of that myself," replied Abigail; "and it will
be time enough for Mr. Masham to fight for me, when I elect him
my champion. What will the whole court say to it! It will be
buzzed about that these rivals, like knights of old, have fought for
me and that I mean to give myself to the conqueror. But I will
disappoint them. I will do no such thing. Mr. Masham, I'll be
bound, thought more of the effect which this duel would produce
upon me than of punishing the marquis for his insolent vaunt.
Such chivalrous motives are quite out of date."

"It may be so," replied Masham; "but unless I have wholly mistaken myself, I was actuated by a better motive than you give me credit for. It was love for you, Abigail, that made me resent the manner in which your name was used. I believed the marquis spoke falsely, and I told him so."

The earnestness with which this speech was uttered dispelled all Abigail's coquetry of manner, as a sudden gust of wind might disperse a rack of clouds hanging over the moon. She trembled, and cast down her eyes. Seeing her emotion, and attributing it to its right cause, Lady Rivers and Harley withdrew to a window, and looked out into the palace-gardens.

"They are likely to come to an understanding now, I think," observed the secretary, in a low tone.

"Very likely," replied the lady, with a smile.

"I cannot carry on this deception further, Mr. Masham," said Abigail, at length. "I have trifled with you too long. It is true the queen is angry, but that is nothing to me. Thinking you would come here, flushed with your success, and anticipating an equally easy conquest over me, I determined to treat you as I have done— lightly. But I find that vanity forms no part of your composition, and it would be unfeeling to pursue such a course further. I am fully sensible of your devotion, and return it. We shall have no more misunderstandings now, depend upon it. Nor shall I again play the coquette—at least, with you."

"Nor with any one else, if I can prevent it," replied Masham, kneeling, and snatching her hand, which he pressed rapturously to his lips. "You are a matchless creature."

At this juncture, the inner door opened, and the queen, attended by Prince George of Denmark, issued from it. Masham instantly sprang to his feet, but not before his situation had been remarked by the royal pair.

A slight smile passed over the prince's countenance, and he glanced at the queen, but her majesty, whose strict notions of etiquette were greatly outraged, did not respond to it. Masham bowed profoundly to hide his confusion; Abigail blushed, and fanned herself; Prince George took a prodigious pinch of snuff, to prevent himself from laughing outright; while Lady Rivers and Harley returned from the window.

"I am somewhat surprised to see you here, Mr. Masham," said the queen, gravely, "after the disregard you have shown to my wishes."

"I am not aware that I have disobeyed your majesty," replied the young equerry.

"You have paid little heed, then, to what was said, sir," rejoined the queen, the cloud gathering more darkly on her brow. "Having sufficiently interested myself in you to express a desire that you should not meet the Marquis de Guiscard, I scarcely expected you would so soon afterwards provoke another quarrel with him, the result of which has been a meeting this morning, at which, I understand, he has been wounded."

"The intelligence came from Marlborough House, I'll be sworn," said Harley, aside. "The devil is not more malicious than the duchess."

"The marquis had used my name most unwarrantably," said Abigail. "He deserved his chastisement."

"For Heaven's sake, don't draw down the queen's resentment on yourself," whispered Harley. "You will put your own place in jeopardy."

"I will risk anything rather than Mr. Masham shall be wrongfully treated!" she replied, in the same tone.

"Faith! your majesty is too hard upon the young man," interposed the good-natured Prince George, in a whisper, to the queen—"sadly too hard. His disregard of your wishes proceeded from inadvertence—sheer inadvertence."

"He shall be taught stricter attention in future," replied the queen. "I am determined to mark my disapprobation of the practice of duelling, and this young man shall be made the first example."

"Nay, madam," entreated the prince.

"I have said it," rejoined the queen, in a tone calculated to put an end to further discussion. "Mr. Masham," she added, "his highness will dispense with your attendance for the next three months, and you will avail yourself of the opportunity to visit your family in Essex, or to travel during the period."

"I understand your majesty," replied Masham, bowing. "I am banished from court."

Anne made a slight movement of the head in assent, and Prince George consoled himself with a prolonged pinch of snuff.

"This is the first time I have known your majesty unjust," said Abigail.

"Cousin, be advised," whispered Harley.

"Perhaps you will also call me unjust, Abigail," said the queen, "when I say, that if any one of my attendants gives away her hand without my consent, she will by so doing vacate her place, and forfeit my favour for ever."

Abigail was about to reply, but a slight pressure upon her arm checked her. The next moment, the adroit secretary passed over to Masham, and whispered to him—"It is proper for you, after what has occurred, to withdraw."

The young equerry instantly advanced to Prince George, kissed the hand which was graciously extended to him, and making a profound obeisance to the queen, was about to retire, when Abigail stopped him.

"I pray your majesty, suffer Mr. Masham to remain a moment longer," she said. "I have a boon to beg of you in his presence."

"If you ask her consent now," whispered Harley, "you will fail. Another time—another time!"

"Mr. Masham, you may go," said Abigail, blushing, and in confusion.

"Nay, since you have called him back, my dear, it is but fair he should hear what you have to say," remarked Prince George, whose good-nature frequently outran his discretion.

"Your majesty has just said, that if any one of your attendants gives away her hand without your consent, she will forfeit your favour for ever," hesitated Abigail.

"Precisely the words I used," replied Anne. "But what have they to do with Mr. Masham? I hope," she continued, in a severe tone, "you have not already taken this step without consulting me."

"Assuredly not, madam," rejoined Abigail, recovering her composure, and disregarding the gestures of Harley, "and though I may have chosen an unfortunate moment for the request, yet I will venture to entreat your gracious permission to answer in the affirmative, in case Mr. Masham should put a particular question to me."

"I must consider of it," replied the queen, coldly.

"Faith, I'm sorry I called the young man back," cried the prince. "Good day t'ye, Masham—good day t'ye!" he continued, accompanying the equerry to the door. "I hope her majesty will be in a better temper when we next meet. Three months is it, eh? I'll try and get the term shortened. But never mind—soon be over—soon over. And as to Abigail, I'll stand your friend. So don't despair—don't despair. Good day!"

And he pushed him gently out of the room.

As soon as the prince returned, the queen took his arm, and was about to re-enter the private apartments, when Abigail advanced towards her.

"Does your majesty require my attendance?" she asked.

"Not now," replied Anne, regarding her with a look of greater displeasure than she had ever before evinced towards her. And she disappeared with her august consort.

"This it is to serve a queen," cried Abigail, bursting into tears, and falling upon Lady Rivers's neck.

"You have to thank yourself for much that has occurred," said Harley. "But the duchess is at the bottom of it all."

"She is," replied Abigail, looking up; "but she shall not profit by her malice. The present turn is hers: the next shall be mine."

"There I am with you, cousin," cried Harley, grasping her hand, warmly. "It will be your own fault if you do not place Masham as high as the proudest noble that presses to Saint James's. Recollect, the fortune of John Churchill was made by Sarah Jennings."

"Meantime, I am in disgrace, and Masham is banished," sighed Abigail.

"Both affairs of a moment," replied Harley. "The wind that blows against us to-day will shift to-morrow. Like the Roman general, we will turn defeat into victory."

CHAPTER XVII.

THE SERJEANT'S "DRUM."

"I TELL you what it is, Proddy," said the serjeant, as they sat together over a bowl of punch at the Marlborough's Head, in Rider-street—a house patronised by Scales, as well on account of the ensign it bore, as of the admirable quality of the liquors dispensed at it—"I tell you what it is. I'm pleased with the way in which those two Mounseers behaved this morning."

"So am I," replied Proddy. "I'm particularly pleased with Savagejohn. I hated him at first — but one always begins by hating. I disliked you consumedly once, serjeant."

"I've been thinking the matter over," said Scales, who was too much engrossed by his own meditations to pay attention to the coachman's remarks; "and I'm resolved to invite 'em to a dance. I know it'll please our women, and it's sure to be to the taste of the Mounseers. They're a merry nation, the French, I will say that for 'em."

"I'm very fond of dancing, myself, serjeant; and a tolerably good dancer, too, though you would hardly think it," observed Proddy. laying down his pipe, and executing a step or two. "Before I grew so stout, I could get through a jig as well as any man. There," he added, cutting a caper, and poising himself on one foot —"what do you think of that?"

"Capital!" exclaimed Scales. "This decides me. We'll have a hop this night week. The quality call a party of this kind a drum, though why I don't know, for I never heard any drumming at their routs; but if I issue invitations to a drum, as I mean to do, it'll be all right and proper, for the only music my guests will get will be such as I myself can produce from a couple of sticks and a piece of parchment."

"And famous rattlin' music, too, serjeant," rejoined Proddy. "Rat-a-tat-a-tat-a-rara! Call it a drum, by all means."

"I don't know, but I may get Tom Jiggins, the fifer of our regiment, to accompany me," said the serjeant, after a moment's reflection; "and in that case we'll keep you alive, for Tom's a first-rate performer. It wont be the first time the Mounseers have danced to the music of the fife and drum, eh, Proddy?"

"Not by a good many," replied the coachman, chuckling; "and to a pretty quick movement, too, if our gazettes speak truth. But we've concluded a truce now, serjeant; so we must have no more jesting. This night week, you say?"

"This night week," replied Scales. "Of course, you'll come?"

"If I'm in the land o' the livin', of course I will," replied Proddy; "we're two inseparables now. What's your hour?"

"Oh! you'll see that in the card," said Scales. "You'll have an invitation—all reg'lar. But I should say eight, or thereabouts; and if you're too genteel to be punctual, don't make it later than nine."

" I'm always punctual, serjeant," replied Proddy ; " every man as holds a office under government is punctual."

" Very right," said Scales. " Come, there's just a glass a-piece in the bowl. May we always be as successful as we've been to-day ! It's time we were movin'. I hear the watchman bawlin' out past ten o'clock. I pay."

" No, you don't," cried Proddy.

" I tell you I do," rejoined Scales, authoritatively. " Here, drawer," he added, flinging down a crown—" here's your dues. Now, comrade, right foot foremost." And they marched forth arm in arm—Proddy strutting as usual, and thrusting out his chin, and the serjeant whistling Marlbrook.

Next morning, as he sat at breakfast with the rest of the household, in the servants' hall at Marlborough House, Scales intimated his intention of giving the drum in the course of the following week ; and the announcement was received with unanimous applause by the whole assemblage, and with especial delight by Mesdames Plumpton and Tipping.

" Well, I declare, serjeant !" cried the first-mentioned lady—" a drum ! what a charmin' idea ! And how impropriate to your profession. My heart quite beats at the thought of it."

" So genteel, too !" added Mrs. Tipping. " So different from the vulgar hop, as they call such things in the city. Ladies of quality give nothing but drums, now-a-days."

" Glad the notion meets with your approval, ladies," rejoined the serjeant. " As Mrs. Plumpton observes, I think it *is* appropriate. I'll do my best to amuse you."

" You've only to drum to amuse me, serjeant," said Mrs. Plumpton.

" Plumpton's sure to take the words out of a body's mouth," cried Mrs. Tipping, sharply.

" I feel the compliment just as much as if it had been uttered, Mrs. Tipping," observed the serjeant, gallantly. " His grace, you think, will have no objection to the party, Mr. Fishwick?" he added, appealing to the cook.

" I'll answer for his grace," replied Fishwick? " and I'll answer also for his gracious permission to provide a good supper."

" As you answer for the solids, I'll answer for the fluids, Mr. Fishwick," said the portly Mr. Peter Parker, the butler, with a knowing wink. " You shall have a bottle or two of wine from my own cupboard, and you shall also have such a bowl of punch as you never drank before. Mrs. Plumpton, I dare say, will lend me the great blue china bowl that stands in the housekeeper's room to brew it in, so that we can have plenty."

" That I will," replied Mrs. Plumpton ; "and as you all contribute something to the feast, I'll add a flask of usquebaugh, that was given me by—by—I forget whom."

" By the late Mr. P——, most likely," suggested Mrs. Tipping, with a sneer. " Well, I don't think *I* shall contribute anything but my company."

" Nothing more is needed," replied Scales, gallantly.

"Of course, you mean to invite Mr. Proddy, serjeant?" said Mrs. Plumpton. "He's such a dear little man !"

"Of course," replied Scales; "and to please Mrs. Tipping, I shall ask Mounseer Bambilot, the Marquis de Guiscard's gentleman, and his friend Corporal Achille Sauvageon,—both magnificent dancers."

"Quite unnecessary to invite 'em on my account, serjeant," replied Mrs. Tipping. "However, I shall be glad to meet any friends of yours."

Soon after this, the serjeant retired to his own room, and with some difficulty wrote out a number of cards, which were despatched by a trusty messenger, and in due time brought responses in the affirmative from most of the parties invited.

Later on in the day, Fishwick came to inform him that the duke had not only given his full consent to the entertainment, but had expressed a hope that it would pass off pleasantly.

"Did his grace say so?" cried Scales, in a transport of delight. "Well, it's just like him. Bless his kind, good heart! No wonder his soldiers love him so much, Fishwick, and fight so well for him. It's a pleasure to die for such a commander."

Some little talk was then held between them as to the arrangements of the night, and they separated with a conviction that the Drum would go off remarkably well.

The six intervening days wore away, and the seventh arrived. During the morning, the serjeant's countenance was charged with unwonted importance. He had undertaken a task of which he evidently felt the magnitude. He was continually going backwards and forwards into the kitchen, and giving directions in a low tone to the scullions. Then he withdrew to furbish his accoutrements, to practise a little on the drum, and hum a song in a low key.

About noon, Tom Jiggins, the fifer, arrived, and made his way at once to the serjeant's room, where they were shut up together till dinner-time, rehearsing, it would seem, from the sounds they produced, the dances of the night.

A gaunt, hard-featured little fellow was Tom Jiggins; not unlike the serjeant himself, on a small scale. He had a long nose, a very long upper lip, and a long chin in continuation. And he made the most of his size, standing as high as five feet would allow him. His eyes had the set stare peculiar to performers on wind instruments and cod-fish. Jiggins was dressed in the regimental uniform—blue, with white cuffs and facings, and wore a broad white belt across his left shoulder, to which was attached by a cord the case containing his fife. The opposite hip sustained a sword. A cap, and powdered wig with a long tail, completed his accoutrements.

Dinner over, the fifer and the serjeant had another rehearsal, after which they esteemed themselves perfect, and whiled away the rest of the afternoon over a mug of ale and a pipe.

Evening at last approached, and the business of the day over, active preparations were made for the Drum. The kitchen was cleared out, and lighted up by candles placed upon the chimney-piece, dresser, and plate-shelves; and at a quarter before eight o'clock,

Just as the clock struck the appointed hour, a scuffling sound was heard in the passage, and the next moment, Mrs. Plumpton and Mrs. Tipping rushed into the room together, both looking very red and very angry.

"You're excessive rude, Plumpton, to push so?" cried Mrs. Tipping. "I declare you have quite disarranged my dress."

"Serve you right, too!" replied Mrs. Plumpton, sharply. "You shouldn't have tried to take proceedings of me. You've almost pulled off my cap and pinners."

"I wish I had," rejoined Mrs. Tipping—"and your wig into the bargain."

"Ladies," said the serjeant, "let me entreat, that on this evening, at least, we may have no quarrelling. You're both beautifully dressed, and would be irresistible, if you didn't look quite so cross."

This had the desired effect. Peace was instantly restored. Mrs. Tipping obligingly arranged Mrs. Plumpton's head-dress, and Mrs. Plumpton pinned up Mrs. Tipping's gown. Both were very finely dressed—the one exhibiting her buxom person in crimson silk, and the other her trim little figure in orange-coloured satin.

Soon after this, Fishwick, Parker, Timperley, and the rest of the household, male and female, amounting to more than a dozen, flocked into the kitchen, and were welcomed by the serjeant, who had a hearty greeting for every one of them. He had scarcely gone the round, when Timperley, who was stationed at the door to usher in the guests, announced "Mr. Proddy and friend."

Habited in his full-dress coat of crimson velvet, striped with yellow, and bound with gold, with a waistcoat to match, and having a large muslin cravat tied loosely round his throat, the coachman presented a very imposing appearance.

Marching up to Scales, he said, "Serjeant, allow me to present to you Mr. Mezansene—a young gentleman who has just been honoured with a place in her majesty's household, and who is desirous of making your acquaintance. I have taken the liberty of bringing him with me."

"No liberty at all, Proddy," replied the serjeant; "you did quite right. Glad to see you, sir."

And he shook hands heartily with Mezansene, who was a tall, slight, and gracefully formed young man, with very good features, except that, like the serjeant, he had a broad black patch across his nose, and another somewhat smaller patch on the left cheek. He was clothed in the royal livery, and wore a full-bottomed, well powdered wig.

"You have been in the wars as well as myself, Mr. Mezansene?" observed the serjeant, in reference to the other's patches.

"These cuts were given me in the street the other night by a party of those wild rakes who call themselves Mohocks, serjeant," replied Mezansene.

"I know the Mohocks well, and nice blades they are," observed the serjeant. "I should like to make some of 'em run the gauntlet for their pranks. That young man's face is familiar to me," he continued, to Proddy, as Mezansene walked towards Mrs. Plumpton and Mrs. Tipping, who were standing near the fire; "I suppose I have seen him at the palace."

"No, you can scarcely have seen him there, serjeant," replied Proddy, "for he only entered the houschold a few days ago. He came in place of Mr. Chillingworth, one of the servants, who, being taken suddenly ill, was allowed to provide a substitute. I met him in the guard-chamber to-day, and was so pleased with his manners, that I offered to bring him here."

Before the serjeant could reply, Timperley announced Mr. Needler Webb, the Earl of Sunderland's gentleman, and Mrs. Loveday, the Countess of Bridgewater's lady's-maid. A coat of green embossed velvet, which had very recently been the property of his noble master—a laced satin waistcoat, pink silk hose, and shoes with pink heels, constituted Mr. Needler Webb's attire. He affected a rakish air, and was very much bepatched and perfumed. Mrs. Loveday was equally gaily attired, and dropping a curtsey to the ground, in reply to the serjeant's bow, joined the other ladies.

Next came Mr. Prankard, Lord Ryalton's chief valet, another smart fellow; and after him, a smarter fellow still, Mr. Lascelles, Lord Ross's gentleman. Then came Lady Rivers' lady's-maid, Mrs. Semple, and Lady Di Cecil's maid, Mrs. Clerges.

Half-a-dozen more arrivals occurred, and the room presented a rather crowded appearance, when Bimbelot and Sauvageon were announced. With a mincing gait, the vain little French valet advanced towards the serjeant, and then bowed to the ladies. It was easy to see that he thought himself the best-bred, the best-dressed, and the best-looking person in the room. His master being still confided to his couch from the effects of the duel, Bimbelot thought it a good opportunity of wearing his full-dress suit, and accordingly he appeared in a coat of scarlet cloth bound with gold, a magnificent waistcoat, a campaign wig, a laced cravat and ruffles. The splendour of his attire won him the admiration of the fairer portion of the company, which he was not slow to perceive, but ogled them very familiarly all round, kissing his hand, grinning, bowing, and chattering. As to Sauvageon, he contented himself with talking to Proddy.

Mulled wine and biscuits were now handed round, and shortly afterwards, the serjeant took possession of a stool at the upper end of the room, and beat a call, while Jiggins perched himself on a chair behind him.

This was understood to be the signal for dancing, and the ball was opened by a minuet, in which Bimbelot and Mrs. Loveday, and Needler Webb and Mrs. Clerges, were the performers; and in spite of the shrillness of the music, which was not exactly in unison with the grave measure of the dance, the two couples not only acquitted themselves to their own satisfaction, but to that of everybody else. Mezansene and Mrs. Semple next stood up for a rigadoon, and executed it with so much spirit that an encore was called for.

"Qui est ce jeune homme là, sergent?" inquired Bimbelot. "Il ressemble diablement à quelqu'un de mes amis, mais qui, je ne puis pas rappeller."

I'm quite as much perplexed as you are, Bamby," replied Scales. "For the life of me, I can't make out who he is like. I'll ask him, when an opportunity offers."

It occurred immediately afterwards. The young man having quitted his partner, came towards them.

"Mr. Mezansene," said Scales, "Bamby and I have discovered a great resemblance between you and——"

"Whom?" demanded the other, with a slight start.

"Nay, don't be alarmed—between you and a friend of ours, whose name we can't at this moment recollect. Have you ever been thought like anybody?"

"Not that I am aware of," replied Mezansene, carelessly. "But it's very possible."

"Mezansene—c'est un nomme François, monsieur!" cried Bimbelot. "Vous êtes mon compatriote?"

"Pas tout-à-fait, monsieur," replied Mezansene; "mais ma mère était Française."

"Ah, votre mère était Française—c'est assez—c'est assez!" cried Bimbelot, embracing him. "J'étois sur que vous étiez François— vous êtes si beau—vous dansez si legerement! je suis fier de vous, mon ami."

And tapping Mezansene on the breast, he led him to Sauvageon, who appeared equally enchanted with their new acquaintance.

Meantime, a cotillon had been called for; then followed a jig, in which Proddy and Mrs. Plumpton distinguished themselves, occasioning immense laughter by their extraordinary and unexpected agility; after that succeeded the fine old dance of "the hay;" and after a breathing-pause had been allowed, and refreshments handed round, the pretty and animating cushion-dance was performed—the serjeant drumming away all the while with untiring spirit, and Jiggins only stopping now and then to whet his whistle.

The cushion-dance concluded, all sat down, and to be sure, such flourishing of handkerchiefs, such puffing and blowing, and such mopping of warm faces as followed! It was delectable to witness it, at least so thought the serjeant.

In the midst of it all, Mr. Parker marched into the kitchen, bearing an immense bowl (Mrs. Plumpton's loan) of cold punch, which he proceeded to set down upon the dresser. The moment was admirably chosen; and as large goblets of the cool and fragrant beverage were handed round, it was pronounced to be more delicious than nectar. And then the laughter and jokes that followed! Talk of champagne!—the best champagne ever grown would not have done its duty half so well, or so quickly as that bowl of punch. Your health, serjeant, in a glass of it.

Again the serjeant's drum beats merrily rat-a-tat, and again the fife pours forth its shrilly notes.

By this time, all are in such tip-toe spirits that nothing but a country-dance will serve their turn, and accordingly partners are chosen, Proddy selecting Mrs. Plumpton, Bimbelot Mrs. Tipping, Needler Webb Mrs. Semple, Mezansene Mrs. Loveday, and the others suiting themselves as they can. In another instant all are in their places, forming two lines, extending the whole length of the kitchen, the fifer playing the liveliest tune imaginable, and Scales coming in every now and then, when required, with a most inspiriting rub-a-dub.

Proddy and Mrs. Plumpton led off, and if they have distinguished themselves in the jig, they surpass their former efforts now. Wonderful is it to behold how lightly Proddy skips about, how he flies down the middle, turns his partner, and winds, without giddiness or apparent fatigue, through all the mazes and labyrinths of the bewildering dance. Even Scales cannot refuse his applause, but cheers him as he bounds along. And well is he seconded by Mrs. Plumpton. She dances with astonishing lightness and energy, and never flags for a moment till they reach the bottom, where a couple of glasses of punch refresh them, and stimulate them to new exertions. Bimbelot and Mrs. Tipping are soon beside them, and in a marvellously short space of time they find themselves at the top once more.

Why, you're not going down again, Proddy," cried the serjeant.

"Yes, but I am though!" cried the coachman, throwing open his coat, and displaying the full breadth of his chest, and the voluminous glories of his striped waistcoat. "I wont be the first to give in, I can promise you. Blow away, fifer! Drum away, serjeant! And do you, girl," he added to a scullion who was standing on a chair near the fireplace, laughingly surveying the group, "take the snuff from those candles, and throw a little more light on the subject. Now Bamby, my boy, stir your stumps!"

And as he spoke, he recommenced, with greater spirit than ever, twirling about, and cutting all sorts of fantastic capers, while his example was followed by Bimbelot, who was excited to a pitch of the most hilarious enthusiasm.

But the coachman was not destined to bring his second passage to an equally successful conclusion with the first. As he was in mid-career, a foot was put forward, whether designedly or otherwise could not be ascertained, but down he came, dragging his partner with him, and upsetting Sauvageon and Needler Webb. Nor was this all. Bimbelot and Mrs. Tipping, who were following closely in his wake at a headlong pace, found it impossible to stop, and tumbled over him, while Mr. Lascelles and Mrs. Clerges in their turn tumbled over them, thus completely burying the poor coachman. Fortunately, he was rescued from his perilous position before he was quite suffocated; but a stop was put to the dance, and Mr. Parker proposed that they should adjourn to the supper, which awaited them in the servants'-hall—a proposition that was eagerly agreed to.

Amply had Mr. Fishwick redeemed his promise to provide a good supper, and the abundance and substantial character of the repast proved his perfect conception of the powers of those who were to be its consumers. The centre of the table was occupied by a large raised pie, shaped like a drum, on the top of which was mounted a little baked model of the serjeant himself, pronounced as "like as life" by Mrs. Plumpton and Mrs. Tipping, and so accurately representing the original that you might see the very patch on his nose.

At the upper end of the table, where the serjeant sat of course, was a noble sirloin of cold beef; and at the other end was a gigantic barrel, or rather tub, of oysters. A goodly ham, tongues, cold fowls, lobsters, and less substantial matters, in the shape of sweets and jellies, constituted the remainder of the repast.

But if the cook had been bountiful in his supply of eatables, the butler was not much behind him in a due provision of drinkables. Jugs of punch were placed at short intervals, with a bottle of wine between each, and a mighty tankard of hot-spiced ale, with a toast floating in it, flanked the sirloin. Altogether, the board presented as inviting an appearance as guests who had earned famous appetites by healthful and agreeable exercises could desire, and they gathered eagerly round it.

Scales was supported on either hand by Mrs. Plumpton and Mrs. Tipping, and carved away at the sirloin as if he were hewing down the ranks of the enemy; while Fishwick faced him, and took charge of the oysters, opening them with a rapidity only equalled by the quickness of their disappearance. Then for a brief while was there silence, broken only by the clatter of knives and forks; but as soon as a few glasses of punch had been swallowed, laughter and jest broke forth anew, with additional force, and were never afterwards hushed—not even by the plates of toasted cheese that followed the removal of the beef and oysters.

The mighty tankard then went round, exciting much merriment as it described its circuit, from the circumstance of Bimbelot and other gallants striving to drink from the particular spots pressed by the sweet lips that had preceded them. Lastly, Mrs. Plumpton's bottle of usquebaugh was introduced, and proved peculiarly acceptable to those who thought the oysters sat rather coldly on the stomach.

The serjeant then rising, requested bumpers to be filled all round, and with great earnestness proposed, "The Queen and the Duke of Marlborough!" The toast was drunk with prodigious enthusiasm. Proddy next got on a chair, and calling out for fresh bumpers, proposed "the giver of the drum," and amid the hurrahs that followed it, unintentionally threw the contents of his glass into Bimbelot's face.

The serjeant returned thanks in a song, and seeing that the spirits of his guests had reached a point of elevation, any increase beyond which might be dangerous, he suggested a return to the dancing-room, and a movement was made thither accordingly.

The fifer played a country-dance, and Proddy would fain have re-engaged Mrs. Plumpton, but Bimbelot had been beforehand with him, which, together with the valet's triumphant grin, so exasperated the coachman, that he presently contrived to jostle the Frenchman, and in doing so, pushed him rather forcibly against Mezansene, who, fancying the attack intentional, replied by a kick, so well applied, that it sent the little valet capering to the other end of the room.

The dancers instantly stopped, and the serjeant, abandoning his drum, rushed to interpose. But all would not do. Bimbelot was furious, and demanded instant satisfaction; upon which Scales declared, if he fought anybody, it must be him, as he was determined to espouse Mezansene's quarrel—the latter being a stranger. The little Frenchman then turned his wrath upon the mediator, affirming that he displayed the grossest partiality, and that, sooner than not fight at all, after the outrageous insult he had received, he *would* fight him—a decision in which he was confirmed by Sauvageon.

After considerable altercation, as no arrangement could be come to, the irate parties withdrew to a back chamber, attended by the male portion of the assemblage, when the serjeant, who had retired to his own room for a moment, returned with a pair of huge horse-pistols, at the sight of which Bimbelot was observed to turn excessively pale.

"Here are pistols, ready loaded," said Scales; "and since you're determined to fight, have it out at once."

"Je suis content," said Mezansene. "Nous tirerons à travers un mouchoir, si vous voulez, Monsieur Bimbelot."

"No," replied Scales. "We'll remove the candles—and then you shall shoot at each other in the dark. That'll be the best way to settle it."

This proposition was not entirely satisfactory to Bimbelot; but on a word from Sauvageon, he acceded to it. Each combatant having taken a pistol, the candles were removed, and they were left together in the dark.

Not a word was spoken on either side, nor any movement made, so as to be audible, for a few moments. Mezansene, who had laughed at the whole affair, was determined to abide his opponent's fire; but as the other appeared so slow, he grew impatient, and came to the resolution of discharging his own pistol. But how to do so without mischief was the question. "I don't want to hurt the poor fellow," he thought; "and in whatever direction I fire I may chance to hit him. Ah, a plan occurs to me!"

The scheme was no sooner thought of than put into execution. He stepped forward noiselessly till his hand touched the wall, and then felt along it till he came to the fire-place. Putting the pistol up the chimney, he drew the trigger, and immediately after the discharge a heavy body came tumbling down.

A strange surmise crossed Mezansene, which was confirmed the next moment, when lights appeared. Poor Bimbelot had taken refuge in the chimney, and his adversary, in his anxiety to avoid him, had chanced upon his hiding-place. Luckily, no damage was done him, further than a few trifling bruises occasioned by the fall, and the serjeant informed Mezansene, privately, that "if Bamby was hit at all, it must have been with the wadding, for he had merely put powder in the pistols."

Mezansene kept this piece of information to himself, though he laughed heartily at it, nor did he say anything of what he knew of Bimbelot's place of refuge. Matters were therefore easily adjusted.

Hands were again shaken: more punch was introduced; more dancing followed; more jokes; a great deal more laughter; and the serjeant's drum terminated as merrily as it began.

CHAPTER XVIII.

ANOTHER LOVE SCENE IN THE ANTE-CHAMBER.

ONE morning, about a week after this merry party, the door of the queen's private apartments in Saint James's palace opened, and Abigail and Lady Rivers entered the ante-chamber. No one was there except the new attendant, Mezansene, who drew back respectfully as they paused.

"I have come with you, my dear Lady Rivers," said Abigail, "to learn if you have received any tidings of Masham."

"I guessed your motive," replied the other; "but I am sorry I can tell you nothing more of him than that it is believed he is gone abroad. He is certainly not with his father, Sir Francis Masham, at High Laver, for a letter was received from the old baronet yesterday, by Lord Rivers, in which he made inquiries after his son."

"How very strange!" exclaimed Abigail. "As far as I can learn, young Masham has written to no one. On quitting the palace, it appears, he immediately went home; after which, giving some directions to his confidential servant, remarking that he should probably not return for two or three months, and that no inquiries need be made about him, he set out unattended, and has not been heard of since. All Mr. Harley's inquiries have been fruitless. I own, I begin to feel very uneasy, and though I try to reason myself out of my apprehensions I cannot succeed."

"Oh! you needn't be alarmed about his safety," returned Lady Rivers. "It's more than likely he has gone to Paris to amuse himself at that gay court."

"Perhaps so," said Abigail. "But then he might write."

"But consider the attractions of the French capital, my dear!" rejoined Lady Rivers, somewhat maliciously. "Besides, he may have fallen in love again."

"I don't think it likely," cried Abigail.

"And do you really—seriously imagine he will remain constant to you during his exile, my dear?" asked Lady Rivers.

"I should not bestow another thought on him if I supposed otherwise," replied Abigail.

"And how as to yourself?" continued her ladyship. "Can you remain constant, too?"

"I may answer for myself more positively than for him," rejoined Abigail. "I can."

"Well, three months is a long time," said Lady Rivers. "It

would try me very hard—especially if I were exposed like you to
the attentions of so many agreeable fellows. Three months—Poor
Masham! he stands but a slight chance—ha! ha!"

"Your ladyship may laugh as much as you please," replied
Abigail, in a tone of pique; "but if I know myself, my sentiments
will continue unchanged."

"So you think now, my dear," rejoined Lady Rivers; "but
scarcely a fortnight has elapsed since his departure. Come, I'll
lay you a wager you forget him before the month is out. Hush!"
she exclaimed, pointing to Mezansene with her fan; "that young
man is listening to us. We'll talk of this another time. Good
day, my dear."

"If you hear anything of Masham, be sure and let me know it,"
said Abigail.

"Be sure I will," replied Lady Rivers. "I hope I shan't have
any unpleasant intelligence to communicate—that he has got a new
lady-love!—ha! ha!"

"In pity, spare me!" cried Abigail.

"Oh, that he could see you now," cried Lady Rivers, screaming
with laughter. But she suddenly checked herself, muttering—
"that young man again."

"Your ladyship is excessively cruel," said Abigail. "To hear
you laugh thus, one would think you had never been in love yourself."

"Perhaps I never have," replied Lady Rivers; "but at all
events, I profess no romantic constancy. And now adieu, for I
really must go." With this she left the room, the door being
opened for her by Mezansene.

"Oh, the pain of being separated from the object of one's regard!"
exclaimed Abigail, half aloud. "Every occupation loses its interest
—every pleasure its zest; and though the surface may appear as
bright and gay as ever, the heart will ache bitterly the while, and
tears—bitter tears flow in secret. Heigho! The queen must not
see I have been weeping," she added, drying her eyes with her
handkerchief.

As she was moving towards the inner door, Mezansene followed
her. He was greatly embarrassed; but Abigail was too much confused to notice him particularly.

"I have a letter for you, Miss Hill," he said, in a voice husky
with emotion.

"For me!" cried Abigail, in surprise. "It must be from him!"
she exclaimed, as she took it.

Unable to resist the impulse, she broke the seal, and eagerly
devoured its contents.

"He has not left London, he writes," she murmured, in irrepressible delight—"he will contrive to see me soon—here—in the
palace! But how, and when, he does not state. Where did you
get this letter?" she asked of Mezansene, but without daring to
raise her eyes.

"I am bound to secrecy," he replied, still in troubled tones;
but, thus much I may say,— he who wrote it is now in the
palace."

"Here!—imprudent!" exclaimed Abigail, placing her hand on her heart.

"You look faint, madam," cried Mezansene; "shall I bring a chair?"

"No, it is passed," replied Abigail; "but are my senses wandering? Have I cheated myself into the belief that I heard his voice? Is it," she added, looking up, and regarding Mezansene, fixedly—"is it you, Masham?"

"It is indeed, Abigail," replied the young man, falling on his knees before her, and pressing her hand rapturously to his lips.

"And you have run this risk for me?" she said, with a look of grateful tenderness.

"I would brave death itself, to be near you, Abigail," he replied, passionately. "I could not obey the queen's harsh mandate. I could not tear myself from you. But not daring to present myself in my own person, I assumed this disguise. I bribed one of the royal servants, Chillingworth, whom I knew to be a trusty fellow, to feign illness, and to engage me as his substitute. I am at present known by my mother's maiden name of Mezansene. Though I have been in the palace nearly a fortnight, until this moment I have not had an opportunity of speaking to you, without incurring needless risk. But I have seen you often, Abigail—often, when you have not noticed me. I have seen you look pensive, and have persuaded myself that the sadness was occasioned by my supposed absence. Oh! how I have longed to approach you—to make a sign to you—to hazard a whisper—but I restrained myself. I was content to see you—to be near you—for I knew a time of meeting would come."

"It is well you failed in making me aware of your presence," said Abigail, "for if I had perceived you suddenly, I should infallibly have betrayed myself. If you are discovered, our hopes are for ever blighted. The queen will never forgive me; and the duchess has so many spies, that the utmost caution is necessary."

"I have hitherto escaped detection," replied Masham; "and now that I have made you aware of my propinquity, I shall be more easy, and therefore less liable to be thrown off my guard. But tell me—are you restored to the queen's favour?"

"Quite," she replied. "For a few days the duchess had regained all her old influence, and during that time made every effort to procure my dismissal. In this object, if she could have controlled her arbitrary temper, she might, perhaps, have succeeded; but, luckily for me, the queen's disinclination to listen to her roused her passion, and she gave vent to it in her customary violence and threats. A breach followed this explosion; and though it is in some degree made up, a coldness still subsists between them. In my own opinion, and in that of Mr. Harley, the queen never will be reconciled to her again, not even ostensibly; but the duchess thinks differently, and has lost none of her confidence. She comports herself with unparalleled haughtiness and insolence towards her majesty, who shrinks from any encounter with her."

"Poor queen!" exclaimed Masham.

"Ay, poor queen, indeed!" echoed Abigail, with a sigh. "She well deserves your sympathy. Never was affection and kindness more unworthily requited than hers has been; never was good-nature more abused; never forbearance more presumed upon. But even her majesty's kindness may be tried too hard, and that the tyrannical duchess will find out ere long."

"Why does not the queen free herself at once?" cried Masham. "Is she not absolute mistress here?"

"Absolute mistress in appearance, but not in reality," replied Abigail; "there is no person in this palace more dependent than its sovereign mistress. Her nature is so affectionate, that love with her is a necessity; and since the loss of all her children, there has been a void in her heart which she has sought to fill up with friendship. How she has been disappointed, you see. But the pang of sundering for ever old ties and old feelings is so great, that she shrinks from it. It is the kindness of the queen's heart that makes her irresolute. This the duchess knows, and takes advantage of. When matters become desperate between them, she adroitly makes some slight concession, soothes the queen's wounded feelings, and all is right again. But if I can prevent it, the present difference shall not be healed."

"You are right," replied Masham; "your duty to the queen demands it. It is intolerable to see such excellence so greatly abused. But how stands Harley with her majesty?"

"His favour increases," replied Abigail. "He is admitted to frequent private conferences, and strenuously urges measures which he affirms would prove beneficial."

"Unfortunately, Harley has only the furtherance of his own schemes in view," observed Masham.

"So the queen suspects," rejoined Abigail; "and therefore she has not entire confidence in him. Poor lady! she is sorely perplexed. She fears the duchess—doubts Harley—and distrusts herself. Ah!" she added, as the inner door slowly opened; "she comes."

Masham had scarcely time to draw back a few paces, when the queen, accompanied by Prince George of Denmark, entered the room.

"Ah! Abigail, I am glad to find you," said Anne. "I thought you long in returning. But what is the matter. You appear agitated."

"I have just received a letter, madam," replied Abigail, in some confusion.

"From Mr. Masham—ha?" said the queen. "Nay, I see it by your blushes. You need not be alarmed. I did not inhibit him from writing to you. Well, and where is he?"

"Pardon me, madam, I am not at liberty to tell you," replied Abigail.

"Well, I will not exert my prerogative, and enforce an answer," rejoined the queen. "Provided he obeys my injunctions, and absents himself from court, I am content."

"Heyday, who have we here?" cried Prince George;—"a strange

face! Come hither, young man. Why don't you move, sirrah, when you're called? Zounds! is the fellow deaf?"

"You frighten him," said the queen, smiling good humouredly.

"What's the matter, sirrah?" cried the Prince, stepping towards Masham.—"'Sdeath! how very like!—It must be——"

"Must be whom?" asked the queen, half turning round. "Who is he like?"

"One of the servants at Hampton Court," replied the prince, adroitly placing himself between her and Masham. "Your majesty recollects Tom Ottley? This young man is the very image of Tom. Oh! you rascal! I've found you out," he added, in an undertone, and shaking his hand at the alarmed equerry.

"You have become very pale again, Abigail," said the queen to her. "You are certainly unwell."

"I shall be better presently," replied Abigail, in a faint voice.

"Your paleness increases!" cried the queen, in some alarm. "A chair!"

Masham immediately flew for one, but the prince took it from him, and carried it to Abigail, who sank into it.

"The salts!" exclaimed the queen; "there is a bottle on that table."

Masham rushed to obey her, and in the hurry knocked down a couple of China ornaments, which were broken in pieces upon the floor. Aghast at what he had done, he stood irresolute, while the prince, darting an angry look at him, ran up, snatched the bottle of salts from his hand, and gave it to the queen.

"That is a very careless person," said Anne, making Abigail breathe at the salts. "What is his name?"

"Masham!" exclaimed Abigail, faintly.

"Masham!—nonsense!" exclaimed the prince. "Her thoughts are for ever running on her lover. The queen desires to know your name, sirrah?" he added, turning towards Masham, and winking at him. "How are you called—Tomkins or Wilkins, eh?"

"Neither, your highness," was the reply. "My name is Mezansene."

"Mezansene—ha!" rejoined the prince. "Well, then, Mr. Mezansene, I hope you'll be more careful in future. I rather liked your looks, and designed to keep you in attendance chiefly on myself; but if you're so confoundedly heedless, I can't do it."

"I crave your highness's pardon," said Masham.

"Well—well, I'll overlook the first fault," rejoined the prince. "Come to my apartments in the evening. My apartments, you understand," he added, with a wink at Masham, who replied with a low bow.

"You look better now, child," said the queen, who had been lavish in her attentions to Abigail. "I hope you will have no recurrence of these attacks."

"I shall never have another, I am sure, gracious madam," replied Abigail, "if you will revoke your sentence on Mr. Masham."

"Do not press me on that point, Abigail," replied the queen. "I cannot do it. You had better retire to your own room. I am going to the library to Mr. Harley, who desires an immediate audience with me. Come, prince, we have detained him long enough. Take care of yourself, child, and think no more of Mr. Masham, if you can help it."

Abigail passed into the inner room without hazarding a look at her lover, while he opened the door for the queen.

Prince George lingered behind for a moment, and said in his equerry's ear—"Confounded scrape you would have got into but for me. Take care you're not found out, or I shall come in for a share of the blame. Coming, your majesty!" And he added aloud—"Don't forget what I've told you, Masham—Mezansene, I mean! Deuce take it! I hope her majesty didn't overhear me."

And he hurried after the queen.

CHAPTER XIX.

WHEREIN MARLBOROUGH AND GODOLPHIN DEMAND HARLEY'S DISMISSAL OF THE QUEEN.

SHORTLY after this, the queen and the prince entered the library, a large, lofty, well-proportioned room, constructed by Charles the Second, and slightly altered by William the Third. It had a semi-coved ceiling, with a deep, richly-moulded cornice, and the windows, which were square and formal, with heavy frameworks, and placed under round arches, supported by pilasters in the worst Italian taste, looked out into the gardens of the palace. Between the springings of each arch, on a pedestal, was set a bust; and there were numerous others disposed in different parts of the room. Well-filled bookcases projected from between the windows, so as to form charming nooks for reading: and the walls on the opposite side were covered with goodly tomes and maps. Throughout the palace, there was not a pleasanter retreat than the library.

Harley was expecting the queen with much impatience, and even exhibited it when she appeared. After returning his salutation, Anne seated herself at a small round table, on which writing materials were placed, and behind which stood a large japan screen, while the prince stationed himself beside her with his arm leaning on the back of her chair.

"The time is at length arrived, madam," said Harley, speaking hurriedly and energetically, "when some positive decision must be come to, and when either I and Saint-John, or Godolphin and Marlborough must retire. It can be no longer averted. Positive assurance has been given me that at the cabinet council which, as your majesty is aware, has been summoned this morning, these lords will announce their intention of resigning, if I am not dismissed. It will therefore be a trial of strength; but if I am supported by your majesty, I can have no fear as to the result."

" I hope their threat will not be put into execution, sir," replied Anne, much alarmed at what she heard. "This is a most unfortunate juncture for a change of ministry."

"It must be avoided, if possible," said Prince George, helping himself to a large pinch of snuff.

"There is no way of avoiding it," replied Harley. "The difficulty must be *met;* and I confess I have none of the apprehensions apparently entertained by her majesty. An outcry will no doubt be raised at first, but it will instantly subside. Marlborough's popularity has reached its climax—nay, is on the decline. The war in the Low Countries has been too long protracted ; the public coffers have been too heavily drained by the vast supplies required, not to have opened the eyes of all thinking persons to the grievance ; and they have begun to perceive, now that the dazzle of victory is over, that this most expensive pastime is only carried on to enrich the commander-in-chief himself. The Earl of Rochester, who will support the new administration, threatens to inquire why the attack on France is ever made through the Netherlands, instead of through Spain, the principal object of the war, where our success might be double what it is, if we had a larger army than that commanded by the brave, though rash, Earl of Peterborough. Public feeling, moreover, is against the continuance of the war. We have bought our honours too dearly ; and though the noisy mob may lose their idol, Marlborough, a new puppet can be bought for them, and at a less ruinous price. As to Lord Godolphin's resignation, with submission to your majesty, it will be scarcely felt, for it can be well supplied."

"By Mr. Harley !" said the prince, somewhat sarcastically.

"No, by a far better man, your highness," replied Harley—"by Lord Poulet. I shall be well content to hold my present office, or any office in which I can effectually serve her majesty ; but she has expressed a wish, in the event of a change, that I should take the chancellorship of the exchequer."

"With the real powers of government," muttered the prince.

"A Tory ministry can be instantly formed," continued Harley, "of which Lords Rochester, Nottingham, Haversham, and Dartmouth, may be members. All your majesty's favourite measures can then be carried. You will never again be thwarted, as you have been, so repeatedly, and so vexatiously, by the insolent and domineering Whigs."

"You promise fairly, sir," remarked Anne.

"I promise what I will perform, madam," replied Harley. "And I also promise your highness," he added to the prince, "an exemption from those sneers and censures with which your administration of the admiralty has been visited. Your highness owes the Tories some favour for a special service they have rendered you, to which I need not allude."

"I am not unforgetful for the handsome provision they have made for me in case of her dear majesty's demise before mine ; but I trust I may never benefit by it, sir," replied the prince, with a low, and somewhat sarcastic bow "I don't see how I can advise the queen to support you now. It is a very critical juncture; and the slightest error in judgment will be fraught with the most perilous consequences."

"At all events, her majesty will determine," replied Harley. "I have used every argument I think right with her."

"My inclinations are with you, undoubtedly," replied Anne.

"If such is really the case, gracious madam," replied Harley, bending the knee to her, "do not hesitate. Consult your own happiness—your own greatness. And do not forget that if Marlborough and Godolphin retire, the duchess retires likewise."

"Enough, sir," replied the queen. "You may rise. I have decided. I will support you."

"Take time to reflect—take time!" cried the prince.

"I *have* reflected," replied Anne. "Whatever the consequence may be, Mr. Harley shall have my support."

At this moment, an usher entered the library, and informed the queen that the Duke of Marlborough and Lord Godolphin were without, and craved an instant audience of her. Anne looked significantly at Harley.

"I will retire," said the secretary. "It were better they did not know of this interview."

"You cannot retire without passing through the room where they are waiting," replied the queen.

"What is to be done?" exclaimed the prince. "Stay, I have it. Perhaps Mr. Harley would not object to step behind this screen?"

Harley signified his ready acquiescence, and as the usher withdrew, ensconced himself as directed. The next moment the usher returned, and announced the Duke of Marlborough and Lord Godolphin.

The commander-in-chief looked grave; and the gloom habitual to the countenance of the lord-treasurer was now almost deepened to severity.

Godolphin's usual deportment, though destitute of haughtiness, was cold and repelling; and so averse was he to flattery, or to the show of it, that he almost resented common civility; while frankness, which passed with him for sincerity, obtained more credit than it deserved. His complexion was black, with thick beetling brows, which added to the sternness of his expression. He was somewhat below the middle size, of a spare frame, and though turned sixty, looked full of vigour, bodily as well as mentally. He seemed one of those men who are made to last. He was plainly attired in a snuff-coloured suit, and wore a black campaign wig that harmonized with his complexion.

Godolphin was one of the best, if not one of the greatest prime-ministers ever possessed by this country. The exalted post which he filled so admirably had been modestly refused when proffered to him, and was forced upon his acceptance by Marlborough, who declared that he himself would not undertake the command of the army, unless Godolphin regulated the supplies. By this great master of finance the revenue was so much improved that, in spite of the debts of the nation, five per cent. interest was paid for money placed in the public funds; and so incorruptibly honest was he in the administration of the treasure confided to him, so utterly free from venality in the disposal of place, that, in spite of the most rigid economy in his own establishment, he quitted office little richer than he entered it. Neither would he ask for the retiring pension which had been promised him.

The customary salutations gone through, but more coldly and formally than usual, on both sides, Marlborough spoke.

"It is with infinite concern that the lord-treasurer and myself present ourselves before your majesty, to advise a course of conduct which we have reason to believe may prove at variance with your own inclinations. Nevertheless, it is our duty so to advise you, and we do not shrink from the task, however painful it may be to us. Of late, to our great grief, we have found that your majesty has withdrawn your confidence from your long-tried and most responsible advisers, and has bestowed it upon one little worthy in any way of such distinction; while the person in question has been further favoured by frequent conferences with you, from which we have been utterly excluded. If we have been misinformed, your majesty will be pleased to say so."

"If your grace refers to Mr. Harley, I have certainly permitted him to visit me rather frequently," replied the queen, fanning herself impatiently.

"Our information was then correct," resumed Marlborough. "The admission made, we demand Mr. Harley's dismissal."

"Demand it?" echoed Anne. "But let that pass. On what grounds do you *demand* his dismissal?"

"On these, madam," replied Godolphin, coming forward. "By lending your countenance to so notorious an intriguer with France, you degrade your own cabinet, and lessen its power, while you increase the confidence of its opponents."

"You do not speak with your wonted calmness, my lord," observed the queen, with asperity. "Can it be jealousy that moves you so?"

"I had hoped that my long services would have saved me from such an unworthy imputation," replied Godolphin. "But if your majesty has forgotten my deserts, I have not forgotten the loyalty and devotion I owe you, and both prompt me to implore you not to commit the honour and security of your kingdom to this traitor. He will be as false to you as he has been to us."

"Though we have hitherto failed in bringing the matter home to Harley through his miserable creature, Greg," said Marlborough, "not a doubt can exist that he has betrayed the secrets of our cabinet to that of France; and I have yet stronger confirmation in these letters," tendering papers to the queen, "which were found upon the persons of two smugglers named Vallière and Bera, who have just been arrested, and who were professedly employed by him to obtain intelligence on the French coast, while the actual nature of their service is thus proved beyond all question. It is true that the correspondence has been so artfully contrived, that Harley may not be implicated by it; but his criminality is unquestionable. On these grounds it is, madam, as well as on the ground of his treachery to us, his colleagues, that we demand Mr. Harley's dismissal from your service."

"And if I should decline to comply with the demand—what then?" said the queen, agitating her fan more violently than before; while Harley, with his finger on his lips, peered from behind the screen, to watch the effect of this question on the duke.

"If, after what has been said, your majesty remains insensible to the prejudice done you by this person, we can only lament your wilful blindness," replied Marlborough, firmly; "but we are bound to regard our own honour and reputation; and we hereby respectfully announce to you, that no consideration shall induce us to serve longer with one whom we hold unworthy of association with men of honour."

"The Duke of Marlborough has fully expressed my sentiments, madam," said Lord Godolphin.

"You will act upon the determination you have so *respectfully* announced, my lords, if you think proper," replied Anne, rising with dignity; "but I will *not* dismiss Mr. Harley."

"Will your majesty grant me a hearing?" interposed the prince.

"Not if your highness is about to support their arguments," replied Anne, peremptorily.

"Bravo!" cried Harley to himself behind the screen. "All is won."

"Your majesty will then consider us as forced from your service," said Marlborough, in a firm, but mournful tone.

And bowing profoundly, he withdrew with Godolphin.

"How shall I thank your majesty?" cried Harley, stepping from behind the screen.

"I know not how I have got through it," said Anne, sinking into the chair. "My mind misgives me."

"And so does mine—terribly!" cried the prince. "You would not listen to me while there was yet time."

"You have acted nobly—courageously, madam," said Harley. "But the blow must be followed up, to ensure a victory."

"True," replied Anne, rising; "and therefore let us attend the privy-council."

CHAPTER XX.

SHOWING HOW THE TABLES WERE TURNED UPON THE SECRETARY.

ONCE again, on that same day, Masham and Abigail met, and in the same place too. Ascertaining that the queen was engaged with the privy-council, the fair attendant took advantage of the opportunity that presented itself to return to the ante-room, where she was not without the hope of finding her lover, and where she in reality did find him.

Delightful was the interview that ensued, but it was, unfortunately, cut short, and at the tenderest point too, by the abrupt entrance of the queen and her consort. Anne was in a state of too great perturbation to notice Masham, who sprang backward as the door opened, and affected to be employed at one of the tables; but the prince shook his head at him, with a look that seemed to say, "You are resolved to be detected, you imprudent rascal!"

"What has happened, gracious madam?" cried Abigail, flying to the queen. "I thought you engaged with the privy-council."

"The council is broken up," replied the queen, hurriedly. "They met not to deliberate, but to dispute; and I therefore put a sudden termination to the meeting."

"I can guess the cause of the dispute," said Abigail. "The treasurer and the duke made their threatened attack on Mr. Harley?"

"Neither the duke nor the treasurer were there," replied the queen; "but you shall hear what occurred. I took my place as usual, the whole of the council being assembled, with the exception of the two important members you have mentioned, for whose absence, however, I was prepared, and was therefore not surprised at it. After a brief pause, during which I observed the council eye each other significantly, I motioned Mr. Harley to open the business of the meeting. He obeyed; but had scarcely commenced, when he was interrupted by the Duke of Somerset, who arose, and exclaimed with great vehemence, 'It is a mockery to proceed further. We cannot deliberate when the two leaders of the cabinet—persons by whose opinions we must be governed—are absent.' The duke had scarcely sat down, when the Earl of Sunderland arose, and said in a stern tone to Harley, 'I demand to know from Mr. Secretary why we are deprived of the attendance of the commander-in-chief and the lord-treasurer? When I parted with them both, an hour ago, I know it was their intention, under certain circumstances, to be present.'—'You have no right to put the question to me, my lord,' replied Mr. Harley, 'and I decline to answer it. But as you state that the duke and treasurer only meant to attend under 'certain circumstances,' perhaps you will state what those circumstances were?'—'The circumstances were these, sir, the earl rejoined: 'they were about to signify to the queen that they would no longer serve with you, whom they find have played them falsely; and, by their absence, I understand that her majesty has accepted their resignation. As their lordships will not serve with you, neither will I, nor will any of the council.'—'There you are wrong, my lord,' cried Mr. Saint-John, 'for *I* will. I will fearlessly and strenuously support her majesty's determination against all opposition.' Sir Thomas Mansell and Sir Simon Harcourt followed to the same effect, all the rest siding with Sunderland; but so fierce a discussion commenced between the conflicting parties, and such opprobrious language was used towards Mr. Harley, and so little respect shown to myself, that I broke up the meeting."

"Your majesty has therefore placed yourself entirely in the hands of Mr Harley?" cried Abigail, joyfully.

"Entirely," replied the queen.

"Oh! how glad I am to hear it," cried Abigail, hazarding a side-look at Masham, who was listening attentively to the conversation. "Your majesty will now have some quiet."

"On the contrary, I am afraid all chance of quiet is at an end," cried the prince, heaving a deep sigh.

"I am expecting a visit from Mr. Harley, to advise what course is next to be pursued," said the queen. "Ha! here he is," she added, as the door opened. "No!" and her countenance fell; "it is the Duchess of Marlborough!"

"The duchess!" exclaimed the prince and Abigail together.

"I am unwelcome, and unexpected, I perceive," said the duchess, maintaining her imperious air and deportment, as she advanced towards the queen. "No matter. I have that to say which *must* be said, and quickly. Before your majesty is finally and irre-trievably committed to this step, you will do well to pause. At all events, I will show you the dangerous position in which you stand. The rumour of the change of administration has spread with light-ning swiftness. The coffee-houses are thronged with members of both houses of parliament, who have expressed their dissatisfaction in no measured terms, and the language they now hold will be repeated when they take their places to-night. Those of the com-mons declare that the bill of supply which was ordered for to-day shall be allowed to lie on the table unread. Already the news of the treasurer's resignation has reached the city, and stocks have fallen lower than they have ever been known during your majesty's reign; while a meeting of the wealthiest merchants has been called to consider what is to be done in a crisis so alarming. As to the people, they are in a state of ferment. The precincts of the palace are surrounded by crowds, who are giving vent to their anger in hootings and groans."

"It is true, your majesty," cried the prince, looking out of the window; "the park is thronged with a vast mob, who appear in a very excited state. There! you may hear their shouts."

And as he spoke, distant groans were heard.

The duchess watched the queen's changing countenance with exultation. She read in it the impression she had produced.

"A popular tumult will ensue," she cried; "and once begun, who shall say where it will end?"

"It is a plot!" cried the queen, enraged and alarmed. "I will not be intimidated!"

"Your majesty had better listen to reason," remarked the prince. "Mr. Harley may find these difficulties unsurmountable."

"Mr. Harley cannot carry on the government, as her majesty will find," said the duchess. "Hated by the Whigs, distrusted by the Tories, he will neither have the confidence of the one party, nor the support of the other; while, labouring as he does under the grave suspicion of trafficking with France, his instant dismissal will be called for by the voice of the whole nation. So circum-stanced, he cannot stand for a day; and her majesty will have to bear all the fearful consequences of the attempt, with the disgrace of failure."

"Your majesty had better reconsider your opinion," urged the prince.

"There is no time to reconsider it," said the duchess. "An instant decision must be made. There is but one way of dispersing those crowds, and of appeasing the popular indignation."

"And that way I will not adopt," replied Anne, firmly. "I have promised to support Mr. Harley; and as long as he chooses to persevere, I will uphold him."

"Worthily resolved, madam," cried Abigail.

"Peace, wench! and deliver your opinion when it is asked," cried the duchess, coarsely. "I take my leave of your majesty. To-morrow, it will be your turn to come to me."

She then moved towards the door, but her departure was checked by the sudden entrance of Harley. His looks bespoke agitation and alarm.

"She here!" he muttered. "I hoped to have anticipated her; but no matter. Stay, duchess," he added, aloud, "you may wish to hear what I have to say to her majesty. Madam," he continued, throwing himself at the queen's feet, "I humbly thank you for the trust you have been graciously pleased to repose in me; but with the most ardent desire to serve you, and to carry out your designs, I am unable to do so."

"He confesses his incompetency!" exclaimed the duchess. "I knew he would be compelled to do so."

"The friends on whom I relied have fallen from me——" pursued Harley.

"It is needless to proceed, sir," interrupted the duchess. "I have already shewn her majesty the utter incapacity of the persons to whom she thought fit to entrust the affairs of her kingdom."

"I hope you have also shewn her majesty that our inability arises chiefly, if not wholly, from your machinations, duchess," replied Harley. "It is with inexpressible concern that I am compelled to tender my resignation to your majesty."

"Resign before he has ever held office!" cried the duchess, derisively. "A capital jest—ha! ha! So ends this farce."

"My friends, Saint-John, Mansell, and Harcourt, retire with me," continued Harley.

"Cholmondely, Walpole, and Montague shall have their places," muttered the duchess.

"I accept your resignation with as much regret as you tender it, Mr. Harley," said the queen; "but though I lose your services, you shall not lose my favour. Duchess, as you have excited this tumult, you will now perhaps take means to allay it."

"Your majesty's happy decision needs but to be publicly announced to change those demonstrations of discontent into rejoicings," replied the duchess. "I will set about it immediately. Poor ex-secretary! He resembles his slippery namesake, Harley-quin, when robbed of his wand by Scaramouch."

"A sorry jest!" exclaimed Abigail—"and ungenerous as sorry."

"If your majesty desires to propitiate the friends you have deserted, and have been obliged to recal, you will discharge your forward attendant," cried the duchess.

"Whatever happens, duchess, Abigail will remain with me," replied the queen with dignity.

"Your majesty has seen how ineffectual your resolutions are," rejoined the duchess, sarcastically. "Again I take my leave."

"To the door, Masham!" cried the prince.

"Masham!" exclaimed the duchess, looking round; "I thought he was banished."

"I meant Mezansene," replied the prince, in some embarrassment. "Deuce take my unlucky tongue!"

"There is something in this," muttered the duchess. "That young man is very like Masham. I go to execute your majesty's behests." And making a profound obeisance, she withdrew.

"I am now nothing more than your majesty's servant," observed Harley.

"You are no longer my minister," returned the queen; "but you are as much my friend—my adviser—as ever"

END OF THE FIRST BOOK.

Book the Second.

ABIGAIL HILL.

CHAPTER I.

OF MASHAM'S PLAN TO DECEIVE THE DUCHESS, AND OF ITS SUCCESS.

THE downfal of Harley, and the resignation of his friends, necessarily increased the ascendancy of the Whigs, and placed the Duchess of Marlborough in a position of greater importance than ever, causing her to be regarded, and with reason, as the sole arbitress of affairs. The contest on this occasion not having been so much a struggle between two conflicting parties, as a trial of strength between the queen and her former favourite, and having resulted in the triumph of the latter, seemed to afford decisive proof of her superior power. "Queen Sarah," as she was commonly styled, by friend as well as foe, was therefore said to have deposed Queen Anne.

But the duchess, though she might well be confident, was not deluded into fancied security. On the contrary, she redoubled her vigilance; strengthened her position as much as possible; and made every effort compatible with her haughty nature to conciliate the queen, and regain her affections.

But Anne was not to be won back. Mortification at the defeat she had endured made her regard her conqueror with positive aversion; and though she masked the feeling carefully during their intercourse, it did not require the penetration of the duchess to discover the true light in which she was now regarded.

The grand subject of uneasiness, however, to the duchess, was Abigail's increasing favour, and her own inability to procure her removal. On this point the queen remained inflexible. Neither remonstrance nor entreaty could shake her constancy to her favourite, and even when told that an address would be presented to her by the House of Commons, requiring Abigail's dismissal, she treated the menace with disdain.

Equally disinclined, also, did she show herself to put a stop to her conferences with Harley, who was admitted to as frequent audiences as heretofore, and the nature of whose counsels soon became apparent in her own mode of conduct. While this great master of intrigue had such constant access to the queen's ear, and while another than herself enjoyed her confidence, the duchess, in the midst of all her triumph, felt ill at ease, and apprehensive of an ultimate overthrow. Cost what it might, therefore, the root of these annoyances must be eradicated, and while debating within herself how to execute her purpose, chance seemed to throw the means of its accomplishment in her way.

It may be remembered that, at the close of a recent interview with the queen, owing to the inadvertence of Prince George of Denmark, the duchess had well-nigh detected Masham's disguise; and though she had repeatedly since that time tried to discover him among the servants, he had managed, by extreme caution, to elude her notice, until one day she met him face to face in the great gallery. Retreat being out of the question, Masham, though filled with confusion, was obliged to brook her scrutiny, and the duchess, after regarding him steadfastly for a few moments, dropped him a profound curtsey, saying, in a tone of bitter raillery, "Accept my congratulations on your advancement, Mr. Masham. I was not aware you had entered her majesty's household."

"Your grace is mistaken," he stammered, in reply. "My name is Mezansene."

"Mezansene!—ha! ha!" laughed the duchess. "How long have you possessed that name, sir?—ever since your banishment from court, I suppose. We shall see whether her majesty knows who she has got in her service. If she is ignorant of the fact, Abigail, I'll be bound, is not. Adieu, Mr. Mezansene—since that's the name you choose to go by—ha! ha!" And with a bow of mock ceremoniousness, she passed towards the royal apartments.

Confounded at what had occurred, Masham stood for some moments irresolute. Persuaded, if the duchess put her threat into execution, and betrayed him to the queen, as he could not doubt she would, that all chance of an union with Abigail Hill would be at an end, and their future prospects blighted, he weighed over every means of avoiding the threatened danger.

After turning over various expedients in his mind, he bethought him of a yeoman of the guard, named Snell, with whom, since he had been forced to consort to a certain degree with the household, he had struck up a kind of intimacy. Snell was a good-looking young fellow, about the same height as himself, not unlike him in features, and might be made, he thought, to pass for him without difficulty. Accordingly, he hurried off to the guard-room in search of him, when, by good luck, he met him coming up the great staircase, on his way to the ante-chamber.

Without pausing to explain his motives, except to say that he wanted to speak to him particularly, Masham seized his acquaintance by the arm, and dragging him quickly along a passage or two, and up a short staircase, pulled him into a small chamber, and closed the door.

"What in the name o' wonder is the meanin' of all this?" asked Snell, almost out of breath.

"It means that we must change dresses—quick!" replied Masham.

"Change dresses!—are you mad?" demanded Snell.

"Not so mad but I can give you a sound and substantial reason for compliance," rejoined Masham. "This purse," tossing him one full of gold, "will speak for my sanity."

"It may speak for your sanity better than your honesty, Master Mezansene," replied Snell, chinking the purse. "How did you come by it?"

"Fairly enough, that's all you need know," replied Masham. "But come, be quick! Each instant is precious." And he began to throw off his own habiliments.

"I'm afraid I shall get into some confounded scrape if I consent," hesitated Snell.

"Tut!" cried Masham. "You've nothing to do but personate me for a few minutes. You can easily do that, you know."

"You're sure there's no treason intended—no popery?" rejoined Snell, taking off his scarlet donblet.

"Treason!—a fiddlestick!" answered Masham, snatching the garment from him.

"And it can't be construed into a hangin' matter?" pursued Snell, as he divested himself of his crimson hose, and black velvet uppers.

"Impossible!" exclaimed Masham, arraying himself in the attire in question. "Recollect that you're me; and whoever questions you, be it the queen herself, be sure and say that you're name is Mezansene. Stick to that, and all will be right."

"The queen!" echoed Snell. "If you think there's any chance of her majesty addressin' me, I'd rather not undertake it."

"It's too late now," replied Masham, who by this time was fully equipped in the other's clothes. "Besides, there's nothing to be afraid of," he said, clapping on the yeoman's little round black velvet cap, ornamented with roses, and taking possession of his halbert; "nothing at all."

He then helped his companion to complete his metamorphosis, which done, Snell looked so like the ci-devant Mezansene, that the other could not help laughing at the resemblance. Speedily checking his merriment, however, he bade the new-made lacquey follow him, and descending the staircase, hurried towards the ante-room, where he indicated to Snell the post he must occupy, while he stationed himself outside an open door, communicating with the gallery.

Snell was in a great flutter, wondering what would happen next, when Prince George of Denmark suddenly issued from the royal apartments, and made towards him with a quick step and mysterious air. The poor fellow turned away his head, and affected to be looking for something on the floor.

"I knew how it would be!" exclaimed the prince. "The duchess has found you out, and has told the queen."

"Told the queen what, your highness?" stammered Snell, not daring to look up.

"Why, who you are, to be sure," rejoined the prince. "What else had she to tell, eh? I slipped away to warn you. Well, what do you mean to do now?"

"I'm sure I don't know, your highness," answered Snell in great

"Imbecile!" cried the prince, angrily. "You've got yourself into a terrible scrape, and must get out of it as well as you can."

Snell groaned aloud.

"One consequence of your indiscretion will be Abigail's loss of her post, I fear," pursued the prince.

"I don't mind what she loses, provided I get off," cried Snell.

"Eh, what? I can't have heard aright, surely," exclaimed the prince. "You don't mind what Abigail loses? Perhaps you don't mind what becomes of her?"

"No, I don't," replied Snell.

"'Sdeath! what have you ventured here for, then?" cried the prince, in a towering passion. "Why did you put on this dress?"

"I'm sorry I ever did so," rejoined Snell. "I was a fool for my pains."

"More craven than fool, I begin to think," said the prince, his anger changing to disgust. "Why, you poor-spirited fellow, you don't deserve a lady's regard. You are not the man I took you for."

"I am not, indeed, your highness," responded Snell.

"You have adopted the soul of a footman as well as the clothes," pursued the prince, impetuously. "I came here to help you, but I'm so thoroughly disgusted, that I cast you off for ever. I wish her majesty would hang you; and if she takes my advice, she will do so."

"Oh, don't say so, your highness!" roared Snell, dropping on his knees. "Pardon me this once, and I'll never offend again."

"Why, what the deuce is this?" cried the prince. "This is not Masham! Some new trickery—eh? Where's your confederate, sirrah?"

"Here, your highness," replied the young equerry, advancing from the door.

"What, in a new disguise?" cried the prince.

"I've changed dresses with this young man, for the purpose of imposing upon the duchess," replied Masham.

"Faith, a good idea, if it can only be carried out," replied the prince, laughing. "But I'm afraid this fellow's stupidity will ruin the scheme. I'll try and frighten him into attention. Hark'ee, sirrah," he added to Snell, "you're in a very awkward predicament—very awkward, indeed. Your only chance of escape lies in discretion."

"I'll do everything your highness directs," replied Snell.

"Get up, then, sirrah," rejoined the prince; "put on a bold countenance; and, as you value your neck, don't leave this spot. I must now go," he added, in a low tone to Masham, "for if I'm found here it may excite suspicion." So saying, he passed on towards the gallery, and Masham returned to his post.

Little time was allowed Snell for consideration. The prince had scarcely disappeared, when the inner door again opened, and gave admittance to Abigail.

"Oh! you are here!" she exclaimed, quickly. "Your disguise has been discovered. Fly as fast as you can!"

"I would gladly do so," replied Snell, averting his face, "but I dare not."

"Dare not!" exclaimed Abigail. "You must. The queen and the duchess will be here instantly, and then we are both lost."

"The prince has just been here, and has ordered me not to stir," replied Snell.

"You had better risk disobeying him than incur the queen's displeasure, aggravated as it is by the duchess's malice," said Abigail. "If you are found here, all chance of our union is at an end."

"Our union!" thought Snell to himself. "This explains it. The rascal has been making love to the queen's favourite! It'll be counted high treason, at the least. I shall be beheaded, and no one will find out the mistake till it's too late. Oh, Lord!—oh, Lord!"

"Don't stand talking to yourself in that way, cried Abigail, "but go. You seem to have taken leave of your senses."

"I believe I have," cried Snell, slapping his forehead, and stamping on the floor, in a distracted manner. "My brain spins round like a top. Would to Heaven I had never entered the palace!"

"These regrets are not very flattering to me," replied Abigail. "But I will not reproach you. They are coming! Fly! fly!"

"I dare not, I tell you," rejoined Snell. "The prince said it was as much as my head was worth to leave this place."

"Your conduct is utterly incomprehensible," said Abigail, in a tone of mingled anxiety and vexation. "You seem determined to ruin us both, and exhibit such unaccountable waywardness and selfishness, that I begin to regret having wasted my affection upon you."

"I wish you never had so wasted it," said Snell.

"How!" exclaimed Abigail, in extremity of surprise and indignation.

"That is, not upon me, but upon him," rejoined the other.

"Him!" she cried. "Whom do you allude to, sir?"

"To—to—to—I don't exactly know his name," he replied.

"This is unpardonable," she cried, "and at such a moment too! But it reconciles me to the discovery. Farewell for ever, sir. I leave you to make your own excuses to the queen. Even if she forgives you, I will not."

"What have I done, madam?" cried Snell, falling on his knees before her, and catching hold of her dress—"what new mischief have I committed?"

"It is idle to ask the question," replied Abigail, trying to extricate herself from him. "Get up—release me!—I hear them coming?"

But before she could free herself from him, the door opened, and the queen and the Duchess of Marlborough entered the ante-chamber.

"There!" cried the duchess, pointing triumphantly to Snell whose back was towards them, and who still remained in a kneeling posture—"behold the confirmation of my statement. Thus it is that your majesty's injunctions are fulfilled. Thus it is that you are betrayed by those in whom you place implicit confidence. After this proof of treachery and disobedience, you cannot hesitate to drive Abigail from your presence for ever."

"You are hasty, duchess," replied Anne, coldly. "This scene may admit of some explanation."

"Explanation!" echoed the duchess, with a contemptuous laugh. "It can admit of no explanation but one. Your majesty, I presume, will not doubt the evidence of your own eyesight?"

"Can this be Mr. Masham?" said the queen. "I am by no means satisfied on the point."

"Her grace is labouring under a most extraordinary delusion," replied Prince George, who was standing near the door with his disguised equerry, laughing at what was occurring. "This person is Mezansene, one of the attendants whom, as your majesty knows, I have lately taken into my service. Let her look at him more closely, and she will instantly perceive her mistake."

"Why, I declare it is not Masham!" cried Abigail to herself, and recoiling in confusion from her supposed lover. "Have I been deceived all this time?"

"It is your highness who is labouring under a delusion, not me," said the duchess. "I affirm that *is* Mr. Masham."

"No, your grace, I'm not Mr. Masham, indeed I ain't!" roared Snell.

"It's not his voice, certainly," cried the duchess, starting forward, and gazing at him in consternation. "This is not the person I met in the gallery."

"Yes it is, your grace, for he has just told me all about it," interposed the prince. "The mistake was very natural, for he is uncommonly like Masham—so like that I frequently call him by the name. Don't I, sirrah?"

"Very frequently, your highness," replied Snell.

"Confusion!" exclaimed the duchess. But instantly recovering herself, she turned to Abigail and said, "Since this is not Mr. Masham, how came he on his knees to you? It is not usual for lacqueys to adopt such a posture to ladies."

"He had a favour to beg from her, of course?" said the prince.

"Yes, I had a favour to beg of her," added Snell.

"Ah, indeed; what was it?" asked the duchess.

"Nay, that's pressing the poor fellow too hardly, duchess," rejoined the prince.

"Pardon me, your highness," replied the duchess, "the whole affair is so mysterious and unsatisfactory, that I shall not rest till I have sifted it thoroughly. Hark'ee, sirrah; as you aver that you met me in the gallery just now, you can of course tell what passed on that occasion. I see you are about to utter a lie. Confess your imposture at once, or you shall be soundly horsewhipped."

"Take care of your neck!" whispered the prince, significantly.

"Speak, fellow!" thundered the duchess.

"Really, your grace quite bewilders me," replied Snell.

"I don't wonder at it," observed the prince; "her grace bewilders most people."

"Are you known to any of the household, knave?" demanded the duchess.

"Yes, to a great many," answered Snell; "that is, I was known—" he added, checking himself in confusion.

"I doubt it," rejoined the duchess. With your majesty's permission, I should like to have some one brought in to identify him."

The queen signified her assent, and the prince, with a covert wink at Masham, told him to fetch some member of the household.

"It is all up with me now!" muttered Snell, groaning internally.

At this juncture, the duchess moved towards the queen, and the prince, seeing her attention occupied, seized the opportunity of whispering a few words to Abigail, which seemed to set her quite at ease, for her face was lighted up with smiles.

The next moment, Masham returned with Proddy. The coachman was dressed in his state livery, and made one of his best and profoundest bows to the queen—another to the prince—and a third to the duchess.

"Step this way, Mr. Proddy," said the latter. "Do you know this person?" pointing to Snell.

"Perfectly well, your grace," replied Proddy. "Perfectly."

"To be sure he does," cried Snell, leaping up joyfully. "I was certain, Mr. Proddy would recollect his old friend——"

"Frank Mezansene," interrupted the coachman, seeing the mistake he was about to commit. "Yes—yes—I recollect you well enough, Frank. I knew him long before he came to the palace, your grace."

"Yes; Mr. Proddy knew me long before I dreamed of becoming a—a—a—yes—"

"A member of her majesty's household," supplied Proddy. "You owe your advancement to me; for if it hadn't been for my recommendation, Mr. Chillingworth wouldn't have engaged you as his substitute."

"Mr. Chillingworth! Mr. Masham, you mean," said Snell.

"No I don't," replied Proddy, significantly. "And you don't either, but you're so confused you don't know what you're sayin'."

"This is a plot, I'm convinced," cried the duchess. "Come, I'll make it worth your while to speak the truth, sirrah," she added to Snell. "You shall have the queen's free pardon, and a reward from me, if you'll confess that you have been put up to this scheme by Mr. Masham."

"Nay, your grace is offering the poor fellow a bribe to forswear himself," said the prince. "Speak at the peril of your life!" he added, in an undertone, to Snell.

"I'm dumb," he replied.

There was a pause, but as Snell remained silent, the duchess turned to the queen, and said—"I pray your majesty let him be detained in close custody, till I have investigated the matter further."

"As your grace pleases," replied the queen; "but it appears unnecessary."

"Remove him!" cried the duchess to Masham.

The supposed yeoman of the guard bowed, and laid his hand on Snell. The latter trembled, and would have spoken, but was silenced by a look from the prince. He was then hurried out of the room by Masham and Proddy.

"So ends your grace's discovery," said the queen, ironically.

"Pardon me, your majesty," replied the duchess; "it is not ended yet. Only promise me that if I lay bare this plot you will punish the contrivers as they deserve."

"The plot exists only in her grace's imagination," remarked the prince, laughing. "But apropos of Masham—I wish we had him again."

"I dare say your highness could produce him at a moment's notice," replied the duchess.

"I wish I could," replied the prince.

"Enough of this," interposed the queen. "Mr. Masham must abide his time. If he appears before the expiration of his sentence, he will incur my displeasure anew."

"I am glad to hear your majesty say so," replied the duchess. "But I wish to confer with you on some other matters, and with your permission we will return to the cabinet."

The queen assented, and they passed into the inner room together.

"How can I thank your highness sufficiently?" cried Abigail, as she lingered behind with the prince. "Without your aid, all must have been discovered."

"'Gad, you've had a narrow escape, it must be confessed," cried the prince, laughing. "But I have thought of a new surprise for the duchess. I can't stop to tell you what it is, for no time must be lost. Follow them to the cabinet, or suspicion may be excited. I'll join you there presently, and perhaps you may see Masham again—ha! ha! Get along with you."

And he hurried through one door as Abigail disappeared through the other.

———

CHAPTER II.

DETAILING THE FURTHER MYSTIFICATION OF THE DUCHESS.

SNELL, meanwhile, was conducted by Masham and Proddy to a closet adjoining the gallery, where the former, having given him some directions and assurances, which restored him, in a measure, to confidence, locked the door upon him.

This done, Proddy took his departure, and the young equerry was setting off in a different direction, when he saw the prince coming towards him. A few words passed between them, at the end of which the prince, having placed a letter in the other's hand, they separated—his highness retracing his steps, and Masham hurrying to his own room.

Shortly afterwards, Masham returned to the closet, wrapped in a loose great coat, and, unlocking the door, entered, and found Snell divested of his attire. Taking a bundle from beneath his great coat, and throwing it to the other, Masham said.

" Here are your own clothes. As soon as you are dressed, come forth again, and take your post at the door. Lock it; act as I have directed; and I will double the reward I have given you."

Snell promised compliance, and Masham, snatching up his own habiliments, which had been tied up in a handkerchief by the other, disappeared.

Half-an-hour after this, and just as the duchess was taking leave of the queen, an usher entered the cabinet, and announced that the Duke of Marlborough begged a moment's audience of her majesty. Anne signified her assent, and Abigail, who with the prince was present, would have retired, but at a sign from her royal mistress, she remained.

The next moment, the duke was introduced. The duchess regarded him with surprise, and plainly expressed by her looks that the visit was wholly unexpected by her.

" I have come to ascertain your majesty's pleasure on a point on which I myself am somewhat doubtful," said the duke; " though I cannot but think you will adopt the course which appears to me most consistent with your character for good-nature."

" A strange preamble, my lord," replied Anne; "to what does it lead ?"

" Ay, what does it lead to ?" interposed the duchess, impatiently. " To the point, your grace."

" Briefly, then," replied the duke, " I have come here on behalf of Mr. Masham, who is just arrived from Paris——"

" Masham again!" interrupted the duchess, "he haunts us. We know not where Mr. Masham has arrived from; but he has been seen here,—in the palace,—not an hour ago."

" Impossible!" replied the duke; " he has only reached London within this half hour. He came straight to Marlborough House, and I saw him not five minutes after he quitted the saddle. His attire bore evidence of the expedition he had used."

" You hear that, duchess?" said the prince, who seemed in a high state of enjoyment at what was going forward.

" He is the bearer of an important letter, which he has been enjoined to place in your majesty's own hands, and no other," pursued the duke, " and he came to consult me as to the course he should pursue, being still under sentence of banishment from your presence. As I have said, I scarcely knew how to advise him, but I consented to come hither to ascertain your pleasure."

" You did wrong!" cried the duchess, harshly.

" I am of a different opinion," rejoined the queen. " Under the circumstances, I *will* see him."

" He is without," replied the duke; " I thought it better to bring him with me."

Bowing to the queen, the duke withdrew, and the next moment returned with Masham. The dusty riding-dress of the latter, his mud-bespattered boots, soiled cravat, and jaded appearance, perfectly bore out the notion of his having just arrived from a long and fatiguing journey.

Abigail was lost in astonishment, and could scarcely believe her eyes; the duchess was disconcerted; and Prince George nearly choked himself between suppressed laughter and large pinches of snuff.

"This is not a fitting attire to present myself in to your majesty," said Masham, with a profound obeisance to the queen; "but I have not had time to repair my toilette; beside——"

"I know what you would say, sir," interrupted the queen, good-humouredly. "You feared to gain admittance to my presence. But do not distress yourself. The necessity of the case excuses the want of etiquette, as well as the violation of my injunctions. His grace of Marlborough tells me you have a despatch for me, which can be delivered to no hands but mine."

"Here it is, madam," replied Masham, offering a letter to her.

"From France, sir?" she asked.

"From France, your majesty," replied Masham.

Before breaking the seal the queen glanced at it, and an almost imperceptible smile dwelt upon her lips; but it speedily faded away, and gave place to a totally different expression as she opened the letter, and scanned its contents.

"You have ill news there, I fear, madam?" said the duchess, after a pause.

"In truth, not very good," replied the queen. "My rash brother has, at length, prevailed upon the king of France to aid him in an invasion of this country, and he calls upon me, as a means of preventing bloodshed, to surrender my crown to him."

"Surrender the crown to *him!*" exclaimed the duchess. "Vanity must have turned his brain. But is the letter from the Pretender himself?"

"It is from my brother," replied the queen.

"The Pretender is no brother of your majesty's, though he passes for such," rejoined the duchess. "We, who are acquainted with the warming-pan history, know better. If the letter is from him, how came it to be intrusted to Mr. Masham? Is he in the Jacobite interest?"

"Assuredly not," replied Masham. "I am prepared to lay down my life in her majesty's service; and in case of a rebellion I shall be found among the first to rally round the throne. But I crave your majesty's pardon for remaining here without licence. Having discharged my mission, I take my leave."

And with a profound obeisance, he retired.

"The letter which your majesty has received contains no idle threat," said Marlborough. "I have just heard, from a source on which I can rely, that an expedition is fitting out at Dunkirk, the command of which is to be taken by the Chevalier de Forbin, a naval officer of great experience and bravery, while it will be accompanied by the Chevalier de Saint George in person."

"This sounds like preparation," said the queen.

"Prompt and effectual measures shall be taken to check it," replied the duke. "I will instruct General Cadogan to obtain assistance from the Dutch government, and with whatever amount of men the French fleet may sail, a corresponding number of battalions shall be transported hither at the same time. The chief aim of the invasion will, doubtless, be Scotland. Several regiments of infantry must therefore be sent to join Lord Leven, the commander-in-chief in that country, who shall have instructions to take possession of Edinburgh Castle. The troops on the north-east coast of Ireland must be held ready for instant embarkation; and with regard to naval defence, if I may be permitted to recommend to the prince, I would suggest that a powerful squadron, under the command of Admiral Sir George Byng, should be sent to lie off Dunkirk, in order to watch the movements of the French fleet."

" It shall be so," replied the Prince. " The Lisbon fleet requires a large convoy, which the enemy no doubt calculated upon, and fancied that our shores would be left defenceless; but we will disappoint them. The squadron shall be sent, as your grace suggests."

" These precautions taken, nothing is to be feared," said the duke. " The attempted invasion will only redound to your majesty's glory, by proving the zeal and devotion of your subjects. Neither will it, as is hoped and intended by the crafty Louis, interfere with the prosecution of the war with France."

"Amen!" exclaimed the queen. "I must now break up the audience, for I am somewhat fatigued, and desire to commune with myself on these unpleasant tidings."

" Before it is broken up, I should wish your majesty to see the prisoner once more," said the duchess.

" It is scarcely necessary," replied the queen, reluctantly; " but if your grace desire it——"

" I *do* desire it," replied the duchess.

" Well, then, let him be brought hither at once," said the queen; " but I warn your grace, that whatever occurs it will make no change in my disposition towards him!"

" In that case, let us bring the matter to an instant issue," said the prince.

Accordingly, an usher was despatched for the prisoner, and he returned shortly afterwards, followed by Snell and Masham—the former in his own garb of a yeoman of the guard, and the latter in the footman's disguise.

" Come this way," cried the prince.

And the pair stood before the queen.

" This young man bears a most remarkable resemblance to Mr. Masham," said the duke. " If I did not know that he had just left us, I should declare that it was him."

" The resemblance is indeed wonderful," said the prince.

" So wonderful that I am convinced it is him!" said the duchess.

" Mr. Masham has just quitted the palace, your grace," replied Snell.

" Oh, yes, I saw him pass the outer court," said the usher.

" Then nothing more need be said," remarked the duchess, " and your majesty will dismiss the prisoner. There has been some trickery in the matter, but what it is I cannot make out at present."

At a gesture from the queen, Snell withdrew with Masham. The others retired soon after, leaving the queen and the prince alone. Anne looked hard at her husband, tapped her fan against her left hand, and shook her head significantly, while Prince George, not knowing exactly what all these expressive gestures meant, relieved his embarrassment by an immoderate pinch of snuff.

"You think you have made me your dupe," said the queen, at length, in a good-humoured tone—"but you are mistaken—I see through it all, and much more plainly than the duchess."

"Your majesty——"

"Nay, if you try to brave it out, I shall indeed be angry," interrupted Anne. "This letter came from France, no doubt—but it was under cover to you; and in making it up again, you have used your own seal. Nay, look. Oh, prince! you are but a poor contriver!"

Her consort took another pinch of snuff.

"This is not all," pursued the queen. "In the folds of the letter there was slipped accidentally, no doubt—a billet from Abigail to Masham, from which I find he has been in the palace all the time, in disguise. Look at it." And she held forth a little note to him.

The prince again had recourse to his snuff-box.

"If your majesty punishes them, you must punish me," he said, "for I am equally to blame. But you will be gracious towards them?"

"I make no promises," she replied. "But I must defer all consideration of this foolish pair of lovers to some other occasion. You must now help me to think over this meditated invasion, and the steps necessary to meet it. Oh, my brother!" she exclaimed— "would there were any way of helping thee, short of surrendering my crown!"

CHAPTER III.

WHEREIN THE SERJEANT RECEIVES AN IMPORTANT COMMISSION FROM THE DUKE.

ON returning from the palace, the Duke of Marlborough retired to his closet, and sent for Serjeant Scales. The serjeant was not long in answering the summons; but he entered so noiselessly, that the duke, who was busily engaged in writing, did not perceive him, and he remained standing motionless and erect for some time, until, chancing to raise his eyes, the duke remarked his presence.

"Oh, you are there, serjeant," he said. "I sent for you to let you know that you will have to sail for Holland to-night,—or rather, early to-morrow morning! for the sloop in which you will take your passage, and which is lying off Woolwich, will set out with the tide, at three o'clock. You must be on board by midnight."

"Good, general," replied Scales, saluting.

"The object of your sudden departure is this," pursued the duke. "Despatches will be entrusted to your care, which you will deliver with your own hand to General Cadogan, at the Hague—with your own hand, mind, serjeant. The general may be at Hellevoetsluys, or elsewhere; for though he has just written to me from Ostend, to say he should take his departure immediately for the Dutch capital, circumstances may alter his route. But you will learn where he is when you reach Briel."

"Very good, general," replied the serjeant. "It shall be done."

Upon this, the duke nodded his head, and resumed his writing; but looking up after awhile, he found Scales still in the same place.

"What, not gone, serjeant?" he said.

"I didn't understand I was done with," replied Scales, saluting, and moving towards the door.

"Stay," replied the duke, noticing a certain hesitation in his follower's manner. "Can I do anything for you before you go? Don't be afraid to ask, if I can."

"I want nothing, your grace," replied Scales, "but what I can't have."

"How do you know that, unless you make the experiment?" replied the duke, kindly.

"Because the errand on which I'm going tells me so," replied the serjeant. "What I want is your grace's company. I don't like leaving you behind."

"Would I *were* going with you, my good fellow!" exclaimed the duke. "I would far rather undergo all the anxieties and fatigues of the most difficult campaign than take part, as I am now obliged to do, in the petty cabals and intrigues of a court. But I am not my own master, as indeed no man is who has sold himself to his country. Content you, serjeant, I shall follow you speedily."

"And who is to clean your grace's boots when I am gone?" said Scales, in a doleful tone, and with a grimace well calculated to provoke the duke's laughter.

"Really, serjeant, I have not given that important matter consideration," said Marlborough, smiling. But fearful of hurting the other's feelings, he added, in a kindly tone, "I shall certainly miss your skilful brush."

"Your grace wont look like yourself without me," said the serjeant, who, being a privileged favourite, indulged in considerable familiarity. "The boots wont take the right polish from any hand but mine. Your grace may laugh; but it's true. You've often admitted it before, and you'll admit it again."

"Very likely, serjeant," replied the duke. "You've many excellent qualities besides a talent for cleaning boots; and I shall be sorry to lose you, even for a short time. Nor would I employ you upon the present commission, but that I know no one so trustworthy as yourself."

"Your grace will never have reason to repent your confidence," replied Scales, proudly.

"I believe you, my good fellow," returned the duke. "I believe you."

"Oh, general!" exclaimed Scales, "how happy shall we be in retirement at Blenheim, after a few more glorious campaigns, when we come to turn our swords into ploughshares."

"That is what I sigh for, indeed, serjeant," replied the duke;

"but it will never happen. I have a presentiment that the fruits of my labour will be snatched from me at the moment of maturity. Louis will accomplish by gold what he cannot achieve by force of arms. There is a faction here at work to oppose all my efforts, and in time they may succeed in neutralizing them. What I gain in the field is lost at court, for there, strange to say, the King of France has a stronger party than I have. Repeated defeats have shewn him we are destined to be his conquerors, and he therefore seeks to retrieve his losses by other means. If he succeeds in obtaining peace on his own terms, it were better the war had never been undertaken—better so much treasure had never been uselessly spent, and so many lives lost—better, far better, Blenheim and Ramilies had never been won."

"It pains me to hear your grace talk thus," rejoined Scales; "but such a disgraceful peace will never be made."

"Heaven grant I may never live to see the day!" cried the duke, "but I fear it. The seeds of treason are scattered so widely throughout this court, that, unless discovered and plucked forth, they will produce a terrible harvest. However, though entertaining this feeling, I do not suffer myself to be disheartened by it, but shall go on as energetically as ever; and as long as the armies of England are entrusted to my command, her laurels shall never be tarnished."

"No fear of that, your grace," said Scales, emphatically.

"The French never have won a battle from me yet, and they never shall win one," cried the duke.

"That's certain!" exclaimed Scales, waving his hat with enthusiasm.

"Steady, serjeant," said the duke, smiling. "But since I forget myself, no wonder you do so. I have spoken unreservedly to you, because I know I am safe with you, and because I desire to relieve myself of some oppressive thoughts. Your fidelity, and the services you have rendered me, entitle you to be treated as a friend."

"Then, as you condescend to treat me as such," replied the serjeant, "I'll make so bold as to offer your grace a bit of advice. Don't have any more misgivings. You'll finish this war as gloriously as you've begun it, and will trample your enemies beneath your foot, as sure as you're a living man. I'll never believe that Englishmen will see the laurels snatched from the brow of their greatest commander—the Duke of Marlborough. If I thought so, I would disown my country."

"No more of this, Scales," said the duke, extending his hand to the serjeant, who pressed it fervently to his heart. "I will see you in the evening, when you shall have the despatches. Make your preparations for departure in the meantime."

The serjeant bowed, and, brushing away a tear, left the closet

CHAPTER IV.

IN WHAT MANNER THE SERJEANT TOOK LEAVE OF HIS FRIENDS.

"A SOLDIER ought always to be ready to march at an instant's notice," thought the serjeant, as he returned to his own room, "and therefore I can't complain. Nevertheless, I should like to have had a little longer furlough. But never mind. 'Tis the fortune of war. My preparations will soon be made, and then I'll bid my friends good bye."

With this, he set to work, and in less than an hour his scanty wardrobe, consisting of half-a-dozen shirts, an undress coat and waistcoat, and some other matters, were packed up in his chest, with military care and neatness. He then dressed himself in his full regimentals, and proceeded to the housekeeper's room, where he found Mrs. Plumpton. Sitting down without a word, he looked fixedly at her, and heaved a deep sigh.

"Why, bless us! serjeant, what's the matter?" cried Mrs. Plumpton, with much concern. "I hope you ain't ill. Take a little ratafia?" And opening a cupboard, she produced a flask and a glass.

"Well, I don't mind if I do, Mrs. Plumpton," replied Scales. "Here's to our next merry meeting!" he added, in a tone somewhat at variance with the hilarity of the sentiment.

"I hope it wont be long first, serjeant," said the lady.

"It may be longer than you think for," replied Scales, mysteriously.

"What *do* you mean, serjeant?" cried Mrs. Plumpton, in alarm. "You ain't a-goin' to leave us soon?"

"Sorry to say I am," replied Scales. "I'm called off when I least expected it, as many a brave fellow has been before me."

"Save us! serjeant, you make me dwither all over," replied Mrs. Plumpton. "You don't mean to say that you're a-goin' to the wars!"

"The trumpet calls him to the field, and to the summons he must yield," apostrophized Scales. "He leaves the mistress of his heart —from her, indeed, 'tis hard to part; but to the battle he must go, for loud the warning trumpets blow."

Mrs. Plumpton sighed dismally.

"Amid the battle's strife," replied Scales, changing his measure, "and when the cannons roar, I'll think of thee, my life, hoping to meet once more."

"Oh! dear! dear!" cried Mrs. Plumpton. "But are you really going?"

"To night the vessel sails, will bear away thy Scales," replied the serjeant. "Though friends elsewhere he find, he leaves his heart behind."

"Don't talk to me in this manner, I beg of you, serjeant," cried Mrs. Plumpton; "I can't bear it. It's cruel of you to trifle with one's feelings."

"I've no intention of trifling with your feelings," said Scales. "Obey I must when honour calls, though doomed to meet the cannon-balls——ha! here comes Mrs. Tipping."

"Oh! Tipping, he's a-goin' to leave us!" exclaimed Mrs. Plumpton, as the lady's-maid entered the room.

"What! the serjeant?" cried the other.

"Yes, the serjeant," responded Scales. "The soldier's is a merry life; he goes when beats the drum; and though he may not like the change,—he takes things as they come."

"And very wise in him to do so," replied Mrs. Tipping. "Well, I wouldn't be a soldier's wife for something."

"You wouldn't!" cried Scales.

"I wouldn't," she repeated. "Suppose I was your wife, for instance, what would become of me when you were away?"

"Why, you must do as the duchess does in his grace's absence," replied Scales.

"The duchess is no rule for me," rejoined Mrs. Tipping. "I shouldn't like it at all. Suppose you were to come back without an arm, or a leg, or an eye?"

"Suppose I was, what then?" replied Scales.

"I don't think I could reconcile myself to it," replied Mrs. Tipping. "I don't like any deficiencies."

"Humph!" exclaimed Scales. "What says Mrs. Plumpton?"

"I should like you just as well if you lost both legs, or a leg and an arm," she replied.

"Well, ladies, this is no jesting matter—at least, not with me," rejoined Scales; "I am really setting out for Holland to-night. It's quite unexpected on my part, or I'd have prepared you for it. But you'll come and take a farewell dish o' tea with me in my room. I'll ask my friend Proddy to meet you. I shall expect you both at five."

Shortly after this, the serjeant repaired to Saint James's Palace, and found Proddy in the kitchen—a lofty and spacious apartment, with a vaulted roof and numerous fireplaces. The coachman was busily engaged with a cold sirloin of beef and a tankard of ale, but on learning the serjeant's intelligence, he declared it quite took away his appetite, and he laid down his knife and fork. It was then settled that they should meet again at five o'clock, and the serjeant taking his departure, Proddy withdrew to a small room contiguous to the kitchen, to smoke his pipe undisturbed, and ruminate on what he had heard. While he was thus occupied, the door opened, and in walked Bimbelot and Sauvageon.

"Good day, gentlemen," said Proddy, shaking hands with them; "how goes the world with you?"

"Passablement, mon cher cocher," replied Bimbelot, "passablement. Mais vous êtes un peu triste—you look down in de mout—chopfallen—vat you call it?"

"I may well look down in the mouth, Bamby," replied Proddy, "seein' as how I'm goin' to lose my best friend."

"Vat, de sergent?" asked Sauvageon.

"Yes, he's leavin' me, and at a moment's notice too," replied Proddy.

"Ventrebleu!" exclaimed Bimbelot; "mais c'est soudaîn. Is Marlbrook going to de wars again?"

"If by Marlbrook you mean the Duke of Marlborough, Bamby," rejoined Proddy, with dignity, "I believe not—not just yet, at all events. The serjeant is chosen as the bearer of certain despatches to General Cadogan, which can only be conveyed by a trusty person. You understand?"

"Oui, je comprend parfaitement," answered Bimbelot, with a significant look at Sauvageon. "And when does de sergent go?"

"He sails for Holland to-night," replied Proddy.

"Vous entendez cela," said Bimbelot to Sauvageon. "Il part ce soir pour la Hollande avec des depêches. Il faut l'arrêter."

"Bon," replied the corporal.

"What's that you say, Bamby?" inquired Proddy.

"I was merely expressing my regret at de great loss we shall sustain in de sergent's absence," replied Bimbelot, "c'est tout, mon brave cocher."

"I, for one, shall miss him greatly," groaned Proddy.

"And I for another!" exclaimed Bimbelot.

"And I for a third," added Sauvageon.

"Si nous pouvons mettre nos mains sur ces lettres, ce sera une bonne chance," observed Bimbelot to his friend.

"Prenez garde," replied the other; "ce drole a des soupçons."

"Eh, what?" cried Proddy; "what's droll? not the serjeant's departure, Savage-john?"

"Not in de least," replied the corporal. "C'est un bien brave homme, le sergent. I sall be excessive sorry to lose him."

"We must call to take leave of him," said Bimbelot. "At what hour does he leave Marlbro' House?"

"I don't know," replied Proddy; "but I'm going to him at five."

"Eh bien, nous passerons chez lui à sept heures—ou un peu plus tard," said Bimbelot, with a look at his friend. "We'll do ourselves de honour to look in upon him, pour prendre congé, in de course of de evening. Oblige us by telling him so."

"I will," replied Proddy; "and I make no doubt he'll be glad to see you."

"Oh! apropos, monsieur le cocher," cried Bimbelot, "I came to ask you a question, but what you tell me about de sergent has put it out clean of my head. Is dat Mezansene vid whom I fight de duel in de dark still in de palace!"

"What for, eh?" demanded Proddy, gruffly.

"Oh, noting very partic'lar," replied Bimbelot. "But I should like to see him."

"Then you can't—and that's flat, Bamby," rejoined the coachman. "He is in constant attendance on the prince, and can't be seen by anybody."

"Ah, Proddy, vous êtes un vieux rusé," said Bimbelot. "You're a cunning old fox. Mais vous ne me pouvez pas tromper. You know very well it's Mr. Masham, en masquerade."

"I know nothin' of the sort," replied Proddy, still more sulkily.

"Bravo!—très bien!" cried Bimbelot, laughing. "But I shan't press you too hard. Don't be afraid of me. I wont betray him. I know what he disguise himself for—une jolie dame—Mademoiselle Abigail Hill—ha, ha! Adieu, mon cher Proddy. We sall meet again in de evening, when we call upon de sergent." And with ceremonious bows the two Frenchmen went their way.

Proddy smoked another pipe, quaffed another mug of ale, and then thinking it time to start, set out for Marlborough House. On his arrival there, he proceeded at once to the serjeant's room, and found him seated at tea between Mrs. Plumpton and Mrs. Tipping, both of whom were in tears.

"Well, this is an affecting sight," said the coachman, pausing, as if arrested by it, near the door—"a wery affecting sight!"

"Yes, it's painful," replied the serjeant; "but having experienced so many sad partings, I'm getting used to it, like the eels. But sit down, comrade—sit down. Wont you join us?"

"Mr. Proddy never takes tea, I recollect," said Mrs. Plumpton. "Ill fetch him some ale."

And quitting the room, she returned in a few minutes with a large pewter jug, holding about three pints.

"Here's to your speedy return, serjeant," said Proddy, applying the jug to his lips, and raising his eyes devoutly to the ceiling, as he took a long pull at the jug. "Nothing consoles a man like ale," he added. "It's balm to the bruised sperrit. We shall be quite lost without him, eh, ladies?"

"Quite lost!" they both agreed.

"The best of friends must part sometimes, my dears," replied Scales; "and we shall be all the happier when we meet again. A little absence teaches us our proper value."

"There's no occasion for absence to teach us *your* valley, serjeant, I'm sure," said Mrs. Plumpton.

"There goes Plumpton again," cried Mrs. Tipping, pettishly. "Al-*ways* taking the words out of one's mouth."

"Then you should be quick, and speak 'em first," rejoined Mrs. Plumpton.

"Oh, serjeant!" exclaimed Proddy, "I wish I was a-goin' with you. Since I've known you, I've had a monstrous longin' to enter the service, and now it comes upon me stronger than ever."

"You'd soon have enough of it," replied Scales; "not that I ever had, though; but then a man must begin young, and get inured to hardship. You can't always recruit yourself with a mug of ale and a pipe after the day's fatigue—and it's but seldom you can get a bed to lie upon. I don't think a soldier's life would suit you, Proddy. You're better as you are."

"Marchin' mightn't suit me," replied the coachman, "'cause I'm pussy and short-winded, but I should enjoy comfortable quarters in one of those old Flemish towns hugely; and as to fightin', I couldn't have too much o' that. One reason why I should like to be a soldier is, that I should then be a favourite with the women. By-the-bye, serjeant, are the Dutch ladies handsome?"

"Very," replied the serjeant, licking his lips; "but not to compare," he added, glancing tenderly at his fair neighbours, " with our own countrywomen."

" Of course not," said Proddy; " but still they may do very well in their absence."

" Why—y-e-s," replied Scales, somewhat embarrassed, " the vrows are not without merit."

" I hope you wont fall in love with any of 'em while you're away, serjeant," said Mrs. Plumpton.

" If you come back with a Dutch wife, it will be worse than returning without a leg," said Mrs. Tipping.

The conversation here dropped. The serjeant made several efforts to renew it, but the ladies were too much depressed to be roused, and as to Proddy, he declared, " he hadn't a word to throw at a dog," so he applied himself for consolation to the jug, the contents of which began to make an evident impression upon his head.

Tea was just finished, and the things removed, when Mr. Timperley entered to say that the Duke of Marlborough desired to see the serjeant. The summons, of course, was instantly obeyed, and Scales was absent nearly half an hour, during which Proddy made no remark to his companions, except to proffer a request to Mrs. Plumpton to replenish his mug, which she complied with, though with some reluctance.

On his return, the serjeant looked grave and consequential, as he usually did when fresh from the presence of his commander. But to gravity he now added an air of mystery, as if fraught with a sense of the importance of his mission. He sat down without a word, and for some moments silence prevailed, which was at length broken by Proddy.

" Well, serjeant, you've got your despatches, I suppose ?" he asked.

" Safe enough," replied Scales, tapping his breast.

As he said this, the door opened, and Bimbelot and Sauvageon entered the room.

" I forgot to mention that I had told these gentlemen you were going," said Proddy, noticing that the serjeant looked surprised, and not altogether pleased.

" Oui, mon cher sergent," said Bimbelot, " nous sommes venus pour vous dire adieu, et vous souhaiter bon voyage."

" Much obliged to you, Bamby, and to you, too, corporal," replied Scales; " but it wasn't at all necessary."

" Vous etes chargé des depêches du duc au General Cadogan, eh, serjent ?" said Bimbelot.

" Why, you didn't tell 'em that, did you ?" said Scales, in a low and reproachful tone to Proddy.

" I told 'em all about it," replied the coachman, whose prudence was completely overcome by the good liquor he had swallowed. " Do you think I'd fail to let 'em know how much you're in the duke's confidence ? Not I ! The serjeant has just left his grace," he added, " and has received the despatches from him."

" Vraiement !" exclaimed Bimbelot, with a furtive look at Sauvageon.

"Silence, fool!" cried Scales, angrily.

"De sergent well deserve de favour he enjoy," said Sauvageon. "'Tis a sure proof of merit to be trusted."

"So it is," said Bimbelot; "but if every one had his due, the sergent would hold a high rank in de army."

"He ought to be a captain," said Proddy. "Captain Scales, here's your very good health, and wishin' you may soon become a general."

"That's the general wish," said Mrs. Tipping.

"This time you've taken the words out of *my* mouth, Tipping," said Mrs. Plumpton.

"I've no desire for preferment," replied Scales, somewhat gruffly. "I'm content with my present station."

"Well, we wont intrude longer, sergent," said Bimbelot. "I suppose you'll be setting out immediately? Can we help you to carry your shest?"

"No, thank you," replied the sergent, somewhat mollified by the attention; "I shall send it on before me. Proddy and I will walk through the Park together."

Bimbelot and Sauvageon exchanged glances.

"A few minutes before nine we shall fancy you crossing the park, and at nine, embarking," said the former.

"If you do so, you wont be far wrong," replied Scales.

"Adieu, then, sergent," said the two Frenchmen, bowing.

"Adieu, gentlemen," replied Scales. And after a further exchange of civilities and professions of eternal regard, Bimbelot and Sauvageon bowed themselves out.

With their disappearance, the conversation fell to the ground once more. Scales cleared his throat now and then, and tried to talk, but in vain; while Proddy quaffed his ale in silence.

This state of things endured for nearly a quarter of an hour, after which the serjeant, as if nerving himself for a great effort, got up, and putting on his hat, said, in a voice which, though he attempted to keep it firm, displayed considerable emotion—"We must part."

"Oh, don't say so, serjeant!" cried both ladies, rising likewise. "You're not going yet?"

"It's useless to postpone it longer," replied Scales; "better get the partin' over. You'll take care of my room during my absence, and clean it now and then?"

"That we will," cried both; "we'll clean it once a week, or oftener, if you wish it."

"Don't meddle with the picters," pursued the serjeant; "for though they're not worth much, I value 'em. And I shouldn't like that piece of shot to be taken down—or that broken sword—or those gauntlets—or those spurs—or the meerschaum——"

"We wont disturb anything," cried both ladies. "You'll find all as you left it, on your return."

"If I do return," said the serjeant, gravely. "There's always an *if* where a soldier's concerned."

"Don't mention such a thing!" cried Mrs. Plumpton, bursting into tears.

"To you, Proddy, I commit the custody of my drum, certain you'll take care of it," continued Scales.

"I'll guard it as I would a treasure!" replied the coachman. "I shall fancy I hear your rat-a-tat-a-tat-a-ra-ra whenever I look at it."

"And now farewell, my dears," cried Scales, in a husky voice. "Take care of yourselves. God bless you!"

"Oh dear!—o-o-o-oh dear! I'm sure I shall never survive it!" blubbered Mrs. Plumpton, applying her apron to her eyes.

"Don't take on so, sweetheart," cried Scales, passing his arm over her shoulder, while she buried her face in his breast; "and don't you, my dear," he added, affectionately squeezing Mrs. Tipping's hand, who was sobbing with equal vehemence, and leaning against his arm for support—"if you go on thus, you'll quite unman me."

There was a pause of a few minutes, during which the serjeant gazed sadly and tenderly from one lady to the other—now drawing Mrs. Plumpton a little closer to him with his left hand, now squeezing Mrs. Tipping rather more affectionately with the right—while the only sound heard was that of their sobs.

At length, Proddy, who had witnessed the scene in silence, and was greatly affected by it, got up, and staggering towards Mrs. Tipping, laid hold of her arm, and offering the jug of ale to her said—"Here, take a drop of this, my dear. It 'll do you good. Nothing like ale to console one in affliction—nothing like ale!"

But Mrs. Tipping would not be so comforted, and she paid no sort of attention to the coachman—so he turned to the serjeant, and offered the jug to him.

"No, I thank'ee, Proddy," said Scales. "You'll take care of these dear creaters while I'm away? I leave 'em to your care."

"You can't leave 'em in better hands," replied Proddy; "I'll be a brother to 'em. You ought to have your picter painted in that attitude, serjeant. You look for all the world like Alexander the Great betwixt Roxylany and Statiry."

An unexpected interruption was here occasioned by the entrance of a couple of stout porters, who came for the serjeant's chest, and, ashamed of being thus discovered, both ladies beat a hasty retreat.

CHAPTER V.

HOW THE SERJEANT WAS WAYLAID IN THE PARK.

THE porters having set out with their load, the serjeant left the room, telling Proddy he would return presently. How long he was absent, the coachman could not tell, for, overcome by grief, and the potency of the ale, he fell fast asleep, and was awakened by a rousing slap on the shoulder. It was now quite dark, and the serjeant held a candle in his hand.

" Come, Proddy, it's time to be off, my boy," he cried—" it's just gone half-past eight, and nine's the hour of embarkation, you know."

" I'm quite ready, serjeant," replied the coachman, with a prodigious yawn, and rubbing his eyes. " I was just a-dreaming of bein' with you in battle; and when you gave me that knock on the shoulder, I thought a cannon-ball had hit me."

" It's well it was only a dream," replied Scales, laughing. " You've had a pretty long nap. Slept off the fumes of the ale, eh?"

" Quite," replied Proddy. " I suppose you've been sayin' good bye to the women again. Took 'em separately this time, eh?"

Scales did not deny the soft impeachment, but coughed slightly, and rubbed his chin.

" You'll not forget what I said to you about 'em?" he observed.

" Oh, about takin' care of 'em," replied the coachman. " Make yourself quite easy. Any more instructions?"

" No," replied Scales. Having taken a last lingering survey of the room, he blew out the candle. " Now then, come along," he cried.

Proddy followed his leader in the dark; but they had not proceeded far, when the serjeant apparently encountered some obstacle in his path, for he came to a sudden halt. Before the coachman could inquire what was the matter, a noise of kissing was heard, intermixed by the words, " Good bye—God bless you!" pronounced in female accents, which, smothered as they were, could be distinguished as those of Mrs. Plumpton. The next moment, a female figure rushed past Proddy, and the serjeant's course was clear—at least for a short distance, for before he reached the end of the passage, he met with another obstruction. Again the sound of kissing was heard. Again pretty nearly the same words were uttered, and in the same stifled tone; but this time the voice was that of Mrs. Tipping, who sobbed audibly as she rushed past the coachman.

" Well, we shall get out in time, it's to be hoped," observed Proddy.

" All right," replied the serjeant, opening the outer door, through which they passed into the garden, and so into the park.

Arrived there, they struck off on the left, in the direction of the Cock-pit. The night was dark; and the gloom was so much increased by the shade of the trees beneath which they were walking, that they could scarcely see each other; but the serjeant, being intimately acquainted with the locality, held on his pace briskly—so briskly indeed, that Proddy could scarcely keep up with him. All at once Scales stopped, and said, " Some one is running after us. Halloa! who goes there?"

The words were scarcely out of his mouth, when two persons rushed forward, and seizing hold of him, endeavoured to drag him backwards by main force; but he disengaged himself by a powerful effort, and uttering a loud oath, drew his sword, shouting to Proddy to run back for the sentinel stationed near the palace.

The coachman endeavoured to obey, but had not got far when his foot caught against some impediment, and he fell with his face on the ground.

While thus prostrated, he could hear the noise of a terrible scuffle going on, intermixed with the clash of swords, and fierce exclamations from the serjeant. Picking himself up as quickly as he could, he hurried on again, roaring lustily for help. To his great satisfaction, he was soon answered by the sentinel, whose footsteps were heard hastening towards him, while at the same time the gleam of a lantern was seen through the trees, advancing in another direction.

The next moment, the sentinel came up, and briefly informing him what had happened, Proddy set off with him to the serjeant's assistance. Both listened intently, in order to discover whether the strife was going forward; but all being now hushed, the coachman's heart died within him. Arrived, as he supposed, within a short distance of his friend, he called out,—"Where are you, serjeant?" and was answered in a faint voice, "Here!"

A watchman arriving on the instant with his lantern, its gleam showed the serjeant leaning against a tree, and supported by his sword. Blood was trickling from his arm, as well as from a gash on his forehead.

"You're hurt, I fear, serjeant?" inquired Proddy, in a tone of the most anxious commiseration.

"Not much," replied Scales. "I've got a thrust through the arm and a cut over the temples, and the loss of blood makes me feel faintish,—that's all. A drop of brandy would set me to rights."

"If that's all you require, serjeant," said the watchman, "I can furnish you with the remedy."

Producing a small stone bottle from his capacious pocket, he drew out the cork with his teeth, and held it to Scales' lips, who drank eagerly of its contents.

"What has become of your assailant, serjeant?" asked the sentinel.

"Fled!" replied Scales—"and I think I've given 'em something to remember me by!"

"Did they try to rob you?" inquired Proddy.

"Ay, of my despatches," replied Scales; "but I foiled 'em. Here they are, safe enough," he added, raising his hand to his breast. "Tie a handkerchief round my head, Proddy, and your cravat round my arm. There—that'll do. Now that the bleeding's stanched, I shall be able to proceed."

"Why, you don't mean to embark in that state?" cried the coachman, in surprise.

"Yes, I do," replied Scales. "I've gone through an action when far worse wounded than I am now. Lend me your arm, comrade."

"You're a brave man, I must say, serjeant," cried the sentinel. "Can I be of any further service to you?"

"No, I thank'ee, friend," replied Scales.

"I'm afraid it's useless to go in pursuit of the villains," said the watchman.

"Quite useless and quite unnecessary," replied Scales. "They've failed in the attempt, and that's sufficient. Besides, as I've said, I've given 'em each a remembrancer. Good night, sentinel."

With this he walked away firmly, though somewhat slowly, and leaning on Proddy's shoulder. The watchman attended him with his lantern as far as the Cock-pit gate, where he took his leave. The two friends then crossed over to Whitehall-stairs, and so quickly had the occurrence taken place, that the abbey clock only struck nine as they reached the bank of the river.

"Just in time," replied Scales, glancing at the wherry which was lying at the foot of the stairs. "I always like to be punctual. Not a word of what has happened, Proddy. I don't want it to come to the duke's ear; it might make him uneasy, and all's right now."

"Do you suspect anybody?" asked the coachman.

"I do," replied Scales; "but that's neither here nor there. Farewell, comrade. Recollect what I told you about the women. Take care of 'em, and take care of yourself."

Grasping his friend's hand cordially, the serjeant marched down the stairs and sprang into the boat, which was instantly pushed from the strand, and disappeared in the gloom.

"The sentinel spoke the truth," said Proddy, turning away with a heart brimful of emotion. "The serjeant *is* a brave fellow—a very brave fellow."

CHAPTER VI.

HOW THE MARQUIS DE GUISCARD HELPED TO RID MR. SAINT-JOHN OF AN INCUMBRANCE.

ABOUT the time of the serjeant's embarkation, two men were staggering along Stonecutter's-alley, a narrow passage near the northeast angle of Saint James's-park communicating with Pall-mall, supporting themselves as they proceeded against the wall, and ever and anon giving utterance to a groan or an execration.

From the difficulty and uncertainty of the progress of these persons, it might have been supposed they were affected by liquor; but when they came within the range of a lamp, burning at the corner of the alley, it was seen from their ghastly looks, as well as from the state of their attire, that they were both severely wounded.

On reaching the lamp-post, the foremost of the two caught hold of it to prevent himself from falling, and declared with an oath that he could go no further. The conversation that ensued between him and his companion was maintained in French.

"Fiends seize him!" exclaimed the man, in accents rendered hoarse with pain. "I believe he has done for me. Who would have thought it would turn out so unluckily! Two to one, we ought to have been more than a match for him; but engaging with that man is like fighting with the devil—one is sure to have the worst of it. He has an arm of iron."

"I wouldn't have proposed the job," groaned the other in reply, "but I thought we could have come upon him unawares. He boasts that he is never taken by surprise, and after this I shall credit the assertion."

"If he had not a scull as thick as a block of marble, and as hard, I should have cut him down," rejoined the first speaker.

"And if he were made of ordinary stuff he must have dropped after the thrust I dealt him," returned the other. "My sword passed right through his body."

"Bah! your blade must have glanced against his ribs, or gone through his arm, Bimbelot," observed the first speaker. "Reserve the description of your feats for the marquis. I know what really *did* happen. I know he has given me enough, and more than I am likely to get over. Go on, and leave me. I may as well die here as elsewhere."

"Don't think of dying, corporal," replied Bimbelot; "that would indeed be making the worst of a bad business. You're badly hurt, I dare say—and so am I; but I hope not mortally. If we can but reach the Unicorn over the way, where the marquis is waiting for us, we shall get our wounds dressed, and then all danger will be over. Come, make an effort. You'll bleed to death if you stay there. I would lend you a helping hand, but my arm is useless."

"It's over with me entirely, comrade," groaned Sauvageon. "This precious scheme was all of your contriving, and you see how it has turned out."

"We both ran equal risk," replied Bimbelot, "and the reward was to be equally divided."

"Reward!" echoed Sauvageon, in bitter derision. "What will the marquis say when we go back empty-handed? We shall get curses from him instead of gold."

"No we sha'n't," replied Bimbelot; "he *must* pay us, or we'll peach."

"The shame of defeat galls me more than my wounds," cried Sauvageon, writhing with anguish. "Would I could have one more blow at the caitiff."

"Don't strike at me, corporal," exclaimed Bimbelot, moving away from him. "I'm not the serjeant. Make an effort, I say, or you'll fall into the hands of the watch. I hear them coming this way."

So saying, he crept off, and Sauvageon, alarmed by the noise of approaching footsteps, staggered after him across the street. A few steps further brought them to the Unicorn—a small inn at the corner of the Haymarket. Guiscard was standing at the door, and without a word led them to a chamber on the right of the passage, on entering which the sight of their blood-stained apparel made him start.

"What the devil is the meaning of this!" he cried. "You have not failed in your enterprise? It was too well planned, and too easy of execution for that. Give me the despatches quickly, and you shall have that which will prove a balsam for your wounds, were they deeper and more desperate than they seem."

"You had better send a surgeon to us, without further question-

ing, monseigneur," rejoined Bimbelot, sullenly, "unless you wish
us to die at your feet."

"You *shall* die, if you have disappointed me, villain!" cried the
marquis, in a terrible tone.   "Give me the despatches, or——"

And he drew his sword.

"Nay, if this is the way we're to be served, it's time to take care
of ourselves," rejoined Bimbelot, moving towards the door.

His passage was barred by the marquis.   Bimbelot would have
cried out, but he was stopped by Sauvageon.

"This is poor usage to men who have risked their lives for you,
monseigneur," said the latter; "if we have failed, it has not been
our fault.   That we have done our best you may be sure, from the
condition we are in."

"I was wrong to blame you, my poor fellow," replied Guiscard,
sheathing his sword; "but it is cursedly provoking to be robbed of
a prey when it seemed actually within one's grasp.   Why, the fate
of this kingdom hung upon those despatches.   With them, the
success of the French expedition would have been decided.   All my
preparations were made for their speedy transmission to France.   A
mounted courier awaits my orders in the next street, prepared to
ride as fast as post-horses could carry him to Deal, where a small
vessel in my pay would bear whatever he might bring, safely and
swiftly, to Dunkirk.   This accomplished, I would have made both
your fortunes."

"We did our best to accomplish it, monseigneur," replied Bimbelot.   "But that serjeant is the very devil."

"Ay, the luck has been against us," added Sauvageon; "but if
we get over it, we'll hope to be more fortunate next time."

"You will never have such another chance," cried the marquis,
sharply.   "These things don't occur twice.   Would I had undertaken it myself!"

"If you had, monseigneur, without disparagement to your skill
and courage, I don't think you would have been more successful
than we have been," replied Sauvageon.   "I never encountered a
man like the serjeant.   We hit him pretty sharply, but he contrived
to walk off, with the queen's coachman, Proddy, and I have no
doubt embarked with the despatches."

"Hell sink him!" cried Guiscard, savagely.

"I hope we shan't lose our reward, monseigneur?" said Bimbelot.
"Consider what we've gone through."

"It was a game of chance, like any other, and having lost it, you
ought to abide by the consequences," replied Guiscard.   "However, as you've suffered so much, you shall have the hundred
pounds I promised you."

"You wont repent your generosity, monseigneur," said Sauvageon.

The marquis then left the room, but returned shortly afterwards
with a surgeon and his assistant, to whom he had accounted for the
disaster, by stating that the two men had been set upon and
wounded by the Mohocks— a circumstance of far too common occurrence in those times of nocturnal riot, to occasion any surprise,
or awaken suspicion.   Having seen their wounds dressed, and

ascertained from the surgeon that no danger was to be apprehended, he ordered his followers to be put to bed, and again quitted the house.

To distract his thoughts, which were by no means of an agreeable nature, he hurried to Little Man's Coffee-house, and joining the faro table, soon lost a considerable sum. He was about to double his stakes, when a friendly arm was laid upon his shoulder, and turning, he perceived Saint-John.

"Come away," cried the latter; "I want to have a word with you. "You're not in luck to-night; and if you go on, you'll repent it."

Guiscard would have resisted, but the other succeeded in dragging him away.

"Come and sup with me," said Saint-John, as they quitted the coffee-house. "I am about to leave town to-morrow."

"Leave town!—and at this juncture, when such great events are on the eve of occurring!" exclaimed Guiscard. "Now, if ever, you ought to be on the scene of action."

"I have done with politics and courts and will try the sweets of retirement," replied Saint-John.

"Is ambition extinct within your breast?" cried Guiscard. "I cannot believe it. If the sovereignty of the realm should be changed by this threatened invasion, you may regret hereafter that you have allowed the opportunity to pass of pushing your fortune to the uttermost."

"I should have more reason for regret if I took any part in the struggle," cried Saint-John. "But a truce to politics."

"By way of changing the subject, then," replied Guiscard, "I have remarked a very pretty woman in your coach of late, and from the hasty glimpse I caught of her features, they seem familiar to me. Who is she?"

"An old acquaintance of yours," replied Saint-John, laughing. "Don't you remember Angelica Hyde?"

"What! the country parson's daughter!" cried Guiscard. "And so, she has taken up her abode with you, eh?"

"It fell out thus," replied Saint-John. "Angelica preferred town life so much to a dull existence in the country, that when the old people returned into Essex, she could not be persuaded to accompany them. And as she threw herself upon my compassion, why—i'faith—I was obliged to receive her."

"No great hardship, I imagine," replied Guiscard, laughing. "She's devilish pretty."

"And devilish extravagant." rejoined Saint-John. "She has almost ruined me in dress and trinkets. Whatever she fancies, she buys, no matter at what cost."

"And is she to be the companion of your solitude?" asked the marquis.

"Deuce knows," replied Saint-John; "I haven't told her of my intention of retiring yet."

"You seem indifferent enough about the matter, at all events," said the marquis, laughing.

"Why, to say truth, I have discovered that she cares very little about me," said Saint-John; "and therefore, though I *have* committed the folly of loving a woman under such circumstances, I sha'n't do so in the present instance."

"A wise resolve," replied Guiscard. "She will sup with us, I suppose?"

"Oh, certainly!" replied Saint-John.

And they continued chatting in the same strain till they reached their destination.

On entering the drawing-room, they found only two persons within it, and these were Prior and Angelica, who were playing picquet, but stopped their game on the arrival of the new comers.

Prepared for some change in Angelica, Guiscard was nevertheless struck with astonishment at the extraordinary alteration that had occurred in her. In the space of a few weeks, the country girl had been transformed into the perfect town lady. There was no end to her finery. Her dress consisted of a blue and gold Atlas gown, with a wrought petticoat edged with gold; shoes laced with silver; lace cap, and lappets; while her fingers glittered with costly rings, and pearls and other precious stones adorned her neck. Her cheeks were covered with patches, and her beautiful locks filled with powder. She looked handsomer than before, but bolder and freer in her deportment; talked loudly; and laughed boisterously and incessantly, probably to display her pearly teeth.

When Guiscard was presented to her by Saint-John, she extended her hand to him, and cried, in a tone of easy familiarity—

"Glad to see ye, marquis. How are ye? Come to sup with us— eh? Been to ridotto, or the masquerade? Saint-John wouldn't take me to either; and of all things I dote on a masquerade. It's so purely funny—one hears and sees so many diverting things—and can do just what one likes. Come and sit by me. Find me changed since we first met in the secretary's ante-room, eh?"

"I then thought you could not be improved," replied Guiscard, bowing; "but I now perceive my error."

"Prettily turned, indeed!" she cried, with a laugh. "I like to extort a compliment. But I *am* improved,—at least, if my glass may be trusted. Hope you admire my dress? It's the ditto of the Duchess of Marlborough's, and was made for me by her grace's own milliner, Madame Alamode; so it must be the thing, you know."

"It's perfect," replied Guiscard. "No dress ever became the duchess half so much—but then, your figure——"

"Far surpasses her grace's!" interrupted Angelica, with another boisterous laugh. "I am quite aware of that, marquis."

"There's no comparison between you," said Guiscard. "We have no such beauty as you at court."

"Always excepting Abigail Hill!" rejoined Angelica, maliciously.

"Not even excepting her!" said Guiscard.

"You really think so?" rejoined Angelica, much pleased.

"On my veracity," affirmed the marquis, laying his hand upon his heart.

"You hear the pretty things the marquis is saying to me, Saint-John," she cried. "Aint you jealous?"

"I should be, if I were not secure of your attachment," he replied, drily. "But, see, supper is ready. Marquis, be so good as to give your arm to Angelica."

Guiscard readily complied, and the folding-doors being thrown open, they proceeded to the adjoining room, where an exquisite repast awaited them, to which ample justice was done by all parties.

The champagne was pushed briskly round, and with every fresh glass he swallowed, the marquis discovered new charms in Angelica, who, on her part, did not appear insensible to his admiration. A bowl of mulled Burgundy closed the feast, and this discussed, the party returned to the drawing-room, where Guiscard sat down to picquet with Angelica, while Saint-John and Prior conversed apart.

"How monstrous dull you'll find the country after the gay life you've been leading," observed Guiscard, in a low tone to his partner.

"Find the country dull!" repeated Angelica, listlessly. "What do you mean, marquis?"

"Oh, I forgot!" said Guiscard. "Saint-John hasn't told you of his intention of——"

"His intention of what?" interrupted Angelica, becoming suddenly animated. "Surely he doesn't think of going into the country?"

"Faith, I don't know," rejoined Guiscard. "Excessively stupid in me to allude to the subject! It's your play, madam."

"I insist upon having a direct answer, marquis!" said the lady.

"Before I comply," he rejoined, "tell me one thing. If Saint-John goes, will you accompany him?"

"Question for question," she rejoined, regarding him fixedly. "Your motive for asking, marquis?"

"My motive is this," he replied, with a passionate glance. "If you prefer staying in town, my house is at your service."

"And you would have me believe you are in love with me?" said Angelica, smiling.

"I adore you!" he answered.

"My heart flutters so that I can play no more," she cried, throwing down the cards, and rising. "Mr. Saint-John, may I ask if you have any idea of going out of town to-morrow?"

"Going out of town?" he replied, glancing at the marquis. "Yes, I think I have."

"Do you mean to remain long in the country?"

"Two or three years," he answered, carelessly. "Just as my inclination holds out."

"Two or three years!" almost screamed Angelica. "And you have settled all this without deigning to consult me?"

"I meant to tell you at breakfast, my dear," said Saint-John, with a comical expression of countenance. "You would have had sufficient time for preparation."

"I should *not* have sufficient time, sir," she retorted; "and, to be plain with you, I wont go!"

"As you please, my dear," replied Saint-John, coolly; "your staying behind will make no difference in my plans."

"No difference!" she exclaimed—"what am I to do for three years? Why, you told me you couldn't live a day without me. Oh, you deceitful wretch!"

"Go, or stay, whichever you prefer, my love," replied Saint-John. "The choice rests entirely with yourself."

Angelica seemed to hesitate between a torrent of indignation and a fit of hysterics. At last, she flung herself violently upon a sofa. Guiscard would fain have offered her assistance, but she pushed him aside.

After a few moments, she arose, and in a tone of forced composure, said—"Will you do me the favour to order my chair, Mr. Saint-John?"

"Certainly, my love,—by all means," he replied, ringing the bell.

And on the appearance of the servant, he gave the necessary directions.

"You were good enough to place your house at my disposal just now, marquis," said Angelica. "I accept the offer."

"Enchanted!" replied Guiscard, though with some confusion. "I hope Saint-John——"

"Oh! no apologies marquis," replied the other." You are doing me an inexpressible favour."

"Adieu, Mr. Saint-John," said Angelica, spitefully. "I hope you will amuse yourself in the country."

"Adieu, ma petite," he replied; "I trust to find you handsomer than ever on my return. I give you a new lover for each month of my absence."

At this moment, the chair was announced, and Guiscard, taking Angelica's hand, led her out of the room.

"I congratulate you, Saint-John, in getting rid of a plaguy incumbrance," cried Prior, laughing.

"The marquis has saddled himself with a nice burthen," replied the other. "His ruin was certain without her assistance, but she will accelerate it."

"Well, I must begone, too," said Prior. "I cannot very well picture you in retirement. But we shall have you back when Harley is again in power."

"Pshaw!" cried Saint-John—"but for Harley, I might remain. He is in my way. If ever I do re-appear——but no matter. Farewell."

As Prior left the room, after shaking hands heartily with his friend, he said to himself—"I shall live to see a terrible conflict yet between Saint-John and Harley."

CHAPTER VII.

SHOWING HOW THE DISINTERESTEDNESS OF MASHAM'S AFFECTION FOR ABIGAIL WAS PROVED.

On the morning after Masham's successful mystification of the duchess, as the queen and the prince were seated together in the library of the palace, Anne remarked to her consort—"Well, prince, notwithstanding all you say about your equerry's devoted attachment to Abigail, I am not at all satisfied that he does not pay court to her as much from interested motives as from a genuine feeling of regard."

"Your majesty does him great injustice by the supposition," replied the prince.

"Nay, if he seeks his own advancement, he only imitates the example of most of those who crowd my court," replied Anne. "I do not blame him for it. But I should be sorry to see her thrown away upon a place-hunter."

"I wish the sincerity of his affection could be tested," said the prince.

"The experiment can easily be made on the first occasion they meet together in my presence," replied the queen.

"Masham can instantly attend your majesty," said the prince; "for he is in my apartments."

An usher was then directed to summon him and Abigail, and the man had scarcely departed upon his mission, when the door opened, and Harley entered. He was received with great kindness by the royal pair, and Anne said to him—"I hope you are come to remind me of my promise, Mr. Harley, to compensate you, so far I am able, for your late defeat."

"I have not forgotten your promise, gracious madam," replied Harley; "and will remind you at a fitting time. But I have just heard that Masham has returned."

"It is true," replied the queen. "You will see him in a moment or two. I have sent for him, and also for your cousin, Abigail, who is in great disgrace."

"In disgrace!" echoed Harley. "I am concerned to hear it. But your majesty is jesting," he added, reassured by the expression of the queen's countenance.

At this juncture, the door again opened, and gave admission to the Duchess of Marlborough.

"Always when least desired," muttered the queen, frowning.

"Her grace has a talent for coming at wrong seasons," observed Harley, in a whisper.

"I am come to tell your majesty," said the duchess, speaking with great precipitancy, and almost neglecting the customary obeisance, "that we were both deceived yesterday. It *was* Mr. Masham whom I met, and he has been for some time in disguise in the palace. I have found it all out by means of ——"

"Your grace's spies," supplied Harley.

"No matter how," rejoined the duchess. "It *is* so; and I can prove it to your majesty."

"It is needless," replied the queen, coldly; "I am already aware of it."

"Then I trust your majesty will punish his presumption as it deserves," replied the duchess. "Oh, he is here!" she added, as the usher announced the offender.

"So, Mr. Masham," she continued, "you played us a daring and unhandsome trick yesterday. Setting aside all else, was it becoming a gentleman to deceive his grace of Marlborough in the way you did, and to make him an unwitting instrument in your scheme?"

"I have explained the matter fully to his grace," replied Masham, "and have obtained his pardon for the liberty I took with him. The duke laughed heartily at my explanation, shook hands with me, and said he hoped the queen would entertain no greater resentment against me than he did."

"I can answer for the truth of this," said the prince, "for the explanation occurred in my apartments this morning."

"The duke's good nature borders upon weakness!" cried the duchess, angrily.

"Your grace keeps the balance even, and makes up his deficiency, in the opposite quality," observed Harley.

"A shrewd retort, Mr. Ex-Secretary," rejoined the duchess; "I am glad you have taken to making epigrams. It will be pleasant and fitting employment for you."

At this moment Abigail entered, and looked round with uneasiness.

"If your majesty allows Mr. Masham to escape with impunity, it will bring scandal on your court," said the duchess, in a whisper to the queen.

"Your grace will be satisfied with the punishment I shall inflict on him," replied Anne. "Abigail," she continued, in a voice of affected severity, "I have sent for you to let you know, that after the deception practised on your part, and on that of Mr. Masham, it will be impossible to retain you longer in my service. You are therefore dismissed."

"Your majesty!" exclaimed Harley.

"Not a word, sir!" cried the queen, peremptorily—"not a word! You are dismissed, I say, Abigail—and you forfeit all my favour. I have ordered Mr. Masham to be present at your disgrace, that, inasmuch as he is the principal cause of it, he may witness the result of his folly and disobedience."

"There is something beneath the surface here," thought Harley. "I shall watch how the game goes, and come in when I find it necessary."

"I applaud your majesty's decision," cried the duchess, unable to conceal her satisfaction. "It is a just sentence. We shall see whether the discarded attendant possesses as much attraction in her lover's eyes as the queen's favourite!"

"Her grace has asked the precise question I desired to have put," observed the queen, in an undertone, to the prince.

The duchess saw the look, and instantly perceiving her error, caught hold of Masham's arm as he was about to speak, and said, in a low, hurried tone—

"Take your cue from me, or you are ruined for ever. Whatever you may feel, do not profess an interest in Abigail now."

"What says Mr. Masham?" cried the queen. "Is he content with the discarded favourite?"

"Madam, I—" hesitated Masham.

"'Sdeath! can you not speak?" cried the prince.

"Don't be guided by the duchess, or you will ruin yourself and Abigail beyond redemption," said Harley, in a whisper to him. "Speak out boldly."

Thus exhorted, Masham threw himself at the queen's feet.

"Do not condemn Abigail for my fault, I beseech you, madam," he cried. "Visit your displeasure on my head as severely as you please, but not on hers! She is not to blame—indeed she is not! I will consent to retire into perpetual exile, never to behold her again, which will be worse to me than death, if you will extend forgiveness to her!"

"Love-sick fool!" exclaimed the duchess.

"Bravo! bravissimo!" exclaimed the prince, clapping his hands joyfully. "Didn't I say so!—didn't I tell your majesty it was disinterested affection on his part? Are you satisfied now?"

"Perfectly," replied the queen. "Arise, sir, you have gained your suit. Abigail is forgiven."

"Oh, your majesty!" cried Abigail, kneeling, and pressing the hand of her royal mistress to her lips.

"I will now let you know that your dismissal was merely a pretence," said the queen. "You deceived me, and I therefore considered myself entitled to deceive you. Trick for trick is only fair play."

"I have been rightly served, gracious madam," replied Abigail; "and I thank you for your leniency."

"Now comes my turn," said Harley, "I shall take this opportunity to remind your majesty of your promise. The favour I ask is a remission of Mr. Masham's sentence, and his restoration to your favour."

"It is granted," replied the queen.

"Lest this silly scene should proceed further, I announce to your majesty, that I forbid any union between Mr. Masham and Abigail," said the duchess, "and you will do well, therefore, to reflect, before you give a promise to that effect."

"On what plea do you forbid the union?" demanded Anne, surprised.

"Your majesty shall know anon," replied the duchess. "My explanation must be for your private ear."

"What is the meaning of this, cousin?" asked Harley, in a low tone, of Abigail.

"Oh! nothing—nothing," she replied, in a confident tone; but

"You think to bring about this marriage," said the duchess, in a low tone, to Harley, as she passed him; "but it will never take place !"

"It *will* take place, as surely as your grace's downfall, of which it will be the precursor," he replied, in the same tone.

CHAPTER VIII.

FURNISHES FRESH PROOFS OF MR. HARLEY'S TALENT FOR INTRIGUE.

SOME days after this interview, a second drawing-room was held at Saint James's, and was followed, as the first had been, by a grand ball in the evening.

So far from diminishing the numbers of those accustomed to attend on such occasions, the threatened invasion, which seemed to call for a demonstration of loyalty and devotion, materially increased them. The drawing-room was crowded ; and the ball, to which the invitations, at the duchess's suggestion, had been very extensive, was equally numerously attended.

The honours of the evening were divided by the queen and the duchess ; and it would be difficult to say which of the two claimed the greater share of attention. Whatever mortification Anne felt, she took care to conceal it, and appeared in better spirits than usual ; but the duchess put no such constraint upon herself, and made it evident how much she was elated by the homage she received. Her deportment had more than its accustomed loftiness and majesty ; her brow was clothed with more than its ordinary pride ; and as she leaned upon the arm of her illustrious lord, and conversed with the noblest and proudest of the realm, who pressed around her, as well as with the more distinguished representatives of foreign powers, she might well have been mistaken for the sovereign mistress of the assemblage.

Much of this homage, though appropriated by the duchess, was paid to her lord. By all, except those arrayed against the duke by faction, he was regarded with admiration, affection, and gratitude, the general feeling being, that if the country was saved from the outbreak of a rebellion, it would be mainly owing to his judgment and foresight.

Amongst others of the duchess's opponents who were present, was Harley, and though bitterly mortified at the unmistakable evidence he witnessed of her unbounded popularity and influence, he took care that her assumption of almost royal state should not pass unnoticed by the queen.

"An invasion seems scarcely necessary to wrest your majesty's crown from you," he observed, in a malicious whisper, "for the duchess appears already to have usurped the sovereignty. See how she keeps the ambassador s around her, and confers with them as if discussing the affairs of her own government."

"I perceive it all, Mr. Harley," replied Anne, quietly, "but it gives me no concern. She is intoxicated with vanity, and discerns not the danger she provokes. This night will be remembered both by herself and others, as that on which her fancied power had reached its climax. Henceforth, it will decline."

"Since your majesty gives me this assurance, I am well content," replied Harley; "but I should like to see her hurled from her pinnacle of pride."

"All in good time," said the queen, with a significant smile.

"Your majesty will forgive my hinting," rejoined Harley, "that the way in which you could wound her most sensibly at this moment, would be to announce to her that you have given your consent to Masham's union with Abigail."

"Oh! apropos of that!" cried Anne. "You heard her declare she would forbid the marriage."

"An idle threat!" exclaimed Harley, derisively. "Your majesty does not attach importance to such a piece of vapouring?"

"There is something in it, I am persuaded," replied Anne. "However, I will try what effect the announcement will have upon her."

"You will deal a harder blow than you calculate upon," said Harley, joyfully. "All her vain-glorious fancies will be put to flight at once. But, with your majesty's permission, I will ask a question or two of Abigail."

And as he mingled with the crowd, the queen commanded an usher to bid the Duchess of Marlborough attend her.

While this was passing, Abigail and Masham were engaged in the dance, and formed the chief object of attraction to the lookers on; for the story of the young equerry's disguises having been buzzed abroad, he had become quite a hero in the eyes of the fairer portion of the assemblage.

As Harley approached the group around the dancers, he perceived the Marquis de Guiscard, watching the graceful movements of his rival with a jealous and vindictive gaze; but not wishing to be troubled with him, he moved in another direction, and stood apart till the dance was over. He then approached Abigail, and claiming her for a moment from her lover, led her into an ante-room.

"Cousin," he said, "I have excellent news for you. The queen, at my request, has consented to your immediate union with Masham."

Abigail uttered an exclamation of delight.

"There is only one obstacle now in the way, that I can foresee," he pursued—"and it may arise from our mutual enemy, the duchess. You recollect she threatened to forbid the union. On what pretence can she do so?"

"Alas!" exclaimed Abigail, turning pale, and sinking into a chair—"I ought to have told you this before."

"Told me what?" exclaimed Harley. "You alarm me. The mischief is not irreparable?"

"I know not," she answered, in a desponding tone; "but you shall judge. When I was introduced by the duchess into the queen's establishment, she required from me a written obligation to consider her in the light of a parent—my own mother, as you know, being dead—together with a full assent to her bestowal of my hand in marriage."

"And you signed such a paper?" cried Harley, in dismay.

"I did," she replied.

"Imprudent!" he exclaimed, striking his forehead. "Then the duchess is indeed mistress of your destiny, and our last and fairest scheme is crushed in the bud."

"Oh, do not say so!" she cried. "I knew not what I was about. The duchess will not enforce fulfilment of the promise,—and if she does, I am not bound by it."

"Be not deceived," replied Harley; "the duchess *will* exact compliance from you; and though you certainly are not bound by the engagement, I know the queen too well not to be sure that she will respect it. If you had told me this before, it might have been guarded against."

"I feel I have been to blame," said Abigail, despairingly. "But it is not too late to remedy the mistake now?"

"I fear it is," rejoined Harley; "nevertheless, the attempt shall be made. The duchess is evidently reserving this blow to the last, and if it can be warded off, nothing more is to be apprehended."

"Accomplish that," cried Abigail, earnestly, "and I swear to you that no efforts shall be wanting on my part to help you to the highest point of your ambition."

"I will do my best," replied Harley, "but unless the document could be abstracted—or—ha!—a plan occurs to me——"

"What is it?" she asked.

"Nay, this is my secret," he replied. "Not a word on the subject to the queen or Masham. Trust me, we will be prepared to meet the danger when it comes."

So saying, he reconducted her to the ball-room, and consigned her to her lover.

A moment after this, as Harley was making his way towards the queen, he perceived the duchess quitting the presence with looks which, in spite of the mask put upon them, plainly bespoke the receipt of disagreeable intelligence.

Satisfied that the queen had made good her words, Harley determined to watch his opponent's movements, and finding that in place of returning to the duke and the brilliant circle around him, she shaped her course toward the green cabinet, as if for the purpose of seeking a moment's repose, he followed her, but at such a distance as not to attract her attention, and, stationing himself near the door, waited to see what would ensue.

He was not long kept in suspense. An usher passed him, and presently returned, accompanied by the Marquis de Guiscard. Seeing this, Harley moved away until the marquis had entered the cabinet. He then stepped forward, and approaching the door, which was left ajar, leaned against the side in such a posture that he could hear what passed in the room, while, to the lookers-on, he appeared solely occupied by the gay scene before him.

The first words that reached his ears were uttered rapidly, and in the voice of the duchess.

"I know you are willing to take a short cut to fortune, marquis," she said, "and I will point it out to you. Notwithstanding the opposition from various quarters—notwithstanding the refusal of the girl herself—notwithstanding the queen's consent within this moment accorded to Masham for an union with her,—you shall still wed Abigail Hill."

"I would hazard everything, as your grace knows, to carry the point," replied the marquis; "but I have, for some time, abandoned it as hopeless; and I see not how my chance is improved by what your grace now tells me."

"Hear me, marquis," rejoined the duchess. "When Abigail entered the queen's service, she resigned the absolute disposal of her hand to me, and subscribed a document to that effect, which I now hold. She stands, therefore, in the position of my ward, and I can bestow her upon whomsoever I please. I offer her to you."

"And I need not say with what eagerness I accept the offer," replied Guiscard. "When does your grace propose to assert your authority?"

"Not till the day of her intended union with Masham," she replied.

"But a secret marriage may take place, of which your grace may be kept in ignorance," said the marquis.

"I am not afraid of that," replied the duchess, significantly. "Will you place yourself in my hands?"

"Entirely," replied the marquis.

"Enough," she rejoined. "I shall now return to the ball-room. Nay, do not attend me, for I would not have us seen together."

So saying, she quitted the cabinet, and just as Guiscard was about to follow her, he was surprised by the sudden entrance of Harley.

"A word with you, marquis," said the latter.

"As many as you please, Mr. Harley," replied Guiscard, bowing.

"To come to the point at once," rejoined Harley, "I have overheard all that has just passed between you and the duchess."

"Then you will have learnt that I can still flatter myself with the hope of becoming your connexion by marriage," said Guiscard with unshaken effrontery.

"A little cool reflection must convince you of the utter impossibility of the scheme being accomplished," said Harley. "Besides, the duchess has offered you no reward——"

"Pardon me, Mr. Harley," interrupted Guiscard, "she has offered me the highest reward in promising me Abigail. I defy you to outbid her. But I am a reasonable man, and always willing to be convinced. What do you offer?"

"Freedom from arrest," replied the other. "I have nothing to do, on leaving this chamber, but to go to the Duke of Marlborough, and inform him that you engaged two of your servants to waylay a serjeant whom he had entrusted with important despatches—I have nothing, I say, but to disclose this—and prove it, as I can do —and you will see that we are not likely to be embarrassed by your presence at the wedding."

"The charge is false!" cried Guiscard, turning very pale.

"Nay, marquis," replied Harley, "it is useless to brave it out with me. I can produce the men at once. But I would rather hush up the affair than reveal it."

"What do you require, sir?" demanded Guiscard.

"Ay, now you are indeed becoming reasonable. I would have you keep on terms with the duchess—acquiesce entirely in her scheme—and when all is arranged, take your final instructions from me. Do this, and you shall not find me ungrateful."

"I shall, indeed, be happy to serve you, if possible, Mr. Harley," said Guiscard.

"We understand each other, marquis," replied the other, drily. "When I purchased the stolen letters from you, you read me a lesson which I shall not speedily forget."

"Ay, and poor Greg's mouth has been stopped by a halter, or I might read you another," muttered Guiscard. "You must undertake to ensure me against the duchess's enmity, Mr. Harley," he added, aloud.

"So far as I am able—certainly," he replied. "But I can more confidently assure you of Abigail's gratitude, and you will find that more than counterbalance her grace's hostility. No further double-dealing, marquis!"

"Nay, I do not merit the reproach, Mr. Harley," said Guiscard. "You yourself make me a traitor now."

"Why, faith, that's true," returned Harley, "and as it is clearly your interest to be faithful to me, I think I may venture to trust you."

So saying he quitted the cabinet.

CHAPTER IX.

IN WHAT WAY MRS. PLUMPTON AND MRS. TIPPING CONDUCTED THEMSELVES DURING THE SERJEANT'S ABSENCE.

ONE day, about a week after the serjeant's departure, Proddy took it into his head to call on Bimbelot, when, to his surprise, his appeal to the knocker was answered by a valet with whom he had no acquaintance, who informed him that his friend was within, but very unwell, and unable to attend to his duties. Proddy, expressing much concern at this intelligence, and a strong desire to see him, was shown into a small room near the kitchen, where he found Bimbelot looking very pale indeed, with his left arm in a sling, while beside him sat Sauvageon, whose head was bound up as if he had received a wound in that region. Both seemed considerably surprised and disturbed at the sight of the coachman.

"Heyday!" exclaimed Proddy, staring at them—"what's the matter? Been fighting another duel, eh?"

"Non, non, mon cher cocher," replied Bimbelot, "we have been wounded as you see by de Mohogs. Ah! terrible fellows dem Mohogs."

"So I've heard," replied Proddy; "but I've always been fortunate enough to escape 'em. Sorry to see you in such a state. When did it occur?"

"Ven!" exclaimed Bimbelot, in some confusion. "Oh, two or tree night ago."

"Well, it's strange I never heard of it," rejoined Proddy; "but they seem to have mauled you desperately. I hope you gave 'em as good as they brought. How many on 'em was there?"

"How many!" repeated Bimbelot. "Let me see—I can't exactly tell. How many should you say, mon caporal?"

"Ventrebleu! I didn't count 'em," replied Sauvageon. "Maybe two dozen."

"Two dozen!" exclaimed Proddy—"that was fearful odds. No wonder you came off so badly. Why, the serjeant found it difficult to——" But remembering his promise, he suddenly checked himself.

"Que dites vous, monsieur?" cried Bimbelot. "Vat vas you goin' to say?"

"I was goin' to say that I've just received a letter from the serjeant, from the Hague," replied Proddy.

"Ah, mon Dieu!" exclaimed Bimbelot. "Is it possible he arrive there safely, after his wounds?"

"Wounds!" echoed Proddy, staring, "who told you he was wounded?"

"Why, you yourself, to be sure," rejoined Bimbelot, eager to repair his inadvertence. "You said just now that he was badly wounded—didn't he, corporal?"

Sauvageon growled an assent.

"Well, if I did, the word slipped out unawares," replied Proddy, reflecting. "It's true he got hurt by some cowardly ruffians on his way to the wherry. But it seems he thinks nothing of the accident, for he makes no allusion to it. However, his assailants wont so easily forget *him*. He said he had given 'em somethin' to remember him by—ha! ha!"

"Indeed!" exclaimed Bimbelot, gnashing his teeth, and glancing at Sauvageon. "Sarpedieu! quand je suis retabli je creverai la tête de ce coquin."

"What's that you say, Bamby?" noticing the angry expression of the other's glance. "It's not polite to talk French in company of a gem'man as doesn't understand it."

"Pardon, mon cher cocher! pardon!" cried Bimbelot. "Je veux dire—vat I mean to say is dis, dat dose who encounter de serjeant, vont forget him in a hurry—ha! ha!"

"No, I'll be bound they wont," replied Proddy, laughing.

"Nor forgive him eider," muttered Sauvageon. "Dey'll pay off deir old debts one of dese days."

"Eh!" what's that, Savagejohn?" cried Proddy.

"Oh! noting—noting"—replied the corporal, "but you're always blowing the sergent's trumpet."

"And he deserves to have it blown," replied Proddy, proudly, "and pretty loudly too."

"I say, Proddy," observed Bimbelot, "did de sergent suspect who attack him, eh?"

"He more than suspected," replied Proddy, significantly. "It was certainty with him. He knew 'em perfectly."

"Ah, diable!" exclaimed Bimbelot. "And he told you deir names—eh?"

"No," replied Proddy, "he kept that to himself, because, as he said, he wished to settle accounts with 'em himself, when he came back!"

Bimbelot and Sauvageon exchanged glances of apprehension, while Proddy muttered—

"Curse the rascals! I believe they're the men, and it'll do 'em good to frighten 'em a bit."

"Et comment se trouvent les dames—how do Mrs. Plumpton and Mrs. Tipping bear de sergent's absence?" asked Bimbelot, anxious to change the subject.

"Oh, pretty middlin',—as well as can be expected, poor things!" replied Proddy. "It's a sad loss."

"A sad loss, indeed,—poor tings!" echoed Bimbelot, secretly grinning. "Pray make our compliment, and say de corporal and I will do ourselves de honour to call and offer dem some consolation."

"I'll deliver your message, certainly," replied Proddy, "but I don't think it'll be of much use. You'd better call some Wednesday evening, for then I shall be there."

"Dat will be an additional inducement," said Bimbelot; "we'll come next Wednesday, if noting occurs to prevent us. But you're not running away?"

"Yes I am," replied Proddy, rising; "good day, mounseers." And with sundry bows on both sides, he took his departure.

"Harkee, corporal," said Bimbelot, in his own tongue, as soon the coachman was gone, "it would be a fair revenge on this cursed Scales to rob him of his mistresses while he's away? How say you? Shall we try it?"

"With all my heart," replied Sauvageon. "Perhaps we may succeed better this way than the other."

"Oh! I've no fear of failure," replied Bimbelot. "I flatter myself I possess as many attractions in a lady's eyes as an old battered soldier. I will lay siege to Mrs. Tipping—you to Mrs. Plumpton."

"Agreed!" rejoined Sauvageon.

Punctual to their promise, the two Frenchmen repaired, on the appointed Wednesday evening, to Marlborough House. Bimbelot was dressed to the point in a velvet coat, satin vest, and silken hose; with a sword by his side, large lace ruffles on his wrists, and a well-powdered flowing peruke on his head. His master's toilette-table had been visited for his perfumes, and his left arm was supported by a silken sash. Thus decked out, he looked, in his own opinion, excessively handsome and interesting—in fact irresistible.

The corporal had brushed himself up a little,—powdered his wig, and put a new tie to his enormous pig-tail; but his personal appearance, never very attractive, was by no means improved by a thick bandage across the brow.

Arrived at their destination, they proceeded at once to the kitchen, where they found most of the household assembled, including Mr. Brumby, the duke's coachman, whom they had not chanced to meet on any former occasion. Mr. Fishwick, who was recruiting himself with a tankard of ale, having been somewhat busily engaged in preparing for a grand banquet on the following day, gave them a hearty welcome; and the ladies professed themselves enchanted to see them. These greetings were scarcely over when Proddy made his appearance.

In pursuance of his scheme, Bimbelot devoted himself to Mrs. Tipping, paid her the most extravagant compliments, and affected to be desperately in love with her; while she, who it must be confessed, was somewhat of a coquette, gave him sufficient encouragement.

The corporal's progress was not equally rapid with Mrs. Plumpton. Whether he was not gifted with the same powers of pleasing as his friend, or whether Mrs. Plumpton was more constant to the sergeant than Mrs. Tipping, it boots not to inquire; but his compliments all fell to the ground, and his fine speeches were wasted on inattentive ears.

A quiet observer of what was going forward, Proddy pretended to be engaged in conversation with his brother whip, Mr. Brumby, but he kept his eyes and ears open to the others, and after some time, seeing encouragement given to Bimbelot by Mrs. Tipping, he thought it his duty to interfere.

"Well, I'm sure, Mrs. Tipping," he cried, "you seem vastly pleased with Mounseer Bamby's attentions. I wonder what the serjeant would say if he was here. It's perhaps as well that he isn't."

"I don't see what the serjeant could complain of, Mr. Proddy," replied Mrs. Tipping, pertly. "I'm not aware that I'm under an obligation not to talk to any one else in his absence."

"And even if you were, ma mignonne, it's of no consequence," replied Bimbelot. "A soldier never expects fidelity; and if he does—ha! ha! But I don't see what de serjeant can do wid two wives. Is it settled vich is to be Mrs. Scale?"

"Did he propose to you, Plumpton?" asked Mrs. Tipping.

"I sha'n't answer the question," replied the other. "Did he propose to *you*, Tipping?"

"And I sha'n't answer the question neither," she rejoined.

"It's plain he's trifling wid de feelings of bote," said Bimbelot.

"That's false!" cried Proddy. "The serjeant is incapable of trifling with anything, or anybody. He's always in earnest. He means to marry——"

"Which of 'em, Proddy," interrupted Brumby, with a laugh, "for I'll be whipped if I can tell. And what is more, I don't think either of the women can."

"It's too bad of the serjeant," cried Mr. Timperley, joining in the laugh. "He don't give other people a chance."

"Not the slightest," cried the portly Mr. Parker, the butler. "I agree with you, Timperley, it's too bad."

"C'est affreux—intolerable!" cried Bimbelot, with an impassioned look at Mrs. Tipping. "I hope he'll be kill'd in de wars," he added, in an under tone.

"No whisperin', Bamby!" cried Proddy, marching up to him. "No squeezin' of hands! I don't allow it."

"And pray, Monseer Proddy, who gave you de right to interfere?" inquired Bimbelot, angrily.

"The serjeant!" replied the coachman, boldly. "These ladies were committed to me by him, and I'll take care of 'em as long as I can."

"Very much obliged to you, Mr. Proddy," rejoined Mrs. Tipping; "but we fancy we can take care of ourselves."

"It's only fancy, then, to judge from what I see goin' forward," observed the coachman.

"Well, I wish the serjeant was back again, with all my heart," cried Fishwick; "it did one good to hear his adventures."

"Ay, I was never tired of hearin' him tell how he beat the mounseers," said Proddy, with a glance at the two Frenchmen. "Did you ever hear him relate how he mounted the half-moon of Ypres, at the siege of Menin?"

"Never," replied Fishwick; "and if you can recollect it, let's have it."

Thus exhorted, Proddy went to the fire-place, and taking down the spit, tied the two corners of his handkerchief to its point, so as to produce something like a resemblance to a flag. This done, he snatched up a ladle, and to the infinite diversion of the Frenchmen, and indeed of the company generally, planted himself before the cook, and commenced his narration.

"Well," he said, "you must know that Menin is one of the strongest forts in Flanders, and esteemed the masterpiece of the renowned Marshal Vauban."

"Marshal Vauban is de first engineer in de world," cried Sauvageon.

"Be that as it may, he couldn't build a fort as could hold out against the Duke of Marlborough," pursued Proddy. "But that's neither here nor there. To proceed: besides being strongly built and well garrisoned, the fort of Menin was rendered difficult of approach, owing to the inundations of the river Lys. Howsomever the duke takes up a position before it, and after the place has been invested for nearly a month, the works bein' sufficiently advanced to allow of an attack, the signal is given by the blowing up of two mines, which have been laid near the angles of a bastion called the half-moon of Ypres. Amid the silence followin' this tremendous clatter, the first detachment of the besiegers, amongst whom was our serjeant, dashes up to the palisades that protected a covered way communicatin' with the fortress, and throwin' a quantity of grenades into it, forces their way in, amidst the confusion occasioned by the explosion. You may guess the strife and carnage that ensues, for every inch o' ground is fiercely contested. Meanwhile, our serjeant works his way on, through a heavy fire, with his comrades dropping around him at every step, over courtine and counterscarp, till he stands in the very face of the half-moon itself. A scalin'-ladder is planted, but so fierce is the fire, that no one will mount, till our serjeant, steppin' before his officer, runs up the ladder, and cuttin' down two of the enemy, and snatchin' up a flag fixed on the bastion, waves it over his head, and shouts at the top of his voice, ' Come on, my lads !' "

As Proddy said this, he sprang upon a small stool, and planting his right foot on a chair near it, raised the mimic flag over his head, and pointing with his ladle towards the imaginary half-moon of his narration, roared out again with stentorian lungs—" Come on, my lads, I say ! We'll give these mounseers another drubbin' Come on ! Victory and Marlborough !"

At the same time, he glared terribly at Bimbelot, who turned aside his head, affecting to be greatly alarmed, though he was convulsed with laughter, while Sauvageon covered his face with his hat to hide his merriment. Fishwick plucked off his cap, and waving it in the air, cheered loudly ; whilst acclamations resounded from the rest of the company.

So delighted was Proddy with the effect he had produced, that he remained for nearly five minutes in the same attitude, continually shouting—" Come on, my lads !—come on !"

" So like the dear serjeant !" exclaimed Mrs. Plumpton, gazing at him in rapt admiration.

" I don't know whether I'm most frightened or delighted," said Mrs. Tipping. "The dear serjeant oughtn't to risk his precious life in this way."

" Well, what happened next, brother Proddy ?" asked Brumby, who was leaning over the back of a chair behind the coachman, and began to be somewhat tired of the constant repetition of the same cries.

" Ay, there's the unfortinatest part of it," replied Proddy ; " just as the words was out of our serjeant's mouth, a bullet comes and hits him slap on the shoulder, and knocks him clean off the half-moon."

In describing which disastrous occurrence, the coachman unluckily lost his own equilibrium. Tumbling backwards, he caught hold of Brumby and Mrs. Tipping, and dragged them both to the floor with him.

The rest of the party flew to their assistance, and on being helped up again, it was found that no damage had been sustained by any one.

By no means discouraged by the accident, Proddy recounted some more of the serjeant's achievements, and seemed to have a malicious pleasure in dwelling upon his frequent threshings of the French.

"I dare say he'll have plenty to tell us when he comes back," said Fishwick. "I anticipate another glorious campaign for the duke."

"It is next to impossible he can go beyond his former successes," said Proddy.

"Fortune may change," observed Sauvageon, "and de duke himself may experience a reverse."

"I don't think it very likely," observed Brumby; "it has been frequently predicted, but has never yet come to pass."

"Nor ever will," said Parker.

Soon after this, supper was served in the servants' hall, and the two Frenchmen required little pressing to induce them to sit down to it. Bimbelot contrived to obtain a place near Mrs. Tipping, and Proddy remarked that he seemed to make further progress in her good graces. Vexation took away his appetite, and he would neither eat nor drink, notwithstanding the jests passed upon him by Fishwick and Brumby.

At length, the hour of departure came. The coachman bade a sullen adieu to his female friends; but remarking that Bimbelot did not come forth with Sauvageon, he went back to see what he was about, and as he traversed the passage leading to the kitchen, he observed the French valet creeping into a cupboard.

Without saying a word, he walked quickly up to the spot, locked the door, took out the key, put it into his pocket, and, chuckling to himself at the trick he was playing, quitted the house.

CHAPTER X.

IN WHICH THE DAY FOR THE MARRIAGE IS FIXED BY THE QUEEN.

THE queen and her consort were alone together in the library of Saint James's palace, when an usher announced that the Duke of Marlborough and the lord treasurer requested an audience.

"Admit them," said Anne. "Some new demand, I suppose," she remarked to the prince.

"Nay, I see not that," he replied. "Most likely they come to tell us that the Chevalier de Saint-George has landed in Scotland. Or he may be captured."

"Heaven forbid!" ejaculated the queen, hastily.

As the exclamation was uttered, Marlborough and Godolphin entered the presence.

"We bring your majesty good tidings," said the duke: "the invasion is at an end."

"Then it is true he is taken?" cried Anne.

"The pretender?—no," replied Marlborough.

"He is not slain?" asked the queen.

"No, he lives to trouble your majesty further," rejoined the duke.

"Heaven be praised!" she ejaculated.

"But what has happened, your grace—what has happened?" interposed Prince George.

"Your highness is well aware," replied Marlborough, "that after the French expedition had encountered Admiral Byng in the Frith of Forth, its commander changed his intentions, and made for Inverness, in expectation that an insurrection would be made in the pretender's favour."

"I am aware of it," said the prince; "and I am also aware that it is mainly, if not entirely, owing to the excellent precautionary measures taken by your grace, that the insurrection has been crushed."

"Your highness does me much honour," rejoined Marlborough, bowing. "But to the point. The very elements seem to have warred in our favour. A violent storm prevented the expedition from landing, and, driven out to sea, they have at last succeeded, after various disasters and severe losses, in getting back to Dunkirk."

"Then we are as much indebted to the weather as to our own exertions for deliverance," said the queen.

"Bloodshed unquestionably has been prevented," replied the duke. "Yet it may be doubted whether the pretender would not have received a severer lesson if he had landed his forces. He might not have lived to repeat the attempt. However, all present danger is at an end, and the lord treasurer and myself are come to offer your majesty our congratulations on the fortunate issue of an affair which seemed fraught with so much perplexity and peril."

"I thank you heartily, my lords," replied Anne.

"Loyal addresses will be presented to your majesty on the occasion from both houses of parliament," said Godolphin, "in which it is to be hoped that our conduct will be approved, (if it shall be found, on consideration, to merit approval,) and that of our enemies, and the enemies of the country, duly censured."

"No doubt of it, my lord," replied Prince George—"no doubt of it. Full testimony will be borne to your deserts, who have managed her majesty's treasure so admirably, and to those of the duke, who has commanded her armies with such distinguished glory."

"One thing I trust her majesty will deign to state in her reply," said Marlborough; "that she will henceforth place her dependence only upon those who have given such repeated proofs of their zeal for the security of her throne, and for the maintenance of the Protestant succession."

"I shall remember what you say, my lord," replied Anne, coldly.

"Your majesty will also remember," said Godolphin, "and it would be well to insist upon it, that all that is dear to your people, and has been secured by your government, would be irretrievably lost if the designs of the Popish pretender should ever take effect."

"Enough, my lord," cried Anne, angrily—"I have been schooled sufficiently."

"All danger of the invasion being over," said Marlborough, "I must crave your majesty's permission to join your forces in Flanders. Prince Eugene is impatiently awaiting me at the Hague, to mature preparations for the ensuing campaign."

"You have it," replied the queen. "And when do you propose to set forth?"

"To-morrow," returned the duke, "unless your majesty has need of me further."

"I shall grieve to lose your grace," said Anne. "But I know that you go to win fresh honours for me, and new laurels for yourself."

"I go with somewhat less spirit than heretofore, gracious madam," rejoined the duke, "because I know that I leave an insidious enemy at work to counteract all my efforts for the advancement of your welfare. I implore you, as you value the security of your government, and the prosperity of your kingdom, to dismiss Abigail Hill from your service. She is a mere tool in the hands of Harley, and as long as she is near you, to pour the poison of that serpent into your ear, it will be in vain to hope for your confidence. All our best efforts will be neutralized. By the zeal and devotion I have ever shown your majesty—and am prepared to show you to the last—I conjure you to listen to me."

"Do not trouble yourself about my domestic arrangements, my lord," replied the queen; "Abigail is merely my waiting woman."

"Ostensibly she is," replied the duke, "but you yourself, gracious madam, are scarcely aware of the influence she exercises over you. It is apparent to the whole court—nay, to foreign courts—and does you and your ministry incalculable mischief."

"It is but a variation of the old cry, your grace," said Anne. "A short while ago, it was said I was governed by the Duchess of Marlborough; now they affirm I am governed by Abigail Hill."

"I trust your majesty will not degrade the duchess by instituting a comparison between her and Abigail," replied the duke, proudly.

"There is no comparison between them, my lord," said Anne.

"A faithful adviser is necessary to a sovereign," rejoined Godolphin; "and it has ever been said that your majesty was singularly fortunate in having such a confidante as the duchess."

"If loyalty and devotion are titles to the office, her grace possesses the requisites in an eminent degree," added the duke.

"She has more than those," said Godolphin, firmly; "she has judgment such as no other woman in the kingdom possesses."

"And arrogance to match it," replied the queen, bitterly.

"I have long felt that her grace has incurred your majesty's displeasure," said the duke, "and I feared the occasion of it. Haughty and imperious she is, I grant. But her whole heart is yours."

"I do not dispute it, my lord," replied Anne, softened. "In spite of her violence of manner, I do believe the duchess loves me."

"She is devoted to you," rejoined the duke; "and my parting entreaty of your majesty is to beseech you to confide in her."

And bending the knee, he pressed the queen's hand to his lips.

"Farewell, my lord," said Anne. "Every good wish attend you."

And with obeisances to the prince, the duke and the treasurer withdrew.

"Your majesty is firm in your adherence to Abigail, I perceive," said the prince, taking a pinch of snuff.

"They take the very means to bind me more strongly to her," replied the queen.

"I am glad of it," observed the prince. "Masham was with me this morning, and implored me to intercede with you to consent to his marriage."

"I am wearied to death with these repeated solicitations," said Anne, good-humouredly, "and must put an end to them in some ·ray or other. Send for Abigail."

"Instantly!" replied the prince, hurrying off to the usher, and muttering as he went, "We must not lose the lucky moment."

A few minutes afterwards, the favourite entered the presence.

"The Duke of Marlborough and the lord treasurer have just been here, Abigail, and have demanded your dismissal," said the queen.

"Indeed, madam," replied the other, trembling. "Am I to understand then——"

"You are to understand that you are to be united to Mr. Masham to-morrow," replied Anne.

"Oh, madam," replied Abigail, throwing herself at the queen's feet. "Pardon me, if I do not thank you properly. My heart would speak if it could."

"Nay, I require no thanks," replied Anne. "I am happy in making you happy, and my conduct will show your enemies that I am not to be diverted from loving and befriending you by menaces or entreaties. Still, as I wish to avoid any scene on the occasion, the marriage shall take place privately, in the evening, in the rooms of my physician, Dr. Arbuthnot."

"Admirably resolved!" cried the prince.

"Oh! I hope the duchess will not hear of it," cried Abigail.

"She is not likely to do so," rejoined the queen. "And now I will no longer detain you. There are times when one desires to be alone—to indulge one's feelings unrestrained. Take this pocket-book. It contains two thousand pounds—your wedding portion."

"Your majesty overwhelms me with kindness!" cried Abigail, in a voice of heart-felt emotion.

"I will take care to apprise Masham of the good fortune in store for him," said the prince; "and I offer your majesty thanks in his name for your goodness. You have made us all very happy," he added, brushing away a tear, "very—very happy."

Abigail attempted to speak, but words failed her; and with a look of the deepest devotion and gratitude at the queen, she retired.

CHAPTER XI.

OF THE MANNER IN WHICH THE DUKE OF MARLBOROUGH SET OUT FOR FLANDERS.

THE Duke of Marlborough adhered to his resolution of departing on the following day. A barge was ordered to be in waiting at White-hall Stairs to convey him on board the vessel he was to sail in, which was moored off Queenhithe. The duke wished to embark privately, but the duchess overruled his desire, and the state carriage was commanded to be in readiness at noon.

Rumours having got abroad that the duke was about to set out for Flanders, on that day, long before the hour fixed for his departure, a vast crowd collected in front of Marlborough house. This was what the duchess had calculated upon, and she congratulated herself upon the success of her scheme, as she watched the momently-increasing throng from the windows of her superb abode.

A little before twelve, the duke requested the attendance of the duchess in his closet. It was to bid her farewell. He seemed deeply affected, and taking her hand, remained for some time silent. The duchess was less moved, but it required the exercise of all her fortitude to prevent her from bursting into tears.

"I go away with an aching heart," said the duke, at length; "for though all seems bright and prosperous at this moment, I discern a storm gathering afar off."

"I am depressed by the thoughts of losing you," replied the duchess, tenderly. "But I have no presentiments of ill."

"My beloved wife!" cried the duke, straining her to his breast. "Heaven knows what I suffer in these separations!"

"I suffer as much as your grace," replied the duchess. "But you are wedded to glory as well as to me, and when my comate calls you hence I do not repine."

"You are an heroic woman!" cried the duke, gazing at her with the deepest admiration. "Oh, Sarah! matchless in beauty as in judgment, Heaven has indeed been bountiful in vouchsafing me such a treasure. But if I look on you longer, I shall never be able to tear myself away. One word before we part. Be prudent with the queen. Do not irritate her further. She is inflexible in her adherence to Abigail."

"Before your grace returns, the minion will be dismissed," rejoined the duchess.

"I doubt it," said the duke, shaking his head.

"You know not the extent of my power," replied the duchess, with self-complacence. "Shall I tell your grace a secret? I have just learnt, from a confidential agent in the palace—the usher who attends the library—that the queen designs to marry her favourite to young Masham this evening."

"This evening!" exclaimed the duke.

"It is intended that the marriage shall take place privately in Dr. Arbuthnot's rooms in the palace," pursued the duchess. "Well, what does your grace say to it?"

"Say to it!" echoed the duke. "What should I say? It cannot be prevented."

"You think so? returned the duchess. "The first letter you receive from me will be to announce that this marriage—arranged by the queen—has been stopped."

"I advise you not to interfere," said Marlborough. "It is too petty a matter to meddle with."

"Small beginnings lead to great consequences," said the duchess. "I will pluck up the weed betimes."

Further remonstrance on the duke's part was interrupted by the entrance of Timperley, to say that the carriage was in readiness. Once more tenderly embracing the duchess, Marlborough took her hand, and led her down the great staircase. As the illustrious pair passed through the hall on their way to the carriage, they found it thronged with the various members of the household, who were drawn up to bid their beloved lord farewell. Amongst these was Proddy, who was transported almost out of his senses by a nod of recognition from the duke.

As Marlborough was seen to issue from the door, a tremendous shout rent the air, and, in spite of all the efforts of the porters at the gates, the court was instantly filled with a mass of persons eager to bid him adieu. Acknowledging their greetings with repeated bows, the duke stepped into the carriage after the duchess. It required all the management of Mr. Brumby, and of the postillion who was mounted on one of the leaders, to manœuvre the carriage out of the gates without injuring some of the throng; but this feat safely accomplished, renewed cheers and huzzas burst from the crowd outside, the whole of whom uncovered their heads, as if by a preconcerted signal, at the sight of the hero they had flocked to behold.

Scared by the shouts, a flight of rooks, which built in the trees near Marlborough House, sprang screaming into the air. They were instantly answered by another flock from the royal gardens, who attacked them in mid-air, and drove them back again to their roosts—a circumstance that did not pass unnoticed by some of the more curious observers.

Meantime, hundreds of faces, in succession, appeared at the windows of the carriage, and benedictions were heaped upon the duke's head. Hats were waved aloft, tossed on the points of sticks, or hurled in the air.

That no part of the triumph might be lost upon the inmates of the palace, the duchess had privately instructed Brumby to drive up Saint James's-street—an arrangement which would have been opposed by the duke, if he had been aware of it; but he was not so, till too late. So on the carriage went in that direction at a foot's pace, for quicker progress was out of the question.

On arriving in front of the palace, the crowd was so dense that it was found impossible to move at all. To the cries of the postillion and Brumby to "make way," the crowd only answered by shouts and vociferations, and pressed closer and closer round the carriage. At last, seeing the difficulty in which the duke was placed, those nearest him exclaimed, "Take out the horses, and we'll draw the carriage!"

The cry was answered by a thousand applauding voices—"Take out the horses! take out the horses!" resounded on every side.

The duke was so circumstanced that he could not refuse consent, and in an instant the wheelers were unfastened by Timperley and another servant, and the leaders driven off by the postillion. The pole of the carriage was then seized by some dozen eager hands, while another band attached a stout rope to the axletree, and harnessed themselves to it.   Brumby still retained his seat on the box, and flourished his whip, though deprived of his reins, declaring "he had never driven such a team before."

The carriage was then put in motion amid the reiterated shouts and applauses of the spectators, hundreds of whom eagerly offered themselves as relays when the others should be tired.

The triumph of the duchess was complete.   As she glanced towards the palace, she fancied she discovered the queen at an upper window, attracted thither, no doubt, by the prodigious clamour of the multitude.

In this way, the carriage was borne up Saint James's-street and along Piccadilly, until it was finally brought to Whitehall-stairs, where, after bidding adieu to the duchess, amid acclamations which the roar of artillery could not drown, the duke entered his barge.

CHAPTER XII.

HOW THE MARRIAGE WAS FORBIDDEN BY THE DUCHESS, AND WHAT FOLLOWED THE INTERRUPTION.

AT seven o'clock on the same evening, a small but very illustrious party was collected together in Dr. Arbuthnot's rooms in the palace. It consisted of the queen and her consort, Masham, Abigail, Harley, and Doctor Francis Atterbury, dean of Carlisle.   Of this celebrated person, who afterwards became Bishop of Rochester, occasion may be found to speak more fully hereafter, as well as of his friend, the witty and learned Doctor Arbuthnot.

The object of the meeting, it need scarcely be stated, was the consummation of Masham's wishes, in regard to his union with Abigail, and Doctor Atterbury was just about to commence the ceremony, when, to the surprise and consternation of all present, except, perhaps, Harley, the door opened, and the Duchess of Marlborough, followed by Guiscard, entered the room.

"I am in time!" she cried, looking around with a smile of triumph.   "You thought to steal a march on me.   But you see I am acquainted with your movements."

"Who can have betrayed us to her?" muttered the queen.

"Why was I not invited to this marriage?" cried the duchess. "Surely I, Abigail's nearest female relation, should have been asked to it?"

"It was an omission, certainly, duchess," said the prince; "but her majesty fancied you would be completely engrossed by the duke's departure for Flanders."

"An evasion, prince!" cried the duchess, angrily.   "Her majesty did not desire me to be present."

"You are right, duchess," replied Anne, coldly; "and you have presumed too much upon my good nature in coming.   Remain or not, as you please, but the ceremony shall no longer be delayed. Proceed, sir," she added to Atterbury.

"Hold!" exclaimed the duchess. "This marriage cannot take place. I forbid it. I told your majesty before, to beware how you gave your consent."

"Your grace is neither Miss Hill's parent nor guardian?" said Atterbury.

"I stand in the place of both," replied the duchess; "and you shall hear the grounds on which I offer my interference. When Abigail Hill entered her majesty's service, she gave me absolute disposal of her hand. Let her gainsay it if she can."

Abigail was silent.

"Since she declines to answer, this document will speak for her," replied the duchess, handing a paper to the queen. "You will find I have not advanced an untruth."

"Why did you not tell me of this before, Abigail?" demanded the queen, somewhat sharply.

"She did not dare to do so," replied the duchess.

"I did not suppose the duchess would act upon it," said Abigail.

"You treat the matter too lightly," cried the queen, with severity. "You have given her full power over you, and must abide by your own act."

"Your majesty!" exclaimed Abigail.

"You must ask her consent to the match, ay—and obtain it, too, before it can take place," pursued the queen.

"I knew your majesty would decide rightly," said the duchess.

"Then it is at an end, indeed!" cried Abigail, "for your majesty well knows it is in vain to appeal to her."

"I cannot help you further," said Anne; "and if I had been aware of this instrument, I would not have allowed the matter to proceed so far."

"Spoken like yourself, madam," cried the duchess. "No one has a nicer sense of justice than your majesty."

"How comes her grace never to have mentioned this instrument before?" asked Prince George.

"I thought it sufficient to forbid the union," replied the duchess. "Abigail ought to have asked my consent."

"Your majesty having admitted the duchess's right to dispose of Abigail's hand under this document," said Harley, advancing, "will, I am sure, agree with me, that if she objects to Mr. Masham, she is bound to say whom she would propose as a husband for the lady."

"You are right, sir," said the queen. "She shall name some one, or the present match shall take place."

"I am willing to abide by your majesty's decision," said the duchess, "and think it influenced by the same high principles of justice as those which have distinguished your judgment throughout. I gave it as my opinion before, that Abigail could not do better than accept the Marquis de Guiscard. Since I am called upon to name some one, I assign her hand to him."

"This cannot be!" cried Masham, indignantly. "The marquis——"

"Peace!" interrupted Harley. "Your grace has made your

nomination. If it is agreed to—good! If not, Abigail is free to make her own choice?"

"Undoubtedly," replied the duchess.

"Hear me!" exclaimed Masham.

"Peace, sir!" cried Harley. "What says the Marquis de Guiscard, then? Is he inclined to accede to the duchess's proposition? Will he consent to unite himself to Miss Hill?"

"I must take time to consider of it," replied the marquis.

"Consider!" cried the duchess—"Consider!"

"He may well do so," rejoined Masham.

"The answer must be at once," said the queen.

"Then I decline the proposed honour, madam," returned Guiscard.

"How, marquis?" cried the duchess, furiously.

"After this declaration, Abigail is free," said Harley.

"Most assuredly," replied the queen.

"I protest against it," cried the duchess.

"Nay, duchess, the queen decides against you," cried Harley, in a tone of bitter irony; "and no one has a nicer sense of justice than her majesty."

"If I had been allowed to speak, I would have disposed of the matter at once," said Masham. "The marquis is married already. He was wedded only three days ago at the Fleet, to Angelica Hyde, the cast-off mistress of Mr. Henry Saint-John."

"I have been over-reached in this matter," cried the duchess, furiously. "It is all Mr. Harley's knavery. As to you, marquis, you shall bitterly rue your share in it."

"Ha! ha! ha!" roared Harley. "Her grace has over-reached herself, and she now visits her rage and disappointment on others. I pray your majesty, let the marriage proceed. The duchess will offer no further opposition to it."

"She will be revenged on you all!" cried the duchess, in extremity of passion.

"Hark'ee, duchess," whispered Harley. "I told you this marriage should precede your downfall, and so it will."

"You have beaten me on this point," rejoined the duchess, in the same tone; "but it will avail you nothing. I will never rest till I have driven you from the palace."

And she flounced out of the room without even making an obeisance to the queen.

The marriage ceremony then commenced. Prince George gave the bride away, and in a few minutes more Masham and Abigail were united.

"I can now claim your promise, cousin," said Harley, in a low tone, as he advanced to salute the bride.

"You can," she replied. "Look upon the duchess's overthrow as certain, and the treasurer's staff as already in your hand."

END OF THE SECOND BOOK.

Book the Third.

ROBERT HARLEY.

CHAPTER I.

GIVES A SLIGHT INSIGHT INTO THE PROGRESS OF HARLEY'S INTRIGUES FOR POWER.

Two years and upwards had elapsed, and Abigail's promise remained unfulfilled. The Whigs were still in power, and the Marlborough family paramount in influence. But neither delay nor defeat discouraged Harley. Resolved to hazard nothing by precipitation, he carefully strengthened himself so as to be sure of holding his place when he obtained it. His measures, at first obscure, and apparently devoid of purpose, began to grow defined and intelligible.

Confident of the support of the Tories, and of those in the Jacobite interest, he at last succeeded in winning over some of the opposite party, and among others, Earl Rivers, who became his confidential agent, and acquainted him with all the designs of his colleagues. By working upon his vanity and jealousy, he managed likewise to estrange the Duke of Somerset, and the queen was prevailed upon to aid in the scheme, by constantly inviting the duke to her private conferences, and flattering his inordinate self-esteem. The Duke of Shrewsbury was also gained over by similar arts, though he hesitated to commit himself by any step which should compromise him with his party.

While thus providing himself with supporters, Harley strove to undermine the stronghold of his opponents. Having long since, as has been seen, succeeded in rendering the Duchess of Marlborough obnoxious to the sovereign, and unpopular with the court, he now turned his weapons chiefly against the duke.

Three more campaigns, which, if not distinguished by victories as glorious as those of Blenheim and Ramilies, still were sufficiently brilliant, had been added to the roll of Marlborough's achievements. The first of these passed off without any remarkable action; but in the summer of 1708, the important battle of Oudenard was gained; and in the autumn of the succeeding year—namely, the 11th September, 1709—the fiercely contested and memorable victory of Malplaquet occurred. In the latter terrible conflict, the French, who, by the admission of both Marlborough and Eugene, performed almost prodigies of valour, lost nearly fourteen thousand men, while the triumph of the confederate armies was dearly purchased. Stigmatizing the battle as a wanton and injudicious carnage, Harley went so far as to insinuate that the duke had exposed his officers to certain destruction in order to profit by the sale of their commissions; and monstrous and improbable as the calumny appears, it nevertheless found some credence amongst those who had lost relatives and friends on that fatal field.

It must be admitted, also, that the duke's ruling passion, avarice, coupled with his wife's undisguised rapacity, favoured assertions like the present, and caused it at last to be generally believed that the war was prolonged rather for his own benefit than for the glory of the nation. There were many, however, who, though fully sensible of the duke's high deserts, and of the groundlessness and malice of such accusations as the above, allowed their desire for peace to outweigh every other consideration, and joined the cry, in the hope of obtaining the object of their wishes.

Marlborough, unintentionally, aided the designs of his enemy. Convinced that he had irrevocably lost the queen's favour, and anxious, while he had yet power, to fortify himself against further opposition, which he foresaw he should have to encounter, he applied to the chancellor, to ascertain whether a patent, appointing him captain-general of the forces for life, could not be obtained. To his surprise and mortification, the answer was, that the appointment would be irregular and unconstitutional; therefore, the grant could not be made; and though further inquiries were instituted through other channels, the replies were equally unfavourable.

Undeterred by these opinions, the duke determined to make a direct application to the queen; and with this view, immediately after the victory of Malplaquet, judging it a fitting season, he was unwise enough to employ the duchess on the mission. Prepared for the request by Harley, and glad of an opportunity of mortifying her former favourite, but present object of unmitigated dislike, Anne gave a decided refusal.

"I shall not remonstrate with your majesty upon your decision," said the duchess; "but since the duke's services are thus disregarded, I must announce to you his positive intention to retire at the close of the war."

"If your grace had said at the close of the present campaign, I should have understood you better," replied the queen, with bitter significance; "but if the duke only means to relinquish his command at the end of the war, I know not when his design may be put into execution."

"Your majesty does not mean to echo Mr. Harley's false and dishonourable cry, that the Duke of Marlborough intentionally protracts the war?" cried the duchess, with difficulty controlling her passion.

"I echo no cry but that of my people for peace," replied Anne. "They complain of the perpetual demand for fresh supplies, and I own that I sympathize with them."

"Well, then," cried the duchess, "you shall *have* peace. But I warn you it will be worse than war."

In spite of her resolution to the contrary, Anne was disturbed by the duchess's implied menace. Left to herself, she could not re-frain from tears ; and she murmured—" Ah ! my dear, lost husband, this is one of the occasions when I should have felt the benefit of your support and counsel."

Anne had now been a widow just a year. Her amiable consort, Prince George of Denmark, expired on the 23rd of October, 1708. Constant in attendance upon him during his illness, Anne made no display of her grief when his sufferings were ended, and might have been supposed by an indifferent or harsh observer to have felt little regret for his loss. But it was not so. She mourned him sincerely, though secretly ; and almost the only person acquainted with the extent of her affliction was Mrs. Masham, who was de-stined to be a witness to her emotion on the present occasion.

"In tears, gracious madam !" cried the confidante, who had approached unobserved. " I trust the duchess has offered you no new indignity ?"

"She has made a request of me, on behalf of the duke, which I have refused—peremptorily refused," replied Anne. " My grief, however, is not caused by her, but by thoughts of my dear lost husband."

"In that case, I can only sympathise with you, madam," replied Mrs. Masham. " I will not affect to lament the prince as deeply as your majesty ; but my sorrow is only second to your own."

"My dear husband had a great regard for you," rejoined the queen—" a great regard. His last recommendation to me was—' Keep the Mashams always near you. They will serve you faith-fully.'"

"And we will make good his highness's words," returned Mrs. Masham ; " but oh ! let us dwell no more on this distressing subject, gracious madam."

"It relieves my heart to open it to you," replied Anne. " It is one of the penalties of royalty to be obliged to sacrifice private feelings to public duties. Abigail," she continued, in a broken voice, "I am now alone. I have neither husband nor children. My brother is in arms against me—my house is desolate—and the crown I wear is a barren one. I dare not think upon the succession to the throne ; for others order it for me."

"Alas, madam !" exclaimed Mrs. Masham.

"Oh that my brother could enjoy his inheritance !" cried the queen, with a look of anguish.

"Let Mr. Harley once be at the head of affairs, madam," re-turned the other, " and I am sure your desires can be accom-plished."

"The season is at hand for his advancement," said Anne. " I have just read the duchess a lesson, and shall lose no opportunity now of mortifying and affronting her. When Marlborough returns, I shall give him clearly to understand that he can expect nothing further at my hands. But where is Mr. Harley ? I have not seen him this morning."

"He is without in the ante-chamber," replied Mrs. Masham " and only waits your leisure for an audience."

"He stands upon needless ceremony," replied the queen. "Bid him come in."

And the next moment, Harley being introduced, Anne informed him what had passed between herself and the duchess.

"I am glad your majesty has acted with such becoming spirit," replied Harley. "The duke will feel his refusal keenly, but I can furnish you with another plan of galling him yet more sensibly. By the death of the Earl of Essex, which has just occurred, two important military preferments have become vacant,—namely, the lieutenancy of the Tower, and a regiment. These appointments, I need not tell your majesty, are usually made by the commander-in-chief."

"And you would have me dispose of them," said the queen.

"Precisely," replied Harley ; "and if I might venture to recommend a fitting person for the lieutenancy, it would be Lord Rivers."

"Why, he's a Whig," exclaimed Anne.

"He is a friend of your majesty's friends," returned Harley, smiling.

"He shall have the place, then," said the queen.

"I have asked few favours for myself, gracious madam," interposed Mrs. Masham; "but I now venture to solicit the vacant regiment for my brother, Colonel Hill."

"It is his," replied the queen, graciously, "and I am happy in being able to oblige you."

Mrs. Masham was profuse in her thanks.

"This will be a bitter mortification to Marlborough," replied Harley, "and will accelerate his retirement. His grace is not what he was, even with the multitude, and your majesty will see the sorry welcome he will experience on his return. I have at last brought to bear a project which I have long conceived, for rousing the whole of the high-church party in our favour, The unconscious agent in my scheme is Doctor Henry Sacheverell, rector of Saint Saviour's, Southwark, a bigoted, but energetic divine, who, on the next fifth of November, will preach a sermon in Saint Paul's, which, like a trumpet sounded from a high place, will stir up the whole city. His text will be, the 'Perils from false brethren ;' and having read the discourse, I can speak confidently to its effect."

"I hope it may not prove prejudicial to your cause," said the queen, uneasily.

"Be not alarmed, madam," replied Harley. "But you shall hear the purport of the sermon, and judge for yourself of its tendency. Its first aim is, to show that the means used to bring about the Revolution were odious and unjustifiable, and to condemn the doctrine of resistance as inconsistent with the principles then laid down, and derogatory to the memory of his late majesty. The second is, that the licence granted by law to protestant dissenters is unreasonable, and that it is the duty of all superior pastors to anathematize those entitled to the benefit of toleration. The third, that the church of England is in a condition of great peril and adversity under the present administration, notwithstanding the vote recently passed to the contrary effect. The fourth and chief article is, that your majesty's administration, both in ecclesiastical and civil affairs, is tending to the destruction of the constitution; that there are many exalted members, both of church and state, who are false brethren, striving to undermine, weaken, and betray the establishment. Reprobated under the character of Volpone, the treasurer himself comes in for the doctor's severest censure. Such is the sum of the discourse, which concludes with the strongest exhortations to the true supporters of the church to stand forth in its defence. Your majesty will agree with me that it is not likely to fail at this juncture."

"It seems a hazardous measure," observed the queen; "but I have no doubt you have well considered it, and therefore I will not oppose you. It may lead to what I chiefly desire, though I dare breathe it only to yourself and Abigail—the restoration of the succession to my father's house."

"No doubt of it, madam," replied Harley, with as much confidence as if he had really believed what he avouched.

CHAPTER II.

HOW DOCTOR SACHEVERELL PREACHED HIS SERMON AT SAINT PAUL'S; AND HOW HE WAS IMPEACHED IN CONSEQUENCE.

ON the fifth of November, 1709, Doctor Sacheverell preached his celebrated sermon, as arranged by Harley, at Saint Paul's, before the lord mayor, Sir Samuel Garrard, and the aldermen, and its effect was quite as extraordinary as had been anticipated. Carried away by the vehemence and earnestness of the preacher, and only imperfectly comprehending the drift of the discourse, the lord mayor highly commended it, and requested that it might be printed. This was precisely what Sacheverell desired; he immediately took the astute citizen at his word, and not only printed the sermon, but dedicated it to him.

Upwards of forty thousand copies were sold in a few days, and it became the general subject of conversation and discussion throughout the city. A firebrand cast into a field of dry flax could not have caused a more sudden and far-spreading blaze than this inflammatory discourse. The cry was everywhere raised that the church was in danger, and that the ministers were its worst enemies. Meetings were convened in various quarters, at which denunciations were hurled against them, and Sacheverell was proclaimed the champion of the high church.

This popular tumult would have subsided as speedily as it rose, if it had not been kept alive and heightened by the arts of Harley and his adherents. Godolphin would have willingly passed the matter over with silent contempt; but this was not Harley's design; and though openly opposing the matter, he secretly contrived to push forward the impeachment of the doctor — well knowing, that the attempt to punish a clergyman was the surest way to confirm the report that the church was in danger.

So much noise, at length, was made about the libellous discourse, that it could not be disregarded, and, acting under the direction of the ministry, Mr. John Dolben, son of the late Archbishop of York, complained in the house of the sermon as factious and seditious; and calculated to promote rebellion; consequently, after some further speeches to the same purpose, nothing being advanced in the doctor's defence, a resolution was passed that the sermon was " a malicious, scandalous, and seditious libel, highly reflecting upon her majesty and her government, the late happy Revolution and the protestant succession, and tending to alienate the affections of her majesty's good subjects, and to create jealousies and divisions among them."

It was then ordered, that Sacheverell, and his publisher, Henry Clements, should attend at the bar of the house next day. The injunction was obeyed; and, accompanied by Dr. Lancaster, Rector of Saint Martin's-in-the-Fields, and a hundred of his brother clergy who had espoused his cause, Sacheverell appeared to answer to the charge, which he boldly confessed. It was therefore agreed that he should be impeached at the bar of the House of Lords, by Mr. Dolben.

Occasion was taken at the same time to pass a resolution in favour of a divine of exactly opposite tenets to the offender— namely, the Rev. Benjamin Hoadley, who, having strenuously justified the principles proceeded upon in the Revolution, was conceived to have merited the regard and recommendation of the house; and it was therefore resolved that an address should be presented to the queen entreating her to bestow some ecclesiastical dignity upon him. The address was afterwards presented by Mr. Secretary Boyle; but though her majesty stated, " she would take an opportunity of complying with their desire," the promise probably escaped her memory, for no further notice was taken of it.

On his impeachment, Sacheverell was taken into custody by the serjeant-at-arms, by whom he was delivered over to the usher of the black rod; but he was subsequently admitted to bail, after which a copy of the articles of accusation being delivered to him, he returned an answer denying most of the charges against him, and palliating and extenuating the remainder. The answer was sent by the lords to the commons, and referred by the latter to a committee.

After much deliberation, in which Harley's influence secretly operated, an address was laid before the queen, purporting " that the house could not patiently sit still and see the justice of the late happy Revolution reflected upon; their own decrees treated with contempt; the governors of the church aspersed; toleration exposed as wicked; and sedition insolently invading the pulpit: and therefore they were under the absolute necessity of bringing the offender to trial." To this address, the queen, acting under advice, gave her assent, and the trial was thereupon appointed to take place on the 27th of February thence ensuing, in Westminster Hall, which was ordered to be fitted up for the reception of the commons.

These proceedings increased the unpopularity of the ministers, while they caused Sacheverell to be universally regarded as a martyr. The anticipated trial, on which the fate of parties was known to hang, formed the entire subject of conversation at all clubs and coffee-houses. The fiercest disputes arose out of these discussions, occasioning frequent duels and nocturnal encounters; while high-church mobs paraded the streets, shouting forth the doctor's name, and singing songs in his praise, or uttering diatribes against his enemies.

CHAPTER III.

OF THE AFFRONT PUT UPON THE DUKE OF MARLBOROUGH BY THE QUEEN.

IN less than a week after Sacheverell had promulgated his seditious discourse, the Duke of Marlborough appeared at Saint James's, having been hastily summoned from Flanders by Godolphin, who informed him of the menacing aspect of affairs, and assured him that the only chance of safety rested in his presence. The duke's return, which had formerly been hailed by the loudest cheers and congratulations of the populace, was comparatively unnoticed, and instead of his own name and achievements forming the burthen of their shouts, he was greeted with cries of "Sacheverell and High Church!" The mob had set up a new idol in his absence.

His reception by the queen was cold and constrained, and though professing to be glad to see him, she made no allusion whatever to the recent victory of Malplaquet. The meeting was further embarrassed by the presence of Mrs. Masham.

After some conversation on indifferent matters, Marlborough adverted to the refusal of the appointment, and expressed his resolution of retiring, as soon as he could do so consistently.

"I am sorry your grace should misconstrue my refusal," said Anne; "there is no precedent for the grant you claim, and I should not be justified in acceding to your request. As regards your retirement, the grief I shall feel at being deprived of your services will be tempered by the enjoyment of a long stranger to my reign —peace."

"I understand your majesty," replied Marlborough, drily. "But even the certainty of misrepresentation shall not compel me to conclude a treaty of peace with Louis, unless upon terms honourable to yourself and advantageous to your subjects."

"What appears advantageous to your grace may not appear equally so to others," remarked Mrs. Masham.

"Possibly not to Mr. Harley and the friends of France," rejoined the duke, sarcastically. "But I will protect the rights of my country, and oppose and confound its enemies as long as I have the power of doing so."

"You are warm, my lord," said Anne—"needlessly warm."

"Not needlessly, gracious madam, when I find you influenced by pernicious advisers," replied Marlborough. "Oh, that I could exlercise the influence I once had over you? Oh, that you would listen to the counsels of your true friend, the duchess, who has your real interests at heart!"

"Her majesty has shaken off her bondage," cried Mrs. Masham.

"To put on another and a worse," rejoined the duke. "She knows not the position in which she stands—she knows not how her honour, her glory, her prosperity are sacrificed at the shrine of an unworthy favourite."

"No more of this, my lord," cried Anne, peremptorily. "I will not be troubled with these disputes."

"It is no dispute, gracious madam," replied the duke, proudly. "As a faithful and loyal servant of your majesty, and as one ready at all times to lay down his life in your defence, I am bound to represent to you the danger in which you are placed. But I *can* have no quarrel with Mrs. Masham."

"Mrs. Masham respects my feelings, my lord," replied the queen, angrily, "which is more than some of those do who profess so much devotion to me. But it is time these misunderstandings should cease. Can you not see that it is her perpetual interference and dictation that have rendered the duchess odious to me, and have led me to adopt a confidante of more gentle manners? Can you not see that I will not brook either her control or yours—that I will govern my people as I please,—and fix my affections where I please? No parliament can rob me of a friend; and if your grace should think fit to attempt Mrs. Masham's forcible removal, as you once threatened, you will find your efforts recoil on your own head."

"I have no wish to deprive your majesty of a friend, and certainly none to dictate to you," replied the duke. "But if it is proved to you—publicly proved—that your confidante has betrayed her trust, and been in constant correspondence with the avowed opponent of your majesty's ministers—to say nothing of foreign enemies—if your parliament and people require you to dismiss her, I presume you will not then hesitate?"

"It will be time enough to answer that question, my lord, when such a decision has been pronounced," said the queen. "I presume our conference is at an end?"

"Not quite, your majesty," said the duke. "I must trespass on your patience a moment longer. You are aware that two military appointments have to be made—the lieutenancy of the Tower, and a regiment."

"I am aware of it," replied the queen, with a glance at Mrs. Masham.

"Lord Rivers requested me to use my interest with your majesty to confer the lieutenancy upon him," pursued the duke; "but on my representing to him that my interest was infinitely less than his own, he entreated my permission to make the request of your majesty himself."

"Has your grace any objection to him?" asked the queen.

"None whatever," replied the duke; "but the person I would venture to recommend to the place is the Duke of Northumberland.

By giving it to him, your majesty will also be enabled to oblige the Earl of Hertford by the presentation of the Oxford regiment, which Northumberland will resign in his favour—an arrangement which is sure to be highly agreeable to the earl's father, the Duke of Somerset."

"I am sorry I cannot attend to your grace's recommendation," replied the queen. "I have already granted the lieutenancy to Lord Rivers."

"How, madam!" exclaimed Marlborough, starting. "Why, Lord Rivers only left me a few moments before I set out, and I made all haste to the palace."

"He has been here, nevertheless, and has received the appointment," rejoined the queen. "He said your grace had no objection to him."

"This is contrary to all etiquette!" cried the duke, unable to conceal his mortification. "I have never been consulted on the occasion! Your majesty will do well to recall your promise."

"Impossible, my lord," replied Anne. "But since your grace complains of violation of etiquette, I beg to inform you that I wish the vacant regiment to be conferred on Mrs. Masham's brother, Colonel Hill."

"Your majesty!" exclaimed the duke.

"Nay, I *will* have it so!" cried Anne, peremptorily.

"In a matter like the present, involving the consideration of very nice points, your majesty will forgive me if I do not at once assent," replied the duke. "Let me beseech you to reflect upon the prejudice which the appointment of so young an officer as Colonel Hill will occasion to the army, while others, who have served longer, and have higher claims, must necessarily be passed over. I myself shall be accused of partiality and injustice."

"I will take care you are not misjudged, my lord," returned Anne.

"It will be erecting a standard of disaffection, round which all malcontents will rally," pursued the duke.

"We will hope better things," said the queen.

"As a last appeal, gracious madam," cried the duke, kneeling, "I would remind you of the hardships I have recently undergone —of my long and active services. Do not—oh, do not force this ungracious and injurious order upon me. Though I myself might brook the indignity, yet to make it apparent to the whole world must be prejudicial to yourself as well as to me."

"Rise, my lord," said Anne, coldly. "I have made up my mind on the subject. You will do well to advise with your friends, and when you have consulted with them I shall be glad of an answer."

"You shall have it, madam,' replied the duke. And bowing stiffly, he quitted the presence.

CHAPTER IV.

IN WHAT GUISE THE SERJEANT RETURNED FROM THE WARS; AND HOW HE BROUGHT BACK A DUTCH WIFE.

THE constancy of Mrs. Plumpton and Mrs. Tipping was severely tried. The campaign of 1707 closed without the serjeant's return; so did that of the following year; and it seemed doubtful whether the winter of 1709 would see him back again. This, it must be confessed, was a long absence, and enough to exhaust the patience of the most enduring. During the greater part of the time, Scales corresponded regularly with his friends, and sent them graphic descriptions of the sieges of Lille, Tournay, and Mons, as well as of the battles of Oudenard and Malplaquet, at all of which he had been present.

Bimbelot and Sauvageon had been constant in their attendance upon the ladies, and though the corporal's suit could not be said to advance, the valet flattered himself that he had made a favourable impression upon the heart of the lady's maid. How far he might have succeeded, and whether he might have possessed himself of the hand of the too susceptible Mrs. Tipping, it is needless to inquire. Suffice it to say, that she was so well watched by Proddy, who guarded her like a dragon, that she had no opportunity of throwing herself away.

It may be remembered, that on the last occasion when Bimbelot was brought on the scene, he was locked up in a cupboard by the coachman, and it may be as well here to give the sequel of the adventure.

For some time the valet remained unconscious that he was a prisoner, not having heard Proddy's manœuvre; but at length, fancying all still, he tried to get out, and, to his dismay, found the means of egress barred against him. While in a state of great anxiety at his situation, he was somewhat relieved by the approach of footsteps, and presently distinguished the voice of Mrs. Tipping, who, in a low tone, inquired, " Are you there ?"

" Oui, ma chère, I'm here, and here I'm likely to remain, unless you let me out," he replied.

" Why, the key's gone !" cried Mrs. Tipping. " I can't open the door. What's to be done ?"

" Diable !" roared Bimbelot. " Je mourirai de faim—je serai suffoqué. Oh, mon Dieu ? Vat shall I do !—ha !"

And in turning about, he upset a large pile of china plates, which fell to the ground with a tremendous clatter.

Mrs. Tipping instantly took to her heels, while, alarmed by the noise, Fishwick, Brumby, Parker, and Timperley, who had retired to a small room adjoining the kitchen to smoke a pipe and regale themselves with a mug of ale previous to retiring to rest, immediately rushed into the passage.

" What the deuce is the matter?" cried Fishwick. " Somebody must be breaking into the house."

"The noise came from the china closet," said Brumby. "A cat must have got into it."

"More likely a rat," said Parker; "but whatever it is, we'll ferret it out. Holloa! the key's gone! I'm sure I saw it in the door to-night."

"This convinces me we've a housebreaker to deal with," said Timperley. "He has taken out the key, and locked himself in the closet."

"Maybe," said Brumby. "But let's break open the door—I'm sure I hear a noise."

"So do I," rejoined Parker.

At this instant there was another crash of china, followed by an imprecation in the French tongue.

"Run to the kitchen, Timperley; fetch the musket, and the pistols, and the sword, cried Fishwick." We'll exterminate the villain when we get at him. I've got a key which will unlock the door. Quick—quick!"

"Ce n'est pas un larron, mes amis—c'est moi—c'est Bimbelot!" cried the Frenchman. "Don't you know me?"

"Why, it sounds like Bamby's voice," cried Fishwick.

"Oui, oui, c'est Bimbelot!" replied the prisoner.

"Why, what the devil are you doing there, Bamby?" demanded the cook.

"I got lock up by accident," replied the valet. "Open de door, I beseesh of you."

At this reply there was a general roar of laughter from the group outside, which was not diminished when, the door being opened by Fishwick, the valet sneaked forth.

Without waiting to thank his deliverers, or to afford them any explanation of the cause of his captivity, Bimbelot took to his heels and hurried out of the house. Their surmises, which were not very far wide of the truth, were fully confirmed on the following day by Proddy.

It has been said that Scales wrote home frequently, but after the battle of Malplaquet, which he described with great particularity, nothing was heard from him, and as this despatch was evidently traced by the hand of a comrade, it was feared, though no mention was made of it, that the serjeant had been wounded.

"Well, I hold to my resolution," said Mrs. Tipping. "If he has lost a limb, I wont have him."

"I don't care what he has lost," said Mrs. Plumpton, "he will be all the same to me."

"I hope he'll come back safe and sound," said Proddy, "and soon, too. I'm sure he has been away long enough."

The campaign of 1709 was over, but yet no serjeant returned. Great was the consternation of the two ladies. Mrs. Tipping had a fit of hysterics, and Mrs. Plumpton fainted clean away. Both, however, were restored, not only to themselves, but to the highest possible state of glee, by a piece of intelligence brought them by Fishwick, who had ascertained from the very best authority,—

namely, the duke himself,—that the serjeant was on his way home, and might be hourly expected.

Shortly after this, Proddy made his appearance, wearing a mysterious expression of countenance, which was very tantalizing. He had received a letter from the serjeant, and the ladies entreated him to let them see it; but he shook his head, saying, "You'll know it all in time."

"Know what?" demanded Mrs. Tipping. "What *has* happened?"

"Something very dreadful," replied Proddy, evasively; "so prepare yourselves."

"Oh, good gracious! how you alarm one!" exclaimed Mrs. Tipping. "He hasn't had a leg shot off?"

"Worse than that," replied Proddy.

"Worse than that!" repeated Mrs. Tipping. "Impossible! Nothing can be worse. Speak—speak! or I shall go distracted."

"Why he has lost his right leg and his right arm, and I don't know whether his right eye aint a-missin', too," replied the coachman.

"Then he's no longer the man for me," replied Mrs. Tipping.

"I'm glad to have such an opportunity of proving my affection for him," said Mrs. Plumpton, brushing away a tear. "I shall like him just as well as ever—perhaps better."

"Well, upon my word, Plumpton, you're easily satisfied, I must say," observed Mrs. Tipping, scornfully. "I wish you joy of your bargain."

"Ah! but Mrs. Plumpton don't know all," remarked Proddy; "the worst's behind."

"What? is there anything more dreadful in store?" asked the housekeeper. "What is it?—what is it?"

"I was enjoined by the serjeant not to tell—but I can't help it," replied Proddy. "He's MARRIED!"

"Married!" screamed both ladies.

"Yes—married!" replied Proddy, "to a Dutch woman, and he's bringin' her home with him."

"Well, I hope he wont let me see her, or I'll tear her eyes out—that I will!" cried Mrs. Tipping. "Bless us! what's the matter with Plumpton? Why, if the poor fool isn't going to faint."

And her womanly feelings getting the better of her rivalry, she flew to the housekeeper, and tried to revive her by sprinkling water over her face.

"This is real love, or I know nothing about it," said Proddy, regarding Mrs. Plumpton, who had fallen into a chair, with much concern. "I wish I hadn't alarmed her so."

And without awaiting her recovery, he quitted the house.

On that same evening, Bimbelot called upon the ladies, and was enchanted by the news which he learnt from Mrs. Tipping.

"Ma foi!" he exclaimed, "here's a pretty conclusion to de sergent's gallant career. So he has lose a leg, and an arm, and an eye, and is marry to a Dush vrow—ha, ha! You say he is hourly expect. I sall call to-morrow evening, and see if he is return."

So the next evening he came, accompanied by Sauvageon, and found the two ladies and Fishwick in the kitchen; but as yet nothing had been heard of the serjeant, nor had even Proddy made his appearance. Mrs. Plumpton seemed very disconsolate, sighed dismally, and often applied her apron to her eyes; and though Mrs. Tipping endeavoured to look indifferent and scornful, it was evident she was quite the reverse of comfortable.

"I hope you'll revenge yourself on de perfidious sergent, ma chère," said Bimbelot to the latter: "let him see dat if he have got a Dush wife, you can mash him wid a French husband—ha, ha!"

"It would serve him right, indeed," replied the lady. "I'll see."

Sauvageon addressed a speech somewhat to the same purport to Mrs. Plumpton, but the only response he received was a melancholy shake of the head.

Just at this juncture, an odd sound, like the stumping of a wooden leg, was heard in the passage, approaching each instant towards the door.

"Sacre Dieu! vat's dat?" cried Bimbelot.

"It's the serjeant!" cried Mrs. Plumpton, starting up. "I'm sure it's the serjeant."

As she spoke, the door opened, and there stood Scales, but how miserably changed from his former self! His right arm was supported by a sling, and what appeared the stump of a hand was wrapped in a bandage. A wooden leg lent him support on one side, and a long crutch on the other. His visage was wan and woebegone, and his appearance so touched Mrs. Plumpton, that she would certainly have rushed up to him and thrown her arms about his neck, if she had not caught sight of a female figure close behind him.

After pausing for a moment in the doorway, and taking off his hat to his friends, Scales hobbled forward. He was followed by his partner, and a thrill of astonishment pervaded Mrs. Plumpton as she beheld more fully the object of his choice.

Never was such a creature seen, nor one so totally repugnant to the received notions of feminine attraction. Mrs. Scales was little more than half her husband's size; but what she wanted in height she made up in width and rotundity, and if she were a Dutch Venus, the Hollanders must admire the same breadth of outline as the Hottentots. Her expansive attractions were displayed in a flaming petticoat of scarlet cloth, over which she wore a short gown of yellow brocade worked with gold, and over this a richly-laced muslin apron. Her stupendous stomacher was worked in the same gaudy style as her gown; immense lace ruffles covered her elbows; and black mittens her wrists. Her neck was so short that her chin was buried in her exuberant bust. Waist she had none. In fact, her figure altogether resembled an enormous keg of Dutch butter, or gigantic runnel of Schiedam. The rest of her array consisted of massive gold earrings, a laced cap and pinners, surmounted by a beaver hat with a low crown and broad leaves; black shoes of Spanish leather, with red heels, and buckles. In her hand she carried a large fan, which she spread before her face, it may be presumed to hide her blushes.

As she advanced with her heels together and her toes turned out, at a slow and mincing pace, the two Frenchmen burst into roars of laughter, and having made her a bow of mock ceremony, which she returned by a little duck of the body, intended for a courtesy, they retired to let her pass, and to indulge their merriment unrestrained.

"What a creature!" exclaimed Mrs. Tipping, tossing her head scornfully, and arranging her pinners; "what an ojus creature! I sha'n't speak to her."

"I suppose I must, though," sighed good-natured Mrs. Plumpton. "Oh, that it should come to this after all his promises and fair speeches!"

"She's no great beauty, it must be owned," said Fishwick, crossing his hands over his paunch, and examining the Dutch lady at his leisure.

By this time, the serjeant had drawn near the group. His countenance grew more rueful each moment, and he had to clear his throat to bring out the words, "Allow me to introduce you to Mrs. Scales. Katryn, myn lief—Mrs. Plumpton."

As the introduction took place, the fat little lady made another ducking courtesy, and lowering her fan at the same time, discovered a broad puffy face covered with patches, a large double chin, a snub nose, and round protruding eyes. She was so very, very plain, that Mrs. Plumpton stood aghast, and stopped midway in her courtesy as if petrified.

"Ah! diable, comme elle est laide!" cried Bimbelot. "J'ai un grand envi du bonheur de notre vaillant sergent—ha, ha!"

"Et moi aussi," laughed Sauvageon. "Sa femme est seduisante comme un tonneau de graisse."

"My wife speaks English very well, Mrs. Plumpton," said Scales. "She will be happy to converse with you."

"Yas, I sbege Englesch bery bell, Mrs. Blumbdon," said the Dutch lady.

"What do you think of her?" demanded Scales. "She's accounted a great beauty in her own country. She was called ' De Vat Haring van den Haag,' or the Bloater of the Hague, which was esteemed a great compliment in that place."

"Yas, I'm taut a grade beaudy in my own coundry," simpered Mrs. Scales.

"There's no accounting for tastes," muttered Mrs. Plumpton. "But do you know, serjeant," she added, aloud, "I think your wife very like Mr. Proddy—so like, that I should almost have fancied she might be his sister."

"Vat does she say?" demanded Mrs. Scales, agitating her fan.

"She says you're very like a respected friend of mine—one Mr. Proddy, the queen's coachman," replied Scales.

"Oh, Mynheer Protty; I've heard you spege of him before," replied his wife. "He musd be a bery gootlooging man, dat Protty, if he's lige me."

"He *is* very goodlooking," affirmed Scales. "You'll see him by and by, I dare say."

"Oh yes, he's sure to be here presently," said Fishwick. "I

wonder he hasn't come before this. Odsbobs! she is uncommonly like Proddy, to be sure!"

"Wont you allow me to present my wife to you, Mrs. Tipping?" said Scales.

"No, I thank'ee, serjeant," replied the lady, glancing scornfully over her shoulder. "Horrid wretch!" she added, as if to herself.

"Well, at all events, you may shake hands with me," said Scales.

"You've only one hand left, serjeant, and it would be a pity to use it unnecessarily," rejoined Mrs. Tipping, pertly.

"Well, I didn't expect such a reception as this," said Scales, dolefully. "I thought you would be glad to see me."

"So we should, if you had come back as you went," replied Mrs. Tipping; "but you're an altered man now. I always told you, if you lost a limb, I'd have nothing to say to you."

"Your wounds would have made no difference to me, serjeant, if you hadn't put a bar between us," said Mrs. Plumpton. "Oh dear! you've used me very cruelly!"

"Hush! not so loud," cried the serjeant, winking, and pointing at his spouse.

"Vat's dat you zay, madam?" demanded Mrs. Scales. "I hope de serjeant hasn't been maagin luv to you."

"Yes, but he has," cried Mrs. Tipping; "he made love to both of us, and he promised to marry both of us, and he *would* have married both of us, but for you, you old Dutch monster!"

"Is dis drue, madam?" cried Mrs. Scales, her face turning crimson. "I ll believe you, but I wond dat saacy slud."

"Barbarous as he is, I wont betray him," murmured Mrs. Plumpton, turning away.

"If you wont believe me, you old mermaid, ask those gentlemen," said Mrs. Tipping. "They'll confirm what I've stated."

"Oui, madame," replied Bimbelot, stepping forward, "je suis bien faché—sorry to tell you dat de sergent did make love to bote dese ladies."

"Silence, Bamby!" cried Scales.

"No, I sha'n't be silent at your bidding," rejoined the valet. "We laugh at your threats now—ha! ha!" And he snapped his fingers in the serjeant's face.

"Yes, yes, we laugh at you now," said Sauvageon, imitating the gesture of his companion.

"Cowards!" exclaimed Scales.

"Whom do you call cowards, sare?" demanded Bimbelot, striding up to him, and grinning fiercely.

"Yes, whom do you call cowards, sare?" added Sauvageon, stepping forward, and grinning on the other side.

"Both; I call you both cowards—arrant cowards!" replied Scales. "You wouldn't dare to do this, for your lives, if I weren't disabled."

The Frenchmen meditated some angry retort, but Mrs. Scales pushed them aside, crying, "Leave him to me. I've an account to seddle wid him. Give me back my gilders, zir. I'll be divorzed. I'll go bag to Holland. I'll leave you wid your fine mizzizes here."

"We'll have nothing to do with him," said Mrs. Tipping.

"Answer for yourself, Tipping," rejoined Mrs. Plumpton. "I can forgive him anything."

"Bless you! bless you!" cried the sergeant, in a voice of deep emotion, and wiping away a tear.

"Give me my gilders, I zay," cried Mrs. Scales, rapping him with her fan. "I've done wid you. I'll go bag."

"Yas, give de lady her money," cried Bimbelot, coming behind him, and trying to trip up his wooden leg. "Ah, ah! mon brave, you are prettily hen-peck—ha! ha!"

"Oui, oui, de gray mare is clearly de better horse," cried Sauvageon, trying to knock the crutch from beneath his arm.

"Ah! rascals—ah, cowards! I'll teach you to play these tricks!" roared the serjeant in a voice of thunder, and shaking them off with a force that astonished them.

But what was their terror and amazement to see him slip his right arm out of the sling, pull off the bandage and produce a hand beneath it, sound and uninjured, and hard and horny as the other. What was their surprise—and the surprise of every one else, except Mrs. Scales—to see him unbuckle a strap behind, cast off his wooden leg, and plant his right foot firmly on the ground, giving a great stamp as he did so!

"Can I believe my eyes!" cried Mrs. Plumpton; "why the serjeant is himself again."

"Mille tonneres!" exclaimed Bimbelot, in affright—"que signifie cela?"

"It signifies that a day of retribution is arrived for you, rascal!" replied Scales, attacking him about the back and legs with the crutch. "This will teach you to waylay people in the park. And you, too," he added, belabouring Sauvageon in the same manner— "how do you like that, eh, rascals—eh, traitors!"

And he pursued them round the room, while Mrs. Scales assisted him, kicking them as they fled before her, and displaying, in her exertions, a tremendous pair of calves. She had just caught hold of the tails of Bimbelot's coat, and was cuffing him soundly, when he jerked himself away from her, and pulled her to the ground. In falling, her hat and cap, together with a false head of hair, came off.

"Another miracle!" exclaimed Mrs. Plumpton, running up to her assistance. "Why, I declare, if it isn't Mr. Proddy, after all!"

"Yes, yes, it's me, sure enough," replied the coachman, getting up—"ha, ha! Oh dear, these stays are sadly too tight for me. I shall be squeezed to death—ho! ho!"

At this moment, the serjeant, having driven out both the Frenchmen, came back, and clasping the unresisting Mrs. Plumpton in his arms, bestowed a hearty smack upon her lips.

"You'll forgive me for putting your affection to this trial, I hope, my dear?" he said.

"That I will," replied Mrs. Plumpton—"that I will."

"I'll forgive you, too, serjeant," said Mrs. Tipping, nudging his elbow, "though you don't deserve it."

Without saying a word, Scales turned and clasped her to his breast. But the embrace was certainly not so hearty as that which he had just bestowed on the housekeeper.

"Well, I hope you've taken care of my room in my absence?" said Scales.

"Come and look at it," cried Mrs. Plumpton; "you'll find it just as you left it."

"Yes, come and look at it," added Mrs. Tipping; "we've cleaned it regularly."

"Thank'ee, thank'ee!" rejoined the serjeant.

"Your drum's as tightly braced as my bodice," said Proddy. "Oh dear! I wish somebody would unlace me."

The coachman being relieved, they all adjourned to the den, and as they went thither, Scales observed to Mrs. Plumpton that he should never forget the way in which she had received him, saying, "It had made an ineffaceable impression on his heart."

"Ineffaceable fiddlestick!" exclaimed Mrs. Tipping, who overheard the remark. "As if she didn't know you were shamming all the while. Why, bless your simplicity, serjeant, did you think you could impose on us by so shallow a device? No such thing. We saw through it the moment you came in."

The serjeant looked incredulous, but at this moment he reached the den, and his thoughts turned into another channel.

Hesitating for a second, with a somewhat trembling hand he opened the door, and passed in. Everything was in its place—the plans, the portrait, the gloves, the sword, the shot, the meerschaum, with the drum standing on the three-legged stool. The serjeant surveyed them all, and a tear glistened in his eye. He said nothing but squeezed Mrs. Plumpton's hand affectionately.

CHAPTER V.

THE TRIAL OF DOCTOR SACHEVERELL.

THE length of time that elapsed between Doctor Sacheverell's impeachment and his trial was so far favourable to him, inasmuch as it gave him ample opportunity for preparing his defence; while no art was neglected to propitiate the public in his behalf, and heighten the feeling of animosity already entertained against his opponents.

The doctor's portrait was exhibited in all the print-shops; ballads were sung about him at the corner of every street; reference was constantly made to his case by the clergy of his party in their sermons, and some even went so far as to offer up public prayers "for the deliverance of a brother under persecution from the hands of his enemies;" the imminent peril of the church, and the excellence of its constitution, were insisted on ; the most furious zealots were made welcome guests at the board of Harley and his

friends, and instructed how to act—the principal toast at all such
entertainments being "Doctor Sacheverell's health, and a happy
deliverance to him."

The aspect of things was so alarming, that long before the trial
came on, the greatest misgivings were felt as to its issue by the
Whig leaders, and Godolphin bitterly repented that he had not
listened to the advice of Lord Somers, who had recommended a
simple prosecution in a court of law as the safest and most judi-
cious course. But retreat was now too late. The task had been
undertaken, and however difficult and dangerous, it must be gone
through with. To quit the field without a struggle would be worse
than defeat.

Warmly attached to the church, and led by Harley and Abigail
to believe that it was really in danger, the queen was inclined from
the first towards Sacheverell, and this bias was confirmed by the
incautious admission on the part of the Whigs of the legitimacy of
her brother, the Prince of Wales—an admission which, coupled
with her dislike of the proposed Hanoverian succession, exasperated
her against them, and increased her predilection for one whom she
believed to be undergoing persecution for promulgating opinions
so entirely in accordance with her own. Additional confidence was
given to the Tories, by the defection from the opposite party of the
Dukes of Shrewsbury, Somerset, and Argyle, all of whom, either
secretly or openly, exerted themselves to throw difficulties in the
way of the impeachment.

Thus embarrassed, and with the tide of popular opinion running
strongly against them, it became evident to the instigators of the
trial, that whatever might be the decision as regarded Sacheverell,
its consequences must be prejudicial in the highest degree to themselves. The only person who seemed unconcerned and confident of
a favourable termination, was the Duchess of Marlborough.

The counsel for the defence included Sir Simon Harcourt, Sir
Constantine Phipps, and three others of the ablest Tory lawyers;
while advice was given on all theological matters by Doctors Atterbury, Smallridge, and Friend. The managers of the prosecution
comprehended Sir John Holland, comptroller of the household;
Mr. Secretary Boyle; Mr. Smith, chancellor of the exchequer; Sir
James Montague, attorney-general; Mr. Robert Eyre, solicitor-
general; Mr. Robert Walpole, treasurer of the navy; and thirteen
others.

The approach of the trial increased the public curiosity to the
highest pitch, and all other considerations of business or amusement were merged in the anticipation of a struggle, which, though
ostensibly for another cause, was to decide the fate of parties.

At length, the 27th of February—the day fixed for the trial—
arrived. About an hour before noon, the courts and squares of the
Temple, where Sacheverell lodged, to be near his lawyers, were
crowded by an immense mob, with oak-leaves in their hats—the
distinguishing badge of the high-church party. A tremendous
shout was raised as the doctor got into an open gilt chariot, lent
him for the occasion by a friend, and as it was put in motion, the

whole concourse marched with him, shouting and singing, and giving to the procession rather the semblance of a conqueror's triumph, than of the passage of an offender to a court of justice.

The windows of all the houses in the Strand and Parliament-street were filled with spectators, many of whom responded to the shouts of the mob, while the fairer, and not the least numerous portion of the assemblage, were equally enthusiastic in the expression of their good wishes.

Sacheverell, it has before been intimated, was a handsome, fresh-complexioned man, with a fine portly figure, and stately presence, and on the present occasion, being attired in his full canonicals, and with the utmost care, he looked remarkably well. His countenance was clothed with smiles, as if he were assured of success.

In this way he was brought to Westminster Hall.

The managers and committee of the commons having taken their places, Sacheverell was brought to the bar, when the proceedings were opened by the attorney-general, who was followed by Mr. Lechmere; after which the particular passages of the sermon on which the impeachment was grounded, were read.

The case, however, proceeded no further on this day, but the court being adjourned, the doctor was conducted back to the Temple by the same concourse who had attended him to Westminster Hall, and who had patiently awaited his coming forth.

The next day, the crowds were far more numerous than before, and the approaches to the place of trial were so closely beset, that it required the utmost efforts of the guard to maintain anything like a show of order. Groanings, hootings, and menaces, were lavishly bestowed on all the opponents of Sacheverell, while, on the contrary, his friends were welcomed with the loudest cheers.

It was expected that the queen would attend the trial, and a little before twelve, a passage was cleared for the royal carriage; notwithstanding which the vehicle proceeded very slowly, and when nearly opposite Whitehall a stoppage occurred. Taking advantage of the pause, several persons pressed up to the window, and said, "We hope your majesty is for Doctor Sacheverell."

Somewhat alarmed, Anne leaned back, but Mrs. Masham, who was with her, answered quickly, "Yes, yes, good people, her majesty is a friend of every true friend of the church, and an enemy of its persecutors."

"We knew it—we knew it!" rejoined the questioners. "God bless your majesty, and deliver you from evil counsellors! Sacheverell and high church—huzza!"

"I say, coachee," cried one of the foremost of the mob—a great ruffianly fellow, half a head taller than the rest of the bystanders, with a ragged green coat on his back, and a coal-black beard of a week's growth on his chin—"I say, coachee," he cried, addressing Proddy, who occupied his usual position on the box, "I hope you're high church?"

"High as a steeple, my weathercock," replied Proddy. "You've little in common with low church yourself, I guess?"

"Nothin'," returned the man, gruffly. "But since such are your sentiments, give the words—'Sacheverell for ever! and down with the Duke of Marlborough!'"

"I've no objection to Doctor Sacheverell," said Proddy; "but I'm blown if I utter a word against the Duke of Marlborough; nor shall any one else in my hearin'. So stand aside, my maypole, unless you want a taste of the whip. Out of the way there! Ya hip—yo ho!"

Scarcely had the royal carriage passed, than the Duchess of Marlborough came up. Her grace was alone in her chariot, and being instantly recognised, was greeted with groans and yells by the crowd. No change of feature proclaimed a consciousness on her part of this disgraceful treatment, until the tall man before mentioned approached the carriage, and thrust his head insolently into the window.

"Good day, duchess," he said, touching his hat, and leering impudently—"you wont refuse us a few crowns to drink Doctor Sacheverell's health, and the downfall of the Whigs, eh?"

"Back, ruffian!" she cried; "drive on, coachman."

"Not so quick, duchess," replied the fellow, with a coarse laugh. And turning to two men near him, almost as ill-looking and stalwart as himself, he added, "here, Dan Dammaree,—and you, Frank Willis,—to the horses' heads—quick!"

The command was so promptly obeyed, that before Brumby could apply the whip, the horses were checked.

"You see how it is, duchess," pursued the fellow, with a detestable grin, "we must have what we ask, or we shall be compelled to escort you back to Marlborough House."

This speech was received with cheers and laughter by the bystanders, and several voices exclaimed, "Ay—ay, Geordie Purchase is right. We must have wherewithal to drink the doctor's deliverance, or the carriage shall go back."

Purchase was about to renew his demand, and in yet more insolent terms, when a strong grasp was placed on his collar, and he was hurled forcibly backwards, among the crowd.

On recovering himself, he saw that he had been displaced by a tall man in a serjeant's uniform, who now stood before the carriage window, and regarded him and his friends menacingly.

"Down with him!" roared Purchase; "he's a Whig—a dissenter—down with him!"

"Ay, down with him!" echoed a hundred voices.

And the threat would no doubt have been carried into execution, if at this juncture a body of the horse-guards had not ridden up, their captain having perceived that the Duchess of Marlborough was molested in her progress. The men then quitted their hold of the horses' heads, and Brumby putting the carriage in motion, the serjeant sprang up behind it among the footmen, and was borne away.

A few minutes after this disturbance, loud and prolonged cheering proclaimed the approach of the idol of the mob. Sacheverell was attended, as before, by a vast retinue of admirers, who carried their hats, decorated with oak-leaves, at the end of truncheons, which they waved as they marched along.

As the chariot advanced, the beholders instantly uncovered to the doctor, and those who refused this mark of respect had their hats knocked off. Sacheverell was accompanied by Doctors Atterbury and Smallridge, who were occupied in examining certain packets which had been flung into the carriage by different ladies, as it passed along, and the contents of most of which proved to be valuable.

When the carriage reached Whitehall, the shouts were almost deafening, and hundreds pressed round the doctor, invoking blessings on his head, and praying for his benediction in return. This was readily accorded by Sacheverell, who, rising in the carriage, extended his hands over the multitude, crying out, with great apparent fervour—"Heaven bless you, my brethren! and preserve you from the snares of your enemies!"

"And you too, doctor," cried the rough voice of Purchase, who was standing near him. "We'll let your persecutors see to-night what they may expect from us if they dare to find you guilty."

"Ay, that we will," responded others.

"We'll begin by burnin' down the meetin'-houses," shouted Daniel Dammaree. "The Whigs shall have a bonfire to warm their choppy fingers at."

"Say the word, doctor, and we'll pull down the Bishop o' Salisbury's house," roared Frank Willis.

"Or the lord chancellor's," cried Purchase.

"Or Jack Dolben's,—he who moved for your reverence's impeachment," cried Daniel Dammaree.

At the mention of Mr. Dolben's name, a deep groan broke from the crowd.

"Shall we set fire to Mr. Hoadley's church—Saint Peter's Poor, eh, doctor?" said Purchase.

"On no account, my friends—my worthy friends," replied Sacheverell. "Abstain from all acts of violence, I implore of you. Otherwise you will injure the cause you profess to serve."

"But, doctor, we can't come out for nothing," urged Purchase.

"No, no, we must earn a livelihood," said Willis.

"I charge you to be peaceable," rejoined the doctor, sitting down hastily in the carriage.

"Notwithstanding what he says, we'll pull down Dr. Burgess's meetin'-house in Lincoln's-Inn-Fields, to-night," cried Dammaree, as the carriage was driven forward.

"Right," cried a little man, with his hat pulled over his brows; "it will convince the enemies of the high church that we're in earnest. The doctor may talk as he pleases, but I know a tumult will be agreeable to him, as well as serviceable."

"Say you so," cried Purchase; "then we'll do it. We meet at seven in Lincoln's-Inn-Fields, comrades."

"Agreed," cried a hundred voices.

"And don't forget to bring your clubs with you, comrades," cried Frank Willis.

"That we wont," replied the others.

"I must keep them up to it." muttered the short man, with the hat pulled over his brows. "This will be pleasing intelligence to Mr. Harley."

The proceedings at Westminster Hall were opened by Sir Joseph Jekyll, who, addressing himself to the first article of the impeachment, was followed by the attorney-general, Sir John Holland, Mr. Walpole, and General Stanhope, the latter of whom, in a spirited speech, declared that if "that insignificant tool of a party, Doctor Sacheverell, had delivered his sermon in a conventicle of disaffected persons, maintained by some deluded women, no notice should have been taken of no nonsensical a discourse ; but as he had preached it where it might do great mischief, his offence deserved the severest animadversion."

At these scornful remarks, the doctor, who had maintained an unconcerned demeanour during the speeches of the other managers, turned very pale, and with difficulty refrained from giving utterance to his angry emotion.

Soon after this, Mr. Dolben spoke, and, in the heat of his discourse, glancing at Atterbury and Smallridge, who were standing at the bar behind Sacheverell, cried—"When I see before me these false brethren——"

The words were scarcely uttered, when Lord Haversham rose, and interrupted him.

"I cannot allow such an expression to pass without reproof, sir," cried his lordship. "You have passed a reflection upon the whole body of the clergy. I move, my lords, that the honourable gentleman explain."

"Ay, ay, explain," cried several voices from the benches of the Lords.

"What mean you by the expression you have used, sir?" demanded the chancellor.

"Nothing, my lord," replied Mr Dolben. "It was a mere inadvertence. I should have said 'false brother,' for I referred only to the prisoner at the bar."

"The explanation is scarcely satisfactory," replied Lord Haversham ; "and I must admonish the honourable gentleman to be more guarded in what he says in future. Such slips of the tongue are unpardonable."

Slight as this occurrence was, it was turned to great advantage by Sacheverell's partisans, who construed it into a complete betrayal of the intentions of their opponents to attack the whole church in his person.

When Mr. Dolben concluded his speech, the court adjourned, and the doctor was conducted to his lodgings in the same triumphant manner as before.

CHAPTER VI.

HOW THE MEETING-HOUSES WERE DESTROYED BY THE MOB.

As evening drew in, the peaceable inhabitants of Lincoln's-Inn. Fields were terrified by the appearance of several hundred persons, armed with bludgeons, muskets, and swords, and headed by three tall men with faces blackened with soot, who, after parading their wild retinue about the square for a quarter of an hour, during which its numbers were greatly increased, paused beneath a lamp-post, when the tallest of the trio, clambering up it, took upon him to address a few words to the mob. As he ceased, shouts were raised of "Well said, Geordie Purchase. Down with the meeting-houses! Down with the meeting-houses!"

"Ay, down with them!" rejoined Purchase. "Let's begin with Doctor Burgess's; it's the nearest at hand. Come on, lads. We'll have all the meeting-houses down before morning. Come on, I say. High church and Sacheverell for ever—huzza!"

With this, he leaped down, and brandishing a naked hanger, ran towards the corner of the square, and entered a little court, at the end of which stood the doomed meeting-house.

Several of the mob who followed him bore links, so that a wild, unsteady light was thrown upon the scene. An attack was instantly made upon the door, which proved strong enough to resist the combined efforts of Purchase and Dammaree.

While these ruffians were hurling themselves against it, and calling for implements to burst it open, a window was unfastened, and a venerable face appeared at the opening.

"What do you want, my friends!" asked the looker-out, in a mild voice.

"It's Doctor Burgess himself!" cried several voices. And a most terrific yell was raised, which seemed to find an echo from the furthest part of the square.

"We want to get in, old Poundtext," replied Purchase; "so unlock the door, and look quick about it, or it'll be worse for you."

"Your errand is wrongful," cried Doctor Burgess. "I beseech you to retire, and take away those you have brought with you. I shall resist your violence as long as I can; nor shall you enter this sacred place except over my body."

"Your blood be upon your own head, then," rejoined Purchase, fiercely. "Curse ye!" he added to those behind him. "Is there nothing to break open the door?"

"Here's a sledge-hammer," cried a swarthy-visaged knave, with his shirt sleeves turned up above the elbow, and a leathern apron tied round his waist, forcing his way towards him. Purchase snatched the hammer from him, raised it, and dashed it against the door, which flew open with a tremendous crash.

But the entrance of the intruders was opposed by Doctor Burgess, who planted himself in their way, and raising his arm menacingly, cried, "Get hence, sacrilegious villains, or dread the anger of Heaven!"

"We are the servants of the church, and therefore under the special protection of Heaven," cried Purchase, derisively. "Let us pass, I say, or I'll cut you down."

"You shall never pass while I can hinder you," rejoined Doctor Burgess. "I have not much force of body; but such as I have I will oppose to you, violent man."

"Since you wont be warned, you hoary-headed dotard, take your fate!" cried Purchase, seizing him by the throat, and dashing him backwards so forcibly, that his head came in contact with the edge of a pew, and he lay senseless and bleeding on the ground.

As the doctor fell, a young man, who had not been hitherto noticed, rushed forward, crying, in a voice of agony and grief, "Wretches, you have killed him!"

"Maybe we have," rejoined Dammaree, with a terrible imprecation; "and we'll kill you, too, if you give us any nonsense."

"You are he who did it!" cried the young man, attempting to seize Purchase. "You are my prisoner."

"Leave go, fool!" rejoined the other, "or I'll send you to hell to join your pastor."

But the young man closed with him, and, nerved by desperation, succeeded, notwithstanding the other's superior strength, in wresting the hanger from him.

"Halloa, Dan!" cried Purchase, "just give this madcap a crack on the sconce, will you?"

Dammaree replied with a blow from a hatchet which he held in his hand. The young man instantly dropped, and the crowd rushing over him, trampled him beneath their feet.

In another minute, the chapel was filled by the rioters, and the work of destruction commenced. The pews were broken to pieces; the benches torn up; the curtains plucked from the windows; the lamps and sconces pulled down; the casements and wainscots destroyed; the cushions, hassocks, and carpets, taken up; and Bibles and hymn-books torn in pieces, and their leaves scattered about.

By this time, Doctor Burgess, who had only been stunned, having recovered his senses, rushed amidst the crowd, exclaiming—"Sacrilegious villains—robbers—murderers, what have you done with my nephew? Where is he?"

"Silence, old man! We have had trouble enough with you already," rejoined Frank Willis, gruffly.

"Make him mount the pulpit, and cry, 'Sacheverell for ever!'" said Dammaree.

"I will perish rather," cried Doctor Burgess.

"We'll see that," said Purchase. "Here, lads, hoist him to the pulpit."

And amid blows, curses, and the most brutal usage, the unfortunate minister was compelled to mount the steps.

As he stood within the pulpit, from which he was wont to address an assemblage so utterly different in character from that now gathered before him, his appearance excited some commiseration

ren among that ruthless crew. His face was deathly pale, and
ere was a large gash on his left temple, from which the blood was
ill flowing freely. His neckcloth and dress were stained with the
anguinary stream. He exhibited no alarm, but turning his eyes
pwards, seemed to murmur a prayer.

"Now then, doctor," roared Dammaree—"'Sacheverell and High
Church for ever,' or the Lord have mercy on your soul."

"The Lord have mercy on *your* soul, misguided man," replied
Doctor Burgess. "You will think on your present wicked actions
when you are brought to the gallows."

"Do as you are bid, doctor, without more ado," cried Dammaree,
pointing a musket at him, "or——"

"I will never belie my conscience," rejoined Doctor Burgess,
firmly. "And I warn you not to commit more crimes—not to stain
your soul yet more deeply in blood."

Dammaree was about to pull the trigger, when the musket was
dashed from his grasp by Purchase.

"No, curse it!" cried 'the milder ruffian, "we wont kill him.
He is punished severely enough in seeing his chapel demolished."

The majority of the assemblage concurring in this opinion, Purchase continued—"Come down, old Poundtext, and make your way
hence, if you don't wish, like a certain Samson, of your acquaintance, to have an old house pulled about your ears."

"God forgive you as I do," said Burgess, meekly. With this he
descended, and pressing through the crowd, quitted the chapel.

Before he was gone, however, the pulpit was battered to pieces
and the fragments gathered together, and in a few minutes more
the chapel was completely gutted by the mob.

Laden with their spoil, the victors returned to the centre of the
square, where they made an immense heap of the broken pieces of
the pews and pulpit, and having placed straw and other combus-
tibles among them, they set fire to the pile in various places. The
dry wood quickly kindled, and blazed up in a bright ruddy flame,
illuminating the countenances of the fantastic groups around it, the
nearest of whom took hands, and forming a ring, danced round the
bonfire, hallooing and screeching like so many Bedlamites.

While this was going forward, Frank Willis, having fastened a
window-curtain, which he had brought from the chapel, to the end
of a long pole, waved it over his head, dubbing it the "high-church
standard," and bidding his followers rally round it.

A council of war was next held among the ringleaders, and after
some discussion, it was resolved to go and demolish Mr. Earle's
meeting-house in Long Acre. This design was communicated to
the assemblage by Purchase, and received with tumultuous applause.

To Long Acre, accordingly, the majority of the assemblage hied,
broke open the doors of the meeting-house in question, stripped it,
as they had done Dr. Burgess's, and carried off the materials for
another bonfire.

"Where next, comrades?" cried Purchase, ascending a flight of
steps. "Where next?"

"To Mr. Bradbury's meeting-house in New-street, Shoe-lane," replied a voice from the crowd.

This place of worship being visited and destroyed, the mob next bent their course to Leather-lane, where they pulled down Mr. Taylor's chapel; and thence to Blackfriars, where Mr. Wright's meeting-house shared the same fate.

Hitherto they had encountered little or no opposition, and, flushed with success, they began to meditate yet more formidable enterprises. Arriving at Fleet-bridge, Purchase mounted the stone balustrade, and claimed attention for a moment.

"What say you to going into the city, and destroying the meeting-houses there?" he cried.

"I'm for somthin' better," replied Frank Willis, waving his flag. "I votes as how we pulls down Salter's Hall."

"I'm for a greater booty still," vociferated Dammaree. "Let us break open and rifle the Bank of England. That'll make us all rich for life."

"Ay, ay—the Bank of England—let's rifle it," cried a chorus of voices.

"A glorious suggestion, Frank," returned Purchase. "Come along. Sacheverell and the Bank of England—huzza!"

As they were about to hurry away, a short man, with his hat pulled over his brows, rushed up, almost out of breath, and informed them that the guards were in search of them.

"They've turned into Lincoln's-Inn-Fields," cried the man, "for I myself told their captain you were there. But they'll be here presently."

"We'll give 'em a warm reception when they come," said Purchase, resolutely. "Here, lads, throw down all that wooden lumber on the west side of the bridge. Make as great a heap as you can, so as to block up the thoroughfare completely. Get a barrel of pitch from that 'ere lighter lying in the ditch below—I'll knock out the bottom and set fire to it when we hear 'em comin', and we'll see whether they'll dare to pass the bridge when that's done. Sacheverell and the Bank of England for ever—huzza!"

CHAPTER VII.

IN WHAT WAY THE RIOTERS WERE DISPERSED.

MEANWHILE, intelligence of these tumults had been received at Whitehall, by the Earl of Sunderland, who instantly repaired to Saint James's Palace, and reported to the queen what was going forward, expressing his apprehension of the extent of the riot.

"I am grieved, but not surprised, to hear of the disturbances, my lord," replied Anne. "They are the natural consequence of the ill-judged proceedings against Doctor Sacheverell."

"But what will your majesty have done?" asked Sunderland.

You will not allow the lives and properties of your subjects to be sacrificed by a lawless mob?"

"Assuredly not, my lord," replied the queen. "Let the horse and foot guards be instantly sent out to disperse them."

"But your majesty's sacred person must not be left undefended at this hour," replied the earl.

"Have no fear for me, my lord," said Anne. "Heaven will be my guard. The mob will do me no injury, and I would show myself to them without uneasiness. Disperse them as I have said; but let the task be executed with as little violence as possible."

Sunderland then returned to the Cock-pit, where he found the lord chancellor, the Duke of Newcastle, and some other noblemen. After a brief consultation together, Captain Horsey, an exempt, was summoned, and received instructions from the earl to mount immediately, and quell the disturbances.

"I have some scruple in obeying your lordship," replied Horsey, "unless I am relieved. Belonging as I do to the queen's body-guard, I am responsible for any accident that may happen to her majesty."

"It is the queen's express wish that this should be done, sir," cried the earl, hastily.

"That does not relieve me, my lord," replied Horsey, pertinaciously; "and I will not stir, unless I have your authority in writing."

"Here it is, then," said the earl, sitting down, and hurriedly tracing a few lines on a sheet of paper, which he gave to the captain. "Are you now content?"

"Humph!" exclaimed Horsey, glancing at the order. "This does not specify whether I am to preach to the mob, or fight them, my lord. If I am to preach, I should wish to be accompanied by some better orator than myself. But if I am to fight, why that's my vocation, and I will do my best."

"Zounds, captain," cried the earl, impatiently, "if you are as long in dispersing the mob as you are in setting forth, you'll give them time to destroy half the churches in London! About the business quickly. Use discretion and judgment, and forbear all violence, except in case of necessity."

Thus exhorted, the captain left the room, and ordering his men to mount, rode in search of the rioters.

As they galloped along the Strand, information was given them of the bonfire in Lincoln's-Inn-Fields, and they shaped their course in that direction, but on arriving there, they found the fire nearly extinguished, and a pack of boys tossing about the embers.

At the approach of the soldiery, these young ragamuffins took to their heels, but some of them were speedily captured, when intelligence was obtained that the mob, having pulled down three or four other meeting-houses, had moved towards Blackfriars.

On learning this, the captain gave the word to proceed thither at once, and putting spurs to their horses, the troop dashed through Temple Bar, and so along Fleet-street. As they came in sight of the little bridge which then crossed Fleet Ditch, a bright flame suddenly sprang up, increasing each moment in volume and brilliancy, and revealing, as they drew nearer, a great pile of burning benches, pews, and other matters. Behind was ranged a mighty rabble rout, lining, to a considerable distance, both on the right and left, the opposite bank of the ditch. The ruddy light of the fire glimmered on the arms of the rioters, and showed the extent of their numbers. It was also reflected on the black and inert waters of the stream at their feet, disclosing here and there a lighter, or other bark, or falling upon the picturesque outline of some old building.

In the centre of the bridge stood Purchase and Dammaree, each with a drawn hanger in one hand, and a pistol in the other, while mounted upon the balustrade, stood Frank Willis, waving his standard triumphantly over their heads.

Meanwhile, the fire burnt so furiously, as apparently to prevent all chance of the soldiers passing the bridge, and a loud shout was set up by the rabble as Captain Horsey halted in front of it.

A few minutes were spent in reconnoitring, after which a trumpet was blown. Amid the silence produced by this call, Horsey raised himself in his saddle, and called in a loud voice,—" In the queen's name, I command you to disperse, and go peaceably to your homes. All shall be pardoned, except your ringleaders."

To this Purchase answered in an equally loud and derisive tone, " We are loyal subjects ourselves. We will fight to the death for the queen—for the High Church and Doctor Sacheverell. No Whigs!—no dissenters!"

" Ay, Sacheverell for ever, and confusion to his enemies!" responded the mob.

" Charge them, men," cried Horsey, spurring his horse towards the fire, and endeavouring to force him through it. But the spirited animal swerved and reared, and despite his master's efforts, dashed off in another direction.

With the exception of two or three, the whole troop were equally unsuccessful. Their horses refused to approach the flames; and a shower of brickbats, stones, and missiles increased the general disorder.

As to the three men who did effect a passage, their horses were so scarred and burnt as to be quite unmanageable, and the poor fellows were speedily dismounted and disarmed. Some dozen others, also, who tried to pass through Fleet Ditch, stuck fast in the mud, and were severely handled by the mob before they could be extricated.

Meantime, loud shouts of triumph were raised by the rioters, and Purchase called upon them to heap more fuel on the fire, which was done by throwing more benches and broken pews upon it. Six stout fellows then approached, bearing a pulpit on their shoulders, which, by their combined efforts, was cast into the very midst of the fire, where it remained erect.

At this spectacle a roar of laughter burst from the rabble, in which some of the guard, in spite of their anger at their discomfiture, joined. Encouraged by this, Purchase shouted out to them, " Don't fight against us, brothers. We are for the queen and the church."

Ordering some of his men to ride round by Holborn Bridge, and attack the rioters in the rear, Captain Horsey caused a discharge of carbines to be made over the heads of those on the bridge, hoping to intimidate them. This was done, but produced no other result than derisive laughter, and a fresh shower of stones, one of which hit the captain himself on the face.

While the soldiers were loading their carbines, a tall man, in a serjeant's uniform, accompanied by a stout coachman, in the royal livery, forced their way up to Horsey.

"Beg pardon, captain," said the serjeant, "but your object is to capture those ringleaders, not to kill 'em, aint it?"

"Certainly, Serjeant Scales, certainly," replied Horsey.

"Then, with your permission, I'll undertake the job," returned Scales. "Come along, Proddy."

And drawing his sword, he plunged into the flames, and was followed by his companion.

Horsey looked on in curiosity to see what would be the result of this daring act, and was surprised to see both men get through the fire without material injury, though the coachman paused to pluck off his wig, which was considerably singed.

"Ha! you are the scoundrel who thrust me from the Duchess of Marlborough's carriage this morning," cried Purchase, glancing menacingly at Scales, "I am glad we meet again."

"We meet not to part till I have secured you, villain," replied the serjeant. "Yield!"

"Not without a blow or two," rejoined Purchase, with a roar of derision.

"He must take me as well as you, Geordie," cried Dammaree, brandishing his sword in the serjeant's face.

"Such is my intention," replied Scales.

And seizing one by the back of the neck, and the other by the collar, by a tremendous effort of strength, he dragged them both through the fire, and delivered them, very much scorched and half suffocated, to the guard.

Meantime, Proddy having contrived to clamber up the balustrade of the bridge, attacked Frank Willis, and tried to force the ensign from his grasp. On the onset of the struggle, the attention of the rabble had been chiefly occupied by Scales, but several persons now rushed to the assistance of the standard-bearer.

Unable to make a stand against so many, Proddy gave way, and dropped into the ditch, but never having quitted his antagonist, he dragged him along with him.

The height from which the coachman fell was not more than twelve or fourteen feet, and the ooze he sunk into was as soft as a feather-bed, so that he ran much greater risk of being suffocated, than of breaking a limb. In fact, he was just disappearing, when a bargeman contrived to pull him out with a boat-hook, and his prisoner, to whom he still clung with desperate tenacity, was consigned to the guard.

On seeing the fate of their leaders, the rioters began to exhibit symptoms of wavering, and shortly afterwards, the detachment of guards sent round by Holborn Bridge coming up, and attacking them with the flat of their swords, the whole rout was dispersed without further resistance.

Almost at the same time, the fire was cleared away with forks, and the blazing fragments cast into the ditch, so as to allow a clear passage for the rest of the troop.

This accomplished, Captain Horsey inquired for the serjeant, and, complimenting him on his bravery, thanked him for the service he had rendered the queen. He would also have made similar acknow-ledgments to Proddy, but the coachman had retired to a neighbouring tavern, to free himself from his muddy habiliments, and prevent any injurious consequences from the immersion by a glass of brandy. Scales, however, undertook to report to his friend the commendation bestowed upon him.

The prisoners were then conveyed to Newgate, as a place of the greatest security: after which Captain Horsey and his troop returned to Whitehall.

CHAPTER VIII.

ON THE SENTENCE PASSED ON DR. SACHEVERELL; AND WHAT FOLLOWED IT.

NEXT day the guards at St. James's and Whitehall were doubled; the train-bands of Westminster were ordered to remain under arms; regular troops were posted in different quarters; and an address having been presented to the queen by the commons, praying that effectual means might be taken to suppress the tumults, and pre-vent their recurrence, a proclamation was immediately made to that effect, and a reward offered for the discovery of the authors and abettors of the late disturbances.

In consequence of these vigorous measures, Sacheverell was obliged to abandon his triumphal chariot, and content himself with a chair, in which he was carried daily to Westminster Hall, very much shorn of his attendants.

The trial having continued upwards of a week, and the counsel for the defence having replied to the different articles of impeach-ment, Sacheverell pronounced the address prepared for him by Atterbury, Smallridge, and Friend, and revised by Harcourt and Phipps. Delivered with the utmost fervour, and with an air of entire conviction, this masterly and eloquent speech produced a strong impression on most of its hearers.

Among them was the queen herself, who appeared much moved by it. It mattered not that it was directly opposed on certain points to the doctrines laid down in the discourse on which the prosecution was grounded; it mattered not that its asseverations were audacious, and its appeals startling; that it was, in short, little better than an artful recantation of the speaker's former opinions; it answered the purpose admirably, and was decisive of the issue of the trial. The research and learning displayed in it astonished the most critical, while its extraordinary power and pathos electrified and enchained the inattentive. The sterner portion of the assemblage yielded it the tribute of their applauses, the gentler that of their tears.

By the publication of this speech, which was almost simultaneous with its delivery, the doctor's popularity reached its apogee, and the most confident anticipations of his honourable acquittal, or of a sentence so lenient as to amount to acquittal, began to be entertained. In any event, the high-church party conceived they had triumphed, and their exultation knew no bounds. Dinners were given at the principal taverns and coffee-houses frequented by the Tories; and the guests sat long, and drank deeply, shouting over the anticipated downfal of the Whigs, and congratulating each other in enthusiastic terms on the brilliant figure cut by their apostle. Not a few disturbances occurred that night in the streets; but the peace-breakers expressing their contrition, when sober, were very lightly dealt with by the authorities. Crowds, too, began to reassemble about the precincts of the Temple and Westminster Hall; but as great decorum was observed, they were allowed to disperse of their own accord.

Throughout this celebrated process, a singular unanimity of opinion prevailed among the lower orders of the people. To a man, they espoused the cause of Sacheverell; stigmatized the prosecution as unjust and inimical to the church; and denounced its authors in unmeasured terms.

As the trial drew to a close, and the managers replied to the doctor's defence, assailing him with virulent abuse, the indignation of the populace was roused to such a degree, that nothing but the precautions taken prevented new riots, worse than those which had previously occurred.

But not only were the people deeply interested in the controversy; it engrossed, from first to last, the attention of the upper classes of society, to the exclusion of every other topic of conversation; and the most feverish anxiety reigned throughout the capital and the larger provincial towns. Public business was altogether suspended, and the close of the trial was ardently desired, as the sole means of allaying the general ferment of the nation.

This did not occur till the 20th of March, when both houses of parliament having taken their seats, the question was put to the vote among the lords, and found Sacherevell guilty by a majority of seventeen.

A plea in arrest of judgment was made, but this was overruled, and on the following day sentence was pronounced.

It was to the effect that Sacheverell should be suspended from preaching for the term of three years, and that his sermon should be burned before the Royal Exchange, by the common hangman, in the presence of the lord mayor and the sheriffs.

Affording indubitable evidence of the weakness of the ministers, this mild sentence was received with every demonstration of satisfaction by their opponents, as well as by the populace generally. The greatest rejoicings were made. Liquor was freely distributed to the mob at certain taverns; and bands of high-churchmen, with oak-leaves in their hats, paraded the streets, chanting songs of thanksgiving for the liberation of their champion.

Bonfires were lighted at the corners of the streets, round which crowds assembled to drink the doctor's health and happy deliverance, from great barrels of ale given them by certain generous Tories. All who passed by were compelled to pledge them.

At night, most of the houses were illuminated, and those who declined to follow the general example had their windows broken by the drunken and uproarious mob. Attempts were made in some quarters to disperse the crowds, and put out the fires; but whether the train-bands were intimidated, or little desirous of putting their orders into execution, certain it is, that the licence of the populace remained unchecked, and numbers continued to occupy the streets to a late hour. Some few stragglers, too much intoxicated to offer resistance, were seized, and conveyed to the roundhouses, but they were discharged next morning with gentle reprimands for their inebriety.

In Pall Mall, nearly opposite Marlborough House, a large bonfire was lighted, and around it some hundreds of persons were collected. Plenty of liquor had been supplied them; and after shouting for some time for Sacheverell and the Tories, they began to yell against the ministers, and prompted by some of Harley's myrmidons, who had mixed with them, gave three groans for the Duke of Marlborough, and one for the duchess.

At this juncture, and as if prepared for the event, two men suddenly appeared, carrying a sedan-chair. Their object being explained, a passage was made for them by the crowd, and they moved on till they reached the edge of the fire. The chair was then opened, and one of the men, who had the air of a valet, dressed in his master's clothes, took forth a figure tricked out in an old black horsehair periwig, a tattered scarlet robe, and a hideous mask. A paper collar was placed round its neck, and a white staff in its hand.

"Here's de lor-treasurer of England, de Earl of Gotolphin!" shouted the man, in a strong French accent, which was supposed to be assumed.

Much laughter followed, and several voices cried, "Into the fire with him! Into the fire with him!"

"He sall go presently," replied the fellow; "but vait till you see his companion."

"Look at dis!" cried the other man at the sedan-chair—a tall, scraggy personage, wrapt in a loose regimental great coat, and having a nose and chin like a pair of nutcrackers—"Look at him!" he repeated, holding up another figure, wearing an absurdly-ferocious mask, a soiled military coat, a laced hat, and a pair of huge jack boots.

"Dis is de commander-in-sheaf—de great Marlbrook!" continued the scraggy man, with the hooked nose, showing the effigy to the spectators, who replied by shouts of laughter, mingled with some expressions of disapprobation. "Dese are de itentical boots he wear at ——."

Further speech was cut short by a great stir amid the crowd, and a loud voice exclaimed, "It's a lie!—an infernal lie! Those are not the boots."

The next moment, Scales, followed by Proddy, rushed forward. Having seen what was going forward from the steps of Marlborough House. they had determined, in spite of every risk, to stop the disgraceful proceedings.

As soon as the serjeant got up to the chair, he snatched the figure from the grasp of the man who held it, and trampled it beneath his feet.

"Shame on you!" he cried, looking round at the mob. "Is it thus you treat the defender of your country, and the conqueror of its enemies? Is it thus you show honour to the victor of Blenheim and Ramilies?"

"Who are you that talk thus to us?" demanded a bystander.

"Who am I?" rejoined the serjeant. "One who has a right to speak, because he has followed the duke in all his campaigns. One who has bled *with* him, and would willingly bleed *for* him. One who would rather have left his corpse on the field of Malplaquet than live to see his commander thus grossly insulted by those who are bound to honour and respect him."

"If that don't touch your hearts they must be harder than millstones," cried Proddy, passing his hand before his eyes. "Are you Englishmen, that you allow a couple of beggarly mounseers to insult your great commander in this way—to say nothin' of his friend the lord-treasurer? If you don't blush for yourselves, I blush for you."

"Mounseers!" exclaimed a bystander. "Vy, you don't mean to say as how these two ill-looking rascals is mounseers?"

"Yes, but I do," replied Proddy. "They're as surely mounseers as I'm her majesty's coachman!"

"It's Mr. Proddy himself!" cried several voices. "We know him very well."

"I wish you knew him better, and copied his manners," replied the coachman; "for then you'd never act in this way. Look at these two tremblin' cowards! Are they men to be allowed to offer an insult to the Duke of Marlborough?"

"No—no," cried a hundred voices. "We didn't know they were mounseers. We ask your pardon, Mr. Proddy. We were wrong —quite wrong."

"Don't ask my pardon," rejoined Proddy. "Ask the duke's. Show your sorrow by better conduct in future."

"We will, we will," replied those nearest him. "What shall we do to satisfy you?"

"Give three cheers for the duke, and then read these rascals a lesson," replied Proddy.

Three lusty cheers followed the coachman's speech, during which the two Frenchmen, almost frightened out of their senses at the change wrought in the temper of the mob, endeavoured to escape.

"Stop 'em!" roared the serjeant—"stop 'em!"

"Ay, ay!—here they are, safe enough," cried several of the bystanders, arresting them.

Bimbelot and Sauvageon besought their captors to let them go, but ineffectually.

"Epargnez moi, de grace," roared Bimbelot, piteously ; "I adore de great Marlbrook."

"Listen to his lingo," cried a waterman. "We must be precious flats not to have found him out sooner."

"I am entirely of your opinion, friend," replied Proddy.

"What shall we do with 'em ?" cried a small-coal-man. "Throw 'em into the fire ?"

"Or cut 'em into mince-meat ?" cried a butcher.

"Or grind 'em to death ?" cried a baker.

"No, let's be merciful, and hang 'em !" yelled a tailor's apprentice.

"Pitié ! pour l'amour de Dieu ! pitié !" cried Sauvageon.

"Oh, mon cher sergent !—mon cher Monsieur Proddy ! do say a word for me," implored Bimbelot.

But the coachman turned away in disgust.

"I'll tell you what we'll do with 'em," said Scales to the bystanders. "The valet shall put on his tatterdemalion attire," pointing to the duke's effigy, "and the corporal shall put on t'other."

The proposal was received with universal acclamations, and instant preparations were made to carry it into effect. The straw bolsters were stripped of their covering, and the two Frenchmen, whose clothes were torn from their backs, were compelled to put on the wretched habiliments of their dummies. The masks were then clapped on their faces, and they looked more complete scarecrows than the effigies themselves.

Bimbelot's appearance occasioned roars of laughter. The old jack boots in which his little legs were plunged ascended to his hips ; the coat covered him like a sack ; and the hat thrust over his brows well nigh extinguished him. Sauvageon looked scarcely less ridiculous.

In this guise, they were hoisted upon the top of the sedan-chair, and exposed to the jeers and hootings of the rabble, who, after pelting them with various missiles, threatened to throw them into the fire ; and would have executed the menace, no doubt, but for the interference of the serjeant and Proddy. In the end, crackers were tied to their tails, and fired, after which they were allowed to run for their lives, and, amidst a shower of squibs and blazing embers, which were hurled at them, managed to escape.

Thus ended the trial of Doctor Sacheverell, which paved the way, as had been foreseen by its projectors, for the dissolution of the ministry. The Whigs never recovered the blow so successfully aimed at their popularity ; and though they struggled on for some time, from this point their decline may be dated.

Six weeks after the termination of this trial, Doctor Sacheverell commenced a progress through the country, and was everywhere received with extraordinary rejoicing. At Oxford, he was magnificently entertained by the heads of the colleges, and after remaining there during a fortnight, proceeded to Bunbury and Warwick, where he was equally well received. But the greatest honour shown him was at Bridgenorth. As he appraoched this town, he was met by Mr. Creswell, a wealthy gentleman of the neighbourhood, attached to the Jacobite cause, at the head of an immense cavalcade of horse and foot, amounting to many thousands, most of whom wore white breast-knots edged with gold, and gilt laurel-leaves in their hats. The roads were lined with people, and, to add to the effect of the procession, the hedges were dressed with flowers to the distance of two miles. The steeples were adorned with flags and colours, and the bells rang out merrily.

This was the last scene of the doctor's triumph.

CHAPTER IX.

SHOWING HOW THE WHIG MINISTRY WAS DISSOLVED.

THE cabals of Harley to effect the dissolution of the Whig ministry were at length crowned with success. Consternation was carried into the cabinet by the sudden and unlooked-for appointment of the Duke of Somerset to the place of lord-chamberlain, in the room of the Earl of Kent, who was induced to retire by the offer of a dukedom; as well as by the removal of Sunderland, notwithstanding the efforts of his colleagues and the Duchess of Marlborough to keep him in his post; but the final blow was given by the disgrace of Godolphin, who, having parted with the queen over-night, on apparently amicable terms, was confounded, the next morning, by receiving a letter from her, intimating that he was dismissed from her service, and requiring him to break his staff, in place of delivering it up in person. A retiring pension of four thousand a-year was promised him at the same time, but it was never paid; nor was it ever demanded by the high-minded treasurer, though he stood greatly in need of it.

The treasury was instantly put into commission, and Lord Poulet placed at its head, while Harley was invested with the real powers of government. Proposals of a coalition were then made to such Whig ministers as still remained in office, but they were indignantly rejected, it being supposed that the Tories could not carry on the administration, inasmuch as they had not the confidence of the country. No alternative, therefore, was left the queen, but to dismiss the Whigs altogether, which was done, and parliament dissolved.

The result of this latter step proved the correctness of Harley's calculations. Hitherto the junta had possessed entire control over the House of Commons, and they relied upon its support, to embarrass the measures of the new ministers, and ultimately regain their lost power. But the returns of the new parliament undeceived them, manifesting a vast preponderance in favour of the Tories.

Mortification and defeat had been everywhere experienced by the Whigs. The recent impeachment was constantly thrown in their teeth: those who had voted for it were insulted and threat-

ened by the rabble; while the name of Sacheverell served as the
rallying word of their adversaries. The new parliament therefore
placed a Tory ministry out of the reach of immediate danger.

Prior to the elections, the ministerial appointments were completed. Saint-John was made Secretary of State; the Duke of
Ormond, lord-lieutenant of Ireland; the Earl of Rochester, presi-
dent of the council; the Duke of Buckingham, lord-steward of the
household; and other promotions occurred, not necessary to be
particularized.

So constructed, the new cabinet commenced its work; and supported as it was by the queen, seemed to hold out a reasonable
prospect of stability. Energy and unanimity at first marked its
progress, and the fierce and unscrupulous opposition it encountered
only added to its strength.

Disunions and jealousies, however, began ere long to arise, in-
spiring the displaced party with a hope that the combination which
had proved fatal to them would be speedily disorganized.

Harley had not yet attained the goal of his ambition; and, now,
at the moment when he was about to put forth his hand to grasp
the reward of his toils—the treasurer's staff—two rivals stepped
forward, threatening to snatch it from him. These were the Earl
of Rochester and Saint-John. Between Harley and Rochester an
old enmity had subsisted, which, though patched up for a time,
had latterly been revived in all its original bitterness. Conceiving
himself entitled, from his long experience, his tried attachment to
the church, and his relationship to the queen (he was her maternal
uncle), to the chief office of the government, Rochester put in his
claim for it, and Anne was too timid and indecisive to give him a
positive refusal. Saint-John, on the other hand, conscious of his
superior abilities, disdaining to be ruled, and master of the Jacobite
and movement sections of the Tory party, was determined no
longer to hold a subordinate place in the cabinet, and signified as
much to Mrs. Masham, to whom he paid secret and assiduous court.
Thus opposed, Harley seemed in danger of losing the prize for which
he had laboured so hard, when an occurrence took place, which
though at first apparently fraught with imminent peril, proved in
the end the means of accomplishing his desires. To explain this,
it will be necessary to go back for a short space.

One night, about six months after Sacheverell's trial, a man suddenly darted out of Little Man's Coffee-house—a notorious haunt of
sharpers—with a drawn sword in his hand, and made off at a furious
pace towards Pall Mall. He was pursued by half-a-dozen persons,
armed like himself, who chased him as far as the Haymarket, but
losing sight of him there, they waited a few moments, and then
turned back.

"Well, let him go," said one of them; "we know where to find
him, if the major's wounds should prove mortal."

"The major has won above five hundred pounds from him," observed another; "so if he has got hurt, he can afford to buy plasters
for his wounds."

"It has been diamond cut diamond throughout, but the major

has proved the sharper in more senses than one," observed a third, with a laugh; "but as the marquis has palmed, topped, knapped, and slurred the dice himself, he could not, in reason, blame the major for using fulhams."

"I shouldn't care if the marquis could keep his temper," said a fourth; "but his sword is out whenever he loses, and the major is not the first, by some score, that he has pinked."

"Defend me from the marquis!" said the first. "I suppose we have done with him now. He's regularly cleaned out."

"Yet he's so clever a fellow, that it wouldn't surprise me if he were to find out a way to retrieve his fortunes," said the third.

"He'd sell himself to the devil to do so, I don't doubt," remarked the first; "but, come! let's go back to the major. We must procure him some assistance."

Finding his pursuers gone, the Marquis de Guiscard, who had retreated into a small street near the Haymarket, issued from his place of concealment, and proceeded slowly homewards. His gait was unsteady, as if from intoxication; and he uttered ever and anon a deep oath, smiting his forehead with his clenched hand.

On reaching his residence, the door was opened by Bimbelot, who started on beholding his wild and haggard looks. Snatching a light from the terrified valet, Guiscard rushed up stairs and entered a room, but presently returned to the landing, and called to Bimbelot, in a loud, angry voice—

"Where's your mistress, rascal? Is she not come home?"

"No, monseigneur," replied the valet. "Madame is gone to the masquerade, and you are aware it is seldom over before four or five o'clock in the morning."

Uttering an angry ejaculation, the marquis returned to the room, and flinging himself into a chair, buried his face in his hands, and was for some time lost in the bitterest and most painful reflection.

He then arose, and pacing to and fro, exclaimed—"Disgrace and ruin stare me in the face! What shall I do?—how retrieve myself? Fool! madman that I was, to risk all I had against the foul play of those sharpers. They have fleeced me of everything; and to-morrow, my house, and all within it, will be seized by the merciless Jew, Solomons, who has hunted me down like a beast of prey. The discontinuance of my pension of a hundred ducatoons a month from the States-General of Holland—the disbanding of my regiment, and the consequent loss of my pay—the extravagances of the woman I was fool enough to marry for the bribe of a thousand pounds from Harley, thrice which amount she has since spent—the failure of my schemes—the death of my stanch friend the Comte de Briançon—all these calamities have reduced me to such a state, that I was weak enough—mad enough—to place my whole fortune on one last stake. And now I have lost it!—lost it to a sharper! But if he has robbed me, he will scarce live to enjoy the spoil."

And with a savage laugh he sat down, and relapsed into silence. His thoughts, however, were too maddening to let him remain long tranquil.

"Something must be done!" he cried, getting up, distractedly;

"but what—what? To-morrow, the wreck of my property will be seized, and I shall be thrown into prison by Solomons. But I can fly—the night is before me. To fly, I must have the means of flight —and how procure them? Is there nothing here I can carry off— my pictures are gone—my plate—all my valuables—except—ha! the jewels Angelica brought from Saint-John!—They are left—they will save me. The necklace alone cost three hundred pounds. Suppose, however, it fetches a third of the sum, I can contrive to exist upon that till something turns up. Money is to be had from France. Ha! ha! I am not utterly lost. I shall retire for a time, only to appear again with new splendour."

Full of these thoughts he proceeded to a small cabinet standing near the bed, and opening it, took out a case, which he unfastened. It was empty.

"The jewels are gone!—she has robbed me!" he exclaimed. "Perdition seize her! My last hope is annihilated!"

Transported with rage and despair, he lost all command of himself, and taking down a pistol, which hung near the bed, he held it to his temples, and was about to pull the trigger, when Bimbelot, who had been on the watch for some minutes, rushed forward, and implored him to stay his hand.

"I know you are ruined, monseigneur," cried the valet; "but it will not mend the matter to kill yourself."

"Fool!" exclaimed the marquis, furiously—"but for your stupid interference all my troubles would have been over by this time. Why should I live?"

"In the hope of better days," returned Bimbelot. "Fortune may smile upon you as heretofore."

"No—no, the jade has deserted me for ever!" cried the marquis. "I shall not struggle longer. Leave me!"

"Only postpone your resolution till to-morrow, monseigneur, and I'm persuaded you will think better of it," urged Bimbelot; "if not, the same remedy is at hand."

"Well," replied Guiscard, putting down the pistol, "I *will* wait till to-morrow, if only to settle accounts with my faithless wife."

"Better let her settle them herself," replied Bimbelot. "If monseigneur would be advised by me, he would quit this house for a short time, and live in retirement, till means can be devised of pacifying his creditors."

"You awaken new hope within my breast, my faithful fellow," replied Guiscard; "I will leave to-morrow morning before any one is astir, and you shall accompany me."

"I wont desert you, monseigneur," replied Bimbelot; "but there's no fear of disturbing the household, for all the servants are gone."

"Gone!" exclaimed Guiscard.

"Yes, monseigneur," replied Bimbelot; "like rats, I suppose, they smelt a falling house. They all quitted this evening, and I fancy, not empty-handed. Mrs. Charlotte, after attiring her lady for the masquerade, dressed herself, packed up her things, and drove off with them in a coach."

"A curse go with her!" cried the marquis.

"I alone have remained behind, because," whimpered the hypocritical valet—"because, my dear and noble master, I would not desert you in your extremity."

"You shall not regret your fidelity, if brighter days shine upon me, Bimbelot," replied Guiscard, touched by his devotion.

"There is one way in which you can readily repair your fortune, monseigneur," replied Bimbelot. "Being on the spot, you can exercise a vigilant espionage over the English court. Our monarch, the great Louis, will pay well for any secrets of importance."

"The secrets may be obtained," replied Guiscard, "but it is difficult to convey them. Everything is easy with money at command, but without it——"

"Monseigneur was not wont to shrink before difficulties," said Bimbelot.

"Nor do I shrink now," replied the marquis. "I will take any means, however desperate, to repair my fortunes. To-morrow, I will make an appeal to Harley and Saint-John to assist me in my emergency, and if they refuse me, I will frighten them into compliance."

"Spoken like yourself, monseigneur," replied the valet.

"I shall try to get a few hours' repose," replied the marquis, throwing himself upon the bed; "and I will then seek a hiding-place with you. Call me an hour before daybreak."

"Without fail, monseigneur," replied the valet. "If Madame la Maréchale should chance to return, what is to be done with her?"

"It will be time enough to think of her when she arrives," rejoined Guiscard, drowsily. "Show her to her room."

"Monseigneur will use no violence?" supplicated the valet.

"Fear nothing," replied Guiscard; "and now leave me. I shall be calmer when I have had a little sleep."

On going down stairs, Bimbelot repaired to a back room, where Sauvageon was comfortably seated, with a bottle of claret before him.

"I was just in time," observed the valet; "he was going out of the world in a desperate hurry, and that wouldn't suit our purpose."

"Not in the least," replied Sauvageon, emptying his glass. "What's he about now?"

"Taking a little repose," returned Bimbelot, "prior to quitting the house. I threw out a hint about renewing his correspondence with the French court, and he snapped greedily at the bait."

"Ha! ha!" laughed Sauvageon. "We shall have him, then."

"Safe enough," replied Bimbelot. "The reward promised us by Mr. Harley for the discovery of his secret practices will not be lost. We shall be able to bring them home to him ere long."

As the words were uttered, a loud knocking was heard at the outer door.

"Sarpedieu!" exclaimed Bimbelot, "Madame la Maréchale has returned before her time. This is unlucky."

So saying, he hurried to the door, and finding it was the marchioness, ushered her in with as much respect as if nothing had happened, and lighted her up stairs, taking the precaution, however, to desire the chairmen to wait.

Entering a chamber at the head of the stairs, Angelica threw down her mask, and divesting herself of a pink silk domino, disclosed a magnificeut dress of white brocade. Her head was covered with a fancy Spanish hat, looped with diamonds, and adorned with ostrich feathers. She was considerably fatter than before, and her features were coarser, but she still looked excessively handsome.

"Send Charlotte to me," she cried, sinking in a chair.

"Mrs. Charlotte is not returned, madame," replied Bimbelot.

"Not returned!" exclaimed Angelica. "How dared she go out without leave! I shall discharge her in the morning. Send Dawson, then."

"Mrs. Dawson is gone out, too," replied Bimbelot. "In fact, all the women have gone out; but I shall be very happy to assist madame, if I can be of any service."

"Assist me!" cried Angelica, starting up. "Marry, come up! here's assurance with a vengeance! A valet offer to be a lady's maid! Leave the room instantly, fellow. I shall acquaint the marquis with your presumption."

"Le voici, madame," replied Bimbelot, grinning malignantly. And he retired, to make way for Guiscard, who entered the room at the moment.

"What is the meaning of this, marquis?" cried Angelica. "Have you discharged the servants?"

"They have discharged themselves," replied Guiscard, coldly. "Having discovered that I am a ruined man, they have taken themselves off."

"Ruined! oh, gracious!" cried Angelica. "Give me the salts, or I shall faint."

"No you wont," he replied, drily. "Now listen to me. Our ruin may be averted for a time, perhaps altogether, by the sale of the jewels you brought with you when I took you from Saint-John. Let me have them—quick!"

"I can't give them to you," sobbed Angelica.

'Why not?" demanded Guiscard, fiercely.

"Because—because I've pledged them to Mr. Solomons, the Jew, for a hundred pounds," she answered.

"He gave you not the tithe of what they're worth," cried Guiscard, gnashing his teeth. "But it matters not, since they're gone. Have you any other trinkets left?"

"Nothing but this diamond buckle, and I shan't part with it," replied Angelica.

"You wont?" cried the marquis.

"I wont," she answered, firmly.

"We'll see that," he replied, snatching the hat from her, and tearing out the buckle.

"I am glad you've done it, marquis," said Angelica. "Your brutality justifies me in leaving you."

"Don't trouble yourself to find an excuse for going, I pray, madam," said the marquis, bitterly. "It is sufficient that I am ruined. I neither expected you to remain with me, nor desired it. I have no doubt you will find some one ready to receive you."

"That's my concern, marquis," she rejoined. "Provided I don't trouble you, you need not inquire where I go."

"Undoubtedly not," said Guiscard, bowing. "We part, then, for ever. And remember, in case you should feel inclined for another union, that a Fleet marriage is as easily dissolved as contracted."

"I shan't forget it," she replied; "but I've had enough of marriage for the present. And now, good night, marquis. I shall be gone before you are up to-morrow morning. I would go now, but——"

"Madame la Maréchale's chair still waits," said Bimbelot, entering the room.

"How purely fortunate!" exclaimed Angelica. "In that case I shall go at once. Tell the men to take me to Mr. Solomons's, in Threadneedle-street. It's a long distance, but they will be well paid."

"Make my compliments to Mr. Solomons, madam," said the marquis, with a sneer; "and tell him that as he has become possessed of all my valuables—yourself the chief of them—I hope he will show me more consideration than he has hitherto done."

"I shall not fail to deliver the message," replied Angelica. "Adieu, marquis!" And she tripped down stairs, followed by Bimbelot.

CHAPTER X.

OF THE MARQUIS DE GUISCARD'S ATTEMPT TO ASSASSINATE HARLEY.

AN hour before daybreak, a coach was brought by Bimbelot, into which such things were put as the marquis thought fit to remove. He then drove to the Red Lion, in Wardour-street, a small tavern, where he hoped to remain unmolested. On the same day, at the hazard of arrest, he attended Harley's levée, but was refused admittance, and, exasperated at the affront, he returned to the inn, and wrote a long letter to the minister, threatening, if assistance were not given him, to reveal all that had passed between them to the Duchess of Marlborough.

On the following morning, he waited upon Saint-John, with whom he had better success. The secretary received him kindly, and, apparently much touched by the account he gave of his circumstances, blamed Harley for his indifference, and promised to represent Guiscard's condition to the queen. And he was as good as his word, for he spoke so warmly to Anne, that she graciously ordered a pension of five hundred a-year to be granted to the marquis.

The order being notified to the commissioners of the treasury, Harley struck off a hundred a-year from the grant, alleging, in excuse, that the funds of the exchequer were exhausted. For this ill turn, as he conceived it, Guiscard vowed revenge, and sought to obtain an audience of the queen, for the purpose of making disclosures to her, but was unable to effect his object.

Some degree of credit being restored to him, the marquis again ventured forth publicly; took lodgings in Ryder-street, and began to frequent the coffee-houses as before. He still played, but with greater caution, and often came off a winner of small sums. Thus encouraged, he proceeded to greater lengths, and in one night was once more beggared by a run of ill luck.

In this desperate extremity he had recourse to Saint-John, who, moved to compassion by his tale, and having, moreover, a liking for loose characters, gave him out of his own purse a sum sufficient for his immediate necessities, recommending him caution in the use of it; but so far from acting up to the advice, the marquis on that very day, as if drawn irresistibly to destruction, lost it all at the faro table.

Shame having by this time utterly forsaken him, he once more applied to Saint-John, but met with a peremptory refusal, and ever after this the secretary was denied to him.

Driven to the most desperate straits, he now subsisted on such small sums as he could borrow—for he had anticipated the first instalment of his pension, and was frequently reduced to positive want. He lodged in Maggot's-court, an obscure passage leading out of Little Swallow-street, where he occupied a single room, miserably furnished. He still continued, however, to keep up a decent exterior, and daily haunted the purlieus of the palace, in the hope of picking up information.

Bimbelot had long since quitted his service, but frequently visited him, under the plea of offering him assistance, though in reality to ascertain whether he was carrying on a correspondence with France. While freely confessing that he was so engaged, the marquis was too cautious to admit his former valet into his plans, until, one day, the latter found him in the act of sealing a packet, when, as if unable to constrain himself, he broke forth, thus—

"Ere many days, Bimbelot, you will see the whole of this capital —nay, the whole of this country, convulsed. A great blow will be struck, and mine will be the hand to strike it!"

"What mean you, monseigneur?" said the valet, trembling with eager curiosity.

"I have just written to the court of France," pursued Guiscard, with increasing excitement, "that a *coup d'état* may be expected, which will cause a wonderful alteration in the affairs of this country; and I have added that this is the most favourable conjuncture for the prince, whom they here wrongfully style the Pretender, to make a descent upon England, where he will find great numbers disposed to join him, and amongst the rest, three parts of the clergy."

"But the blow you mean to strike—the blow, monseigneur?" demanded the valet.

"Will be aimed at the highest person in the realm," replied Guiscard, smiling savagely. "The prince will find the throne vacant."

"Ha!—indeed!" ejaculated Bimbelot, unable to repress his surprise and horror.

"Villain!" cried Guiscard, seizing him by the throat. "I have trusted you too far. Swear never to repeat a word I have uttered, or you are a dead man!"

"I swear it," replied Bimbelot. "I have no intention of betraying you, monseigneur."

Reassured by the valet's protestations, Guiscard released him, and as soon as he could venture to do so with safety, Bimbelot quitted the house. He did not, however, go far, but entered an adjoining tavern, whence he could play the spy on the marquis's movements.

Shortly afterwards, Guiscard came forth, when Bimbelot followed him, but at such a distance as not to attract his notice.

Shaping his course to Golden-square, the marquis stopped at the Earl of Portmore's residence, and delivered a packet to one of the servants. As soon as the coast was clear, Bimbelot came up, and learnt that the packet was addressed to the Earl of Portmore (then commander-in-chief in Portugal), and was to be forwarded to his lordship, with his other letters, by his wife, the Countess of Dorchester.

Somewhat puzzled by the information, Bimbelot resolved to lay it before Harley, and he accordingly proceeded to Saint James's-square for that purpose. He was quickly admitted to an audience with the minister; and the intelligence appeared so important to the latter, that a queen's messenger was instantly despatched for the packet, and in a short time returned with it.

On breaking the cover, its contents proved to be a letter addressed to a merchant at Lisbon, and within that was another cover, directed to M. Moreau, a banker in Paris, which being unsealed, the whole of the marquis's atrocious projects were disclosed.

After perusing these documents, Harley ordered Bimbelot to be detained, and repaired to Mr. Saint-John, by whom a warrant was issued for the marquis's arrest.

Three queen's messengers were then sent in search of the offender By good fortune they found him in Saint James's Park, and before he could offer any resistance, secured and disarmed him. The marquis besought them to kill him on the spot; but, turning a deaf ear to his entreaties, they conveyed him to the Cock-pit, where he was placed in a room adjoining the secretary of state's office. His clothes were then carefully searched, and everything taken from him; but the scrutiny was scarcely concluded, when he contrived, unperceived, to possess himself of a penknife which chanced to be lying on a desk near him, and to slip it into his sleeve. Possessed of this weapon, all his audacity and confidence returned, and he awaited his approaching examination with apparent unconcern.

Meanwhile, the news of Guiscard's capture was conveyed to Harley; and shortly afterwards, a privy council, consisting of himself, Saint-John, Sir Simon Harcourt, the Earl of Rochester, the Dukes of Newcastle, Ormond, and Queensbury, together with Lords Dartmouth and Poulet, assembled in the secretary's room,—

a plainly furnished chamber, containing merely a large table covered with green cloth, round which a number of chairs were set, a small side-table for the under-secretaries, and a full-length portrait of the queen by Kneller.

Saint-John officiated as chairman. After a brief conference among the council, the prisoner was introduced. He looked pale as death, but maintained a stern and composed demeanour, and glanced haughtily and menacingly at Saint-John and Harley.

"I am surprised and sorry to see you in this position, marquis," observed the latter.

"You may be sorry, but can scarcely be surprised, sir," rejoined Guiscard.

"How so?" demanded the other, sharply. "Do you mean to infer ——"

"I infer nothing," interrupted Guiscard; "let the examination proceed."

"You are brought here, prisoner, charged with treason and *leze majesté* of the highest class," commenced Saint-John.

"By whom am I thus charged?" asked Guiscard, impatiently.

"No matter by whom," rejoined the secretary. "You are accused of holding secret and treasonable correspondence with the court of France. How do you answer?"

"I deny it," replied Guiscard, boldly.

"The next allegation against you, prisoner, is one of the blackest dye," pursued Saint-John: "you are charged with plotting to take the life of our sovereign lady the queen, to whom you, though a foreigner, are bound by the strongest ties of gratitude, for many favours conferred by her majesty upon you."

"Heaven forbid I should be capable of harbouring a thought against the queen!" cried the marquis, fervently. "I should indeed be a monster of ingratitude."

At this asseveration, there was an irrepressible murmur of indignation among the council.

"I know the miscreant who has thus maligned me," continued Guiscard. "He is a man who served me as valet—a man of infamous and unscrupulous character, who has forged this story to obtain a reward from Mr. Harley."

"I would now ask, prisoner," pursued Saint-John, "if you have any acquaintance with M. Moreau, a banker, at Paris? and if you have held any communication with him lately?"

At the mention of this name, in spite of himself, Guiscard trembled.

"I used to know such a person," he replied; "but I have had no correspondence with him for many years."

"That is false!" replied Harley, producing the packet. "Here are your letters to him, in which you make the most diabolical proposals to the French government."

At the sight of the packet, a terrible change came over Guiscard. His limbs shook, and the damps gathered thickly on his brow.

"It is useless to brave it out further, wretched man!" said Harley. "As some slight atonement of your offence, I recommend you to make a full confession."

"I *will* confess, Mr. Harley," replied Guiscard, "and I may say more than you may care to hear. But first, I beg to have a word in private with Mr. Saint-John."

"That is impossible," rejoined the secretary. "You are here before the council as a criminal, and if you have anything to advance, it must be uttered before us all."

"What I have to say is important to the state," urged Guiscard; "but I will not utter it, except to you. You may make what use you please of it afterwards."

"The request is unusual, and cannot be granted," replied Saint-John, coldly.

"You will repent your non-compliance with my wishes, Mr. Saint-John," said Guiscard.

"This pertinacity is intolerable," cried the secretary, rising. "Let the messengers remove the prisoner," he added, to one of the under-secretaries.

"A moment—only one moment," said Guiscard, approaching Harley, who had taken the seat just quitted by Saint-John. "You will intercede with her majesty to spare my life, Mr. Harley? You were once my friend."

"I can hold out no hope for you, prisoner," replied Harley, sternly. "The safety of the state requires that crimes of such magnitude as yours should not go unpunished."

"Where are the messengers?" cried Saint-John, impatiently.

"Will you not endeavour to prove my innocence, Mr. Harley?" said Guiscard, drawing close to the minister.

"How can I, with such damning evidences as these before me?" cried Harley, pointing to the letters. "Stand back, sir!"

"Can nothing move you?" repeated Guiscard.

Harley shook his head.

"Then have at thee, thou blacker traitor than myself!" thundered Guiscard.

And plucking the penknife suddenly from his sleeve, he plunged it into Harley's breast. The blade came in contact with the bone, and snapped near the handle, but unconscious of the accident, Guiscard repeated the blow with greater violence than before, exclaiming—"This to thy heart, perfidious villain!"

The suddenness of the assault for a moment paralyzed the spectators. But recovering themselves, they sprang to Harley's assistance. Saint-John was the first to attack the assassin, and passed his sword twice through his body; but though Guiscard received other wounds from the Duke of Newcastle, who, being seated at the lower end of the table, leapt upon it, and thus made his way to the scene of action, as well as from Lord Dartmouth, he did not fall. Some of the council nearest Guiscard were so much alarmed by his infuriated appearance, that, fearing he might turn his rage upon them, they sought to protect themselves with chairs. Others shouted for help, while the Earl of Poulet called loudly to Saint-John and Newcastle not to kill the assassin, as it was most important to the ends of justice that his life should be preserved.

Amid this confusion the messengers and door-keepers rushed in, and threw themselves upon Guiscard, who, wounded as he was, defended himself with surprising vigour, and some minutes elapsed before he could be overpowered. In the struggle he received many severe bruises, one of which chancing in the back, occasioned his death.

While the messengers were in the act of binding him as he lay upon the ground, he said to the Duke of Ormond, who stood near him, "Is Harley dead? I thought I heard him fall."

"No, villain! he lives to balk your vindictive purpose," replied the duke.

Guiscard gnashed his teeth in impotent rage.

"I pray your grace dispatch me!" he groaned.

"That is the executioner's business, not mine," replied the duke, turning away.

Nothing could exceed the calmness and composure exhibited by Harley on this trying occasion. Uncertain whether he had received a mortal wound, he held a handkerchief to his breast to stanch the blood, patiently awaiting the arrival of a surgeon, and conversing tranquilly with his friends, who crowded round him, expressing the most earnest solicitude for his safety.

And well might he be content, though he knew not then why. That blow made him lord treasurer and earl of Oxford.

CHAPTER XI.

WHEREIN HARLEY ATTAINS THE HIGHEST POINT OF HIS AMBITION; AND THE MARQUIS DE GUISCARD IS DISPOSED OF.

SHORTLY afterwards, Mr. Bussiére, an eminent surgeon, residing near Saint James's Park, arrived, and while examining the extent of injury sustained by the sufferer, the penknife-blade fell from the waistcoat into his hand. Seeing this, Harley took it from him, observing with a smile, that it belonged to him, and requesting that the handle of the knife might be preserved. He then demanded of the surgeon, whether his hurts were likely to prove mortal? "If you think so," he said, "do not hide your fears from me. I profess no idle disregard of death, but there are some family affairs which it is necessary I should arrange before I am driven to extremity."

"I am not apprehensive of any serious consequences, sir," replied Bussiére; "but as a slight fever will probably ensue, it may be well not to allow anything to disturb your mind. If you have any arrangements, therefore, to make, I would recommend you not to postpone them."

"I understand you, sir," returned Harley; "and will not neglect the caution."

His wounds were then probed and dressed. He bore the operation, which was necessarily painful, with great fortitude, not once uttering a groan, and jestingly remarking, as the incision was enlarged, that the surgeon's knife was sharper than Guiscard's

The dressing completed, Bussiére declared that there was not the least danger, and that he would be answerable for his patient's speedy and perfect cure—an announcement which was heard with the liveliest satisfaction by every one present except the assassin, who, as he lay bound in a corner, gave vent to his disappointment in a deep execration. This drew Harley's attention to him, and he begged Bussiére to examine his wounds.

"Better let me die," cried Guiscard; "for if I recover I will make such revelations as shall for ever blast your credit."

"Ungrateful dog!" exclaimed Saint-John; "actuated as you evidently are by vindictive motives, any statement you may make will be disregarded."

"You yourself are equally guilty with Harley, Saint-John," rejoined Guiscard. "I denounce you both as traitors to your country and your queen, and I desire to have my words written down, that I may subscribe them before I die."

"It is useless," cried the Duke of Ormond. "No one will believe the accusation of an assassin."

"You are all in league together," cried Guiscard. "If you will not listen to me, let a priest be sent for. I will make my confession to him."

"Better let the villain speak," remarked the Earl of Rochester, who, it may be remembered, was Harley's opponent, "or it may be said hereafter that his charges were stifled."

"I perfectly agree with you, my lord," said Harley. "Let one of the secretaries take down his declaration."

"Do not trouble yourself further," interposed Bussiére. "Any excitement will retard your recovery, and may possibly endanger your safety."

"Be advised, Harley," urged Saint-John.

"No," replied the other; "I will stay to hear him. I am well enough now. Say on, prisoner. What have you to allege against me?"

Guiscard made no reply.

"Why do you not speak, villain?" demanded the Earl of Rochester.

"He cannot, my lord," replied Bussiére; "he has fainted. Some time must elapse before he can be brought round, and then I doubt whether he will be able to talk coherently.

"If such is your opinion, sir, it is useless to remain here longer," rejoined Harley. "Saint-John, will you acquaint her majesty with the attempt made upon my life, and assure her that, so far from repining at the mischance, I rejoice in the opportunity it affords me of testifying my fidelity. Had I not been true to the queen, her enemies would not assail me thus."

"I will faithfully deliver your message," replied Saint-John; "and I am sure the queen will be as sensible of your devotion as we are of your courage."

With this, Harley, assisted by Bussiére and the Duke of Ormond, entered the sedan-chair which had been brought into the room, and was conveyed in it to his own residence.

Bussiére next turned his attention to the prisoner, and after dressing his wounds, which were numerous and severe, a litter was brought, in which he was transported to Newgate, under the care of two messengers, who had orders to watch him narrowly, lest he should attempt his life.

In compliance with Harley's request, Saint-John hastened to the queen to inform her of the disastrous occurrence. She was much shocked by the intelligence, as well as touched by Harley's message, and expressed the most earnest hopes for his recovery, that she might have opportunity of proving her sense of his devotion. Next day, addresses were made by both houses of parliament, expressive of their concern at the "barbarous and villanous attempt" made upon Mr. Harley's person, and beseeching her majesty to give directions for the removal of all papists from the cities of London and Westminster. An act was afterwards passed, making it felony, without benefit of clergy, to attempt the life of a privy-councillor.

For nearly a week Harley continued in a precarious state, owing to the sloughing of his wound, and more than a month elapsed before his perfect recovery was established. His first step was to wait upon the queen at Saint James's, to offer thanks for her frequent inquiries after him.

"Heaven be praised!" exclaimed Anne, "that the malice of our enemies—for your enemies are mine—has been disappointed. I shall take care to let them see that each demonstration of their hatred only calls forth fresh favours from me."

On Harley's first appearance in the House of Commons, congratulations on his escape were offered him by the speaker, to which Harley replied with much emotion:—"The honour done me by this house so far exceeds my deserts, that all I can do or suffer for the public during the whole course of my life, will still leave me in debt to your goodness. Whenever I place my hand upon my breast, it will put me in mind of the thanks due to God, of my duty to the queen, and of the debt of gratitude and service I must always owe to this honourable house."

Harley's return to business was signalized by the introduction of a grand project which he had long entertained for paying off the national debts and deficiencies, by allowing the proprietors of such debts six per cent. interest, and granting them the monopoly of the trade to the South Sea; a scheme which afterwards gave rise to the establishment of the South Sea Company. This scheme, though little better than a bubble, as it eventually proved, was admirably adapted to the speculative spirit of the age, and met with a most enthusiastic reception. The bill was instantly carried, and a new mine of wealth was supposed to be opened. Most opportunely for Harley, just at this juncture, while his popularity was at its zenith, his rival, the Earl of Rochester, died suddenly; and the queen, having no longer any check upon her impulses, at once yielded to them; and having first created Harley Earl of Oxford and Mortimer, on the anniversary of the restoration of her uncle, Charles the Second, to the kingdom, placed the treasurer's staff in his hands.

Thus Harley's ambitious designs were at length crowned with success.

Brought to Newgate, Guiscard was taken to an underground cell on the common side of the gaol, the dismal appearance of which struck him with so much horror, that he implored his attendants to let him have another chamber; and absolutely refused to lie down upon the loathsome bed allotted to him. His condition was supposed to be so dangerous, that force was not resorted to; and he was allowed to lie on a bench until the following morning, when the surgeon visited him, and found him in so alarming a state, that he instantly caused him to be removed to an airy apartment in the master's side. Here his attire was taken off, when another wound was discovered in the back, which, from want of attention, had already assumed a very dangerous appearance. As soon as it was dressed, he was put to bed; but his sufferings were too great to allow him to obtain any repose. About the middle of the day, the door was opened by the turnkey, who informed Guiscard that his wife desired to see him, and the next moment Angelica was ushered in.

"What brings you here, madam?" demanded Guiscard, fiercely.

"I have come to see you—to know whether I can be of use to you—to implore your forgiveness," she replied, in trembling accents.

"Then you have come on an idle errand," he rejoined. "Begone! and take my curse with you."

"Oh! pity me!" she cried, still lingering—"pity and forgive me!"

"Forgive you!" echoed Guiscard. "But for you, I should not be what I am!—But for you, I should now be the inmate of a magnificent mansion, reposing on a downy couch, full of hope and health, instead of lying here on this wretched bed, and in this narrow chamber—a felon—only to go hence to the gallows! Off with you, accursed woman! your presence stifles me. May your end be like mine—may you die in an hospital, shunned by all, a leprous, loathsome mass!"

"Horrible!" shrieked Angelica. "Oh! let me out! let me out!"

As the door was opened for her by the turnkey, another person was introduced. It was Bimbelot, who could not repress his curiosity to behold his victim.

"Ah, monseigneur! ah, my dear master! do I behold you in this deplorable condition!" whimpered the hypocritical valet.

"Ha!" exclaimed Guiscard, starting bolt upright in bed, and glaring at the valet with so fierce an expression that the latter retreated towards the door. "Are you come here to deride my misery?"

"On the contrary, monseigneur," replied Bimbelot, trembling, "I am come to offer my services. I deplore your situation, and will do anything in my power to relieve it."

"Get hanged, then, at the same tree as myself," rejoined the marquis, savagely.

"I am sorry I cannot afford you that satisfaction, monseigneur," replied Bimbelot ; " but there is no need to talk of hanging at all. I am the bearer of good news to you. Her majesty offers you a pardon, if you will make a full confession."

"Ah, villain, you are at your damnable practices again !" cried Guiscard. "You think to delude me further. But you are mistaken."

"No, monseigneur, I am your friend," replied the valet.

"Well, I will trust you once more," said Guiscard, changing his tone. "I have something to say to you. Come near, that I may whisper in your ear."

"You may place perfect reliance on me," replied Bimbelot, winking at the turnkey as he advanced towards the prisoner.

But as he came within reach, Guiscard caught him by the throat, dragged him upon the bed, and would have strangled him, if the turnkey had not flown to the poor wretch's assistance. As he was dragged out of the cell, more dead than alive, the marquis gave vent to a loud demoniacal laugh.

But the exertion proved fatal to him. Ere long, he became delirious, uttered the most frightful blasphemies and imprecations, and evinced his terror of the ignominious death which he fancied awaited him, by clasping his hands round his throat, as if to protect himself from the hangman. An attempt was made later in the day, when he became calmer, to obtain a confession from him ; but he was so oppressed by an extravasation of blood which filled part of the cavity of the chest, that he was unable to speak, and indeed could scarcely breathe. His wounds had now become excessively painful, and some operations were performed by the surgeons for his relief. In this state of suffering, he lingered on till late in the following night, and then expired.

A shameful indignity was offered to his remains. The surgeons having received instructions to preserve the body, placed it in a large pickling-tub, in which state it was exhibited to a host of lovers of horrible sights by the jailors. The body was afterwards interred, without any ceremony, in the common burying-place of the malefactors dying in Newgate.

Such was the end of the gay and once admired Marquis de Guiscard ! the shame of his race.

CHAPTER XII.

CONTAINING THE FINAL INTERVIEW BETWEEN THE QUEEN AND THE DUCHESS OF MARLBOROUGH.

ALL friendly intercourse between Anne and the Duchess of Marlborough had for some time ceased, and the latter, becoming sensible, at last, of the ascendancy of her rival, Mrs. Masham, and of the utter impossibility of regaining the influence she had lost, wrote to remind the queen of a promise she had extorted from her in a moment of good-nature, to bestow her places upon her daughters, and entreated permission to retire in their favour.

Anne replied, that she could not think of parting with her for the present; but being again importuned, peremptorily desired not to be troubled again on the subject. Notwithstanding this interdiction, the duchess addressed another long letter of remonstrance and reproach to her royal mistress; after which she withdrew altogether from court, and retired to the lodge at Windsor, held by her in virtue of her office as keeper of the Great and Home Parks. Advantage was immediately taken of her absence to circulate a number of reports to her disadvantage, some of which reaching the ears of the duchess, she immediately returned to court, with the intention of exculpating herself before the queen. Anne received her with the greatest coldness in the presence of the Duchess of Somerset and Mrs. Masham, and refused to grant a private audience. Unable to brook the sneers with which she was regarded, the proud duchess drew herself up to her utmost height, and glancing scornfully at Mrs. Masham, observed—" Since your majesty compels me to do so, I declare openly, and in the hearing of all, that the basest falsehoods have been propagated concerning me by your unworthy favourite, and that she now prevents my justification from being heard."

" It is false, duchess!" replied Mrs. Masham. " But for my intercession her majesty would not have received you, after your insolent letter to her."

" But for *your* intercession, minion!" cried the duchess, advancing towards her, and seizing her arm with violence. " Is it come to this? Can I have indeed sunk so low, that you—a creature whom I have raised from abject poverty—should tell me that you have interfered in my behalf with the queen?"

" Duchess!" exclaimed the queen, angrily.

" You will find her out in time, madam," rejoined the duchess, " and you will then learn whom you have trusted. The best proof of her uneasiness is afforded by the fact that she dares not let me speak in private with you."

" I would spare her majesty a scene—that is my only motive for opposing the interview," replied Mrs. Masham.

" So you admit that you *do* control her majesty's actions, minion!" cried the duchess, bitterly. " She is governed by you—ha!"

" Whenever the queen deigns to consult me, I give her the best counsel in my power," replied Mrs. Masham.

" And most pernicious counsel it is," observed the duchess, furiously, " venomous serpent that you are!"

" To put an end to this dispute, duchess," interposed Anne, with dignity, " I will grant you a final interview. Present yourself at six this evening."

" I thank your majesty," replied the duchess, " the rather that your permission is accorded against the expressed wishes of Mrs. Masham. You will bitterly repent the favour you have shown her!"

" Her majesty cannot repent it more bitterly than she regrets the favours she has lavished upon you, duchess," observed Mrs. Masham, " and which have been requited by such base ingratitude."

" It is for her majesty to judge my conduct, and not you, minion!"

cried the duchess, proudly. "I will justify myself to her, and to the whole nation. Nay, more; I will open her eyes to your duplicity and treachery."

"I am too secure of her majesty's good opinion, and too confident in my own honesty, to fear your threats, duchess," replied Mrs. Masham, derisively.

"Hypocrite!" exclaimed the duchess.

"Insolent!" responded Mrs. Masham.

"No more of this," cried the queen; "these broils distract me. I agreed to an interview with you, duchess, on the understanding that nothing more should pass here. If you persist in this quarrel, I withdraw my assent."

"I have done, madam," rejoined the duchess, restraining herself. "It shall not be said that I failed in proper respect to your majesty; neither shall it be said that any court favourite insulted me with impunity. This evening, I shall not fail to avail myself of your gracious permission to wait upon you." And with a profound obeisance to the queen, and a look of haughty defiance at the others, she withdrew.

"Her insolence is insufferable!" exclaimed the queen. "I almost repent that I have promised to receive her."

"Why not retract the promise, then, madam?" said Abigail. "Bid her make her communication in writing."

"It shall be so," replied Anne, after a moment's hesitation.

"I am glad your majesty has so decided," said Mrs. Masham. "It is not likely that the duchess will be satisfied with the refusal; but it will convince her that she has nothing to expect."

And so it proved. The message being delivered to the duchess, she begged the queen to make a new appointment. "Your majesty cannot refuse me one last interview," she wrote; "neither can you be so unjust to an old and faithful servant as to deny her an opportunity of justifying herself before you. I do not desire any answer to my vindication, but simply a hearing."

"What shall I do, Masham?" said the queen to her favourite, who was present when the message was delivered.

"Decline to see her," replied Mrs. Masham; "but if she forces herself upon you, as will probably be the case, take her at her word, and do not vouchsafe any answer to her explanation, which, rely upon it, will rather be an attack upon others than a defence of herself."

"You are right, Masham," returned the queen. "I will follow your advice."

Mrs. Masham's conjecture proved just: on that same evening, without waiting for any reply from the queen, the duchess repaired to Saint James's Palace, and proceeding to the back staircase, of the door of which she still retained the key, mounted it, but was stopped on the landing by a page.

"Do you not know me, sir?" cried the duchess, angrily.

"Perfectly, your grace," replied the page, bowing respectfully; "but I am forbidden to allow any one to pass through this door without her majesty's permission."

"And the Duchess of Marlborough especially, sir—eh?" she rejoined.

"It would be improper to contradict your grace," returned the page.

"Will you do me the favour, sir, to acquaint her majesty that I am here, and add, that I crave a few minutes' audience of her—only a few minutes," rejoined the duchess.

"I may incur her majesty's displeasure by so doing," answered the page. "Nevertheless, to oblige your grace, I will hazard it."

"Is the queen alone?" asked the duchess.

"Mrs. Masham, I believe, is with her," replied the page. "Her majesty has just dined."

"Mrs. Masham—ha!" exclaimed the duchess. "No matter. Take in the message, my good friend."

Nearly half an hour elapsed before the page returned, during which time the duchess was detained on the landing. Apologizing for the unavoidable delay, he begged her to follow him.

"You have tarried long enough to settle all that is to be said to me, sir," observed the duchess.

"I know nothing, your grace," replied the page, walking forward discreetly.

The next moment, the duchess was ushered into a cabinet, in which she found the queen alone.

"Good evening, duchess," said Anne. "I did not expect to see you. I was just about to write to you."

"I am sorry to intrude upon your majesty," replied the duchess; "but I have some important communications to make to you."

"Ah—indeed!" exclaimed Anne. "Can you not put them in writing?"

"They will be quickly told, gracious madam," said the duchess.

"Better write to me," interrupted Anne.

"But, madam——"

"Write—write," cried Anne, impatiently.

"Oh, madam! you are indeed changed, if you can use me thus!" cried the duchess. "You never yet, to my knowledge, refused to hear any petitioner speak, and yet you refuse me—your once favoured—once beloved friend. Be not alarmed, madam. I do not intend to trouble you on any subject disagreeable to you. I simply wish to clear myself from the imputations with which I have been charged."

"I suppose I must hear," cried Anne, with a gesture of impatience, and averting her head.

"Oh! not thus, madam," exclaimed the duchess—"not thus! For pity's sake, look at me. You were not used to be so hard-hearted. Evil counsellors have produced a baneful effect upon your gentle nature. Be to me, if only for a few minutes, while I plead my cause, the Mrs. Morley you were of yore."

"No, duchess," replied Anne, in a freezing tone, and without looking at her—"all that is past. You have to thank yourself for the change which has been wrought in me."

"Hear me, madam," cried the duchess, passionately; "I have

been much wronged before you—grievously wronged. There are those about you, whom I will not name, who have most falsely calumniated me. I am no more capable of saying aught against your majesty, than I am of taking the lives of my own offspring. Your name never passes my lips without respect—never, I take Heaven to witness!"

" You cannot impose upon me thus, duchess," said Anne, coldly. "Many false things are told of you, no doubt, but I judge not of them so much as of your own deportment and discourse."

"I am willing to amend both, madam," returned the duchess.

"It is useless," said Anne, in the same tone as before.

"Is the quarrel, then, irreparable?" demanded the duchess. " Notwithstanding your majesty's assurance, I am certain my enemies have prevailed with you. Give me an opportunity of clearing myself. What has been told you?"

" I shall give you no answer," replied Anne.

"No answer, madam!" cried the duchess.—"Is this kind—is it just? Is it worthy of you to treat me thus? I do not ask the names of my accusers. Nay, I promise you not to retort upon them, if I should suspect them. But tell me what I am charged with?"

" I shall give you no answer," replied the queen.

" Oh, madam—madam!" cried the duchess, "the cruel formula you adopt convinces me you have been schooled for the interview. Be your kind, good, gracious self, if only for a moment. Look at me, madam—look at me. I am not come here with any hope of winning my way back to your favour, for I know I have lost it irrecoverably; but I have come to vindicate my character as a faithful servant. You cannot refuse that plea, madam."

" You desired no answer, and you shall have none," replied the queen, rising, and moving towards the door.

"Oh! do not go, madam!" cried the duchess, following her, and throwing herself at her feet—" do not go, I implore you."

" What would you more?" demanded Anne, coldly, and still with averted looks.

" I would make a last appeal to you, madam," said the duchess, as soon as she could command herself. " By all that is right and just, I implore you to answer me. Have I not despised my own interest in comparison with serving you well and faithfully? Have I ever disowned the truth? Have I ever played the hypocrite with you? Have I ever offended you, except by over-zeal and vehemence —or, if you will, arrogance? If this is true, and it cannot be gainsaid, I am entitled to credit, when I avouch that my enemies have belied me behind my back. Do not turn a deaf ear to my entreaties, madam; but tell me what I am charged with? Answer—oh, answer!"

" You compel me to reiterate my words," replied the queen. " You shall have no answer."

" You deny me common justice, madam," cried the duchess, losing all patience, " in refusing me a hearing—justice, which is due to the meanest of your subjects. You owe it to yourself to speak out."

"Just or unjust, I will give you no answer," replied the queen. "And here our conference must end."

"So be it, then," returned the duchess, resuming all her haughtiness. "I have loved you sincerely, madam—ay, sincerely—because I believed my affection requited; but since you have cast me off, I shall crush all feelings of regard for you within my breast. If you were but an instrument in my hands, as some avouch, I at least used you to a noble purpose. Such will not be the case with her who now governs you. She will degrade you; and the rest of your reign will be as inglorious as its opening was splendid and triumphant. Let my words dwell upon your memory. Farewell —for ever, madam." And without another word, and without an obeisance, she quitted the apartment.

As soon as she was gone, Mrs. Masham entered from an adjoining chamber.

"Your majesty acted your part to admiration," she cried. "I did not give you credit for so much firmness."

"I had hard work to sustain my character," replied Anne, sinking into a chair. "I am truly thankful it is over."

"It is not yet quite over," said Mrs. Masham; "one step more requires to be taken."

"True," replied the queen, "I must call upon her to resign her places. But I do not like to give them to her daughters; and yet I believe I made a promise to that effect."

"Heed it not, madam," said Mrs. Masham. "Her grace has forfeited all title to further consideration on your part."

"I must own I should like to make you keeper of the privy purse, Masham," said Anne.

"And I admit I should like the place excessively, madam," replied Mrs. Masham.

"Would I could get rid of my scruples," said Anne, ruminating.

"I will relieve you of them, madam," replied Mrs. Masham. "The promise was extorted, and is therefore *not* binding."

"I will make another, then, freely, that shall be so, Masham," rejoined the queen. "You shall have the place."

"I am bound to you for ever, madam, by this and a thousand obligations," returned the artful favourite, in a tone, apparently, of the most fervent gratitude.

CHAPTER XIII.

IN WHAT MANNER THE GOLD KEY WAS DELIVERED UP BY THE DUCHESS.

THE duchess's dismissal, though fully resolved upon, as has just been shown, was, with Anne's customary irresolution, long postponed. At length, however, on the duke's return from the campaign of 1710, it was resolved to bring matters to a crisis; and, accordingly, when he waited upon her, the queen received him very coldly, studiously avoiding making any allusion to his successes, but observing, with some harshness, "I trust your grace will not allow a vote of thanks to be moved to you in parliament this year, because my ministers will certainly oppose it."

"It pains me to hear your majesty speak thus," replied Marlborough. "Such unmerited honours have ever been unsought by me, and I have welcomed them chiefly because I thought they redounded to your glory. I shall take care to avoid them in future."

"You will do well, my lord," replied Anne.

"Here is a letter from the duchess, which she entreated me to present to your majesty," pursued the duke. "Will you deign to take it?"

"I pray you excuse me," rejoined Anne, with freezing dignity; "all communication is closed between the duchess and myself."

"It is a letter of apology, madam," replied the duke—"of humble apology. Her grace wishes to give you an assurance, under her own hand, of her contrition for any faults she may have committed. She is willing and anxious to do anything that may be deemed reasonable, to prove the sincerity of her regrets; and since her presence has become irksome to your majesty, she is desirous of resigning her offices."

"I am glad to hear it, my lord," interrupted the queen, quickly.

"On the understanding, of course," pursued the duke, "that she is succeeded as groom of the stole by her eldest daughter, Lady Ryalton; and as keeper of the privy purse by Lady Sunderland. With your gracious permission, she would willingly retain the Great and Home parks, as well as her pension from the privy purse."

"I assent to the latter part of the proposition," replied the queen. "She shall have the parks and the pension, which will give her three thousand five hundred a-year; but the other offices I shall reserve for my friends."

"How, madam!" exclaimed the duke. "I trust it will not be necessary to remind you of your promise."

"It was extorted from me," replied the queen.

"Even if it were so, madam, which it was *not*," rejoined Marlborough, proudly, "your royal word, once passed, should be kept."

"There must be some reservation in these matters, my lord," replied Anne, colouring; "my promise was conditional on her grace's good behaviour."

"Your pardon, madam," returned the duke; "I have always been given to understand by the duchess—and she is incapable of asserting an untruth—that it was unconditional. Nay, the very nature of the boon bespeaks it to be so."

"My word is as good as that of the duchess, my lord," cried the queen, angrily, "though you would seem to insinuate the contrary."

"Your majesty misunderstands me," replied the duke. "I do not design to cast a shadow of imputation on your veracity. That you made the promise with the tacit understanding you describe, I am satisfied; but that the duchess was unconscious of any such mental reservation, I am equally satisfied. It is with this conviction that I beseech your majesty, on parting with your old friend and servant, not altogether to overlook her many services, nor give to strangers what is due to her."

"I have done all I think needful," said the queen; "and more, much more than I am advised to do. I accept her grace's resignation. You will bid her deliver up the gold key to me within three days."

Marlborough looked as if stricken by a thunderbolt.

"Three days!" he exclaimed. "If your majesty is indeed resolved upon the duchess's dismissal, and is deaf to my remonstrances, at least grant me an interval of ten days, during which I may concert means of rendering the blow less mortifying to her."

"On no account," replied the queen, alarmed. "I now repent giving so much time, and shall limit the space to two days."

"Well, it matters not, since it is to be," sighed the duke. "I would now speak to your majesty on another subject."

"Do not trouble yourself, my lord," replied the queen, sharply. "I will talk of nothing till I have the key."

"I take my leave, then, madam," replied the duke, "lamenting that I should have lived to see you so changed."

And he bowed and departed.

"Well, Masham," said the queen, as a side-door in the cabinet opened to admit the favourite, "are you satisfied?"

"Perfectly, madam," replied Mrs. Masham. "You will have the key to-night."

"You think so?" cried Anne.

"I am sure of it," returned the other. "I would not for all the honours the duke has gained be the bearer of your message to the duchess."

"Nor I," replied the queen, with a half smile.

Marlborough fully sympathized with these opinions. He had never felt half the uneasiness before the most hazardous engagement he had fought, that he now experienced in the idea of facing his wife. He would willingly have broken the disagreeable intelligence he had to communicate by a note, or in some indirect manner, but the duchess met him on his return, and rendered his intentions nugatory. Perceiving from his looks that something had gone wrong, she came at once to the point, and asked—"You have seen the queen—what says she?"

"Give me a moment to recover myself," replied Marlborough.

"If you are afraid to answer the question, I will do so for you," rejoined the duchess. "My resignation is accepted. Nay, do not seek to hide it from me; I know it."

"It is so," replied the duke.

"But she has granted the places to our daughters? At least she has done that?" cried the duchess.

"She refuses to fulfil her promise," returned Marlborough.

"Refuses! ha!" cried the duchess. "She is the first queen of England who has acted thus dishonourably. I will tell her so to her face. And all the world shall know it."

"Calm yourself," replied Marlborough. "This passion is useless. The queen requires the key within two days."

"She shall have it within two minutes," rejoined the duchess, snatching it from her side. "I will take it to her at once."

"But consider——" cried the duke.

"I will consider nothing," interrupted the duchess. "She shall at least know how much I hate and despise her. If I perish for uttering them, I will let her know my true sentiments."

"You shall not go forth in this state, Sarah," cried Marlborough, detaining her. "Tarry till you are calmer. Your violence will carry you too far."

"Are you, too, joined with them, my lord?" cried the duchess, furiously. "Let me go, I say! I will not be hindered! My indignation must out, or it will kill me."

"Go, then," replied the duke, releasing her. And as she rushed out of the room, while he sank upon the sofa, he ejaculated, "No rays of glory can gild a life darkened by tempests like these!"

Still in the same towering passion, the duchess reached the palace. In spite of all opposition, she forced herself into the ante-chamber of the cabinet, and Anne, who chanced to be there, had only time to retire precipitately, ere she entered. She found Mrs. Masham alone, who could ill disguise her uneasiness.

"Where is the queen?" demanded the latter.

"You see she is not here," replied Mrs. Masham. "But I must demand, in her name, the meaning of this strange and most unwarrantable intrusion."

"So you are the queen's representative, hussy!" cried the duchess. "It must be confessed that the majesty of England is well represented. Bnt I will not bandy words with you. I wish to enter the cabinet to speak with the queen."

"You shall not enter," replied Mrs. Masham, planting herself before the door.

"Dare you prevent me?" cried the duchess.

"Yes, I dare, and I do!" replied Mrs. Masham; "and if you advance another footstep, I will call the guard to remove you. Her majesty will not see you."

The duchess looked as if she meditated further violence, but at last controlled herself by a powerful effort. Glancing at Mrs. Masham with unutterable scorn, she said, "Your mistress has required the key from me. Take it to her." And as she spoke she flung it upon the ground.

"Say to her," she continued, "that she has broken her word—a reproach under which none of her royal predecessors have laboured. Say to her, also, that the love and respect I once entertained for her are changed to hatred and contempt."

And with a glance of defiance she quitted the room.

"Is she gone?" cried the queen, half opening the door, and peeping timidly into the room.

"She is, madam," replied Mrs. Masham, picking up the key; "and I am thankful to say she has left this behind her. At last you are rid of her for ever."

"Heaven be thanked!" ejaculated Anne.

"Will it please you to take the key?" said Mrs. Masham.

"Keep it," replied Anne. "Henceforth you are comptroller of the privy purse. The Duchess of Somerset will be groom of the stole. But I have better things in store for you. The Duchess of Marlborough shall not insult you thus with impunity. On the earliest occasion, I will give your husband a peerage."

"The duchess says you do not keep your promises, madam," cried Mrs. Masham; "but I have found it otherwise."

"It is the duchess's own fault that I have not kept them with her," returned Anne. "I loved her once as well as you, Masham—nay, better."

CHAPTER XIV.

SHOWING HOW THE SERJEANT QUITTED THE SERVICE.

RECALLED to scenes of war in Flanders, the serjeant remained with his regiment till the termination of the campaign of 1711. He had been absent nearly two years, and having been severely wounded at the siege of Bouchain, in the autumn preceding his return, had been incapacitated from writing home; neither had he received, for nearly three months, tidings from those in whom he was interested, in consequence of which his heart misgave him so much, that he determined, before proceeding to Marlborough House, to seek out Proddy. Accordingly, he repaired to the palace, and inquiring for the coachman, was told he was in his room, whither he directed his steps. Full of the pleasurable surprise which he imagined his appearance would occasion the coachman, he entered the room, and closing the door after him, made a military salute to Proddy, who was seated beside a table, in a semisomnolent state, with a pipe in his mouth, and a mug of ale before him. On raising his eyes, and beholding the unlooked-for apparition, the coachman dropped his pipe, pushed his chair back, and with eyes almost starting out of their sockets, and teeth chattering, remained gazing at him, the very picture of terror and astonishment.

"What! don't you know me?" cried Scales, greatly surprised.

"I *did* know you once, serjeant," gasped Proddy; "but I don't desire any further acquaintance with you."

"Pooh, pooh!" cried the serjeant; "what's the matter—what are you afraid of? You must come with me."

"Oh, no, thank'ee—much obleeged, all the same," replied Proddy, getting as far back as possible.

"Well, if you wont go with me, I must stay with you," replied Scales, taking a chair. "I don't mean to leave you any more, Proddy."

"You don't!" exclaimed the coachman, with a look of increased affright.

"No, we shall part no more," replied Scales. "I've got a pretty long furlough, now."

"Why, you don't mean to say they give leave of absence from below?" cried Proddy.

"From below!" echoed the serjeant. "Oh, I see—you mean from the Low Countries."

"You may call it by that name, if you please," rejoined Proddy; "but we generally give it another and less pleasin' happerlation."

"Well, we wont quarrel about names," returned the serjeant. "What I mean to say is, I'm no longer in the service. I'm the same as a dead man."

"I know it," returned Proddy, shuddering.

"But I sha'n't give up my former habits," said Scales. "I shall beat the drum, as heretofore—and clean the duke's boots. I shall still haunt the old spot."

"Oh, don't—don't!" cried Proddy.

"Why not?" returned the serjeant. "Has anythin' happened to prevent me? Why do you stare so hard at me, man? D'ye think me altered?"

"Not so much as I expected," replied Proddy.

"I dare say I *am* changed," ruminated the serjeant. "The last three months have tried me hard. I've had terrible quarters—hot as h——"

"Oh, don't mention it," interrupted the coachman. "What a relief it must be to get away!"

"You'd think so if you tried it," replied Scales. "How cool and comfortable you feel here! I shall often pass an hour with you."

Proddy groaned audibly.

"By the by," pursued the serjeant, "talkin' of my looks, do you think they'll find me changed?"

"What, the women-folk?" cried Proddy. "Do you mean to appear to them?"

"Of course,—and this very night," returned Scales.

"Lord help 'em!" cried Proddy; "how frightened the poor creaters will be. It's as much as I can do to bear you. Why, you don't mean to say you care for 'em now?"

"Not care for 'em!" replied Scales. "It's anxiety about 'em as has brought me to you!"

"Well, this beats everythin'," said Proddy. "I thought your last bullet must ha' settled that long ago."

"Not a bit of it," replied Scales. "Here's your health, and glad to see you, Proddy!" he added, taking up the mug and emptying it, very much, apparently, to his satisfaction.

"What! can a ghost drink ale?" cried Proddy, in surprise.

"Why, zounds! you don't take me for a ghost, sure*ly*?" cried the serjeant, looking up.

"I *did*," replied the coachman, drawing nearer to him; "but I begin to think I must be mistaken. We heard you were killed at the siege o' Bushin."

"Wounded, but not killed, Proddy," replied the serjeant. "My hurt was at first supposed mortal; but here I am, as you see, alive and kicking."

"Oddsbodikins! how delighted I am!" cried the coachman,

throwing his arms round his neck. "I never expected to behold you again."

"Well, I thought your reception rayther odd," said the serjeant, as soon as he had extricated himself from his friend's embrace. "So you took me for a sperrit, eh!—very flatterin', ha! ha! You ought to have known that ghosts never walk in broad daylight—to say nothin' o' my substantial and earthly appearance."

"I was puzzled woundily, I must own," returned Proddy; "but arter the han'kicher stained wi' blood, and torn into two pieces, which you sent home to Mrs. Plumpton and Mrs. Tipping, none of us could doubt your disserlution."

"Eh! what!" cried the serjeant. "Do *they* think me dead, too!"

"To be sure," replied Proddy. "There came a letter from the fifer o' your regiment, Tom Jiggins—him as played at your ' Drum,' you remember, enclosing the bloody relics, and saying you was grievously wounded, and couldn't recover."

"But I *have* recovered, howsomedever," replied the serjeant. "Poor Tom Jiggins! two days after he wrote the letter, he was shot through the head by a carabineer."

"Poor fellow!" echoed Proddy; "then *he* really is dead?"

' Dead as your great-grandfather, if you ever had one," replied Scales. "But I'll tell you how my mischance came about. Bouchain, you must know, is a strongly fortified town, with the river Sanzet flowing right through it, and the Scheld almost washin' its walls. Round about it, there are broad, deep ditches, filled to the brim wi' the waters o' the two streams I've mentioned, and besides these, there are miles o' great flat swamps capable of inundation, so that the place is as difficult of approach as a besieged garrison could desire. Our general's object, you must understand, after investing the place, was to draw a line o' circumwallation round it; but, in accomplishin' this, he experienced great obstacles. It would be no use tellin' you how Marshal Villars, who was posted wi' his army in the open space betwixt the two rivers, threw bridges across the Sanzet—and how we demolished 'em—how entrenchments were constructed under General Albergotti, by means o' which, and the batteries o' Bouchain, Villars intended to sweep the intermediate ground wi' a cross-fire—how the duke passed over the Scheld in the night-time to interrupt these operations, and how he was foiled by the marshal, and obligated to return—how he covered the front from Haspres to Ivry wi' a line of redoubts and lunettes—and again crossed the Scheld at the head o' fifty battalions and as many squadrons—when perceivin' that the enemy were rapidly extendin' their works, he ordered the line o' circumwallation to be forthwith commenced between their entrenchments and the town Upon which, four thousand men were set to work, and notwithstandin' a heavy fire from the garrison, and repeated volleys from the hostile entrenchments, the line o' circumwallation was continued to the inundation o' the Sanzet——"

"Come to the point, serjeant," interrupted Proddy. "Your circumwallations and nunindations confuse me sadly."

"To make a long story short," replied Scales, laughing, "the marshal, finding himself driven hard, was more than ever anxious to keep up a communication with the garrison; and he contrived to introduce a reinforcement o' fusileers into it by means o' a small dam, together wi' a supply of powder and flour, of which they were runnin' short. Havin' accomplished this, he next attempted to fortify the dam by means o' fascines attached to an avenue of willows, though the water was at least four feet deep."

"D—n the dam," cried Proddy. "I'm a-gettin' out o' *my* depth again."

"I'll land you presently," returned Scales. "Behind the dam ran a cattle-track, on which were posted four companies o' French grenadiers, together wi' the king's brigade, to protect the work. To dislodge these troops, and check the operations of the workmen, was the duke's object. Accordingly, a fascine road was made across the inundated morass; and under cover o' night, six hundred British grenadiers, sustained by eight battalions o' infantry, made the attempt. It was a hazardous enterprise; for we had to wade for near a quarter of a mile, sometimes up to the middle, and sometimes up to the very shoulders in water, and to keep our muskets high and dry above our heads all the time. Two-thirds of the distance had been safely accomplished, when the duke, who was with us, and who had been sufferin' from ague, began to feel fatigued. I besought him to mount upon my shoulders; he consented; and, nerved wi' the glorious burthen, I pressed forward wi' redoubled ardour. It was impossible to advance so silently as not to betray our approach to the enemy; and when we came within shot, they fired a volley at us, but, owing to the darkness, it did little execution. A ball, however, had struck me in the breast; but I said nothing about it, determined to go on as long as my strength lasted. Despite my exhaustion, I was the first to reach the traverse, where I deposited the duke, and then dropped, luckily not into the water, or I must ha' been drowned. I had no share, as you may suppose, in what followed; but I afterwards learnt that the French were compelled to evacuate their posts, while the duke was enabled to extend the road across the marsh, and so complete the circumwallation."

"Bray-vo!" exclaimed Proddy, rapturously. "I'm sure the duke didn't forget you, serjeant."

"Hear it out, and then you'll learn," replied Scales. "When I came round, I found myself in my tent, whither I had been conveyed by the duke's orders, and with the surgeon dressin' my wounds. I asked him what he thought o' my case; and he said that, knowin' as how I didn't fear death, he must say he thought my chance but a poor 'un. 'Very well,' says I, 'I sha'n't go unprepared.' So I sends for Tom Jiggins, and I bids him write a farewell letter for me to the two women; and I tears the han'ker-cher, with which the blood had been stanched, in two, and encloses a half to each of 'em. This done, I felt more comfortable. Half an hour afterwards, the duke himself came to see me, and expressed the greatest concern at my sitivation. 'I owe my life to you, my brave fellow,' he said; 'and if you recover, I'll give you your discharge, and make you comfortable for the rest o' your days. Live for my sake.' 'Always obey orders, general,' I replied; 'since you command me to live, I *will* live.' And so I did."

"Bray-vo, again!" exclaimed Proddy. "Walour ought to be rewarded. I've no doubt when I'm superanivated, and no longer able to drive, that her majesty 'll perwide for me."

"No doubt of it," returned Scales. "Well, as soon as I was able to be moved, I was taken to the hospital at Douay, where I remained till the end o' the campaign. I wasn't able to write, but I got a comrade to indite a letter for me; but I dare say it miscarried."

"Most likely," said Proddy.

"It's an awkward question to ask," said Scales, hesitating; "but did the women seem at all afflicted at the news o' my supposed death?"

"Werry much," replied Proddy—"werry much, especially Mrs. Plumpton. Mrs. Tipping cried a good deal at first, but her eyes soon got as bright as ever. As to Mrs. Plumpton, she looks like a disconsolate widow."

"Poor soul!" cried Scales. "Poor soul!"

"I may say a word for myself, serjeant," pursued Proddy: "I was as much grieved as if I'd lost a brother."

"Thank'ee—thank'ee!" cried Scales, in a tone of emotion, and grasping his hand with great cordiality. "You are a true friend."

"You've just come back in time, serjeant, if you still have any likin' for Mrs. Tipping," remarked Proddy, significantly.

"How so?" asked Scales, becoming suddenly grave. "Isn't she true to her colours, eh?"

"She encourages Bamby a great deal more than I like," replied Proddy; "and I've been half expectin' her to throw herself away upon him."

"The devil!" exclaimed Scales, angrily. "That little rascal is always in the way. But I'll settle him this time."

"I say, serjeant," said Proddy, after a moment's reflection; "have you made up your mind which of the two women you'll take for a wife?"

"Pretty nearly," replied Scales; "but why do you ask, Proddy?"

"For a partik'ler reason o' my own," returned the coachman.

"Very likely I may decide to-night," said Scales. "Do you mind which I choose?"

"Oh, no; it's quite immaterial to me," answered Proddy, with an air of unconcern, "quite immaterial."

"An idea has just struck me, Proddy," said the serjeant; "they suppose me dead. What if I appear to 'em as a ghost, to-night?"

"Don't frighten 'em too much," replied the coachman, "or the consequences may be ser'ous. I know how I felt just now. But how will you contrive it?"

"Oh, it's easily managed," replied the serjeant. "As soon as it becomes dark, I can steal into the house unperceived, and get into my den."

"You'll find it undisturbed," said the coachman. "Mrs. Plumpton wouldn't suffer a single article in it to be moved. She cleans it regularly."

"Bless her!" exclaimed Scales, in a voice rendered hoarse with emotion.

"Bamby and Savagejohn are sure to be there to-night," pursued Proddy, "so that any scheme o' wengeance you may meditate can be put into execution."

"All falls out as I could desire," said Scales. "Now, then, lets lay our heads together, and arrange our plans of attack."

"First of all, let me get you a pipe, and replenish the mug," said the coachman.

This done, they held a close conference, which lasted till about eight o'clock in the evening, by which time they had smoked nearly a dozen pipes, and discussed at least three mugs of strong ale. They then thought it time to set forth, and while Scales stole into Marlborough House, through the garden-gate in St. James's Park, Proddy entered boldly from Pall Mall.

CHAPTER XV

IN WHICH THE SERJEANT'S GHOST APPEARS TO HIS OLD FRIENDS; AND IN WHICH MRS. PLUMPTON AND MRS. TIPPING FIND EACH A HUSBAND.

PREPARATIONS were making for supper, and most of the household were assembled in the servants' hall, including, of course, Fishwick, Parker, Brumby, and Timperley. Neither Mrs. Plumpton nor Mrs. Tipping, however, were present; but as Proddy was inquiring after them, the last-named tripped into the room. She had evidently been taking unusual pains with her toilette, and it must be confessed, looked extremely piquante and pretty. A rose-coloured paduasoy dress, with short open sleeves edged with crowsfoot, displayed her trim little figure; a laced cap and lappets adorned her head; and a patch here and there set off her complexion and heightened the brilliancy of her eyes. Her roguish and coquettish air proclaimed that she was bent upon conquest.

"You expect Mounseer Bambyloo, I see," said the coachman.

"Why, yes; it's just possible he may come," replied Mrs. Tipping; "he and Corporal Sauvageon generally drop in about supper-time; and very pleasant company we finds 'em."

"Werry pleasant, indeed!" echoed Proddy, drily. "You seem to have quite forgotten the poor serjeant."

"The serjeant! puff!" cried Mrs. Tipping. "What should I think about him for, eh? Would you have me sit sighin' and groanin' all day, like that poor fool Plumpton?"

"Ay; she's a model o' constancy,' said Proddy; "there are few o' your sex like her."

"The fewer the better, to my thinkin'," cried Mrs. Tipping, spitefully. "Oh, here she comes! I declare it gives one the wapours to look at her."

As she spoke, Mrs. Plumpton entered the room. She was clad in deep mourning, and evinced by her altered demeanour the sincerity of her affliction.

"You must take care o' yourself, my dear Mrs. Plumpton," said the coachman, kindly; "you are quite-a-losin' your good looks."

"Why should I preserve them, supposing that I ever had any?" she answered, with a melancholy smile.

"You may find another admirer—one you may like as well as the serjeant," he urged.

"Never!" she replied, firmly.

"Mrs. Tipping has done so," he said, glancing maliciously at the lady's maid.

"Mrs. Tipping is no rule for me," returned Mrs. Plumpton, gravely.

At this moment, a great shuffling in the passage announced the arrival of Bimbelot and Sauvageon. The former was dressed with extraordinary smartness, wore a laced velvet coat, diamond, or what looked like diamond, buckles, speckled silk stockings, a full-bottomed peruke, a clouded cane, and a silver-hilted sword. He was patched and perfumed as usual, and carried his feathered hat in the points of his fingers.

Nodding in reply to the little Frenchman's bow, Proddy inquired gruffly, "if he had got a place, seein' he was so sprucely rigged out?"

"Oui, mon cher Proddy, oui," he replied; "I have got a new place, certainly; but I am no longer a valet. I am employed by my Lord Oxford."

"Oh, indeed!" exclaimed the coachman. "May I ask, in what capacity?"

"I regret I cannot answer you; c'est un secret," he replied, mysteriously, "un grand secret."

"But you will tell me?" said Mrs. Tipping.

"Tout à l'heure, ma chère," he replied; "dans un tête-à-tête. Oh! I must tell you, I have sush a sharming aventure dis mornin' on the Mall. I meet sush a pretty lady, and she give me sush tender glances. Oh, ma foi!"

"And you returned them, no doubt?" said Mrs. Tipping, in a tone of pique.

"Oh! mon Dieu! oui," cried Bimbelot. "You wouldn't have me insensible to a lady's advances! Ven she ogle me, I ogle her again."

"Very pretty proceedings, indeed!" cried Mrs. Tipping, bridling up. "And you've the audacity to tell me this to my face."

"Ah, pauvre chérie—dear little jealous fool!" cried Bimbelot. "don't fly into a passion."

"Leave me alone—I don't wish to speak to you—I hate you!" cried Mrs. Tipping.

"Au contraire, chère petite; you love me so mush you can't live vidout me," rejoined Bimbelot. "Soyez raisonnable, cher ange."

Q

"Vain coxcomb!" muttered Mrs. Tipping. "I'll lower his pride."

At this moment supper was announced. Bimbelot offered his arm to Mrs. Tipping, but she turned from him disdainfully, and took that of Proddy.

The supper passed off pleasantly enough, for Mrs. Tipping, to mortify Bimbelot, chattered incessantly to Proddy; and the latter, who was secretly anticipating the fun that was to ensue, was in high good-humour. The only person who seemed out of place was Mrs. Plumpton. She sat silent and abstracted, ate little or nothing, and neither the lively sallies of Bimbelot, nor the tender assiduities of Sauvageon, who still continued to pay court to her, could draw a smile or a word from her. But an occurrence took place which somewhat altered the complexion of the party. When supper was nearly over, a loud knocking was heard at the outer door of the passage, and Timperley got up to answer the summons.

"Who can it be, I wonder?" said Proddy, wondering whether the serjeant had made any alteration in his plans.

"Perhaps it's the fair lady that Monsieur Bimbelot met this morning on the Mall," observed Mrs. Tipping, maliciously.

"Oh non, ce n'est pas cette dame, j'en suis sûr," replied Bimbelot, with an uneasy look.

"It's a woman, however," cried Fishwick, as female tones in a high and angry key were heard in the passage.

As the voice reached his ears, the little Frenchman turned pale, and rose suddenly.

"Bon soir, messieurs et mesdames," he stammered; "I feel very ill; de supper disagree vid me—bon soir!"

"Stop a bit," cried Proddy, laying hold of his arm. "What's the matter?"

There was a slight struggle heard outside, and a shrill female voice exclaimed, "Let me come in! I know he's here. I *will* see him."

"Oh, je suis perdu!" cried Bimbelot, with a distracted look at Sauvageon; "c'est elle! Vat sall I do?—vere sall I go?"

"Sit down, I tell you," cried Proddy, still detaining him in his grasp.

"No, I tank you—no; I must go," cried Bimbelot. And in his efforts to extricate himself, he pulled the coachman backwards upon the floor, while his own coat was rent in the effort up to the very shoulders. Just at this moment, an enraged female burst into the room, and shaking her hand menacingly at Bimbelot, who retreated from her, cried, "I knew you were here. Oh, you base little deceiver!"

And she forthwith proceeded to pull off his peruke, and cuff him tremendously about the ears.

"Pardon—pardon, ma chère," cried Bimbelot. "C'est la derniere fois. I vill never do so again—never, je te jure!"

"I know better," cried the lady. "You've deceived me too often. Oh, you wicked little creature!—there's for you!" And she gave him a sounding buffet, that made him put his hand to his ear.

"He has deceived me as well as you, ma'am," said Mrs. Tipping, getting up, and boxing him on the other side.

"He hasn't married you, I hope," cried the strange lady. "If so, I'll hang him for bigamy."

"No, he's only perposed," replied Mrs. Tipping.

"That's nearly as bad," cried Madame Bimbelot.

"Very nearly," replied Mrs. Tipping. "Oh, you base little wretch!"

Upon which, they both began to box him again, while Bimbelot vainly endeavoured to shelter his head with his hands.

"We'll teach you to play these tricks again," cried Madame Bimbelot.

"Yes, we'll teach you," added Mrs. Tipping.

The well-merited punishment of the little Frenchman gave great entertainment to the spectators, and even drew a smile from Mrs. Plumpton. Proddy, who had got up from the floor, was so convulsed with laughter, that he had to hold his sides. At length, however, thinking the chastisement had proceeded far enough, he good-naturedly interfered.

"Come, come, ladies, let him alone," he said. "You, at least, ought not to be so hard upon him, Mrs. Tipping, for you're quite as much to blame as him."

"I don't doubt it," cried Madame Bimbelot, gazing spitefully at her. "I dare say she gave him every encouragement."

"Oui, ma chère," cried Bimbelot, piteously, "dat she did."

"Oh! you base hypocritical little monster!" cried Mrs. Tipping, in a fresh access of passion. "Didn't you give me to understand you were single?"

"Well, never mind if he did," said Proddy; "you can't misunderstand him now. Come, make it up, and let us finish supper."

Fishwick and Brumby, joining their solicitations to those of Proddy, peace was at length restored; and Bimbelot, having resumed his peruke, sat down again with a very crestfallen air. Madame Bimbelot was accommodated with a seat near Mr. Parker. Now that she was a little more composed, and the company were at leisure to examine her features more narrowly, she proved to be a very fine woman—a little erring on the score of *embonpoint*, but far surpassing Mrs. Tipping in attraction. She was very tawdrily dressed in a blue and silver sack, highly rouged, with her neck considerably exposed, and covered, as were her cheeks, with patches. Her features were small, but excessively pretty, the mouth inclining to the voluptuous, and the eyes bright and tender. Her hair was powdered, and dressed in the *tête de mouton* style. As Proddy looked at her, he thought he had seen her before, but could not recollect when, or under what circumstances. Madame Bimbelot wanted little pressing from Parker to partake of the supper. She ate of everything offered her—cold fowl, ham, game pie, pickled oysters, stewed cheese, fish *rechauffée;* and when the butler himself thought she must be satiated, begged for a taste of th corned-beef,—it was so very tempting,—and devoured a large plateful. Notwithstanding this inordinate display of appetite, her charms produced a sensible effect upon Mr. Parker, and without saying a word, he went in search of some choice old Madeira, which he kept in a little press in his pantry. Returning with a bottle under each arm, he drew the cork of one of them, filled a bumper for Madame Bimbelot, who, requiting the attention with a tender look, tossed it off in a twinkling, and held out the glass to be replenished. Parker gallantly complied, drank a bumper to her health, and passed the bottle round the table. The effect of this generous wine on the company was magical and instantaneous. All tongues were loosened at once, and the conversation became loud and general. Even Bimbelot recovered his spirits, and ventured to cast an imploring look at Mrs. Tipping, who, however, took no notice of him, but put on her most captivating airs to Proddy. One person only amid this noisy assemblage was silent—one person only refused the wine—need it be said it was Mrs. Plumpton? As time flew on, and the bottle went round, Mr. Parker seemed to grow more and more enamoured of Madame Bimbelot; they drew their chairs close together, whispered in each other's ears, and a complete flirtation seemed to be established between them.

"I say, Bamby," said Proddy, nudging him, "where are your eyes, man? Don't you see what love Mr. Parker is a-makin' to your wife?"

"He does me great honour," replied Bimbelot, shrugging his shoulders with an air of supreme indifference. "A jealous husband is a fool."

"Well, he has *one* recommendation, at all events," observed Mrs. Tipping. "I suppose *you* would be jealous, Mr. Proddy?"

"Of you,—werry," replied the coachman, with a slight wink.

"La, Mr. Proddy, how am I to understand that?"

"I'll tell you more about it an hour hence," returned the coachman.

"Oh gimini! you quite confuse me," she rejoined, casting down her eyes, and forcing a blush.

In this way another hour passed. More Madeira was brought by Parker, who was unwilling to let the flame he had excited expire for want of aliment. Proddy discovered beauties in Mrs. Tipping which he had never discerned before, and the lady on her part almost gave him to understand that if he found his bachelor life solitary she was ready to enliven it with her society. All were extremely happy and comfortable, and all apparently very unwilling to separate.

About this time, Proddy cast his eye towards the clock, and seeing it only wanted a few minutes to twelve, thought it high time to turn the conversation into another channel.

"Mrs. Plumpton," he said, calling to her across the table in a voice calculated to attract general attention—"I hope you haven't lost the poor serjeant's han'kercher."

"Lost it!—oh no," she replied, drawing forth the ensanguined fragment, "it's my only comfort now."

"I've mine safe enough, too," said Mrs. Tipping, drawing the other half from her pocket. "Here it is—heigho!" And she heaved a deep sigh.

"Those are the halves of a han'kercher sent home by poor Serjeant Scales when he was mortally wounded," observed Parker to Madame Bimbelot. "They're stainded with his blood."

"So I see," she replied. "How purely shocking!"

"Talkin' o' the serjeant," said Proddy, mysteriously, "somethin' werry extraordinary happened to me last night."

"About the serjeant?" cried Mrs. Plumpton, starting.

"About the serjeant," replied Proddy, still more mysteriously.

"In Heaven's name what is it?" demanded Mrs. Plumpton, eagerly.

"Thus adjured, I must speak," replied the coachman, in a solemn tone, "but I don't expect you to believe me."

There was a general movement of curiosity, and all conversation ceased. Mrs. Plumpton seemed as if her very being were suspended.

"I had been a-bed and asleep, as far as I can guess, about an hour," proceeded Proddy, "when I suddenly waked up wi' a strange and unaccountable feelin' o' dread about me. Why, I can't tell, but somehow the poor serjeant came into my head, and I thought of his lyin' far away in a gory grave."

"Oh, dear!" cried Mrs. Plumpton, bursting into tears, and pressing the handkerchief to her lips.

"Oh dear! oh dear!" sobbed Mrs. Tipping, folding up her half, preparatory to putting it into her pocket.

"Don't cry, ladies, or I can't go on," said Proddy. "Well, I was a-thinkin' of the serjeant in this way, and a-tremblin' all over, when all of a sudden, wi' a rattlin' o' rings that made my blood rush to my 'art, the curtains was drawn back, and I saw—*the serjeant!*"

"The serjeant!" exclaimed Mrs. Plumpton.

"Or rayther his ghost," replied Proddy. "There he was, lookin' as pale as a corpse, and holdin' his hand to his left breast, just where the bullet as caused his death struck him. I tried to speak, but my tongue clove to the roof o' my mouth, and I couldn't get out a word. After lookin' at me steadfastly for a short time, the spirit says, in a hollow voice, 'You wonder what I'm a-come for, Proddy. I'll tell you. I want that 'ere torn han'kercher again. I must have it to-morrow night.'"

"Oh dear! did he say so?" cried Mrs. Plumpton.

"Here's my half," screamed Mrs. Tipping; "I wouldn't keep it another minute for the world."

"And what happened next?" asked Fishwick.

"Nothin'," replied Proddy. "The happarition wanished."

"Why didn't you tell me this before?" asked Mrs. Plumpton, reproachfully.

"I didn't want to spoil the pleasure of the evenin'," answered Proddy; "besides, I thought midnight the fittest season for a ghost story."

As he spoke, the clock struck twelve,—slowly and solemnly.

There was a deep silence. Each one looked round anxiously, and Mrs. Tipping whispered to Proddy, that she was sure the lights burned blue.

All at once, the ruffle of a drum was heard, proceeding apparently from the other end of the passage.   Every one started, and the women with difficulty repressed a scream.

It was a strange, mysterious, hollow, death-like sound.

Rat-a-tat-a-tat-a-ra-ra !—rat-a-tat-a-tat-a-ra-ra !

Then it stopped.

"Surely, my ears haven't deceived me !" cried Fishwick. "I heerd a drum."

"Oh, yes, I heerd it plain enough," returned Brumby. "and so did all the others."

"Oh, yes ; we all heard it," they rejoined.

There was a pause for a few moments, during which no one spoke. Alarm and anxiety were depicted in every countenance.

Again the drum was heard, but more hollowly than before.

Rat-atat-atat-a-rara !   Rat-atat-atat-a-rara !

"It's the serjeant's call," cried Proddy.   "I shall go to his room.   Who will accompany me ?"

There was no reply for a moment.   At length Mrs. Plumpton got up, and answered—" I will."

"Don't be so wentersome !" cried Fishwick ; "you don't know what you may see."

"I shall see *him*, and that will be sufficient," replied Mrs. Plumpton.

"I should like to go, if I durst," said Mrs. Tipping, her curiosity getting the better of her fears ; "but I'm sure I should faint."

"I'll take care of you," said Proddy.

"We'll all go," said Fishwick ; "we'll see whether it really is a ghost."

"Yes, we'll all go," rejoined the others.

At this moment, the drum sounded for the third time, but so hollowly and dismally, that the hearers shrank back aghast.

Rat-atat-atat-arara !   Rat-atat-atat-arara !

"Come away," cried Proddy, taking Mrs. Plumpton under one arm, and Mrs. Tipping under the other.

"Yes, we're all a-comin'," replied Fishwick, half repenting his temerity.

Emboldened, however, by numbers, he followed Proddy and his companions down the passage.   Parker and Madame Bimbelot brought up the rear, and the lady was so terrified, that the butler found it necessary to pass his arm round her waist, to support her, though his own apprehension did not prevent him from stealing a kiss,—an impropriety which escaped the notice of her husband, no lights having been brought with them.   All was silent, for the beating of the drum had ceased.   Arrived at the door of the den, Proddy paused before it.   It was a thrilling moment, and Mrs. Tipping declared she was ready to faint.

After a brief delay, the door was thrown open, and a cry of terror was raised by all the spectators as they beheld the serjeant at the end of the room.   There he stood, erect as in life, in his full regimentals, with his three-cornered hat on his head, his sword by his side, and a drum-stick in either hand.   Before him, on his three-legged stool, was his drum.   The black patch was still visible on his nose, so was the other on his forehead. A lamp, placed out of sight in a corner, threw a ghastly green glimmer upon his face, which had been whitened with pipe-clay.

At the sight of this frightful spectre, a universal cry of alarm was raised by the beholders. Mrs. Tipping screamed aloud, and threw herself into the arms of the coachman, while Madame Bimbelot sank into those of Parker, who carried her off as fast as he could to the servants' hall.

Amid this terror and confusion the spectre struck the drum,

Rat-a-tat!

"What d'ye want?" demanded Proddy.

Rat-a-tat-a-r-r-r-r-a-r-a!

"What d'ye want, I say?" repeated Proddy, as the hollow ruffle died away.

"My han'kercher," answered the ghost in a sepulchral tone.

"Here's my half," said Mrs. Plumpton.

"Give him mine," murmured Mrs. Tipping to Proddy.

"You must give it yourself," replied the coachman; "the sperrit wont take it from any other hand."

"I da-r-r-r-aren't," she rejoined.

Meanwhile, Mrs. Plumpton had advanced slowly and tremblingly, and holding out the fragment of the handkerchief. When she came within reach, the ghost stretched out its arms, and folded her to its breast.

"He's alive!" exclaimed Mrs. Plumpton; "alive!" And she became insensible.

"Holloa, Proddy!" shouted Scales, in most unspiritual tones; "she has fainted. Some water—quick!"

"Why, what the devil's the meaning o' this?" cried Fishwick. "Are you alive, serjeant?"

"Alive?—to be sure I am," he replied. "But stand aside for a moment. You shall have a full explanation presently."

And hurrying off with his burthen, he was followed by most of the spectators, who could scarcely credit their senses.

"Oh! good gracious, Mr. Proddy," cried Mrs. Tipping, who had remained behind with the coachman. "Is the serjeant come to life again?"

"He has never been dead at all," replied Proddy.

"Not dead!" echoed Mrs. Tipping. "Oh, then, let's go after 'em immediately." And she flew to the servant's hall, where she found the others crowding round the serjeant and Mrs. Plumpton.

A little water sprinkled in the housekeeper's face revived her. As she opened her eyes, she gazed fondly and inquiringly at the serjeant.

"I see how it is," she murmured; "you have played me this trick to try my fidelity."

"At all events, it has quite satisfied me of it," replied Scales, pressing her to his heart. "I'll tell you how I recovered from my wound, which at first was supposed mortal, anon. At present, I shall only say that I have quitted the service—that my noble master has promised to provide for me—that I mean to take a wife—and that wife, if you will have me, shall be yourself. How say you?"

She buried her face in his bosom.

"Serjeant!" exclaimed Mrs. Tipping, reproachfully.

"You're too late," said Proddy, detaining her. "Since you've come to the resolution o' marryin', I can't do better than follow your example; and since you've at last made a choice, the only difficulty I had is removed. Mrs. Tipping, have you any objection to become Mrs. Proddy?"

"None in the world," she replied; "on the contrary, it will give me a great deal of pleasure."

"Then we'll be married at the same time as our friends," said the coachman.

"And that'll be the day after to-morrow," cried Scales; "I can't delay my happiness any longer."

"Pray accept my best compliments and congratulations, mon cher sergent," said Bimbelot, stepping forward.

"And mine, too, mon brave sergent," added Sauvageon, advancing.

"I had an account to settle with you, gentlemen," said Scales, stiffly; "but I'm too happy to think of it."

"Oh! pray don't trouble yourself," replied Bimbelot. "Allow me to present Madame Bimbelot. Angelique, ma chère, où es tu?"

"Madame's too much engaged with Mr. Parker to attend to you," replied Proddy.

"So it seems," said Bimbelot, with a disconcerted look.

At this moment, the door suddenly opened, and two tall men, of stern appearance, with great-coats buttoned to the throat, pistols in their belts, and hangers at their sides, entered without ceremony. They were followed by an elderly man in a clerical cassock, and a female about the same age.

"Hippolyte Bimbelot," said one of the men, advancing, "and you, Achille Sauvageon, we arrest you of high treason in the queen's name. Here is our warrant."

"Arrêté!" exclaimed Bimbelot, in extremity of terror. "Oh, mon Dieu! what for?"

"You are accused of treasonable correspondence with France," replied the messenger. "Come along. We have a coach outside. We learnt at your lodgings that you were here."

"Ma pauvre femme!" cried Bimbelot. "Vat vill become of her, if I'm taken to prison?"

"Don't be uneasy about her—I'll take care of her," rejoined Parker.

"Here are two of her relations, who wanted to see her, so we brought 'em with us," said the messenger.

"Jelly!" cried the elderly lady, rushing forward, "don't you know me—don't you know your poor distracted father?"

"What, mamma, is it you?" cried Madame Bimbelot. "Well, this is purely strange."

"I meant to scold you severely," cried Mrs. Hyde, embracing her, and shedding tears, "but I find I cannot."

"Come along," said the messenger, laying hold of Bimbelot's shoulder. "We can't wait here any longer."

"Eh bien, I sall go," replied Bimbelot; "but you'll find yourself in de wrong box, bientôt. Mr. Harley vill take up my case."

"Why, it's by Mr. Harley's order you are arrested," rejoined the messenger, with a brutal laugh.

"Oh dear, it's all over vid us," groaned Bimbelot. "Ve sall be hang like de pauvre Greg."

"Most likely," replied the messenger. "Come along." And he dragged forth Bimbelot, while his companion led out Sauvageon.

As this was passing, Angelica threw herself at her father's feet, and, with tears in her eyes, implored his forgiveness.

"I will forgive you, my child," he said, "and grant you my blessing, on one condition—namely, that you return with us into the country at once. The Essex wagon starts from the 'George,' Shoreditch, at three o'clock to-morrow morning. Will you go by it?"

"Willingly, father," she replied, rising; "willingly. I have not known a day's real contentment since I left your roof."

"Then you shall have my blessing," cried her father, extending his arms over her.

"And mine, too," added her mother.

And fearing if they tarried longer that her resolution might change, they took a hasty leave of the company, and hurried to the George, from whence they left for Essex in the wagon about two hours afterwards.

Angelica, it may be added, became a totally changed person. The former fine lady would not have been recognised in the hard-working, plainly-dressed woman, who was to be seen, ere a month had elapsed, actively employed in her daily duties in Mr. Hyde's humble dwelling.

The day but one after this eventful evening, two couples were married at Saint James's Church. They were Serjeant Scales and Mrs. Plumpton—Proddy and Mrs. Tipping. Both unions turned out happily, though Mrs. Proddy became a widow two years afterwards, her husband dying of apoplexy, about a week before the decease of his royal mistress. The serjeant was appointed superintendent of the gardens at Blenheim, and had a pretty cottage allotted him by his noble master, which was charmingly kept by his wife, who made him a most excellent and affectionate helpmate. And here they both passed many happy years, enlivened occasionally by a visit from Mrs. Proddy.

CHAPTER XVI.

SHOWING HOW THE GREATEST GENERAL OF HIS AGE WAS DRIVEN FROM HIS COUNTRY.

THE removal of the Duchess of Marlborough being effected, the Tories next directed their machinations against the duke. Assailed with the grossest and most unjustifiable abuse; lampooned and libelled by petty scribblers; attacked in the most rancorous manner by Swift, Prior, and Saint-John; accused of fraud, avarice, extortion—of arrogance, cruelty, and ungovernable ambition, a sensible decline was effected in his popularity.

During his absence from England in 1711, these attacks were continued with unabating virulence; his successes were decried; his services depreciated; his moral character calumniated; his military skill questioned; even his courage was disputed. Preparation was thus made for the final blow intended to be levelled against him on his return. Though despising these infamous attacks, Marlborough could not be insensible of the strong prejudice they created against him, and he complained to Oxford, who thus characteristically endeavoured to vindicate himself from any share in the libels. "I do assure your grace," he wrote, "that I abhor the practice, as mean and disingenuous. I have made it so familiar to myself, by some years' experience, that as I know I am every week, if not every day, in some libel or other, so I would willingly compound that all the ill-natured scribblers should have licence to write ten times more against me, upon condition they would write against nobody else." Oxford was the more anxious to excuse himself, because, at this particular juncture, he wished to effect a coalition with Marlborough.

A charge was subsequently brought against the duke, which more deeply affected him. He was accused of receiving a large per centage from Sir Solomon Medina, the contractor for supplying the army with bread; and though he immediately exculpated himself by a letter, declaring that what he had received was "no more than what had been allowed as a perquisite to the general as commander-in-chief of the army in the Low Countries, even before the revolution and since," yet still the charge was persisted in, and inquiries directed to be instituted.

By these means the public mind was prepared for Marlborough's downfal. On his return, at the latter end of the year, he experienced insults and indignities from the populace whose idol he had formerly been, while by the queen and her court he was treated with coldness and neglect.

On the opening of Parliament, in the debate upon the address, the Earl of Anglesea remarked, that "the country might have enjoyed the blessings of peace soon after the battle of Ramilies, if it had not been put off by some persons whose interest it was to prolong the war."

To this unjust aspersion the Duke of Marlborough made a dignified and touching reply, which, as the queen herself was present, though merely in the character of a private individual, had the greater weight.

"I can declare, with a good conscience," he said, "in the presence of her majesty, of this illustrious assembly, and of God himself, who is infinitely superior to all the powers of earth, and before whom, in the ordinary course of nature, I shall soon appear, to render an account of my actions, that I was very desirous of a safe, lasting, and honourable peace, and was always very far from prolonging the war for my own private advantage, as several libels and slanders have most falsely insinuated. My great age, and my numerous fatigues in war, makes me ardently wish for the power to enjoy a quiet repose, in order to think of eternity. As to other matters, I had not the least inducement, on any account, to desire the continuance of war for my own particular interest, since my services have been so generously rewarded by her majesty and her parliament."

The amendment on the address, moved by Lord Nottingham, and supported by Marlborough, being carried in the House of Lords, occasioned great alarm to the Tories, and rumours began to be raised that a new ministry was to be formed, of which Lord Somers was to be the head, and Walpole secretary of state. Mrs. Masham owned that the queen's sentiments were changed. Saint-John appeared disconcerted, and even Oxford could scarcely conceal his apprehensions. The Tory party was disunited, and the knowledge of this circumstance gave additional encouragement to the Whigs. Fresh advances were secretly made by the treasurer to the duke, but they were repelled like the first.

Finding that his salvation depended upon the most vigorous measures, Oxford bestirred himself zealously, and by his artful representations, frightened the queen from recalling the Whigs. He convinced her, that if they returned to office, she must necessarily reinstate the Duchess of Marlborough, and submit to the domination of a tyrannical woman, whose temper had been aggravated by the treatment she had experienced. The latter argument prevailed.

The storm being weathered, Marlborough's immediate disgrace was resolved upon. The commissioners of public accounts were ordered to examine the depositions of the bread contractor, Medina, and to lay their report before the house. In answer to these accusations, the duke published the letter to which allusion has been previously made, and which afforded a complete answer to the charge. Notwithstanding this, and without waiting the result of the investigation, the queen, at the instance of Oxford, dismissed him from all his employments.

Thus, unheard and unconsidered, was the greatest general England had then ever possessed, dishonoured and degraded. His disgrace occasioned the liveliest satisfaction throughout France; and on hearing it, Louis the Fourteenth exclaimed, in a transport of joy, "The dismissal of Marlborough will do all we can desire." His minister, De Torcy, declared—"What we lose in Flanders, we shall gain in England;" and Frederick the Great of Prussia broke out indignantly, thus:—"What! could not Blenheim, Ramilies, Oudenarde, nor Malplaquet, defend the name of that great man? nor even Victory itself shield him against envy and detraction? What part would England have acted without that true hero? He supported and raised her; and would have exalted her to the pinnacle of greatness, but for those wretched female intrigues, of which France took advantage to occasion his disgrace. Louis the Fourteenth was lost, if Marlborough had retained his power two years more."

Such were the sentiments entertained by the different potentates of Europe. It is grievous, indeed, to think that so great a man should have been destroyed by faction. It is still more grievous, to think that some of the obloquy which the bitter and unprincipled writers of his own time endeavoured to fasten to his name, should still cling to it.

In the latter part of the same year, the duke voluntarily exiled himself from an ungrateful country. He embarked from Dover on the 28th November, and sailed to Ostend, where he was received with every demonstration of honour and respect. Proceeding to Aix-la-Chapelle, he afterwards retired to Maestricht, to await the duchess, who was not able to join him till the middle of February.

Marlborough never saw his royal mistress again. Apprised of her dangerous illness, at Ostend, he reached England the day of her decease. As he approached the capital, along the Dover road, he was met by Sir Charles Cox, at the head of two hundred mounted gentlemen, and on the way the cavalcade was increased by a long train of carriages. On entering the city, a company of volunteer grenadiers joined them, and firing a salute, headed the procession, raising a cry which found a thousand responses—"Long live King George! Long live the Duke of Marlborough!"

CHAPTER XVII.

QUEEN ANNE'S LAST EXERCISE OF POWER.

THE rivalry between Oxford and Saint-John ended in producing a decided rupture in the cabinet. While the treasurer endeavoured to sacrifice his colleague, by artfully misrepresenting his conduct to the queen, the secretary was enabled to counteract his designs, through the influence of Lady Masham, whose husband had been raised to the peerage with nine others, to strengthen the government, immediately after the dismissal of the Duke of Marlborough.

Saint-John's successful negotiation of the peace of Utrecht rendering it impossible to withhold from him the distinction, he was created Viscount Bolingbroke, though he himself expected an earldom; but he was refused the Garter, on which he had set his heart, while Oxford took care to decorate himself with the order. Bolingbroke never forgave the slight, and from that moment utterly renounced his friend, and bent his whole faculties upon accomplishing his overthrow. He found a ready coadjutor in Lady Masham, who was equally indignant with the treasurer for having opposed the grant of a pension and other emoluments which the queen was anxious to bestow upon her. Thus aided, Bolingbroke soon gained a complete ascendancy over his rival, and felt confidently assured of supplanting him in his post as soon as Anne's irresolution would allow her to dismiss him.

Oxford's fall, however, was long protracted, nor was it until his secret overtures to the Elector of Hanover, after the death of the Princess Sophia, had been made known to the queen, and that the court of Saint Germain had exposed his duplicity, and urged the necessity of his removal, that she consented to the measure. The Jacobite party, of whom Bolingbroke was the leader, had become paramount in importance during the latter part of Anne's reign ; and as her dislike of the Hanoverian succession and her predilection for her brother the Chevalier de Saint George were well known, the most sanguine anticipations were entertained, that on her death the hereditary line of monarchy would be restored. That the period was fast approaching when the question of succession to the throne would be solved, the rapidly-declining state of the queen's health boded, and little doubt existed in the minds of those who considered the temper and bias of the public mind, and were aware of the preponderating influence of the Hanoverian party, as to the way in which it would be determined. Still, to an ambitious spirit like that of Bolingbroke, the chance of aggrandizement offered by adherence to the fallen dynasty of the Stuarts, was sufficiently tempting to blind its possessor to every danger ; and although aware of the terrible storm he should have to encounter, he fancied if he could once obtain the helm, he could steer the vessel of state into the wished-for haven. The moment, at length, apparently came, when it was to be submitted to his guidance. On the evening of Tuesday, the 27th July, 1714, Oxford received a sudden and peremptory intimation from the queen to resign the staff into her hands without a moment's delay ; upon which, though it was getting late, he immediately repaired to the palace.

Ushered into the queen's presence, he found Lady Masham and Bolingbroke with her, and their triumphant looks increased his ill-dissembled rage and mortification. Anne looked ill and suffering. She had only just recovered from a severe inflammatory fever, attended with gout and ague, and had still dangerous symptoms about her. Her figure was enlarged and loose, her brow lowering, her features swollen and cadaverous, and her eyes heavy and injected with blood. She scarcely made an effort to maintain her dignity, but had the air of a confirmed invalid. On the table near her stood a draught prescribed for her by her physician, Sir Richard Blackmore, of which she occasionally sipped.

Moved neither by the evident indisposition of the queen, nor by any feelings of gratitude or respect, Oxford advanced quickly towards her, and eyeing his opponents with a look of defiance, said, in an insolent tone, and with a slight inclination of the head—
"Your majesty has commanded me to bring the staff.—I here deliver it to you."

And as he spoke, he placed it with some violence on the table.

"My lord !" exclaimed Anne, "this rudeness !"

"Lord Oxford has thrown off the mask," said Bolingbroke. "Your majesty sees him in his true colours."

"It shall not be my fault, Bolingbroke," replied Oxford, bitterly, "if her majesty—ay, and the whole nation—does not see you in your true colours—and they are black enough. And you, too, madam," he added to Lady Masham, "the world shall know what arts you have used"

"If I have practised any arts, my Lord Oxford, they have been of your teaching," rejoined Lady Masham. "You forget the instructions you gave me respecting the Duchess of Marlborough."

"No, viper! I do not," cried Oxford, his rage becoming ungovernable. "I do *not* forget that I found you a bedchamber-woman; I do *not* forget that I used you as an instrument to gain the queen's favour—a mere instrument—nothing more; I do *not* forget that I made you what you are; nor will I rest till I have left you as low as I found you."

"My lord!—my lord!" cried Anne. "This attack is most unmanly. I pray you withdraw, if you cannot control yourself."

"Your pardon, if I venture to disobey you, madam," replied Oxford. "Having been sent for, I shall take leave to stay till I have unmasked your treacherous favourites. So good an opportunity may not speedily occur, and I shall not lose it."

"But I do not wish to hear the exposure, my lord," said Anne.

"I pray your majesty, let him speak," interposed Bolingbroke, haughtily.

"Take care of your head, Bolingbroke," cried Oxford; "though her majesty may sanction your correspondence with the courts of Saint Germain, her parliament will not."

"Your majesty can now judge of his baseness and malignity," said Bolingbroke, with cold contempt, "knowing how he himself has duped your royal brother."

"I know it—I know it," replied Anne; "and I know how he has duped me, too. But no more of this, if you love me, Bolingbroke."

"Oh, that your majesty would exert your spirit for one moment," said Lady Masham, "and drive him from your presence with the contempt he deserves."

"If your majesty will only authorize me, it shall be done," said Bolingbroke.

"Peace! peace! my lord, I implore of you," said Anne. "You all seem to disregard me."

"Your majesty perceives the esteem in which you are held by your *friends!*" said Oxford, sarcastically.

"You are all alike," cried the queen, faintly.

"What crime am I charged with?" demanded Oxford, addressing himself to the queen.

"I will tell you," replied Bolingbroke. "I charge you with double-dealing, with chicanery, with treachery, with falsehood to the queen, to me, and to the whole cabinet. I charge you with holding out hopes, on the one hand, to the Elector of Hanover, and to Prince James, on the other. I charge you with caballing with Marlborough—with appropriating the public monies——"

"These charges must be substantiated—must be answered, my lord," interrupted Oxford, approaching him, and touching his sword.

"They *shall* be substantiated, my lord," replied Bolingbroke, haughtily and contemptuously.

"Bolingbroke, you are a villain—a dastardly villain!" cried Oxford, losing all patience, and striking him in the face with his glove.

"Ha!" exclaimed Bolingbroke, transported with fury, and partly drawing his sword.

"My lords!" exclaimed the queen, rising with dignity, "I command you to forbear. This scene will kill me—oh!" And she sank back exhausted.

"Your pardon, gracious madam," cried Bolingbroke, running up to her, and falling on his knees. "I have indeed forgotten myself."

"Oh! my head! my head!" cried Anne, pressing her hand to her temples. "My senses are deserting me."

"You have much to answer for, Bolingbroke," whispered Lady Masham; "she will not survive this shock."

"It was not my fault, but his," replied Bolingbroke, pointing to Oxford, who stood sullenly aloof in the middle of the room.

"Let Sir Richard Blackmore and Doctor Mead be summoned instantly," gasped the queen; "and bid the Duke of Shrewsbury and the lord chancellor instantly attend me—they are in the palace. The post of treasurer must be filled without delay. Lose not a moment."

And Lady Masham ran out to give the necessary instructions to the usher.

"Shrewsbury and the chancellor—what can she want with them?" muttered Bolingbroke, with a look of dismay.

Oxford, who had heard the order, and instantly divined what it portended, softly approached him, and touched his arm.

"You have lost the stake you have been playing for," he said, with a look of triumphant malice. "I am now content."

Ere Bolingbroke could reply, Lady Masham returned with Sir Richard Blackmore, who chanced to be in the ante-room, and who instantly flew to the queen, over whose countenance a fearful change had come.

"Your majesty must be taken instantly to bed," said Blackmore.

"Not till I have seen the Dukes of Shrewsbury and Ormond," replied the queen, faintly. "Where are they?"

"I will go and bring them instantly," replied Blackmore; "not a moment is to be lost."

And as he was about to rush out of the room, Bolingbroke stopped him, and hastily asked, "Is there danger?"

"Imminent danger!" replied Blackmore. "The case is desperate; the queen cannot survive three days."

And he hurried away.

"Then all is lost!" cried Bolingbroke, striking his forehead.

And looking up, he saw Harley watching him with a malignant smile.

Lady Masham was assiduous in her attentions to her royal mistress; but the latter became momently worse, and continued to inquire anxiously for the Duke of Shrewsbury.

"Has your majesty no commands for Lord Bolingbroke?" inquired Lady Masham.

"None whatever," replied **the queen**, firmly.

At this juncture Sir Richard Blackmore returned with the Duke of Shrewsbury, the lord chancellor, and some other attendants.

"Ah! you are come, my lords," cried Anne, greatly relieved. "I feared you would be too late. Sir Richard will have told you of my danger—nay, it is in vain to hide it from me; I feel my end approaching. My lords, the office of treasurer is at this moment vacant; and if anything should happen to me, the safety of the kingdom may be endangered. My lord of Shrewsbury, you are already lord chamberlain and lord-lieutenant of Ireland; I have another post for you. Take this staff," she added, giving him the treasurer's wand, which lay upon the table, "and use it for the good of my people."

As the duke knelt to kiss her hand, he felt it grow cold in his touch. Anne had fainted, and was instantly removed by her attendants.

"So," cried Oxford, "if the queen's fears are realized, Lady Masham's reign is over; while your fate, Bolingbroke, is sealed. You have to choose between exile and the block."

"If I fly, you must fly with me," cried Bolingbroke.

"No, I shall wait," replied Oxford; "I have nothing to fear."

"So end the hopes of these ambitious men!" observed the Duke of Shrewsbury to the chancellor; "the queen found they were not to be trusted. Her people's welfare influenced the last exercise of power of GOOD QUEEN ANNE."

THE END.

Savill & Edwards, Printers, 4, Chandos-street, Covent-garden.